MW00799377

Table of Contents

Title Page
Copyright
Dedication
Disclaimer
Prologue
Chapter One
Chapter Two
Chapter Three
Chapter Four
Chapter Five
Chapter Six
Chapter Seven
Chapter Eight
Chapter Nine
Chapter Ten
Chapter Eleven
Chapter Twelve
Chapter Thirteen
Chapter Fourteen
Chapter Fifteen
Chapter Sixteen
Chapter Seventeen
Chapter Eighteen
Chapter Nineteen
Chapter Twenty
Chapter Twenty-One
Chapter Twenty-Two
Chapter Twenty-Three
Chapter Twenty-Four
Chapter Twenty-Five
Chapter Twenty-Six

The Final Charade

Talia Dayne

ISBN-13: 9798991976213

Cover design by: Mollie Javellana and AJ Javellana
Edited by: CJ Editing
Printed in the United States of America

You are very blessed if you have one person who truly supports and cheers you on. My cup runneth over as I am not even able to mention by name all of the cousins, aunts, siblings, children, married-ins and friends who have supported me and cheered me on.

I hope that as you read this dedication and wonder if you are meant to be in it, that you pause and smile, because you are.

A special shout out to my parents who read this in its rough form shortly after my college career.

To my husband who told me, "Let's just do it" and supported me as I sat down to really focus.

To my daughter who was an amazing pre-reader who caught so many mistakes before I sent it on its way. She also taught me a few important things about how to use my computer more efficiently.

To my daughter-in-law who edited and helped with all of the logistical and grammatical stuff that comes with writing and publishing a novel.

To my son who put together my book cover and is helping with marketing.

And finally, to all of you who are probably sick of hearing about Hayden and Kayra. Thank you for putting up with my obsession.
You make me feel loved and I don't take that for granted.

Disclaimer

I love fiction. I hope that as a reader you can find yourself wrapped up in the world that I created as you journey with my heroines on their adventure west. As fiction goes, I'd like for you to understand that this novel is fiction at its core, despite some historical influences.

I went back and forth about how to best represent my characters and groups of people. Being from an Indian reservation myself, I decided it was better to fully make up cultures, traditions and customs rather than to misrepresent a tribal nation. If you see a similarity or wonder what people during this time period did or didn't do, remember, it's only a coincidence and not intended to be taken as historically accurate.

I ask you to enjoy the creative aspects of this fictitious novel and to allow for artistic license as you are transported back into the late 1800s.

Trigger Warning

This book contains mentions of sex work, rape, violent acts, and familial deaths. None of these topics are graphic and are intended to eventually demonstrate grace, repentance, and resilience. Please read at your own discretion or skip through parts that may be harmful to your mental health.

Prologue

Hayden

Pink flames streaked the sky as the sun began to show itself. Peering out from the safety of her wagon, Hayden swiped tendrils of hair from her face to better see her cousin Kayra's wide eyes. It was entirely too early for this. "Wait, what? You have to calm down! There's no way he is actually dead."

Together the women turned their gaze, taking in the sight of their uncle lying face down in the dirt, mere steps from the campsite. Blood at the back of his head matted greasy, gray curls. Maybe they really did need to get all riled up, as Kayra suggested.

"You better hurry. I ain't going over there," Kayra insisted.

Hayden, slipped a dress over her already-perspiring body. "I'm coming, give me a second."

Lifting her skirt with one hand, she pushed through the curtain above the buckboard. It creaked and whined as she hopped to the ground. Kayra stepped aside to allow her cousin past. Whiskey and bad hygiene filled her nostrils as she strode closer to where he lay. Covering her mouth, she bent down and pulled an empty bottle of booze from his gripping fingers.

Kayra, a good ten feet away, held her arms tightly in front of her chest. "I think he's dead, but I don't know how to tell for sure," her voice cracked as she spoke.

Hayden poked their uncle's shoulder with a finger. No response. The creaking sound of her cousin struggling to hold back sobs was both frustrating and possibly warranted.

"Kayra," she said, not masking the irritation in her voice, "what happened?"

"All I know is, I woke up, climbed down and there he was. He hasn't budged," Kayra held a hand to her cheek. "The horse is gone too."

"Great." Now all they had were a pair of mules. Hayden frowned. Gleaming tears glossed Kayra's big, round eyes. If she allowed her cousin to become hysterical, she would have two dramas to sort out.

"Cousin, it's alright," Hayden softened her tone. "He probably just passed out. It's not like it's the first time we've had to haul him around while he sleeps it off. On the bright side, at least today he's got clothes on."

Kayra looked anything but amused. The fear in her eyes was reminiscent of the terrified little girl she had once been. Hayden shook that memory from her head. One bad situation at a time.

"Come on, we gotta flip him," Hayden held out a hand, waving her forward.

Kayra backed farther away, "No, Hayden, please," her words came out in a spooked whisper. "Touch him...he's cold."

Afraid to do just that, Hayden slowly placed a hand to their uncle's beefy arm. His skin completely lacked temperature. This really did look bad.

"You're right. He doesn't seem to be breathing either." Hayden learned a trick for managing panic whenever she felt it sneaking up on her.

She counted in her head, *one, two, three, four, five* before imagining all the fear being tucked away into a box. *Control your mind, control the situation.* She repeated the mantra she'd taught herself.

Hayden squatted beside their uncle. "We got to turn him over," Hayden stated matter-of-factly. "Get over here and help."

Uncle John was a big man. Rolling him was not a one-woman job.

Kayra raised an eyebrow, refusing to move.

Her cousin was many wonderful things, but being brave wasn't one of them. Unfortunately, there was no way Hayden could manage alone. "I need you," with fists planted on her hips she added, "Please."

"Fine," Kayra gave in. She was mumbling under her breath as she tread warily ahead, but at least she was coming.

Hayden grabbed Kayra's arm, offering what she hoped was a reassuring smile, "We're alright, no matter what. I got you. You know that, right?"

Kayra nodded.

"Now, when I count to three, we do it."

Sliding her hands under their uncle's thick belly, Kayra's nose scrunched up in distaste. "It's wet!" she squeaked.

Ignoring the complaint, Hayden continued, "One, two, three."

With painstaking effort, they raised the body up on its side, then over. His back fell against the ground with the *thwack* of a roped steer. An arm slid from his chest, resting with a thud on the hard earth.

Shrill screams sounded out across the prairie as the women darted away from their uncle's lifeless bulk.

No longer was Kayra making any pretense of holding in tears. Her sleeves were covered in blood. Frantic, she began smearing them down the front of her dress, painting the worn fabric with maroon streaks.

Hayden tuned out the tantrum. Her uncle's normally red face was gray as pigeons. Dark brown blood soaked his chest. The parched ground greedily drank in the liquid pooling at his side.

"He's definitely dead," Hayden sighed before taking her cousin's bloodied hands in her own. "We have to think, and I can't with you carrying on like this. Sweetie, go wash up, okay?"

Kayra nodded again.

"And try not to waste water, we're too low as it is."

Kayra was still nodding her mute obedience, sucking in the cry trying to escape her mouth. Hayden smoothed the dark hair on top of her cousin's head. "You'll feel better once you're clean," she managed a smile. Kayra headed toward the water barrel.

Hayden needed a moment to get a hold of herself. She opened and closed her hands to stop their shaking. *Control your mind, control the situation. Control your mind, control the situation.*

One foot in front of the other until they got to where they needed to be. They had to figure out how desperate their situation really was.

"Kayra," Hayden directed, "you need to go see how much money we got left in the can or if he's hidden anything."

Kayra's mouth dropped open, "He just passed, and you want me to go through his things? I don't think that's right."

It did sound callous, but what choice did they have? Hayden walked to Kayra. She tucked a stray lock of dark hair behind her cousin's ear. "He's dead, honey, and I'm sorry about that," she shrugged. "Uncle John has put us in some difficult spots before but this one is big. I'm trying to be sensible. We need to know what we're dealing with. That can of money is all we have and we're going to need every cent now that he's not here to take care of us."

"I guess that makes sense."

As soon as Kayra was gone, Hayden bent over, sick. She sucked in deep breaths, holding and exhaling, until her heart rate slowed.

Half afraid that their uncle would jump up and scare her, Hayden began rifling through pockets. One brief moment of hope filled her heart when she felt a wad of something in his left boot, but upon pulling it out, she realized it was nothing more than a grubby old deck of cards.

She tossed the faded box at his chest. It landed in the blood and left a trail as it slid to the ground beside him. His pockets were as empty as the field they'd camped in.

Kayra's long skirt caught on the splintered wood of the wagon as she climbed out shaking her head. "It's gone, all of it."

A couple of birds circled overhead, cawing. Hayden tore a thumbnail off with her teeth and spit it to the ground, "Ugh! How could he do this? He's got nothing on him either. Our medicine show in the springs brought in a lot. There must have been some two hundred dollars in that can. I should have known he wasn't gonna make wagon repairs. How is it gone? Think, think, think!" she tapped her forehead.

Kayra, like a lamb who's realized they were next in line at the chopping block, whispered, "What are we gonna do?"

The reality of the situation landed square on Hayden's shoulders. Their uncle had never been a loving guardian, but he had taken care of them the last five years. Oddly, it was death that brought the girls to him in the first place, and once again death was leaving them to fend for themselves. They would never catch a break, it seemed.

Like a bad dream, five years worth of scams flew through her mind; hoards of cons pulled, tonics sold, disguises worn. It all morphed together with the faces of people they had masterfully manipulated. All of it to make a paltry living, and what had it gotten them? Nothing. Their derelict uncle had once again wasted it all. Her gut tightened as anger swelled. Now, they were penniless and alone on the plains of Colorado dealing with his dead body.

Another fingernail flew from Hayden's lips. "We gotta stay calm and do things logical. First, we're gonna bury him. In spite of everything, he's our family and we can't just leave him to rot, as much as I'm tempted to do it."

"Hayden," Kayra chastised, "Don't speak ill of the dead. His spirit will hear you and it just ain't right."

Grabbing the hand her cousin offered, Hayden squeezed, "I won't then. Not right now anyways, but I don't think it works like that. He's already gone wherever he's going."

A plan set her mind at ease. She tucked in her blouse and smoothed her worn gray skirt. The shovel was right where she knew it would be, tied underneath the bed, behind the front wheel. Tools clattered to the ground as she yanked it free. "You see," she smiled, "all we need to do is dig a grave and when we are done burying him, we'll plan our next move. One thing at a time."

The sun was already baking as Hayden began stabbing the ground. It did not immediately give, so she grunted and pounded harder. With her feet planted apart, she continued to assault the dirt, more aggressively. The dry earth, marked by the curved blade, did little more than pool with dust. She placed a foot on top of the shovel raising her whole body to rest there, balancing on the metal edge. After minutes of fruitless labor, she was wet with sweat.

Rage filled her chest. "Why!" she yelled. If God heard her, she would be glad.

Blonde strands of flyaway hair danced in her face, sticking to her brow. The anger, fear and frustration she was trying so hard to keep at bay flew from her lips. Hayden threw the shovel. It clanked to the ground. There was something satisfying about the dramatic way it landed. In a huff, she flopped down in the patch of shade the wagon offered.

Several minutes passed before Kayra came into her peripheral view. Without comment, Hayden took the cup of water her cousin offered. Kayra sank down to the ground, resting her head on Hayden's shoulder. Her arm snaked through the nook of her cousins.

Kayra spoke softly, "We could take his body with us till we get to town."

"You think I haven't thought of that? Well, I have and it's a bad idea. We don't even know where 'town' is. It could be days. His body will stink by the time we get anywhere." Hayden heard the bite in her words but couldn't bring herself to soften them.

Kayra nodded, "Then we're going to have to burn it," Sse whispered.

"It's too dry!" Hayden pointed out the flaw. "We could start a grass fire and burn ourselves up?"

Kayra lifted her head, sucking in a deep breath before speaking. Her tone of voice remained in check but there was a firmness to how she held her jaw. "Well, I been thinking too. And what I know is that the river over that way isn't running," Kayra motioned toward the creek bed.

"So?" Hayden stared at Kayra until understanding hit her. A small smile spread across her face. Maybe there was something to the idea. *Yes, yes that was it*, she decided, rubbing her neck. "It's not going to be easy to haul him all that way."

Kayra let out the breath she had been holding, "If we can get him on a blanket and attach it to Chloe and Amos," she motioned toward the mules, "I think we could drag him easy enough."

"Let's do it," Hayden grabben the wagon wheel and pulled herself up before offering a hand to her cousin. Any idea was better than none. This might just work.

Hours later the sun was straight up in the sky punishing the prairie around them as they finally caught a glimpse of the creek.

Apparently, moving a dead body by blanket and wary mules was no quick task.

It took hours hauling that precarious load across the rutted prairie. They were waist high in yellow grass, yanking the bits of the mules as they forced them ahead.

It had been much harder than either woman had anticipated. Hayden's shirtfront was soaked with sweat and her hair curled by the time they reached their destination. Together, they mustered their strength, heaving the body off the ledge. They winced as it landed with a thud. Uncle John's dead eyes stared up at them. Hayden looked away, remembering.

Hayden forced her mind back to the present as they looked down on their uncle. John was family and he deserved some words, a song or something. Hayden wanted to feel sorrow, she tried to work up the sadness. She scrunched her face and bit the inside of her cheek.

Nothing.

What did that say about her or about him? No, he hadn't been anything like a father, but he'd never laid a hand on them or let anyone else. That alone was more than a lot of orphaned girls could say. For that she would honor him. For teaching her how to see a situation and use it to her advantage, she would always be grateful. The rest of what he was and wasn't lay between him and God.

"Did you bring the liquor?" Hayden asked.

Kayra went to the mule and pulled three bottles from a pack hanging around Amos' belly.

Uncorking the bottle, Hayden sniffed. Her eyes slid shut as the sour odor filled her nose. When she opened them, Kayra was staring.

"Are you done?" Kayra shook her head.

"Tell me you aren't curious. He never gave us a taste, but he drank from sunup to sundown." Before she could be talked out of it, Hayden put the bottle to her lips and took a large gulp, swallowing several bitter drinks. The instant burn that slid down her throat was almost as bad as the horrible flavor. She stuck out her tongue and shook her whole body.

Kayra swiped the bottle away, "We aren't becoming drunks tonight, so just stop that, right now," she held the whiskey up, "This is for burnin', not drinkin'."

Hayden let out a giggle blowing hard liquor fumes into the air, "It's awful. How did he like that stuff?"

"Hayden, please," Kayra's eyes filled with tears. "Can we just take care of this?"

Hayden nodded, her mind a little cloudy. "Of course. I'm sorry," she bit her lower lip to keep from smiling. She blinked several times. Was she drunk? Could you get drunk that fast?

Kayra gave her a scathing look, "Let's do what we came to do."

Hayden opened her eyes wide, refocusing, "I'm sorry cousin, really." She'd pushed too far. Kayra seemed genuinely upset. It's not like Hayden was trying to make her mad. She'd only taken one drink. One long drink that made her feel funny, but just one.

Kayra shook her head. Her eyebrows creased together.

So, what was the best way to go about the next step in their plan? Hayden tilted her head thinking out loud, "You think maybe we should put kindling over him?"

Kayra's eyes grew into silver dollars. "I don't have any idea. You know better than me," she begged Hayden to take charge.

Hayden scoffed, "I don't know better. I ain't never burned a body before."

Kayra's fearful eyes pleaded with her to handle this next part. Guilt crawled up Hayden's neck. She was not making this easy for her cousin. It was easy to forget that Kayra was a year-and-a-half younger. At nearly twenty, it was Hayden who should take care of things.

Hayden closed her eyes, "You're right! I'm sorry. It just makes sense to cover him so that he catches easier and I don't want to have to see him when we...."

"Alright, alright, alright," Kayra interrupted, waving her hands back and forth. "I agree, let's just gather some brush and not think about it." Kayra walked towards a nearby bush and started collecting its fallen branches.

Once Uncle John's bulk was sufficiently blanketed, Kayra doused the pile with the whiskey he'd left in the wagon and Hayden started a fire. She dropped a flaming branch over the brush below and both girls jumped back as the kindling quickly crackled into ash.

Hayden put a hand on Kayra's shoulder before leading her away. "We can come back later to make sure it's done. We don't have to watch him..." the words trailed off.

Kayra nodded. The two tired women walked towards the only shade tree in sight. Quietly, they sat as the sun dipped lower and lower. A breeze picked up and the prairie began to cool. With the gentle wind came the foul odor of smoke and something else. Something neither girl recognized, but knew. Hayden made no mention of it while Kayra covered her mouth burying her face in her skirt.

When the air stilled, Kayra spoke,"You're awful quiet. Are you sad?"

Hayden wiped her nose with the hem of her dress,"No. It may be unchristian, but I'm not."

"Me neither," Kayra traced a finger through the dirt beside her cousin, "Well, it's not like you to be so quiet."

"I suppose not. I've been thinkin'. See, Uncle John was certainly killed. So, there was someone in our camp last night. It may have been his murderer who took our money. Someone may have climbed into the wagon with us while we were sound asleep and stolen it," Hayden sat up straight. "So, why didn't they hurt us, and what did Uncle John do to get himself killed? Kayra," she paused, "are we in danger?"

Kayra was thoughtful before responding, "I think Uncle John must have taken the money with him over to that horse camp we passed. He'd said that he wanted to gamble before we hit Denver City. I imagine he cheated and got caught. Simple as that," Kayra folded her legs in, moving to face her cousin, "but if someone was in our wagon last night, what if they come looking for us to finish the job?"

Hayden felt her face bloom into a smile. That was exactly where she needed Kayra's mind to go. "You don't need to worry about that anymore. They won't recognize us a second time."

"Oh no, Hayden. No you don't. I know that smile," she accused, pointing to her cousin. "You got some crazy idea in that brain of yours, and we can't. I won't. I won't, I tell you. With Uncle John gone, we don't have to play any parts or cheat anyone ever again. After all that has happened today, that is the one good thing. We're free. We don't have to lie anymore."

"Just hear me out. It's not really lying; it's just allowing people to reach their own conclusions based on what they imagine."

Kayra raised her voice, "That's lying! I'm terrible at it and I hate it."

Hayden gave Kayra a good-natured shove. "I got a whole plan and it's foolproof. Just give us one more run and then we can be done for good. We're in a bad place here," Hayden reminded.

"I know we are," Kayra agreed, "but I want to just get to the city and then we can figure it all out, the right way."

"That's my plan, we absolutely are headed for the city," she stated slyly, "but as nuns."

"No!" Kayra repeated. Wide eyes stared incredulously at her cousin. "No more lies and no more scams," Her chin was set like stone.

"You haven't even listened," Hayden beamed, excited over her idea, "I don't have all the details worked out, but I know we can do this. We still have those nun habits that we used in Nebraska. We put them on, spend a few weeks in Denver at that, Our Lady of Something-or-Other, we talk about the mission we are traveling to in California. We play up our desire to minister to the Indians, and we take off in two, maybe three weeks with money and prayers." Hayden held her hands together, bowing for effect, "We say that we are headed out West to help the Indians find Jesus. I know this will work. We can do this."

"No! You're crazy. Let's just go into Denver City and when we get there, we contact the Sheriff, tell him about Uncle John and get jobs like normal people?"

"Jobs! Doing what, cousin?" Hayden looked down her nose, "You know what happens to young penniless girls in big cities. Uncle John never let us forget what he had saved us from by taking us in, and in that he was right. We escaped that fate once, and I'm not about to get us into a situation that will turn bad ever again."

Kayra was quiet. They had seen way more in their lives than most women their age. Hayden meant it when she said that she would do anything to keep them from a life like that.

Hayden continued explaining the flaws in Kayra's idea, "If we go to the sheriff, whoever killed Uncle John will wonder if we saw him and if he wonders he may shut us up, just in case, or better yet, we get blamed for the murder."

Both women sat back in disagreeable silence.

Finally, Kayra sighed, "If, and I repeat, *if* we do this nun deal. Where will we go when the gig is up?" Kayra's mouth was drawn taut, but Hayden could see that she was winning the battle.

"That's the beauty of it, Cousin," Hayden jumped to her feet, "When else in life, will we get the opportunity to do anything grand? When?" she paced back and forth as she spoke. "Have we ever gotten to make our own choices? No. Think about it. We have no guardian, not a single family member besides each other. That means we've no identity. We could leave Denver with a little money and the ability to recreate ourselves." Hayden stopped and knelt in front of Kayra. "I know how you hated the pity we got from everyone after the killings, the charity Uncle John was too quick to accept. Remember how glad we were just to leave Oklahoma so we could get away from it?"

Hayden brushed a dark brown lock of hair from Kayra's forehead. She had promised to protect them no matter what and this could finally change their lives. "We can forget all of that and be whoever or whatever we want."

"I'm happy being me. Why do you always want to be someone else?"

Hayden lurched back as if she'd been slapped, "Where's the fun in that? We can do literally anything we want without being told otherwise. We can go wherever we choose and make the life that we want. I promise it will be better. Better than anything we've pretended was good."

"Where?" Kayra cut in, "Supposing I agree to this foolishness, Just where are we going to reinvent ourselves?" She folded her arms across her chest.

Hayden pointed to the dark mountains looming in the distance. "West, where everybody is going for a fresh start full of possibilities."

Chapter One

Hayden

Sister Hannah and Sister Mary-Katherine drove their wagon straight down a rutted dirt road on the outskirts of town. Underneath the long, dark robe, Hayden's body was slick with perspiration. Thankfully, the worst of the day's heat was past them. Colorado was drier than Hayden had ever seen it. The intensity of the sun burned the skin peeking out from the habit around her face. The mules must have smelled water because they picked up the pace and marched straight toward the trough in town square.

Relief that they had made it to wherever they were bolstered Hayden's confidence. She had said they could find their way and they had. Sure, it had taken longer than expected and they had no idea where they were, but they were going to be fine. Just like she'd promised.

Yesterday they had completely run out of water. Hayden had stopped drinking her share the night before, only pretending to sip from the canteen. Chloe and Amos had suffered more, and it showed. Their ribs poked out and foam dripped from their bits to the ground. Kayra thought they looked rabid and feared they'd been bitten by some infected animal, but as is the nature of mules, they kept on steadily until they rode into town and now made a beeline for the life-giving liquid.

As the mules drank their fill, Hayden followed suit, slipping from the wagon seat to join them. She cupped her hands and brought the mossy water to her parched mouth. She was desperate. "It's better than thirst," she encouraged Kayra who climbed down and did the same.

After they all had some water, Hayden wrapped the reins around her wrist and led the animals to a railing where she tied them. "There's the supply store," Hayden pointed out. "Go along with whatever I do in here. I don't remember the name of the church, so we'll have to figure this out as we go." Hayden smiled confidently.

"Can't I be a deaf and mute sister?" Kayra muttered plodding up the few steps onto the wood planked porch outside a general store. "Just promise me we can eat today."

The ladies paused outside the shop and Hayden took a deep steadying breath holding her hand to her belly before turning the knob.

A cowbell jangled as Hayden stepped inside. Together the pair stopped, waiting for their eyes to adjust to the dim room. It was a well-supplied, tidy store. An array of fabric lay on the shelf ahead of them. To the right was a cutting table and behind it stacked floor to ceiling were plenty of dry goods and candies. All sorts of houseware items were creatively displayed, and a catalog lay open on the counter.

An older man appeared from a doorway at the back of the store. He was as wide as he was tall. His head gleamed where a large island of scalp rose above a graying wreath of hair. Whatever was missing from his head had found its place on his chin. It looked as if he had pinned the bristles of a paintbrush under his lip. At the sight of the two ladies his face brightened into a sunny smile, "Well, sisters, how can I be of help?"

Hayden looked the man in the eye and put on her best smile. She cleared her throat. It was so dry, her voice sounded like it came from someone else. She decided to throw in an accent as well. "You are a very good man," she spoke in what she was sure would pass for an Irish brogue,"The good Lord gives us gifts and mine is the ability to see into people's hearts. The Lord has shown me that we should come to you. You must be the kindest man in this place." She stepped forward and grabbed his hand looking pensively at his palm. "I'm right again, clever and faithful as well."

Kayra had lowered her head as soon as Hayden started speaking. Her eyes remained focused on the plank floor.

The storekeeper's chest swelled. "Well, I won't brag to my smartness," he chided, "but kind I am and faithful too, though I regret I am not of the same faith as you servants of the Lord. I'm Lutheran. In fact," he leaned in to speak private like to the ladies, "my brother, Reverend Stephen, is the minister in this here town and I am deacon of the month."

Hayden closed her eyes and smiled as if she'd known it all along, clapping her hands together. "Ha!" she laughed, "I could tell." She waved her finger at him, "You are a man of boundless leadership. I assure you that our flock would greatly benefit from a gentleman such as yourself."

The storekeeper stammered at her words and blushed, making his round face appear like a sunburned walrus. "Oh!" He waved her comments away, "Tell me, what it is I can help you with."

Hayden had to recollect her story. She'd been distracted using her accent and flattery. After a moment's pause, she spoke, "Well, my friend, I am Sister Hannah and this meek soul is Sister Mary-Katherin," she motioned toward Kayra, "We sir have traveled by sea and land and are bound for the poor heathens out west, to teach them better the way of the Lord and to guide their children in the paths of rightness."

"Righteousness," Kayra supplied under her breath before again bowing her head.

"That is right Sister Mary-Katherine and the only way to righteousness is in rightness of one's life with God, isn't that correct sir?"

"Oh, yes,Sister," the man nodded his enthusiastic agreement, "that is what my book says. It surely does."

Kayra sighed and stepped up beside her cousin. "What we need is any food and water you can share with us. We are without money. We also will need directions to the church so we can prepare for our journey."

The shopkeeper leaned on his counter and frowned at the women, "I'm afraid there ain't no Catholic church in Willow Creek," He tapped his finger on the mahogany and made a clicking sound with his cheek, "but I do know of a Catholic family that I'm sure would be willing to take you in and get you rested up. And you're in luck," He smiled expectantly at Hayden, "They're German too. Just came this way from the old country a few years ago. In fact, Oma doesn't speak a word of English. I'm sure this will be a treat for them. You can surely see the Lord's hand in this unexpected meeting."

Hayden's smile wavered. She felt as if the floor had fallen out from under her. The storekeeper grabbed a key ring and his hat from under the counter. "Let me close up shop a minute and I'll take you there straight away."

Before Hayden could work up a reason for not accepting his offer, the man had disappeared into the back room. Hayden turned to meet Kayra's angry scowl.

"You had to use an accent, didn't you?" she pinched Hayden's arm and furrowed her brows. "What was it anyway?"

Hayden smiled, gaining her composure, "I'm good at accents. And if we had run into trouble, I could just act like I didn't understand."

"Well now you've done it. A piece of bread and a cup of water was all we needed and look what a mess you made. How are you gonna get us out of this one?"

Hayden fluttered her eyelashes. "Alas Sister Mary-Katherine, tis near sundown and my vow of silence regrettably must begin."

"Oh, no you don't!" Kayra seethed. Her fists tightened and her jaw set in for battle. Hayden's smile never left her face as she bit her lips together.

"Don't you dare do that to me. Don't you dare." Kayra's hands were raised to shake her cousin when Hayden giggled at the reentrance of the storekeeper.

All smiles and sweat, the storekeeper handed an apple to each sister and reached for a pail of water and a dipper. Kayra took it with her free hand and drank for several long moments. It felt like an eternity before Hayden got it. The water splashed across her cracked lips. It was the best thing that she had ever tasted. That apple was going to be the second-best.

The barrel of a man, insisting the ladies call him Jonas, slapped a straw cowboy hat onto his head and ushered the women outside.

"Shall we, ladies?"

Kayra was stiff as a washboard as the two cousins marched in silence behind Jonas. The mules were waiting just as they had left them. The storekeeper piled a bag of dry beans into the wagon and climbed in to drive.

Hayden made a silent dash toward the back. If she hurried, Kayra would have no choice but to sit beside their overly helpful friend. Kayra snatched the apple from her hand as she scurried past. Hayden turned an angry scowl toward Kayra. Why on earth would she do that?

"You'll have to excuse my cou--" she cleared her throat. "My Sister. Her vow of silence, fasting and prayer must start at sundown. And so it appears the sun is setting now."

Hayden's mouth dropped open at Kayra's statement. It would be just like her to try and get even. The self-satisfied smile Kayra shot Hayden was enough to earn her a scolding, but she couldn't exactly do anything about it right now. Hayden covered her ears at the sound of her cousin biting into that juicy, beautiful apple.

Kayra spoke between bites, "Where is the nearest church for us to take mass?"

"That would be Our Lady of Peace. It's a two-days ride into the heart of Denver City. I believe the Mayer's–them's the folks we're going to see–their son is planning to leave in the spring to become a Priest. You'll be a real blessing for them."

Hayden silently repeated the information in her head, memorizing it.

Kayra

Kayra had no idea how long they had driven but finally, Jonas slowed the mules to turn down a dirt path. Like a welcoming beacon, a small home glowed in the night. A black and white dog barked wildly, announcing their arrival. Two men emerged from the house. Little faces poked up against the window behind them. The porch creaked as the men approached the wagon and their guests.

"Hello there Gregor, William," Jonas called from his seat, extending a hand. The older men shook it firmly, "I have a treat for you folks," he declared, hopping from the wagon and stretching his legs. "This is Sister Mary-Katherine," he held the reins, motioning toward Kayra, "and her traveling companion is Sister Hannah. She's in the back of the wagon but you'll have to meet her tomorrow. She's taken a vow of prayer for the evening. These women are traveling to serve the Lord out West and need a few days rest before continuing their journey. I know how you miss having people in a parish here, so I thought, what a wonderful opportunity." He held his hands out to his sides like a circus ringmaster.

Kayra held her breath. This was so embarrassing and absurd. What would they do if they were turned away? The two men from the house looked at each other, the older man nodded. "There is always room at the inn," He smiled and put a hand on Jonas' shoulder. "Of course, they are welcome for as long as they like. William, why don't you help Sister Mary-Katherine inside while Jonas and I go tell your mother that we have guests."

As the men entered the home, Kayra overheard Jonas telling the older Mr. Mayer what a shame it was that Sister Hannah was in prayer because she was so looking forward to speaking with Oma.

Kayra felt her shoulders relax. They could stay. That meant food.

The younger of the two men approached the wagon and stopped short when his eyes met Kayra's. "I uh ...am William."

Kayra swallowed her nerves, "I'm Sister Hannah," butterflies filled her stomach, "No. I'm sorry, that's wrong. I'm Sister Mary-Katherine. Hannah's in the back...praying." Another pause, "I need to speak with her."

William offered his hand toward Kayra. She knew she had to take it but looked at the friendly gesture as if it were a snake.

Hastily, she gave him her hand and hurried out of the wagon. William held her palm a moment after she was safely on the ground.

"Sister, we are honored that you are here with us."

Kayra nodded. She felt flush, desperate to get out of the habit draping her from head to toe. "Excuse me." She curtsied and went to the back of the wagon. *Did I just curtsy?* she asked herself. Unbelievable.

Hayden was crouched inside the canvas, waiting like a bandit for Kayra to tell her what was happening.

"I'm famished back here." Hayden hissed, "You aren't seriously going to hold to that whole fasting thing, are you?"

A smile tugged at Kayra's lips, "I should." From the pocket of her robe, she produced the perfect red apple that had tempted Hayden earlier, handing it over. "You got us into this and you know that I'm a terrible liar."

Try as she might, Kayra just couldn't be angry. The whole situation was just preposterous, the humor too obvious. She put a hand to her mouth to shush her cousin. "I will try to bring you something to eat. But you truly had better pray that I don't stammer around too badly in there and mess up. Remember, Cousin," Kayra used the name Hayden reserved for her. "You owe me." The curtain fell and Kayra disappeared.

++← →++

Kayra

"Good night Jonas," Kayra called to the storekeeper as he climbed on one of the Mayer's horses. "Truly, thank you for your help today." Kayra waved as he strode off into the dark night. She really meant that. It had been such a blessing that he had decided to bring them out here.

Kayra climbed up into the back of the wagon and passed a hunk of bread and cheese toward Hayden. Hayden's eyes shone brightly as she began devouring the food. "Well, tell me." Hayden pleaded, her mouth full of bread. Kayra jerked off her headpiece.

"Shhh." Kayra put a finger to her mouth. "William is filling a water bucket for us. He's the oldest son. Did you see him?" Hayden shook her head.

Kayra sighed. "They're the most wonderful family, Hayden. They have a whole slew of children." Kayra leaned back, relaxed for the first time in days. "They said that we can stay for as long as we need. They offered space for us to sleep inside but I figured your vow of silence was easier to keep out here where you can talk," Kayra teased, putting her hand to her lips at the sound of approaching footsteps.

"Sister Mary-Katherine?" William's voice sent a shiver down her spine.

"I'll be right there." Kayra took a deep breath and opened the canvas to reach out and get the bucket of water.

William was standing there with his hat in his hand. The bucket of water rested on the ground beside him.

Kayra felt her face redden. Why? She hated her emotions. At 18, she was a grown woman but her face catching fire as easy and often as it did made her feel like such a child

"Thank you," She reached out.

Quickly, William grabbed the handle of the pail and held it for her until she had a good grip. She smiled and pulled it inside.

"Uh, Sister," He spoke to the curtained wagon.

Kayra's eyes widened. "Yes?"

"I know it's late and you're tired, but I was hoping that you would have a few moments to talk with me."

Hayden's brows shot up in alarm. She covered her mouth. Kayra went still. If she didn't breathe maybe he would assume she hadn't heard.

There was shuffling outside the wagon. Was he leaving?

"It's about the priesthood. I have so many questions. I was hoping that you would help me understand my place."

Hayden pushed Kayra toward him. "*Go*" she mouthed.

Kayra shook her head in terror. "*I can't*," she mouthed back.

"Sister?" William asked again.

"One moment!" Kayra punched her cousin in the arm as she climbed out of the wagon. When her feet hit the ground, she looked up at William and gulped. She couldn't do this. She was awful at talking to strangers, especially men.

"Let's walk." He suggested as he led the way past the house and towards a trail. He offered Kayra his arm. "It's dark." He explained.

Unease threatened to strangle Kayra. It was incredibly dark. She placed her hand in the crook William held towards her. It was as unsettling as she had feared it would be. Where was she supposed to rest her hand? She'd never been offered a man's arm.

Uncle John was no gentleman, and he didn't let the women so much as talk to any of the men in the towns they had worked in, although Hayden always had found a way. Was she supposed to rest it on his forearm or link elbows? This was a disaster.

Too late she remembered that her hat thing was still in the wagon. Her wet hair must look like a matted mess. At least it was clean now. Mrs. Mayer had seen to that.

A coyote howled in the distance. Kayra stepped closer to William as if she had never heard that before. He chuckled and patted the hand linked in his arm. "We're safe."

Kayra was incredibly aware of the man beside her. The feel of his skin under her hand made her conscious of every jumbled emotion in her body. A pulse beat steadily through his arm. How could it remain so constant while hers was thumping like a drunken rabbit?

Quietly, she sucked in air and blew it out, trying to get control of herself. She needed to focus on something besides William. The night sounds caught her attention. She forced her concentration to the crickets and toads. As they played a symphony of rustling and chirps a calm blanketed itself around her. The evening was warm but a gentle breeze felt heavenly against Kayra's face.

Thankfully, William chatted about his family and their farm because Kayra was so nervous she doubted that she could string a sentence together if she had to. That would have made this awkward walk even worse. He led her a short distance from the homestead.

Kayra did her best to say 'uh huh' at the right time so he wouldn't realize how off kilter she had become. They stopped at the edge of a pond.

"This is it," He pulled his hat off and Kayra released his arm.

"It's so peaceful." She meant it.

Kayra felt his eyes on her face and again wished that she had something to cover her hair. She ran her hand through the long strands.

William looked away and walked closer to the water. Not knowing what she was supposed to do, Kayra found a large rock and sat down.

Kayra

"It's just," William started, "they want me to become a priest. Of course I want to serve the Lord, but do I have to give up my dreams to be who God wants me to be? I definitely want to be married."

His face was a mixture of anguish and confusion. His troubled blue eyes pleaded for understanding. He was so sincere about his faith. Kayra felt her face burn again, shame spread through her.

"My parents gave up a lot for us to have this life in America. My sister Karla," William paused and swallowed heavily. He broke a small branch from the tree and started peeling the bark from it. "She died in passage. They blame themselves. Then, we come here and there is so much open land. It was unlike anything we'd ever experienced in Germany. My Father believed that this is 'our God given path.' That, 'We had been led here for a purpose.' So, we settled in Willow creek, even though there is no parish. We implored the Mission in Denver City, but no Priest will take on a flock this small."

William sat beside Kayra. Heat radiated from his body, making her want to scoot away, but there was no place to scoot.

He turned, facing her. The entire side of his thigh was touching hers. She tried very hard to keep her leg from flinching.

"That was the first time my father asked me to consider becoming a priest. He said that we could really make a difference here if we had a church. I would never do anything to disappoint my parents. I said, yes... but, I'm turning 19 in two months and it's time to do what I promised, except I don't know if I can."

Kayra felt for him with everything in her. Having lost both of her parents, if given the opportunity, she believed that there was little she wouldn't have done to please them. William's family was everything that she imagined hers would've been. Ingrid, William's mother, had treated her like the most special guest ever to darken their door. Even though they had just met, she felt comfortable with the woman and Kayra always felt awkward around people.

She could only be herself with Hayden. The whole family had made her feel at ease in a situation that normally would have sent her over the edge.

And Oma, who Hayden had worried so much about, had slept in her chair the whole evening, only awakening when William helped her into bed. He was incredible if what she'd seen tonight was a true glimpse of the man.

His devotion to his family and his true desire to serve God shamed her. Guilt twisted her gut.

How could she allow all the deception she and Hayden concocted to continue? How could she use the Mayer's this way when they trusted them without any reservation?

William's voice interrupted her culpable thoughts, "You were an answer to my prayers. I've prayed to talk with someone already serving God." William paused before continuing, "And then I saw that you were young and beautiful. I've never met a nun that decided to enter into service as young as you. That made me see that a person can be sure of what they want and dedicate themselves because they know, not because they have no choices.

"As beautiful as you are, you didn't join the clergy because you wouldn't find a husband. You joined because you wanted to, because you believe in it, like I should." An awkward smile spread across his face. "The nuns that I knew in Germany were all old and not women that I wanted to spend time with. If you were ever in their presence, it was because you were in trouble. I've been in their company a time or two and it was not like this."

His words incited new feelings in the pit of Kayra's stomach.

She tried to squelch them down.

Kayra flushed, bowing her head to hide her face. No one had ever said that she was pretty before. With Hayden by her side, people hardly noticed her at all.

"You shouldn't say things like that," She whispered.

"I know." William came to his feet and threw the branch he'd been holding to the ground. "I'm sorry, Sister Mary-Katherine, but this is what I'm talking about. I can't help but notice.

Here I am, a future priest with a woman who has already given herself to the church and I..." He shook his head and ran his fingers through his blond hair. "I'm sorry. It was wrong." William stood facing the water.

Bewildered, Kayra bit her lip. She was not the one who should be in this situation. It was Hayden who could convince this man to go into the Priesthood and put at bay all his fears of failure. Hayden could handle his compliment without falling out of character. But Hayden wasn't here.

Kayra was still nervous, but she didn't want to escape anymore. She stared into his troubled face. The hard lines of his features were drawn up in concern imploring her to put his fears at rest.

Kayra was alone with a man for the first time, a man who was kind and handsome. He had even said that she was pretty. She had always dreamt of a moment like this, and wouldn't you know it, she's supposed to be a nun.

"How do you do it?" His question sounded desperate. "How do you turn off that part of yourself that needs another person?" He sighed, "I must be wicked." He lowered his head, shoulders slumped. "Me and my mouth. We should go back to the house. This was a bad idea."

"William," She waited until he looked at her. Kayra didn't know where that came from, but somehow, she found the words to speak. "The cloth is not for everyone. People need to be truly called to serve in this way, you can't do it because someone wants you to."

"But being a good son means that you listen to your parents. I do love God and I do want to serve him with all of my heart."

Kayra was thoughtful before responding, she had no parents to consider the way that he did. "Being a Priest is not the only way to please God."

William swatted at a mosquito. "I have struggled with this for so long. Can I do it? If I can't then how do I tell my father?"

"Of course you have struggled because you are a good son. They know you. They know your heart, and I don't think that they would want you to live a life that wasn't what you desired."

William stood straighter. "Sister, you have no idea how badly I needed to hear that." Relief flooded his eyes. "Now, I just need to figure out how to tell my dad. This will not be easy. I'll pray on this."

Kayra came to stand beside him. In a moment of compassion, she smiled, taking his hand in both of hers.

She wasn't uncomfortable any longer. She had his full attention now. His wide, unblinking eyes locked with hers. "And more than that, God created all feelings. I don't believe that they are wicked and you, William, definitely aren't."

"I have tried to keep my mind pure and devote myself only to the Lord, but I want to have a partner in life, a wife."

"You're a good man. One day there will be some very lucky woman who finds such a faithful husband and father for her children. Farming is a good life. God will bless it."

William gripped her hand. "Sister, that's just it. These things everyone sees for my life, they are my father's dreams, not mine. He's the farmer." William shook his head. "I have been stuck, fearing what my life was going to be like. But neither the priesthood nor farming were things that I wanted. Then you showed up tonight and inspired me to do something different. When Jonas talked about you and Sister Hannah heading toward California, I thought, that's what I should do. Drop everything and go try on a new life, a life that I create for myself. You know, there's a wagon train leaving Denver City in a couple weeks?" William laughed at his words, "Of course you know, that's why you're here."

Things were happening too fast. She had wanted to reassure this man and now he was not only dropping his plans to become a priest but wanting to stop farming and leave his family as well, to go what? Pan for gold?

"Whoa, whoa, whoa," Kayra said. The excitement on his face was like Hayden's when she gets an idea in her head and it needs to happen *right now*. "Slow down. You have a lot going on in your mind. One big decision at a time. Maybe talk to your parents about the first thing before uprooting your world because of my advice."

William smiled. One crooked smile that made her all too aware that he was so close and still holding her hand.

"That's a good point. You are wise. And I know I can't go now. There's too much work for my father and brothers alone, but I can start planning." William looked into Kayra's eyes and her belly danced. His eyes were so clear, so imploring, so hopeful. "Maybe next year I can head west. Thank you, Sister Mary-Katherine."

Powerful arms surrounded her. Not sure of what else to do and liking the touch, she slid her arms around him, flattening her hands against his wellbuilt back. Surely, nuns hug. She only allowed the moment to last a few seconds before pulling herself away.

"Sister Mary-Katherine, you are unlike any nun that I have ever known."

Kayra gulped. He was looking down at her with an intensity that made her want to climb back into his embrace. Not knowing what else to do, she smiled and turned, heading in the direction of the house. She had to pull her emotions together. They were all over the place.

After saying goodnight from a safe distance, she climbed quietly into the wagon so as not to wake Hayden.

Once inside, she was slugged in the arm. "What do you think you're doing?" Hayden was not only awake, but had obviously had enough time to work herself up. "You're a nun, Sister Mary-Katherine, or did you forget?"

"Hayden," Kayra corrected, "I'm not a nun, and I did nothing wrong."

Hayden harrumphed, frowning. More calmly she asked, "What was that all about back there?"

"You were spying, weren't you?"

"I only followed to protect you," Hayden raised her chin, daring Kayra to challenge her statement. "You might have been in trouble."

"I don't need protection." Kayra pulled her robes up exposing long legs. It was so stuffy in the wagon.

Hayden paused before speaking, "I'm sorry, Cousin."

Kayra looked back at her feeling too many things to know where to start. Finally, she smiled. "Alright, but my goodness, you really did it to us this time, *Sister Hannah*. You won't even believe it."

"Tell me! Tell me everything and don't leave anything out." Hayden sat crossed-legged on the feather mattress that she shared with her cousin. She'd already stripped herself of her habit and was sitting in only her cotton gown.

Kayra began peeling off her robe. "You know Hayden, I'm not sure that nuns have to wear all this stuff all of the time. Do they?"

"How would I know?" Hayden exclaimed, "You're the one giving out advice on the priesthood."

Both girls giggled and sank down to lie next to each other.

"Well," Kayra began. She grabbed Hayden's hand and held it. "William is really handsome. Did you see him?" Hayden shook her head and waited for Kayra to spill it. "His folks want him to become a priest and serve here in Willow Creek."

"But they're the only Catholics, aren't they?" Hayden asked, wrapping a lock of long, blonde hair around her finger.

"Yes, but more than that, he doesn't think he can fulfill all of his priestly obligations." She looked at Hayden meaningfully.

Hayden's eyes lit up and her mouth gaped open. "He talked to you about that?"

She raised her eyebrows and nodded. "Well yes," Kayra continued. "He wanted to know how I dealt with IT."

"Wow," Hayden said, "You told him about being married to the church right, and how much more fulfilling that is?"

"No," Kayra smiled softly. "I told him the truth."

"You what?" Hayden jerked her hand away. "This was our last scam and then I swore you didn't have to lie anymore. You promised to give me a couple of weeks. That's all I asked. I can't believe you would do this."

"Calm down." Kayra gave her pillow a fluff and resettled against it. "I didn't tell him that much of the truth. I only said that the Priesthood was not intended for every man and that he can serve God and have a family too."

"Oh!" Hayden conceded. "That's not bad."

Kayra shook her head. "I can't lie like you, but I'm not stupid you know."

Hayden jumped in, "I know you're not. I just get in my head...you know."

Kayra's lips curled into a smile. "It's a good thing that I love that head so much. You make me crazy." She turned and looked at her cousin. "He told me something else. There's a wagon train leaving Denver City in two weeks. Do you think we can make it in with them?"

"Well, aren't you just full of useful information tonight." Hayden grinned like a bear with an abandoned bee hive. "It's all falling into place. Two weeks?" She blew out a long breath. "I tell you what, let's work Willow Creek for seven days. No, eight. Because there are no other Catholics here, it will be easier to fake our way through it with the townsfolk. Then we can head that way. That is, if you think you can handle being a nun for that long?" She winked at Kayra.

"I'll do my best."

"It'll be tight but we should be able to swing it. I don't think that I can wear this nun get up all the way out west anyhow, but we need the cover to raise some cash. Are you with me on this?"

"Sure, Hayden, but why would two single, unchaperoned women be headed out west? Plus we will only have a small--smaller than you think--wad of cash?"

"Oh, we won't be single. At least I won't. Wait, you won't. Wait. You don't have to pretend unless you want to, but it will be an easy one. I need to work on the details." Hayden began concocting their next sham. "Your husband could already be in San Francisco, and he struck gold, that way you don't have to play any big part and people will just imagine what they want to. He just sent for his beautiful wife that he desperately misses and her sister who is a teacher. I'm the sister, see. I'll pull my hair back tight and get out those spectacles and be a fantastic teacher type person."

"School wasn't your thing, Hayden. You hate teachers," Kayra said doubtfully.

"I know. It'll be fun. You can even call me Mrs. White."

Kayra smiled into the darkness, her eyes heavy. By morning, Sister Hannah would be full of all sorts of ideas for this next charade. If all she had to do was act married to someone who wasn't even around, she could do that.

For Hayden, she would do that. But nothing more.

Chapter Two

Kayra

Morning came too quickly. Sunlight streamed through a hole in the canvas and shone like a beam into Kayra's eyes.

She tried moving on her side, but, as usual, Hayden was sprawled out, taking up three quarters of their mattress. She always took up far more than her share of the bed. It would be a hassle to resituate, so Kayra decided to start the day.

As she dressed in her habit, the farm sounds became clear. The children were up and quarreling. Ingrid's voice scolded from the house, "Elias, Judah, you stop that bickering." The distant call of sheep and the tinkling of bells about their necks reminded Kayra of her childhood.

A pang of sadness tugged at her. The crack of an ax brought her back to the present. Who was swinging it? She peered through a hole in the canvas covering the wagon.

Her intake of breath was audible, she covered her mouth with her hand, darting her eyes to see if Hayden was still asleep.

William, his shirt crumpled on the ground beside him, raised his golden arms above his head and swung downward. A log split and fell beside the block. Kayra could see clearly what she'd felt last night. That was an oddly intimate thought. She knew what those arms felt like. His broad shoulders were dark. Apparently, he went shirtless often. His face shone with sweat. His features hardened with each swing of the ax. He paused his work to wipe his brow and move sandy blond hair from his face. William's eyes roved over to the wagon. Guilty, Kayra shrunk from the hole she had been peering out. Hayden moved. Kayra swallowed and tried to gather herself.

"You okay?" Hayden asked in a groggy voice.

"Nothing. I mean, yes." Kayra grabbed her head covering and began pinning it. "I was just looking outside...checking the weather."

Hayden's eyebrows arched. She smiled with sleepy amusement. "And what did we see? Did a snake strike at you?" She jerked her hand out from under the quilt.

Hayden sat up and crawled to where Kayra had been spying. She pushed her cousin aside. Kayra sat back in annoyance, tugging on worn brown shoes.

"Wow! Cousin," Hayden mused. "You said he was good looking, but that doesn't do him justice. Bobby from Cheyenne," She glanced back at Kayra, "remember him? Now Bobby was good looking but...wow!" Hayden tilted her head. "His nose is a bit large though, don't you think? What's his name again?"

"William, and you'd better leave him alone. He's a good man."

"Well, he certainly is good looking. You are mighty protective for only knowing him for less than a day." Hayden sat down again and began dressing. "Listen, you don't have to worry about me. I'm a nun for heaven's sake. I decided last night that we need to make a trip into town, spread news of our arrival. What was the shopkeeper's name again?"

"Jonas," Kayra recited.

"We'll pay him another visit, and meet the townsfolk. He sure was a talker, which is good. By now, hopefully word of us has already spread. Curiosity can only be rewarded with cash if we act while it's fresh." Hayden put a couple pins in her mouth and arranged her hair under the headpiece.

Kayra shook her head and climbed from the wagon. It was just Hayden being Hayden, but everything out of her mouth this morning rubbed her the wrong way.

How could her cousin have zero qualms about this awful charade?

Hayden

"Wait up! Sister Mary-Katherine, wait for me!" Hayden made quick work of her clothes. Why was Kayra being so difficult this morning? Like a mouse, Hayden scurried from the wagon running straight into William.

"Good morning." He smiled a brilliant smile with remarkably straight teeth. No one has teeth like that. He extended his hand.

Shaking it, Hayden returned his greeting. "I'm–" she began.

"Sister Hannah," he offered. "William. It's a pleasure to have you here."

"Thank you," Hayden replied. She cleared her throat, remembering to use an accent this time. "Have you seen Sister Mary-Katherine?"

"Yes, I saw her climb from here a moment ago. I was just going inside to say good morning." He stepped onto the porch and motioned Hayden ahead of him. "I'm sure mom will have saved you breakfast. You're talking now, so I suppose you can eat."

"Yes, I'm famished," she admitted stepping into the clapboard house.

It was simple and cozy inside. A large table with mismatched, rustic chairs, a very clean fireplace, and a small but functional kitchen crowded the room. A piece of dark gray fabric hung in front of a doorway separating the main house from a bedroom. The other doorway was open and neatly made pallets lined the wall. Standing at the table with sticky dough covering her hands, a middle-aged woman frowned at the sight of the man standing in the doorway.

"William, button your shirt for heaven's sake," She chided in a thick accent, "We have guests, you know."

Kayra looked up from her breakfast and met William's eyes.

The corners of his mouth curved into a crooked smile. It was personal, the way they held each other's gaze.

That was not good. Once her emotions got involved, Kayra was always putting the brakes on Hayden's schemes. Color flooded Kayra's cheeks. Nope, this needed to be squelched.

Interrupting Hayden's thoughts, William's mother was instantly at her side. She wiped her hands on a towel and ushered Hayden to an empty seat at the table.

"I am Ingrid." She motioned to a chair. "Welcome to our home, Sister Hannah." A sudden single cough turned into a fit of them. Ingrid looked embarrassed as she tried to regain her voice. She cleared her throat. "We are so blessed that you have come." She set a plate of fried potatoes, two eggs and beans in front of Hayden.

Ingrid clicked her tongue at her son.

"William?" Ingrid asked, "Are you done with the firewood? If you are, go." She shooed him toward the door. "Get it loaded and fill the buckboard for the Frenches."

William nodded and stepped outside. "Yes Ma'am."

Ingrid shook her head, "I don't know where that boy's head is sometimes." She poured Hayden a cup of coffee. The aroma of these wonderful foods were almost more than Hayden could take. She took a big forkful and gulped it down with the coffee. It had been such a long time since she had eaten at a real table in a real home.

"The Frenches are neighbors of ours," Mrs. Mayer explained, returning to her worktable, "Mr. French died when whooping cough spread through here. It just about took our Jonathon too. Victoria, his wife, has had a difficult time out here by herself. She only has daughters, so she hires William to do most of her plowing and planting." Ingrid stopped her work and smiled at Hayden. "It would be wonderful if you ladies could go along with him. I'm sure they would love meeting you."

"We need to go into town this morning." Hayden answered quickly. Kayra took a sip from her coffee mug, cutting her eyes at her cousin.

Too bad, Hayden thought. They did need to go to town and Kayra really didn't need to be spending any more time with William than was absolutely necessary.

"Oh, that's a shame." Ingrid said, unaware of the cold-front Hayden sensed brewing from Kayra's side of the table. "The Frenches are good people. You know Mrs. French has such devotion to this land. She could leave if she wanted. Her Father is mayor in Denver City and has offered to help her move so that she could have an easier life. But she says she loves the people in Willow Creek." She placed a damp rag over her bowl. "We are blessed to have a wonderful community here. People help each other like family."

Hayden caught that tidbit and rethought her decision to go into town. Mayor in Denver City? *This woman would have a lot of connections that could prove useful.*

"Well, we are servants of the Lord," Hayden said. She made small changes in her accent to mimic Ingrid's. "I suppose I could go visit this woman. Sister Mary-Katherine could run our errands in town."

Ingrid's face brightened, "That would be wonderful." Just then, a child crying in the yard made Hayden and Kayra crane their necks to see out the window above the table. Ingrid shook her head. "All day, every day. I'd better go see what horrible travesty has happened now." She headed out onto the back porch.

"I hate you!" Kayra whispered. "You know that I wanted to go with Will."

"So, he's Will now? That is precisely why you shouldn't go, but we can use this woman's connections. One of us needs to accompany him."

Kayra rushed to her feet. The legs of the wooden chair scratched the floor as she turned to leave the kitchen.

"Kayra!" Hayden called after her

Ingrid returned smiling. "I just told mother. She likes visiting the French's homestead. She loves the ride you know, but I think she also likes the fancy treats that Victoria always has in her candy dish. Imagine owning a dish just for sweets." Ingrid bent to look inside a cupboard. "Oma is looking forward to meeting you."

Oh no. Everyone thought that she spoke German. Quick change of plans. Hayden made a show of sighing. "Sister Mary-Katherine will have to go in my stead. The errands in town may require my personal attention." With that, Hayden stood up and shoved the last bite of potatoes in her mouth and exited the house.

Kayra

Hayden fled from the farm in a hurry to 'attend to her errands.' Kayra knew full well that she was dodging William's grandmother. She acted as if the old woman was rabid. Kayra giggled to herself. As usual, Hayden had apologized to her before drilling her on the details of their story. Kayra was more pleased than she should be that Hayden was not with her today.

An hour later, she sat next to William on the buckboard's bench. He had on different clothes.

Boyish curls glistening in the sun were still wet. Had he gone to all of that effort to bathe and change because he was making a visit or because she was going along?

Oma was seated in the bed of the wagon propped up by soft hay tucked around her. William explained that she couldn't stay awake long enough to sit on one of the benches. He smiled warmly at the steel haired woman behind them.

Only minutes had passed when gentle snores sounded from the bed of the buckboard.

Kayra looked over at William. He chuckled, "I told you. She's 93 and sleeps as much as a new babe."

They bounced along a shady path, William and Kayra side by side, careful not to bump legs or rub shoulders. Kayra's arm was sore from the effort to stay on her side on the bench.

"Did you always have a faith in God, or did it come on as you became older?" William asked.

Kayra wasn't at all ready to answer such a direct question. She'd never been able to lie and not feel guilty. The silence was starting to get uncomfortable so she just started talking. "My mother was a believer and I remember when I was a small child she would sing hymns to me and tell Bible stories. I remember when I was afraid and she sang songs about God's love or protection, it always made me feel safe, peaceful. We didn't attend services much. My father was not interested in church. I have always believed in God. As I got older and life changed, I didn't pay a whole lot of attention to his role in my life." She decided to skirt the truth without lying. "I have only recently taken on the Habit. I guess, I'm searching for meaning and truth too. Just like you."

"My mother also taught us when we were young. I have so many questions and it was just natural for me to be alone and ask God about all of the things that were on my mind. We have a Bible in the house and I started taking a few verses or a chapter a day and just thinking about what they meant. That was when I really started to have my own faith. It was like my parents showed me the door, but I had to go through it. As you know, I still have a lot of unanswered questions, but if you can put all of your faith in God even if you didn't grow up focusing on him, I can do that too. Don't you think?"

"William, Your desire to do what is right is humbling." And boy was it. How had she not wondered about spiritual things before? Basic morals, she had. But faith? What exactly was that? Was it the same as simply believing? For the first time since childhood, she wanted to hear some of those old stories her mother had told her at bed time.

"Whoa boy," William brought the rig to a stop pointing high into a tree. "Can you see that nest up there?"

Kayra followed his gaze and nodded. "Wow! Yes. I would have missed it if you hadn't shown me."

"It's a Hawk's nest. I raised one a few years back. Jonathan was 12 and made a bad choice while hunting. He shot the mother. Dad tore him up for that. We don't kill anything that we won't eat unless we have to. None of us were going to eat that beautiful creature. We kept hearing the babe in the tree and after a couple of days, I climbed up and got him. He was young but already huge. He pecked my hand real good that first day." William held his knuckle up showing where several scars were visible. Kayra ran a finger over the puckered skin. He flinched.

"I'm sorry, did I hurt you?" She looked up to find him staring at her.

"No," he said, "I just..." he glanced away and continued his story. "I handled him with gloves after that. Even when he didn't need my care anymore, he would come around. I made long leather gloves that went up to here." He touched the curve of his bicep. "I'd hold out meat. He would swoop down and take it from my hand. I haven't seen him in over a year though. Hawks are amazing creatures. They mate for life, you know."

"That's incredible." Kayra began. "My Uncle knew a fellow in Oklahoma City that trained elephants. My cousin and I loved watching him work."

"Oklahoma City?" William's head leaned back. His brow furrowed. "That's where you're from?"

Angry with herself for forgetting her role for a moment, Kayra stuttered. "N-no... Stillwater, Oklahoma." There was nothing wrong with sharing some truth.

"So, Sister Mary-Katherine, how did you end up here with Sister Hannah?"

Kayra was spared the necessity to lie because Oma asked William a question in German. He answered and took up the reins. To Kayra's relief, when they started bumping down the path again, he didn't repeat the question.

Kayra

Kayra found herself enjoying the visit with Victoria French and her charming girls. Oma seemed to as well, though she couldn't speak a word to any of them. While sipping tea from delicate little teacups and eating what Victoria called biscuits, though they looked a lot more like cookies, Victoria chatted about her children and the land and let Kayra in on a lot of local gossip.

Hayden had been right, this woman knew a lot about everything that went on in the area and she shared it with ease. No need to pry information out of her. All the frivolity of the afternoon came to a screeching halt when Victoria mentioned word of a man burned in a creek bed two days' ride east of Willow Creek.

Apparently, people were speculating and buzzing about the possibility of a deranged murderer.

"Killing is bad enough, but to burn a poor man like that is just unconscionable." That had been Victoria's opinion on the matter.

Kayra nodded her agreement but said nothing. She held the teacup to her lips but couldn't bring herself to sip it despite her rapidly drying mouth. Her stomach churned. That stench of death. The unique odor of it mixed with brush and smoke. In an instant, she was there by the creek bed.

The delicate cup in her hand was suddenly a leaden weight. She set it clinking against the saucer on the table beside her.

"Are you alright?" Victoria leaned toward Kayra. Awkward silence filled the space. Kayra knew polite conversation required her to respond but she couldn't formulate a single word. Finally, Victoria cleared her throat, "I'm going to refill the tea pot."

Kayra focused on breathing. Hayden taught her that if she just breathed in and out, over and over she could readjust her mind. Sometimes it helped.

When Victoria returned, she opened the door and a warm breeze carried the clean scent of her farm into the stale room. Kayra managed a smile and lifted her tea cup again.

Kayra

William came to the house just before sundown. Victoria excused herself to speak with him. As much as Kayra tried to eavesdrop, the cumbersome headpiece she was wearing was too thick to hear a thing. All she could make out were muffled voices.

"Sister Mary-Katherine," Victoria paused at the edge of the room, "William has requested that I take in your habit for you instead of accepting pay for his work today." Victoria looked almost mischievous in the way her eyebrow arched up, her smile almost a smirk. "It's quite alright with me. It would be an honor to alter it. Isn't that thoughtful of our William?"

Could she do that? *What would Hayden say?* The Mayer's needed that money. Ingrid was very generous but they obviously were not well off. "Um, I don't know..." Too many thoughts all at once.

Victoria put a hand on Kayra's shoulder. "Let him do this for you. I think it means a lot to him."

Kayra nodded. Again, she was unable to find her voice.

Victoria ushered her into her bedroom.

It was unlike anything Kayra had ever seen. From the look of the room, Victoria did come from money. The home itself was modest but her room was ornate. In all their wandering, she and Hayden had met wealthy women, ladies who wore hats instead of bonnets, and hoops under their skirts. This was what the cousins had imagined their homes were like.

Victoria slept in a brass bed with a shiny rose-colored coverlet. Next to her bed was a tall wardrobe with a barely tarnished mirror on the outside of the door. Red velvet curtains adorned the windows and portraits of people Kayra imagined were family hung in wooden frames along one wall.

A bureau with a porcelain pitcher and bowl sat along one side, and a table with a silver tray with what must be a perfume bottle sat near the door. In a corner of the room was a shiny black sewing machine. Even the treadle looked polished. Kayra took it all in.

"I'm sorry Sister." Victoria put a tentative hand on Kayra's shoulder. "I know owning things is of little importance to a lady of the cloth. It is a bit much."

Realizing that her reaction had made Victoria uncomfortable, Kayra was quick to reassure her. "Don't apologize. This room is breathtaking. I could spend the rest of my life right here."

Victoria laughed and went to rummage through a box under her bed. Kayra climbed from underneath the habit, setting it on the polished railing at the foot of the bed. Heat crept up her neck, her face was probably splotchy and red telling exactly how she felt. Her slip, also what she slept in, was the same one she'd had since she was 15. It fit about as well as the habit did, only it was too small instead of too large.

It wasn't anything anyone saw, so it didn't matter, but here, in this room, it felt like even the curtains were laughing at it. Tears showed where the fabric had just given up trying to hold their weave together. Then there were the seams that she had restitched with black thread.

Those tidy lines mocked her. Kayra held her hand over the hem covering a repair.

Victoria pulled a basket from a box and took out a tape measure. Kayra had never been measured before. What did it matter? The habit was nearly a square black garment. She wouldn't be wearing it much longer anyhow. Another stab of conscience joined her distressed emotions.

After writing down the measurements, Victoria opened her wardrobe doors and fingered several dresses before making a selection. She handed a light blue skirt and beige blouse to her. "I know this will feel awkward, wearing these things, but it will only be for a few days." Victoria offered a sympathetic smile.

Kayra could have kissed Victoria for the clothes. That awful habit was miserable. The dark color attracted the sun to its thick, scratchy material and the thing was so roomy that Kayra found herself constantly tripping over the garment. As she rejoiced at the freedom of her new wardrobe, she couldn't help but wonder what Hayden's response would be to her change in attire.

Kayra finished dressing and paused in front of the long mirror, smoothing her dark hair. Wisps framing her face refused to lay straight. If only she had a ribbon to tie it back. No matter.

She felt so much better. Dare she think even pretty? The clothes Victoria had chosen were simple, no frilly collars or lace. That was probably on purpose so that Sister Mary-Katherine wouldn't feel uncomfortable. The soft texture of the cotton against her skin was like feathers. The hem came clear to the floor. How many yards of material must have been used to make up this skirt?

She held her arms out and spun in a circle, baby blue hues whirling about her legs in soft, feminine waves

Kayra nibbled on her bottom lip. She couldn't stop smiling. The shirt seemed tailored to her. Five dresses were all that she and Hayden had between the two of them. And none of the dresses hugged her shape like this blouse did. The creamy blouse cinched in at her waist and flared out at the hips. Tiny white buttons met at a straight collar. Kayra decided to leave the button at the top undone.

She felt pretty and daring. She may be playing a role, but this costume she loved. Would Will notice?

A small pang of guilt coursed through her as she thought of Hayden. She opened the door and poked her head out, taking a deep breath to steady her nerves.

"Come, Sister. I'm waiting." Victoria waved her forward.

Kayra took a few small steps into the living room. Victoria rushed to her side. She took her hand and spun her around. "Sister Mary-Katherine, you are a vision of loveliness. I doubt I will ever be able to wear that again. It looks much better on you." She embraced Kayra tightly and held her out for a second inspection. "The only thing you need is for me to set your hair. May I?"

Kayra nodded. She tried to stop smiling as she followed Victoria. In moments, her dark hair was pinned and arranged on top of her head so stylishly that Kayra felt a little foolish. It was hair that should be worn to a dance or maybe the theater, not on a farm.

Oma once again was asleep in an armchair by the door when they reentered the living room. Victoria went to the kitchen and began setting the table. Unsure of what else to do, Kayra followed. "Can I help?"

"No, dear. The stew is simmering and the bread is in the oven. You could call to the girls that it's time to clean up for supper."

Glad for anything to occupy her, Kayra stepped onto the porch and waved the girls toward the house.

It was dark before William made his way into the kitchen. His face was clean and his hair wet again. He smelled of soap. Had he had the forethought to bring soap? Because of her? Surely not. Kayra focused on breathing. Her heart leapt in her chest as she tried to act normal.

William glanced first in the stewpot. "Smells wonderful, Victoria." He remarked, then turned toward the table and stopped as if he'd come to the edge of a cliff.

Kayra fingered her silverware, feeling so vulnerably self-conscious. But how interesting could the table setting be? She had to look up. Desperate for something to do, she reached for a glass and stood to fill it with water.

"You," William started, "You look beautiful." He stared until even Victoria became uncomfortable.

"William," Victoria teased. "You did know she was a girl didn't you?" Easily, she walked past him, patting his arm. "She is remarkable isn't she?"

Kayra bit her lower lip, her eyes filling with unwelcome tears. She wouldn't let them fall. Her face was as if she'd fallen asleep too close to the campfire.

This was her first time feeling seen and admired as a woman. Not everyone stood out. The fact that she didn't had never bothered her before.

Now, suddenly she was playing a lead role and wasn't at all used to the attention. How could she be so pleased but hate the moment all the same?

"Now sit down and let's eat." Victoria ordered.

They all found places around the table. William was unusually quiet throughout dinner and Kayra could tell that Victoria was amused. Oma seemed unaware that anyone was in the room but she spooned herself bite after bite. Luckily, the girls rushed in and after a squabble over who got the big chair, settled down to spoon stew into their bowls. Their chatter about everything from how much they hated the chickens to the boy at school who had been pestering Sonya, was a godsend at a tense dinner.

William

William took a deep breath.

He'd done that several times already. The night was darker than it had been the evening before. Cloud cover hid the stars obscuring the moon, making the drive home feel almost treacherous. Oma's soft snores were a comfort reminding William that he wasn't alone with Sister Mary-Katherine. He hadn't said anything to her since supper and definitely didn't assist her climb onto the buckboard.

Before, he had been captivated by this woman and now, he was going to have to work *very* hard to not make a fool of himself.

After riding a short way listening only to the creaking wagon and Oma's symphony with the crickets, Sister Mary-Katherine spoke, "Thank you, William, for what you did today."

"It was nothing."

Kayra looked down at her lap where her hands were clasped. She looked uncomfortable too, probably because she was being made to wear clothes that she wasn't used to. This must be hard for her. He should have thought of that.

"It was my pleasure." He purposely kept his response short, not wanting to say anything that might reveal his thoughts. It had been more than his pleasure and he would have worked a month just to see the transformation in Mary-Katherine. *Sister Mary-Katherine*, he reminded himself. She had taken him completely by surprise.

His usual confidence was shaken and he found himself trying to think of something to say. All he could do was breathe.

Again, it was Sister Mary-Katherine who broke the silence. "William, have I done something wrong?"

"Mary-Katherine–Sister. No, no you have...I just–" He sighed. "I guess I just don't know how to act with you now." He spoke truthfully. "This must sound foolish because honestly I haven't acted myself ever since you came here." Through the corner of his eyes he glanced her way.

"Me neither." Mary Katherine admitted shaking her head. Her neck was beautiful. The curve of her jaw. The pucker of a lip. Even in the darkness, he could see the lines of her perfect profile. He returned his eyes to the road.

"This is silly." She turned to him. "I'm dressed differently, but nothing has changed."

Everything has changed, William thought.

She turned to him. "For now, can we just be ourselves? Is that even possible?"

This was what he wanted but was it a good idea? He battled thoughts racing through his mind before purposely relaxing his shoulders. "Alright, we'll just be ourselves. So, Mary-Katherine," he said, pointedly leaving out the sister part. "I want to know something about you, besides that you are a nun and beautiful." He cast a sideways glance at her and was pleased to find his charm wasn't wasted.

"Alright. Let's see, something about me," She thought aloud, "Sister Hannah is my cousin."

"Really?" William looked at her. She seemed delighted with his surprise.

"Now it's your turn." Her voice held laughter as she spoke.

"I hate potatoes."

They both laughed. "You can't hate potatoes. You have an entire field of them."

"My father insisted that the ground was perfect for spuds, but it's true. Much to my mother's frustration, I simply hate them. If they aren't fried I hardly eat them."

They continued easily together, laughing and sharing little things about themselves. She told him a few stories about what she and Sister Hannah had been like as children and he was shocked to get insight into this side of the nun's life.

His impression of Sister Hannah was nothing like what Mary-Katherine was telling him now. His initial impression had been that she was serious and boring and not at all comfortable to be around. He gathered by their conversation that Hannah was not at all as she first seemed and that Mary-Katherine was devoted to her.

He sensed that Mary-Katherine was holding back. If they had grown up together, why didn't Mary Katherine have an accent like Hannah's? *An accent could be lost*, he supposed. He had worked very hard for that. His father insisted that if they were to fit in and get work, the boys had to speak like Americans, not Germans. It was obvious that only Hannah spoke German.

There were so many things that William wanted to understand, but they were having such a good time, so he decided to let those questions wait. He didn't want her to clam up now that she was finally sharing.

"I guess that's about all there is to me." Mary Katherine sighed and a smile curved her lips. She had no idea the beautiful image she made. She could be an angel. Everything about her was so good. Had God sent her to him?

"No, it's not." William flirted. "You left out that if you weren't a nun, you would be secretly crazy for me." His heart beat powerfully in his chest as he waited to see if he had taken it too far.

Her eyes widened. She looked like a deer caught in his sight. *Oh no.* He'd said the wrong thing. She clasped her hands in front of her and sat up straight, leaning toward him. "William," she whispered, her throat raspy with the words. "I'm not a nun."

"I know." He said, slowing the wagon. "Right now, we are just us." They stared at each other. Somehow, their faces were mere inches apart. He felt the warmth of her breath steam against his trembling lips. He closed his eyes and leaned in to fill that last aching distance. As soon as the moment began, it abruptly stopped. He felt her pull away. She lowered her face.

Well, he'd definitely read that wrong. Instantly righting himself, his heart racing, he swallowed.

His face burned.

He gripped the reins in his hands. What was he thinking? He'd almost kissed her, a woman of the cloth, a woman who was much purer than he ever could be. She had already taken vows and he wouldn't try to make her break them.

God had better realize the sacrifice he felt at this moment. He'd try to stop thinking about Mary Katherine in that way.

Almost imperceptibly, She leaned toward the opposite side on the bench. Oma stirred in the back of the wagon reminding William that they were not alone.

William distanced himself and ran his fingers through his hair clicking to the horses to speed them. Mary Katherine smoothed her skirt and rechecked the pins in her hair. The rest of the ride back was made in silence. William didn't trust himself to speak and not finding anything appropriate to say they rode side by side, careful not to touch.

When they arrived at the house, not a light burned, although the cloud cover had given way to the glory of the night and the moon made Sister Mary Katherine all too visible. William hurried to the side of the wagon and helped Mary-Katherine down. It creaked as she stepped from the rail. Was it his imagination or did she hold onto his hand a moment longer than necessary?

He had to apologize. William whispered, "I'm sorry about what almost happened tonight." He stared at the ground and shuffled his booted foot. He'd been trying to figure out how to undo the awkwardness.

"William," Mary Katherine whispered. He forced himself to look at her. She didn't look angry or afraid. "If things were different, if we had met at a different time…" She shook her head and continued, "If you had kissed me, we would both be sorry later."

"Right now, I'm doubting that." He smiled, shy over the truth of that admission.

Her lips turned up at the side and it took the breath from his chest when she came up on tiptoe and brushed her lips on his cheek before running toward her wagon.

William looked up into the stars. "WHAT ARE YOU DOING TO ME?" He was confused and frustrated and happier than he remembered ever being.

Kayra

Kayra climbed slowly into the wagon. The last thing she wanted was to be put through an interrogation. Hopefully Hayden was asleep and stayed that way. To her relief, Hayden was sprawled out and breathing deeply. More cautiously than ever, she lay down beside her cousin and closed her eyes. She knew that there would be a lot of questions to answer come morning. For now, she had this moment alone with her thoughts and feelings.

Except guilt kept her awake. The horrible feeling in her stomach infected her heart and mind. She'd drift off, only to awaken shortly after, unease wrestling inside her belly. She couldn't keep this up.

So many things were happening in her heart and mind. Things that she hadn't considered or understood. When had all of this God stuff crept up on her? Over the past few days she'd found herself thinking more and more about what she and Hayden were doing with their lives. When she analyzed it, she was deeply ashamed.

Everything that they did was for themselves and they did horrible things in order to take care of themselves.

They lied.

They took from people.

They were dishonest with anyone who wasn't the two of them.

Immense guilt replaced her usual discomfort in taking advantage of people.

It was like God had sent them to this farm so that she had to face all of these wrong things in her life. Confrontation was so not her thing. She rolled over, squeezing the feathered pillow in her tight grip.

If she was true to what she thought might be the Lord prodding her, that meant that she would have to talk to Hayden about it. That was terrifying in and of itself because for one thing, she had more than an inkling that Hayden would not feel the same way. That blonde mixture of crazy and fierce protection was her world, her best friend, security and comfort. Kayra closed her eyes, but should she be? According to William, God was that for him. Yet, how did one put that trust in something they couldn't see? Faith, she answered her own question. That very faith that William had asked her about.

That very faith that did not exist in her mind and heart, even though she was wearing the robes that indicated it did.

Guilt washed over her as hard and fast as any river rapids could. It was that guilt she dozed off to, only to awaken again and again in the night. She tried to toss and turn quietly. The last thing she wanted right now was for Hayden to wake up and ask her what was on her mind. She'd have to tell her soon enough.

Because if she continued to pretend that she was okay with lying to these very good people, she was sure either the guilt or God himself would smite her. *Tomorrow.* Tomorrow, she'd be brave and tell Hayden everything.

Chapter Three

Greely

The still night was unnerving. He'd left Jimson a ways off. The crazy animal paced in a circle always making too much noise, but if Greely showed him the circle the horse would stay occupied until called for. That animal was both a curse and a blessing. No one could handle the beast except Greely, thanks to the time he'd found the stallion nibbling on Jimson weed. The smart horse had become crazy. *Ain't nothing wrong with crazy though.*

A few hundred yards away, Greely sat, unmoving, gun in hand, finger on the trigger. His mustache twitched at a sound up ahead.

He sniffed the air like a dog searching for a scent. How could he've been followed? He spit out the side of his mouth, tobacco just missing his leg.

Someone was out there. He could feel their gaze. He scanned the black forest for a glimpse of the white in his pursuers eyes. Another crackle of sticks, barely audible, then a flash where the moonlight caught a shadow.

With practiced speed, he aimed and shot. The ring of the bullets echoed throughout the woods. *Boom, boom, boom,* one after the other. Then he heard the thud of his fallen prey. Hefting himself off the ground he whistled and stiffly limped toward his kill. Arthritis always acted up after he sat too long. The brush crackled beneath his feet. He saw the mound ahead of him laying motionless in the dark. He had no idea who it could be. He'd been traveling at a rapid pace for days, trying to reach Denver before news of that man he killed did.

Earlier in the day, he'd dozed, but at the change in Jimsen's gait, he startled awake. The horse's ears had been set forward. Following the animal's lead he'd looked around.

That was when he first saw the rider coming up behind him. Quickly, he'd darted into the pines waiting patiently for the hunter to become the hunted.

It hadn't taken long. He figured his pursuer wasn't law or a professional.

Men who lived by the gun were wise in their traps. They knew that patience was the key to survival. This fellow had to be strong though, because the pace that he had set was a lot to handle.

Perhaps he had missed something with the drifter camping on the prairie. The gambler had said he was alone but maybe he'd had a son or brother lagging behind. They'd played poker and the man was drunk.

Rule number one, you don't come to a game drunk.

Rule number two, you don't brag about how much money you've got to play with.

He'd done both. After the game had broken up, and he'd started for his camp, he was so drunk that he could barely heft himself onto his horse.

One cowboy slapped the animal on the rump, howling with laughter as they darted away, that fool bobbing back and forth in the saddle.

Greely had excused himself, making a show of going in the opposite direction before looping around. When he'd found John, the sorry man had already taken a nasty fall from his mount, who was nowhere in sight. Blood streamed down the man's neck. Greely was careful not to touch it as he rifled through the strangers pockets. In the distance, there was a beat up wagon and a pitiful pair of mules. Obviously the man drank and gambled more than he cared for his stuff. The wad of cash the man had been bragging about was folded in his breast pocket. Greely began counting as soon as he pulled it out. One hundred twenty dollars. Not a bad night's work.

Then, Greely's legs came out from under him. The drunk had come to, and planned to fight. Greely pulled a knife from his waist. The man lunged forward, barely an attack. The man ran dead ahead straight into the knife. Greely jabbed the blade deeper into his stomach. The man's face registered shock as he stumbled back, staggering toward the wagon. Greely watched him fall. He'd wanted a fight and he'd gotten one. Greely whistled and mounted Jimson.

Now, approaching his latest kill, he cocked the gun again, cautiously toeing the man lying before him. When the form failed to move he kicked the body over. He'd never laid eyes on this fellow before. He set the rifle down and bent to dig through his pockets, only three dollars. Maybe it had just been a coincidence and he'd just been traveling the same route. That made for an unfortunate day, hadn't it? He took the butt of his rifle and smashed it into the man's face until blood drenched the ground. Satisfied, he wiped the end of his rifle on the dead man's pants and whistled.

Jimsen obediently trotted up and pawed at the ground sniffing wildly at the iron smell. "Like that, do you?" Greely asked, stroking the horse's neck. "Me too." Then he hopped into the saddle and they rode, making up for lost time.

Fineese

Fineese sat contentedly on the new bench she'd just been given. She stroked the graying blond hair of the man she loved. He was amazing.

A smile curved her lips. Before him, she couldn't remember being loved. She'd never had things, let alone the likes of the gifts he lavished. She knew little about his life outside her cabin. She knew that he had a family with children as old as she was, but when he was with her, she pretended that she was all he had.

She wondered at times why a man so mature and settled would be drawn to her. She was street trash compared to him. He was sophisticated, and traveled. He spoke two languages, one of which only came out when he was drunk.

She remembered the first time they had met, well more accurately, when he had caught her. After having been turned out of the orphanage in Denver City where she had lived until she was 17, she found herself alone in a new place. Alone and starving.

She had been about to resort to thievery for her next meal when he'd found her in his chicken coop in the middle of the night. They had startled each other. She took in his messy hair and the look of shock on his face when she crawled out of the coop, eggs in hand. She was sure he was gonna use the gun in his hand, but he had set it down and coaxed her to him. She was talking and explaining when he took her into his arms and hushed her, smoothing her head.

She told him everything. How she had been kicked out of the orphanage because she was too old, and how she had no money or idea of where to go. He just jumped into action. Before dawn, she was taken to a trapper's cabin outside of town and given clean blankets and enough food to make it until he could bring her more.

She never had to worry about her next meal after that, and out of the goodness of his heart, he'd arranged for her to stay in that cabin and he would help her by paying the rent on it; all so that she would have a safe place to call her own. In two years, he never once missed a payment. What a lucky night that had been for her, for them.

After a couple weeks of his help setting up her new home, she was finally able to make him a meal to repay him for some of his kindness. He had been almost shy when he'd told her she was beautiful and asked if she would allow him to kiss her. Imagine, a man so thoughtful that he asked before kissing you. That was when she realized that she loved him and that he loved her too.

She didn't care why he had helped her so long ago. She was sure now that he kept helping her because of love. A smile curved her lips, remembering.

As if out of nowhere, a wave of nausea rushed over her. She hurried from the bench and wretched into a basin. Her stomach muscles burned. Her face did too. She grabbed a glass of water and sipped it, then turned to him, forcing a smile.

His eyes however held not even a hint of the pleasure she was used to seeing. She went to the kitchen and grabbed an apron, tying it just above her barely-there waist. She knew the moment understanding dawned in his eyes.

He sat up straighter, glaring, "How long have you known?"

She laid a towel over the basin. "A couple months, I suppose," She spoke softly, not meeting his eyes. Of course he was shocked and it would take him a while to warm up to the idea of becoming a father with her.

He stared, not flinching, not smiling, not even breathing. Fineese tidied her long red braid.

"When were you going to tell me?" He growled the question at her.

"When the time seemed right." She faced him now and forced a smile. "Surprise."

"Whose is it?"

Tears scalded her eyes.

What?

She swallowed and bit down the bile rising in her throat. She'd remain calm and not cry. Sometimes, he was unpredictable. How quickly his behavior could change.

"It could only be yours and you know it." She put her hands on her hips, chiding him.

"With a girl like you it could be anyone's." He jerked his work boots on and stood. "How could I possibly believe that the child is mine?"

"It's only you and me, and you know it." She said again and went toward him, but he held up a hand, halting her.

"Do you have any idea how expensive this is going to be to take care of? I heard of a lady in the Denver area that can give you some concoction to stop it, if it isn't too late." He shook his head. "I pay you to make sure that this type of thing doesn't happen."

"I did the things you told me and evidently it still happened, and I'm not having this 'taken care of'."

"Are you not joking?" He froze in place and went silent.

Maybe he was coming to his senses. Maybe all he needed was time to sort things out in his mind. Fineese reached out her hand to touch his shoulder.

He jerked away. "You really think you can have this baby? And what, send him out to play while you work?" He pointed to the bed.

Fineese held her chin up. "I think *we* can have this baby, and that we'll raise him out here far away from town. Things don't have to change. We just get another person to love. A person who came from the love we share."

"*We*," he snorted. "This is *your* problem." He grabbed his hat and turned to leave.

"This is our child, mine and yours. How…"

He held his hand up and instantly she fell silent.

"I got kids Fineese. I have a family with them. That's not what I wanted with you."

She grasped a nearby chair steadying herself. She couldn't believe how he was acting. Could he really mean the things he said?

He stomped toward a cabinet and poured himself a shot of whiskey, drinking it down in one swig. He shook his head. "Your rent is paid through the month," He announced, not meeting her eyes. "I won't be back, and I never knew you."

She dared not move. He had never been quite like this before.

He walked toward her. For a moment she didn't know if she should run or fall into his arms. He took the decision out of her hands and pulled her against him, capturing her mouth in a kiss. Would it really be their last? If only he would stop and think this through. His fingers snaked up into her red hair and she felt them squeeze. *He wasn't angry, he was sad,* she told herself.

"You ruined it." He held her face in his hands, and suddenly he looked old in her eyes. "You ruined it all." He stepped toward the door. "I will never come to you again and you'd better not be seen around town like this either." He pointed to her stomach.

"You can't mean that." Fineese shook her head.

He reached in his pocket and handed her ten dollars. She dropped her hand, refusing to take it. The breeze from the window carried the cash in circles to the floor. "Don't push this, Fineese. You're not my wife, you're a… a whore. I can't risk my real family playing daddy to yours. Why'd you let this happen?"

She couldn't breathe. A whore? She wasn't a whore. He was the only man she'd ever been with. He loved her, she was sure of it. Why else had he set her up out here if not to be together?

"I guess I'll be in trouble again for gambling away our money." With that said he strode from the cabin.

Fineese tried to swallow her cries but before long she was sobbing. The peaceful life in the country she'd grown in love with was over. He was not coming back. Staying here even to finish out the month would only make things harder. She had to get away. With rash purpose she strode to her closet, pulled out her carpet bag and began dumping what few belongings she had inside.

She reached under her mattress and counted her savings. In two years, all she came up with was sixty-three dollars, seventy-three if she included the ten Gregor had just given her.

Fineese

Five months later, Fineese leaned against the wall outside the saloon trying to look appealing while feeling miserable. Her feet hurt and her back ached, but earning a few more bucks before leaving was the responsible thing to do.

All the sacrifices she made now would make life easier for her and the baby in the future. She would make those sacrifices even though all she wanted to do was to go lay down and rest.

When she first came to Denver, she had an end goal in mind: get far away and make a fresh start for herself. Knowing that supplies for her trip west would cost more than her meager savings, she'd made friends with a local tender and he had set her up in a room above the saloon, rent free. *It was only temporary.* She reminded herself of that fact every day. What was a girl to do?

Denver had been bustling with excitement as visitors from all over flocked to its stores, restaurants, and saloons. A wagon train was leaving town in three days, headed for California. The town's people were geared up for the festivities that came with such an unusually large crowd. Ladies wore their best outfits and the men gambled more frivolously than usual. All in all, it was great for the town's economy. Hers too.

Anyway, she was treated well here and she had what she needed to survive and that is what she had to do right now: survive. The past was the past and soon this would be her past.

She'd done what she needed to do and in the first couple months since agreeing to work this way, she'd almost tripled her money. And with all the new men coming into town, she figured she would be able to cover her supplies and maybe have some leftover to start her new life when she finally reached San Francisco.

With only a few other ladies in town to compete with for business, even her obviously protruding belly had not proven to be a deterrent.

Fineese had no idea how much it would cost to start over in California. She was determined though, that no matter what, she was about to end her career as a sporting lady. She protectively placed a hand over her belly. "I will make things different for you." She choked out the broken words. "We will start a new life. I promise. People won't know about any of this. I swear it."

Kayra

When morning dawned, her resolve to come clean had dwindled. Could she actually go through with it? What they were doing was deplorable. He would hate her and Hayden would hate her and in the end. In the end, they would still not live happily ever after, so what was the point in causing them both all of that hurt? As she dressed, she rationalized that it was better to be a nice memory than a horrible reality.

Hayden was at the water pump when Kayra climbed from her bed. She waved Kayra over.

Hyden was all smiles. "Hey, you didn't wake me up when you got back last night, and what do you have on?"

Kayra took over the pumping and started to tell Hayden about the French family and what had led to her new outfit.

Hayden had been angry with Kayra for allowing Victoria to alter her habit, but not furious, admitting that it provided a wonderful opportunity to personally meet when she came to drop off the habit.

Kayra shared with Hayden about the town gossip. She knew that Hayden would know how to use the information. Hayden said that she already got an earful on that very thing. Apparently, news of the burning was the only gossip in town. Hayden brushed off her concerns as if she didn't want to talk about it, which was just fine with Kayra. She didn't even want to think about it.

Hayden changed the subject and went on about how well she had done in town. To hear her tell it, the town was liable to build a church and name her Saint. Somehow, this success didn't cheer Kayra up. It made her feel even more unsettled. Hayden was celebrating, but Kayra was shriveling.

Finally, Hayden asked about how the trip alone with William and his Oma had gone. Kayra fought with herself about whether or not she should tell Hayden about the almost kiss they had shared...then decided against it. She would keep that special memory for herself.

Hayden

Hayden wondered if Kayra was telling her everything about the trip to Victoria's, but after asking over and over, she decided to let it go. Kayra and William were acting stranger than usual. Both seemed uneasy when they were around the family. In fact, they hardly acknowledged one another, focusing instead on whatever they were occupied with, and then there were times when Hayden would see them alone together. Perhaps they thought no one was looking. Of course, Hayden was always looking.

Once, she had awakened in the night to find Kayra missing from the wagon and, after investigating, found the two by the pond. They were sitting opposite each other talking. She watched them for a while before boredom and the desire to sleep won out over her nosiness. She decided it was harmless enough. She could demand that Kayra tell her what was going on, but it was better to wait. Sooner or later, Kayra would come enlisting help or advice. And of course she'd be there to help her through it. It bothered her that it hadn't happened yet.

I've been pretty preoccupied with raising the money for the trip, Hayden reasoned. Still, being left out of something that she was sure was a big deal to her cousin, stung. Obviously, Kayra was taken with this man.

Hayden wouldn't begrudge her this infatuation, friendship, or whatever it was as long as it didn't interfere with their plan. The hoax was almost over anyway. She'd managed to collect nearly 180 dollars in donations for the mission from the very good people of Willow Creek. Since they already had a wagon and mules, that was more than enough and if it wasn't, she would come up with something else, but this town had been drained nearly clean. It was almost time to move on.

Two more days in Willow Creek and then they would assume different identities and head west. It was thrilling to consider all the possibilities. It wasn't so much the destination that excited her as it was the adventure of getting there.

Kayra

Kayra lay beside Hayden faking sleep. She'd done this each night, waiting until it was safe to sneak out and meet Will. Most nights they just talked. She could talk to him about things that Hayden had never acted interested in. Big things. He challenged Kayra to consider things about God that she had never even thought about. She found herself praying for the first time since she was a child. He believed so much and made her want to. Not all of their time was spent debating the universe. Often, he would grab her hand and not let go. She wanted to be close to him with everything in her. They were careful not to 'almost kiss' again. The guilt over what was hidden wore heavier and heavier around her neck with each conversation and thing that they shared about their souls. This was not who she wanted to be.

Victoria had come earlier in the day and, once again, Kayra was dressed as Sister Mary-Katherine. The alterations had been fantastic. Although it weighed less and she moved easier in it, slipping into the garment was like dressing in her lies. Its heaviness was felt all the way into her soul.

When she walked out of the house wearing the robe, William was out in the field. He waved but she couldn't make out his expression. Things were bound to be different now. Somehow, wearing normal clothes had made their friendship easier. Will had said it made him feel less guilty for his feelings, even though he was not going to act on them again.

They hadn't gotten a moment alone together since the arrival of Victoria and her girls. Throughout the evening, she had searched his face, but he kept himself guarded. She smiled, remembering Victoria's whispered comment, "You'd better be careful honey or that boy just might forget he is going to be a priest." It was said in jest but it hit much closer to home than she realized.

Finally, Hayden's breathing evened out. Kayra remained still a few minutes more just to be sure. Like a burglar, Kayra slipped into her new habit. She held the headpiece in her hand and closed her eyes battling over the decision to put it on. In the end, she folded it up and left it. With hurried strokes, she ran a brush through her hair before slowly climbing from the wagon in an effort to hush the worn bones of their home.

Kayra's heart beat like a hummingbird's as she raced to their meeting place by the pond. She stepped off the path, slowing her pace, not wanting to appear over-anxious. William saw her approach and jogged to meet her. He was carrying a blanket and basket.

"What's all this?" She motioned.

He took her hand in his free one and his lips opened into a smile. She had come to adore the warmth in that crooked grin. "Have you ever been on a night-picnic, Mary-Katherine?"

She had eaten outside at night many times because, for the past five years, the wagon had been the only home she'd known. Not wanting to spoil William's surprise, she shook her head.

"Wonderful." He reached for her hand and led her into the trees. "I know the most beautiful place back here for watching the stars."

How was entering the forest going to lend itself to star gazing? she wondered, but the idea of being secluded with William made it unimportant. She held tightly to his hand as he guided her up a hill. As they came to the top, the thick trees thinned out. They found themselves in a small open meadow. Kayra was trying to catch her breath. She breathed in the deep scent of the trees. Will set the blanket in the center of the field.

It was breathtaking. The moonlight played in the branches, which were pointing toward the heavens, as its glow cascaded gently down until it kissed the grass. The quaking sound of Aspen leaves rustling in the breeze added to the perfection. It was like a private paradise. A place where she and Will could say goodbye.

"To see the stars really well you have to come over here and lay down." He was resting lazily on his side. He patted the blanket beside him.

Kayra gave him a warning smile, but she was willing to risk being that close. He laid back, tucking his hands behind his head. Kayra sat with her legs crossed at his side, watching him admire the sky.

He looked so peaceful. When was the last time she'd felt peace?

Will reached for her hand. "When I was young, I would come here to think and sometimes pray." He smiled and Kayra was sure that she had never seen a more attractive man. "It amazes me that there is so much out there."

Kayra had only a moment's hesitation before she lay down beside him. She rested her head against his shoulder, comfortable and safe.

"Will, I don't want to leave tomorrow." Kayra's words whispered in the moonlight made William's breathing halt.

William squeezed her hand. He cleared his throat, his voice unsteady. "I said that I would not try to change your path, but if you feel like I do, don't go. Mary-Katherine, stay... with me! Wait and then in a year we can go out west together."

Kayra turned to face him. "You don't understand. It's not that simple." Her eyes filled with tears that threatened to spill down her cheeks.

"You're wrong." He sat up. "It's not that complicated." With his calloused finger, he tenderly stroked Kayra's cheek. "Look at me. You said, 'one can have a family and serve the Lord.' Why not you? Why not us?"

"William, stop. Please, just stop. There is so much that you don't know."

"I know that I love you and I am pretty sure that you love me." He spoke as if that alone was enough.

Kayra held her face in her hands and allowed the flood gates to open. Once she started she couldn't stop. William placed a palm across her heaving back.

Kayra turned into his arms and buried her head in the crook of his neck.

"My sweet Mary Katherine, please don't cry. We can work this out." He stroked her head. "I have thought about this. Every night you leave me, I think about this. We could go into Denver, find Father Christopher and..."

His words made her cry even more. She shook her head, unable or unwilling to explain. She had never before felt so secure. He was what she'd dreamt of. His heart beat against her cheek. He sighed, holding her. After a while, her tears had run their course. She hiccupped. He laughed, relieving the tension. She giggled as another one shook her body.

"Can we talk about this?" There was so much hope in his voice.

"I can't."

"And there is nothing I can do to change your mind?" William stroked her hair

"No," She whispered.

She heard the air escape in frustration from his mouth. "How can–"

"Stop," she begged. "It is what it is and what we have is only going to last a few more hours. Let's not spend it arguing. Please, William. Give us right now, a time that we can always remember."

He raised her hand to his lips and kissed her knuckles. He was her dream but her lies were keeping it from becoming a reality. The weight of deception hung like a millstone around her.

Wrapped in his powerful arms, her head buried in his neck, she clung to him allowing his strength to fill her weakness. He kissed the crown of her head, smoothing her hair. His fingers ran the length of her tresses, returning to the tender spot at the nape of her head. She raised her face to find his eyes closed.

His full lips were there, just a breath away. How many times had they been this close? How many more times would they have left? Fighting against everything her good sense was telling her not to do, she closed the space between them.

Will's shocked intake of air was replaced by the gentle accommodating encouragement he offered, turning her face to an angle that allowed him to explore her kiss. It was tentative at first, like the caress of a butterfly tasting and trying her will. The moment she responded, he did too, filling her heart with the emotion she had been craving from him.

"You can never leave now." William uttered the words that she hated most. She was horrible. She was going to leave. She was not going to tell him how many lies had piled up between them. She was going to break his heart.

She pulled away as abruptly as if he had hurt her. "No, no, we have to stop this."

He straightened himself and bowed his head. When he brought his eyes up to meet hers, they crinkled at the edges. He was smiling. Even now, he was not angry with her. "It always comes to this, Mary-Katherine. I say it won't, but it always does. I can't seem to help it."

"I'm so sorry."

"Shh." He quieted. "You have nothing to be sorry about. But we do need to figure out what is happening between us. You can't walk out of my life tomorrow. That would destroy me."

Kayra adamantly shook her head. She didn't trust herself to speak. William was quiet and she assumed he was waiting for her to explain or come to her senses or something that made sense. In silence, they settled beside one another and Kayra forced her attention to the sky overhead. God was watching and she knew that he was well aware of the string of lies she was continuing to tell.

Please forgive me.
They rested until sleep finally claimed them both.

Kayra

It was still dark when Kayra awoke. William's hand held hers and his deep breaths bordered on snores. She dared not move for fear of waking him. Dew covered the ground around them and glittered through the grass. It had to be near sun up. Her mind began whirling around the possibilities of what the new day would bring.

William had asked her to stay with him. Actually, she reminded herself, he had asked Sister Mary-Katherine. No matter what decision she made, people were going to be hurt. Either direction she went on this, William was going to be hurt. Wondering whether or not he would be able to forgive made her sick to her stomach.

Leaving made the most sense but it brought angry tears to her eyes. How could she do that to him? To Hayden? Once word got out of their deception, surely they'd be run out of town leaving the Mayers to clean up their mess.

More than anything, fear of telling William the truth and being rejected is what made up Kayra's mind.

Slowly, she slid from his side. He began to awaken and smiled. It stabbed through her like a sword. Tears blurred her vision. She blinked them away. He sat up and moved to pull her to him. She dodged his embrace and stood. Her throat burned as she broke out in uncontrollable tears. In an instant, he was at his feet. He grabbed her wrist and forced her into his arms. Sobs came before she found the strength to push him away.

"I want to help. Why are you doing this? I love you Mary-Katherine."

Startled, she stepped far away from him. "You can't. Things aren't as simple as they seem." Angrily, she brushed a stream of tears from her face only to be immediately replaced with another one. "I'm not what I seem. This hurts but..."

William stepped toward her but she avoided him. "It doesn't have to hurt." He raised his voice. "You convinced me that I can serve God and have a family. Well I plan on that, and I want you to be a part of it. Please, don't leave."

"I'm sorry. I have to. Hannah will be awake soon." Refusing to endure a moment more she ran, out of the meadow and into the trees.

Kayra heard him calling after her. "Mary-Katherine!" Through blinded tears, she sprinted faster putting as much distance as she could between them.

William

When William arrived back at the house, fear clenched his heart. The wagon was gone. Fresh tracks marred the dirt road where she had left his world. She really was gone. From the pit of his gut he felt a hurt unlike any he had experienced before. He hurled the basket. It hit the porch post, spilling out its untouched contents. The snacks that he had so hopefully packed the night before.

The door creaked on its hinges. Ingrid padded outside in her bare feet. "William?" she coughed. She cleared her throat before continuing. "What's going on out here?" She pulled a blanket around her small shoulders.

"Nothing, mother," The words were spit through a clenched jaw.

"Son, where are the sisters?" She looked so alarmed.

"They're gone." William choked on the words

"But they...I..." She fell silent.

Ingrid bent down to collect the contents of the uneaten picnic.

"Mother, don't. It's my mess." William stooped to help.

Crouched on the porch, Ingrid spied silver at the same time William did. Slowly she lifted the smooth band. When her eyes met his, the love and compassion he saw in their depths was all it took. He couldn't hold in the anguish he felt a moment longer. He collapsed to his knees and cried. Ingrid wrapped her arms around him, pulling his body against her small frame.

"Oh, son, I was afraid this was happening. I'm sorry, my dear boy, so sorry."

He wanted her arms to comfort him. He felt about as defeated as any little boy could, but even his mother's arms couldn't help.

She took a deep breath and he felt her chest shake. She was crying too. "I wish I could feel this for you."

William sat up. "No, Mother, you don't. I'd not let you." He forced a smile. "I'll be okay." He said the words doubting their truth.

Ingrid held her hand to his cheek. The coolness of her small palm felt good on his burning face. "I'm no stranger to heartbreak, son. It does get better."

William nodded. Losing his sister had been a heartbreak, but somehow she hadn't allowed it to keep her down. She'd held the family together by sheer will. Her tiny shoulder's had carried so much. Looking at her now, wrapped in a shawl, graying hair wisping about an untidy braid, lines creasing her forehead, she looked old. When did that happen?

A coughing fit overtook her. William stood, pulling her up beside him. She'd had a cough for at least a month and it only seemed to be getting worse. Her energy had diminished and she'd been sleeping a lot more. "We need to get you back inside."

She handed him the ring. "I'm okay, too." Her eyes crinkled when she looked at him. Was she also lying?

Chapter Four

Hayden

While the sun still slept, the sound of Kayra hitching up the team startled Hayden into consciousness. Before she was even dressed, Kayra was driving the wagon down the road, leaving the Mayer's farm behind them.

Hayden crawled into the seat beside her friend and waited for an explanation. It was rare for Kayra to drive the team. That job usually fell to Hayden, but somehow Hayden could see that her cousin needed this time to be in control.

What could have caused this? Kayra hadn't slowed their pace in about twenty minutes. The mules resisted her stamina, refusing to keep up with her demands. She still hadn't offered an explanation. Whatever it was, it must have to do with William.

Hayden couldn't stand the silence a moment longer.

"Cousin, did William hurt you?"

Kayra scoffed. "No, he did nothing wrong. It was all me."

Hayden paused. She needed to be delicate here and not say the wrong thing. "What did you do?"

"You mean besides lying to him for days and days, leading him on and then chickening out when it came time to face my actions?" Her response required no answer but Hayden answered anyway.

"No, you are the best person I know. You could never do anything wrong."

That didn't seem to help. Kayra snorted her disbelief. "Truly, if I am the best person you know, then you need to make a new friend because I'm feeling pretty bad about myself right now."

"Stop that, right now. You're amazing. I don't want another friend. We're family. More than that, we're a team and I couldn't live without you. I know that you liked William but...he's just one man. I promise when we get to Denver I will have you falling in love with someone else, someone better."

Kayra shook her head and sighed. "Thanks Hayden, but stop. I know you don't understand but that won't fix this. It can't be fixed." Tears filled her eyes and Hayden wrapped her arms around Kayra, forcing her close. The mules slowed their pace.

Hayden sighed, "I love you Cousin, so I'll stop. Unless I find a really dreamy, perfect beau for you. Then I would have to intervene. Are you going to be okay?"

"Of course. It just hurts right now." After a moment, Kayra opened up. "He said he loved me. He asked me to stay with him."

"He *what*?" Hayden pulled her cousin away to see her face and jerked the reins from her hands, halting the grateful mules. "But you're a nun!"

"No I'm not." Kayra stomped her foot, "but he doesn't know that."

"What did you say?" Hayden couldn't believe what she was hearing.

"Nothing. Nothing at all, I just ran. Literally."

The girls stared at each other. Hayden knew that a romance was developing between her cousin and that Mayer boy, but she'd figured it was a harmless flirtation. After her initial reaction wore off, she'd been pleased that Kayra had gone along with it at all, feeling only slightly worried that it might compromise their cover. She should have given the crush more credence.

"I should've known that you would fall hard the first time." Hayden quickly hugged her cousin again. "Don't worry, it'll pass." Hayden took up the reins moving the animals into action. "I bet you haven't slept much. Go ahead," Hayden motioned behind them. "I can manage here."

A much calmer Kayra climbed into the back of the wagon which gave Hayden time to begin working on the next portion of their plan.

Hayden

The girls stopped for the night before reaching Denver City. Hayden wanted to go over the details of their next charade and fine-tune characters before playing the parts.

They camped along a stream. The Rocky Mountains stood tall and powerful in the distance. How would they ever climb them? It was a scary thought that filled her with excitement.

While Kayra prepared to make a fire, Hayden took their rifle and set out in search of supper. She knew how to shoot but had never really hunted before. Uncle Johnny had provided the meat. It was kind of empowering to have this newfound responsibility. The sun kissed the mountain. Soon, seeing would be next to impossible. Lucky for them, Hayden was confident that she'd have dinner before it was dark.

A good distance from camp, Hayden entered a treeline. The earthy smell of pine filled her lungs. Maybe her luck would be better with some cover. She shot at two rabbits but didn't come close to hitting either. It felt like she'd been walking for an hour. Her enthusiasm waned. She crouched in the shadows of a tree. Maybe she should just rest and wait for something to come to her.

Some hunters did that. She rested her back against a large tree trunk, the heavy weapon poised across her lap. She decided that hunting wasn't fun after all. Before long, boredom got the better of her and she began thinking.

Soon after that, she was asleep.

Her dreams were rarely peaceful. When she slept she was always a frightened child running from her burning home. In the distance, she can hear her aunt's tortured scream and she can see her mother's face as life leaves it. She hides behind a huge rock, waiting. Tears run down her cheeks and she fights back any noise attempting to escape her throat.

Then, Kayra is running through the field. Someone is chasing her. He is lean and strong with that terrifying face painted with red stripes shining in the moonlight, eyes like black diamonds. His jaw is held in a grimace.

As he closes the distance between him and Kayra, her cousin's gown catches on a thorn bush and tears. As she stumbles the warrior scoops her up onto his horse. Hayden sees herself running from the safety of her hiding spot, rock in hand. It flies through the air and lands smack into the back of the Indian's head.

His arms go limp and Kayra falls to the ground. Then the girls are running like mad through the trees, hearts beating so hard they think they will die.

There are lights ahead. When they reach Uncle Johnny's house it's completely dark.

Hayden awoke with a start. It was only one of her nightmares. The eerie cold that always follows her dreams seemed exaggerated as darkness blanketed everything around her. Empty handed, she came to her feet. With or without dinner, it was time to head back to camp, back to Kayra. A chilling breath of air rushed through Hayden's lungs, compelling her to freeze. Crackling in the trees up ahead drew her attention toward a small figure. Slowly, not wanting to scare her prey she lifted the rifle to her shoulder taking aim.

At the click from charging her weapon, a fox she realized, peered from its activities only long enough to make a better target. The echo of her shot sounded like thunder in her ears. "I did it!" A feeling of exuberance and pride rushed through her veins. "I did it. Maybe hunting is fun." Hayden set the gun down and darted in the direction of their dinner, her stomach growling in anticipation. It might not be a deer but what would they do with all that meat anyway? How would she have even gotten a deer back to camp?

As soon as Hayden was within ten feet, she stopped short. Something was wrong. 'Knock it off, Hayden. You're no chicken.'

With purposeful steps, she continued. Leaves danced above her as the wind carried a horrific stench in her direction. Covering her mouth and nose she halted. Her eyes fell on her prey. A small, limp ball of fur lying lifeless on top of... a man, his body, bloated in death.

His head smashed so brutally, was she looking at his face or not? His clothes were shredded. A bone jabbed through tattered pants and most of his right leg was gone altogether.

She opened her mouth to scream but no sound would escape. Her mind begged her legs to run, but they were frozen in place. Odor permeated the air. Her chin jerked forward several times before her stomach tightened and she vomited at the dead man's singular foot.

Kayra

Kayra was seated by the fire imagining awful scenarios when she finally saw her cousin. Hayden was frantic. Indians must be after them. The only other time that she had ever seen Hayden this afraid was that night long ago. Kayra ran to meet her. "Did they hurt you?"

Hayden shook her head, her eyes gleamed with terror.

"Who's after you?" Kayra demanded, grabbing Hayden's arm. She scanned the dark prairie behind her cousin.

"Don't...think...anyone..." Hayden jerked her arm free, darting from the camp to dry heave into the brush.

Kayra followed, she wasn't letting her out of her sight. "What happened?" Gently she moved Hayden's cornsilk hair away from her flushed face.

"He was dead. It was awful..." Hayden turned into her cousin's outstretched arms but didn't cry.

"Dead?" Kayra searched the darkness for any sign of trouble. "What's going on? Who is dead? Are we safe?"

Shaking her head, pupils dilated, Hayden replied, "I don't know. The man must have been killed a while ago, He was swollen and stunk... but... I just don't know. I don't think I'll ever feel safe again."

"Wait, killed? How do you know he was killed?" Kayra asked.

Hayden dipped her face avoiding Kayra's eyes. "His head or face or whatever it was had been smashed in. No animal could have done that."

Kayra gasped. "Maybe a bear could..."

"No!" Hayden lifted her intense eyes and locked them with her cousins. "It was just like... It must've been Indians. I never heard of anything like this."

Not Indians. Please God, not Indians. Kayra nodded her understanding. They had seen firsthand what Indians on a warpath were capable of. No further explanation was necessary. Kayra's eyes filled. Would they never have a moment's peace? Could this day get any worse? Kayra's stomach churned, panic rising inside of her. "Please, no."

Too quickly, Hayden's face softened. She pulled herself away straightening her dress, running a hand down her disheveled hair. "Cousin, I didn't mean to scare you. It just startled me. I'm sure we're safe, well... probably. Don't worry. We'll leave at first light."

Still unconvinced, Kayra nodded. If Hayden was going to pretend to be okay, so should she, but her stomach was flopping around like a dying fish.

Hayden grabbed her by both shoulders forcing her to look into her eyes. "We're fine. You've nothing to be afraid of. I was spooked."

Kayra swallowed her fear. "First light."

"I didn't get us any dinner," Hayden said.

"I couldn't eat anyway." Kayra motioned to the small fire she built. "We might should put this out. No need to draw attention."

"I think it's fine. It's been burning. Anyone in the area will have already seen the smoke."

Kayra was glad. The last thing she wanted was to spend the night in darkness.

Every sound surrounding them felt like a threat. Kayra held her cousin's hand and prayed for morning.

Hayden

Morning had finally come and with their early departure, it hadn't been a full day's travel before they were driving the wagon down the crowded streets of Denver City. They passed dozens of wagons, both new and old. People scurried about their business dressed in everything from hats with long feathers curling down their smiling brims to threadbare muslin dresses.

Music and laughter spilled onto the bustling sidewalk from an overfull saloon. Just outside the swinging doors stood a young, and very pregnant, woman.

Her overflowing bosom nearly poured out of the constricting purple bodice of her gown. Her red hair set high on her head like a crown. Rust colored ringlets fell in long coils down her white shoulders. The gentleman she was talking to, ran a finger along her neckline.

Boldly, the woman grabbed his hand and the two disappeared. The saloon doors swinging behind them.

"Did you see that?" Hayden's eyes were wide.

"I tried not to stare. That girl must be younger than we are," Compassion was thick in Kayra's voice. "How sad for her, for that child."

"It's disgusting," Hayden countered.

Kayra frowned. "Remember what you said about young girls alone in a big city and what became of them. She's probably a lot like us and never wanted that for her life any more than we do."

"Yes, but I would never let us become that. There are plenty of other ways to earn money."

"Oh you mean morally, like lying to people's faces and taking their hard earned money for causes that you don't even care about, and furthermore don't even exist. Face it Hayden, at least that girl is honest with the people she takes money from. How can you be so condemning? We aren't exactly living righteous lives either."

"We only pulled that last scam to get here. For heaven's sake, it didn't hurt anyone"

Kayra shook her head. A pregnant pause then she spoke. "Yes, Hayden, it did hurt someone. It hurt two people actually, very badly." She crossed her arms in front of her and darted her eyes up and down the street. "Stop the wagon. I'm going to find the sheriff and tell him what you found."

"Kayra." Hayden pulled the wagon off the road. "I'm sorry." She put a tentative hand on Kayra's shoulder. "That was thoughtless of me."

"I know you didn't mean to be hurtful. It's just... sometimes you're so selfish. What anyone else wants, or feels, or needs doesn't matter. It's always about what you want and how you want to get it. I love you cousin, but that's wrong."

Kayra's words landed on Hayden like a brick. Never in all her memories had Kayra ever spoken with such calm judgment, not to her. Her cousin's words hurt. She was only trying to make things better for them, to protect her.

"Cousin, I'm sorry. I don't know what else to say. I care about you. Honestly, other people don't really matter to me, but you do. You're the most important thing in my life."

"But I shouldn't be." Kayra spoke softly. Through the din of town noise, Hayden leaned in giving Kayra the attention she needed. She continued. "We should be doing something good with our lives. Don't you feel empty at night when you lay there and know that not a single thing you did that day meant anything to anyone except us? I'm not just talking about you Hayden. I've done it too. The Mayer's think about everyone else. The way they help Victoria and what they did for us... I want to be like that."

"I had no idea you felt this way." Hayden was very still. .

"Well, I really didn't either, but spending time with William showed me how awful we are." She shook her head. "I can't be like that anymore. I won't pull any more scams that could hurt someone. I'm sorry,I just can't do it anymore."

Guilt was not an emotion that Hayden was used to feeling, but she felt it now.

She never wanted to hurt her and she hated to see such a good person feel bad about themselves.

She'd pushed her to do things that she knew she was uncomfortable with, but it had always seemed like an adventure, a way to pretend they were someone else if even for a little while. And people seemed to enjoy the roles she came up with. They liked helping, but if it really bothered Kayra, she would stop. If there was ever a person that she wanted to feel valued, it was her and if this was how, she'd do it. No more taking from people under false pretenses.

"Kayra, I never wanted to make you feel bad. If you want, we really can become nuns. I'd do anything for you, cousin." Hayden meant every word that she said.

Kayra snickered. She ran her fingers through her hair squeezing it at the roots. "No, I don't want to be a nun. I just want for us to be the kind of people that God would want us to be."

"Alright. I get it. From now on we will do one unselfish thing a day, one thing that doesn't benefit us at all. And more than that, we can pick someone every week and do nothing but nice things for them. It will be like a project for us. This is going to be fun. How does that sound?"

"I don't know what to do with you Hayden. It sounds fine to start with, but I am serious. No more hurtful scams."

"Can I still be a teacher for the trip to California?" Hayden asked hopefully.

Kayra was thoughtful. "I suppose there's no harm in what you have planned. Just please don't make it elaborate. And no accents."

Hayden smiled and held her hand out for her cousin to shake. "I think we have a deal." Kayra shook it.

"Thank you. Now we have to report the body you found. Do I have to do it, or will you take care of this?" Kayra asked.

Hayden feigned offense, "Of course I'll handle it and I will be completely honest about everything. Just let me find those fake spectacles."

Hayden

The sheriff's office consisted of a wooden desk and chair. Not at all as impressive as what Hayden had hoped to see in the big city.

On the wall behind the desk were a half dozen reward posters. There were two cells with bars. Each cell had a cot and chair. Having never been inside a jail before, Hayden was disappointed to find no prisoners. The sheriff sat behind his desk flipping through a stack of papers.

"Can I help you?" He asked without raising his face.

"Um, yes. I'd like to report a murder."

His finger held its place and he brought his eyes up to meet Hayden's. "A murder? Tell me about it." He eased back in his chair, setting the pile aside. The chair creaked beneath him.

"Okay," Hayden paced back and forth in front of the desk. She adjusted the glasses on her face and nervously cupped the tight bun at the nape of her head. "My sister and I," she began, "camped last night about seven miles outside of Denver in the direction of Willow Creek. Anyway, I went out hunting..."

"Hunting. You hunt, do ya?" The sheriff leaned forward, folding his hands in front of him. Amusement flickered across his face. His brown mustache twitched as his mouth softened.

"Yes, I hunt." Hayden's reply was terse.

"Continue." The sheriff reached for a pad of paper and a pencil.

Annoyed at his disbelief, Hayden elaborated. "I had just killed a large buck when I came across a body. It was a man and he had been obviously dead for several days."

"What did he look like?"

"Well, he'd been torn apart by animals. His head was beaten in so I couldn't make out any facial features. I couldn't say how old he was. Indians did it."

He cocked an eyebrow. "Why you supposin' that?"

"Because it was inhumane." Hayden said matter-of-factly.

"You probably don't know this little lady, but we've discovered three other bodies out on the plains. None of the killings seem to be related and one of the poor fellows was actually burned in a crick. Indians don't do random killings. They kill for a purpose and are inclined to take a trophy." He tugged at his hair. "I'm sure that you couldn't have known the danger you were in out on the plains or your husband wouldn't have let you go out hunting alone. You'd best stay closer to town from now on. If you'd fetch your husband, I'd like to hear his take on this."

Hayden stood tall in front of him. "My report of the murder is sufficient and besides that, I already told you that I was with my sister! I have no husband. Are you going to do something about this or not?"

"Didn't mean to offend, ma'am. You two ladies got no business traveling alone, with or without a murderer on the loose. It ain't safe or proper."

Hayden's blood began to boil, her eyes bored into the man like a knife. "I am completely capable of taking care of myself and my cousin."

"Uh, your sister isn't it?"

Flustered Hayden stomped her foot and walked closer to his desk. "And I'll have you know that propriety is of no importance to me either. I will do as I please, and if it suits me to travel unchaperoned, I will. In fact, my sister and I are leaving for California with the next wagon train." Hayden's nostrils flared. She took her spectacles off, smiling curtly. "Now, if you'll excuse me, I have some business to attend to and I expect you to attend to some as well. Good day, sir."

Hayden spun to leave. The scratching of the chair beneath the sheriff signaled his abrupt stand. "Ma'am, I apologize."

Hayden cast a glance over her shoulder. "I don't need nor want your apology. Just do your job."

Quickly, he came from behind his desk, extending his hand. "My name is Derrick. Derrick Jones."

Hayden paused before shaking his hand with a firm, terse grip. "I'm Hayden and my sister Kayra is waiting outside. If you'll excuse me…" She turned to leave. He followed her onto the walkway.

"Miss, where are you staying? I'll escort you back." Gently, he took her elbow in his hand to help her off the sidewalk.

She jerked free. "I told you before, I don't need any assistance or an escort. That hasn't changed since you found out that I don't have a husband." With that, she turned on her heel, hastily grabbing the bench seat of the wagon and hoisted herself up. She made a show of taking the reins from a startled Kayra and clicked her tongue.

Kayra

They registered with the wagon train that was scheduled to leave in two days. Kayra sat alone in their hotel room. Her mind wandered to the upcoming trip. She doubted that Hayden had any real idea what lay ahead of them, which was made more apparent as they argued over which supplies were necessary and which weren't. Hayden declared themselves ready and decided that it wouldn't be too frivolous to stay in a hotel for a couple of nights.

Neither girl had ever had the occasion to stay in a hotel before. Hayden reasoned that it would probably be the last couple nights of restful sleep that they'd have for a long time.

The room was not by any means luxurious, but having lived in a wagon for nearly five years, it seemed decadent. The bed was softer than anything Kayra remembered sleeping on and the sheets were crisp and white. Adjoined to the hotel was a bathhouse. Both girls had treated themselves to a very long, warm soak. Feeling fresh and pampered, Kayra walked to the window. The lace curtains danced in the breeze. Looking out onto the streets of Denver City, Kayra spied her cousin.

Hayden was nearly dancing up the walk. She looked like anything but a schoolmarm. Her hair hung in loose golden curls. She had ditched her spectacles and wore her best dress. Simple as it was, she looked anything but plain. Next to her, holding a brown paper package, was a young man. He stood a good foot taller than Hayden who hung on his arm. He wore creased, new clothes and an impeccably clean cowboy hat, set low on his forehead. He had to be a local man because he nodded to several passersby in greeting. Hayden's eyes gleamed with mischief. Giggling, she stopped at the hotel entrance.

Hayden

"Thank you, Denny, for bringing me back and for the gift." Reaching out, she took the package from him. As a prize for his attention Hayden gave him her most polished smile.

The fellow shuffled his feet, studying the ground. "It was my pleasure Ms. Hayden." Then, he just stood there.

Hayden made no effort to excuse herself or fill the silence. She was becoming impatient with him for not already asking her to the celebration tonight. Determined to get an invitation, she decided to make herself a bit less threatening. "I was so pleased to come across you today, knowing so little about the city and being alone in such a big place without a brother or father here to protect me. It was nice to have found a handsome man like you to help me find my way back to the hotel." *That ought to do it.*

"I didn't realize that you were here without any family." Denny looked a little braver.

"Did I not mention that?" She touched her hand to his arm. "It's just me and my sister Kayra. As I said, we're going to California by wagon train."

"You mentioned that." He took the hat off of his head and held it in his hands. Another awkward pause. What is it going to take? Never leaving things to chance, she fished around again. "This city is so big. I guess I'm going to have to spend the next couple days in my room so I won't get lost."

"Oh, you aren't going to the celebration tonight?" He was clearly disappointed.

Almost got him, she hoped.

"No, it would be too overwhelming. We'd be swallowed up in a big crowd like that." Hayden shook her head, making her eyes appear large.

"Well, if you'd like, I'd be glad to take you. Your sister too. We only get a crowd like this every so often. It'd be a shame to miss out. Besides, I'd like to see you again."

Hayden displayed her most innocent expression of pleasure. "Really, you would?" She looked up at him with practiced adoration. "That would be fantastic. It'll be so exciting. Are you sure you don't mind?"

"Not at all, I'd love it." His too-wide smile was actually very sweet.

"It's settled. We will meet you here at seven." Hayden concluded the deal.

"Sounds great." He fumbled, releasing Hayden's arm. Stepping backwards he waved. "Bye, then." His foot stepped unevenly off of the walkway and he tripped but righted himself before stumbling too badly. Immediately his face reddened and he looked up.

Hayden's eyes widened. She darted forward. "Denny, Are you alright?"

"I'm fine. I feel like a fool, but I'm fine."

She offered a sympathetic smile. "Bye then, until tonight."

He nodded, putting his hat back on his head, then turned in humiliation heading down the street from where he had come.

Chapter Five

Hayden

At ten till seven, Hayden sat by the window watching the street for Dennison, her finagled date. She wore Kayra's new skirt and blouse from Victoria. It didn't fit as perfectly as it had on her cousin, but it was nicer than anything either girl owned. Kayra had insisted that Hayden borrow it and dressed in one of her common day dresses.

"Cousin, aren't you going to do anything with your hair?" Hayden clucked her disapproval and walked over to the dressing table where Kayra combed her dark brown locks. "If you want, I could fix it for you."

"No thanks."

Hayden frowned at her cousin's reflection. "I sure hope that you snap out of this mood you've been in. This could very well be the most exciting night we have ever had. We've never been to a party like this. Besides, we're starting our new lives." She knelt down in front of the dressing table taking Kayra's hands in her own. "Tell me what I can do to make this better."

Kayra took a deep breath, exhaling like a steam engine. "I'm sorry I haven't been good company. It sounds silly. I only knew William for one week, but I miss him and I still feel really bad about what I did to him. I can't bear the thought of never seeing him again, never apologizing. We couldn't have made it work even if I had fessed up to who we really were... I just feel completely... alone." A tear ran down her cheek.

Hayden wiped it away. "How can you feel alone? I'm right here and always will be. We are enough. I'm your family cousin, and I'll take care of you."

Hayden sighed. *Would Kayra ever come out this melancholy?*

"Come on sweetie, get up. You're going to have a glorious night and forget all about William." She pulled Kayra to her feet. "Let's go. I'm sure Denny's downstairs by now."

"Who's this fella anyway?"

"Just a man I met in the general store this morning. You'll like him. He's sweet and very generous." She lifted her skirt displaying new shoes.

Kayra shook her head. "I hope that you know what you have gotten yourself into. You did tell him that we are leaving with the wagon train?"

"Of course. He knew exactly how long I was staying in town and he offered to buy the shoes for me. I didn't ask. Oh," Remembering the rest of their conversation, she clued Kayra in, "I also told him that I was an artist from Boston, but that's all. No elaborate lies. I promised you and I kept it. Just one small, simple one." Hayden opened the door and they left their room headed for the staircase.

"Did you give him your real name or am I to call you Contessa all evening?"

"No, Hayden will do," She winked at Kayra. "but I like Contessa. Let's see if we can work it in sometime."

Hayden shushed Kayra as they exited the hotel lobby. Denny was quick to extend his hand. Kayra shook it.

"Hi," He nodded. "I'm Dennison Harvey. Denny for short. I was lucky enough to bump into Ms. Hayden this morning and am pleased to escort the two of you to the dance."

"I'm Kayra, Hayden's cousin."

Denny looked up at Hayden, confusion clouding his eyes. "Cousin? I thought you two were sisters."

Unphased, Hayden shook her head. "No, you must've misheard. But you look fantastic," she gushed. "I'm sure that every girl in Denver is going to be boiling in jealousy over us stealing you."

Denny cooperated beautifully with her change of topic. "I doubt that, Ms. Hayden." He held his arm out. "I will be the one making people envious. You look real good."

Real good? Hayden thought as she placed her hand in the crook he offered, that's all I get? Real good. A pie is "real good" for heaven sake. Her smile betrayed none of her thoughts as she allowed her escort to lead the way. Kayra tagged along behind.

Hayden

The square was a mass of people, music, food and laughter. Lanterns hung from strands around the dance floor. Red and white-checkered cloths covered tables creating a barrier for the celebration. A band on a platform plucked their instruments. A banjo twanged over the hum of voices.

They passed a group of girls hunched together, whispering and looking over toward where several young men had assembled. Hayden was in her element, her confidence growing by the moment. She smiled openly to several strangers all the while not skipping a beat in the flirtatious conversation with Denny.

"If you'll excuse me," Kayra motioned to the refreshment table. "I think I'll go get a drink."

Hayden shook her head behind Denny's and gave Kayra an annoyed look. "Why don't you stay with us? I'm sure Denny would love the first dance with you." She took his hand and placed it in her cousin's. Kayra's eyes scolded Hayden for what she was doing but her mouth turned into a gallant smile as she accepted his hand.

"Let's dance then!" Denny said, leading her into the center of the square where couples were lining up. He fell in line with the men bowing all the while scanning the crowd for his date.

Hayden, however, had strategically positioned herself by the punch. She made herself look bored, standing there all alone. In a matter of moments, it paid off.

As soon as Hayden entered the square, she'd noticed a tall, handsome man laughing with a group of rowdy looking cowboys. He looked older than she was. His hair was slicked back and shining like a raven's wing. Hayden forced herself not to stare. If she wasn't mistaken, he was admiring her as well. She gave away nothing, acting oblivious to the attention.

Now, her stranger was walking directly her way.

He strode right past her to the refreshment table. "Hi, Amy. You look nice tonight. I hope your ma don't got you at the tables all night."

The girl was a little breathless as she spoke. "Hi, Randy. You look good too. Want some punch?" Hayden thought this Amy was just average. Not like Randy.

"Are you sure this hasn't been spiked?"

The girl giggled a little too heartily at his predictable jest. "Of course I'm sure! Why do you think I have to stand here?"

"Then fix me up." The girl handed him a cup and he drank it down in one gulp. "Thanks Amy, now make sure you come and find me if you get a chance. I'll teach you something new out there." He nodded in the direction of the band.

"Will do." The girl nodded eagerly. Randy turned to watch the dancers. As if noticing Hayden for the first time, he tilted his head to the side.

Hayden glanced at him from the corner of her eye.

"I don't think we've met." He extended his hand. "My name's Randy. Who do I have the pleasure of addressing?"

Hayden placed her hand in his and cocked her head. "It's a pleasure to meet you. I'm Hayden."

He took her hand and raised it. His ebony eyes never leave hers.

Hayden arched her eyebrow and smiled. He's a charmer? "Well, Randy, are you from here?"

He released her hand and stepped closer.

"I am, but you certainly are not. I make it a practice to know all the prettiest girls. Are you with the wagon train?"

"Actually, yes. I'm traveling with my cousin to California. Are you headed that direction?"

"Until now, I'd never considered it. Perhaps there is something worth going to California for after all."

His directness intrigued Hayden but she played off his comment and pretended to misunderstand. "Oh, yes. I've heard wonderful things about the west. It all sounds so romantic and exciting. Men are striking gold every day. I'm sure they'll save a nugget or two for someone like you."

He nodded. "And what does the west hold for you, Hayden? Are you going in search of fortune?"

"I, sir," she offered him a winning smile, "am in search of adventure."

"Is that so? If that be the case I'm sure that you won't be able to pass up the opportunity of dancing with me."

"Perhaps," She couldn't hide the gleam in her eye. "But for now you'll have to excuse me. My escort is heading this way. This dance belongs to him."

"Then you can count down the minutes til ours." He took her hand a second time and held it.

Dennison hustled to where they stood, clearing his throat. "Hello, Randy."

"Hey there, Den. I hope you don't mind my visiting with your date. She's been eagerly waiting for you to finish your dance. I don't know how you could have let her out of your sight." He politely handed her over to the confused man at his side.

Denny half smiled at the pair. "Hayden, would you like a dance?"

"Yes, Denny. That would be wonderful." She followed him out into the crowd, not once satisfying Randy with a glance in his direction. As far as Dennison Harvey could tell, he had her undivided attention and she was sure that she had succeeded in acquiring Randy's.

Denny was as clumsy as Hayden was smooth. He pushed her around the floor, his arms stiff. Hayden could tell that he was uncomfortable. She could feel his pulse as he held her hand.

It crossed her mind that she was mistreating him solely for her own good. She was sure Kayra disapproved. Remembering the promise that she'd made to her cousin, she decided to play a little matchmaking. It would be her good deed for the day.

"Denny," She began. "I was so flattered that you invited me tonight that it didn't occur to me about your sweetheart and how she might feel."

"My sweetheart? I don't know where you could have gotten that idea. I don't got a sweetheart."

"Oh, you don't? That doesn't make a lick of sense." She said as if talking to herself.

"What doesn't make sense?" Denny spun Hayden in a circle.

"Well, I went over to get some punch and the real pretty girl working the table, I think Amy is her name, anyway she seemed a little upset that I had come with you."

Denny laughed. "Amy Simmons? That's about the craziest thing that I ever heard. I've known her my whole life."

"I'm sure that I'm not mistaken. She was asking all kinds of questions about us and never took her eyes off of you."

Denny pulled his head back. "Are you sure? She hasn't ever let on that she might have any interest in me."

"Have you let on that you were interested in her?" Hayden raised her eyebrows.

"Well, no."

"Trust me on this Denny. I'm a woman. You two would make a fantastic couple. You should give it a shot."

"I wouldn't even know how. Besides, I'm with you."

"But I'm leaving in two days." She reminded him. "And she's all the things you love right here. Let me help you. Here's what you do." Hayden stopped dancing and led Denny towards a table.

They sat close and she whispered in his ear, "This will make her jealous, then when I go over there, upset because you were preoccupied with her, she'll feel very special." Hayden was quick to notice that Randy was watching. This was working out to both of their advantages.

"Now, wait here a minute. I'm going to go over to the punch table and plow the way. When I leave the table you wait the length of one song, then head over and talk to her. Do you understand?" She met his eyes encouragingly.

"I don't know. If she likes me, why doesn't she just tell me?"

"Because she's a girl and you are so amazing that it makes her nervous. Why haven't you ever told her?"

Denny smiled and nodded, "You got me there."

"Alright. You want me to do this right?" Hayden needed his approval.

"I definitely want you to do this," Denny looked about as happy as he'd been when she stumbled into him in the drygoods store.

With that, she was gone.

Hayden took purposeful steps toward the refreshments. Ten full cups of punch lined the oiled cloth. Amy's brown curls bounced as she clapped to the music. Hayden felt a pang, she'd been mean.This girl wasn't unattractive at all. She only lacked a spark. Denny might be just the thing to bring this dull girl to life.

"Hi." Hayden said, reaching for a cup.

Amy smiled.

Extending her hand Hayden introduced herself. "I'm Hayden."

Amy shook it. "I'm ..."

"Amy, I know." She laughed giving Amy a knowing look. "You're all that my date has been talking about."

The girl's eyes burrowed together and her smile turned crooked. "Surely you're mistaken. There must be another Amy here."

"No." Hayden shook her head. "It's you. He keeps looking over here and suggesting that we get a drink. He about ran over here earlier when some tall man was talking to you."

"Randy? Oh that's silly. He flirts with everyone. Besides, I'd never be brave enough to go after him."

"What about Dennison Harvey?" Hayden cocked her head and raised her eyebrows.

"Denny?" Amy made a dismissive sound through her teeth. "I don't know. I guess I've never thought of him like that." As the words came out of the girl's mouth her eyes twinkled just a bit.

"He's fantastic, isn't he? He's so sweet and strong.That shyness just hides what he really wants to say. If only I weren't leaving for California. I guess it wouldn't matter anyway." She looked directly into Amy's eyes. "His heart I believe is already spoken for."

"I have always thought he was handsome... His eyes are so big and brown."

"Oh, I think that the two of you would make a striking couple. Give him a shot. Heaven knows he'll stammer around. He said that he can hardly think when he sees you."

"What would I even say?" Amy placed a hand to her neck fingering the lace along her collar.

"Just be yourself. I better go, here he comes and we both know he's not looking for me. Good luck." Hayden winked at her new friend then headed towards the dance floor. It took only a moment before she was whisked around by a skinny cowboy in new boots.

She danced back to back with several different partners. As the song ended she complained that her feet hurt and walked toward a table where Kayra sat watching the show.

"Hayden, what are you doing?" She asked. "I just don't know how you get away with it. You have at least three beaus now all following after you like sheep. Here comes one now."

"Good evening, ladies." Randy approached the table nodding at Hayden but smiling in Kayra's direction. "I presume that you must be the cousin."

Kayra smiled, the uncomfortable kind that didn't make it past her nose.

"Although, sometimes I go by Kayra." She extended her hand. Randy took her hand and bowed to her like a duke from a story book.

"It's a pleasure to meet you, Kayra. It appears that they're starting a song. I would feel like the luckiest man here if you would agree to dance with me."

Startled, Kayra looked at Hayden as if asking permission. Hayden winked, granting approval.

In the blink of an eye Randy had twirled Kayra onto the dance floor. *So, that is how it is to be played?*

Nonplussed, she waited for the song to near its end before heading from the square. Out of the corner of her eye she watched Randy actually kiss Kayra's hand. He stopped for a glass of punch and then went out of sight.

Hayden strolled toward the stables. *He'll follow*, she assured herself. Her belly was a flutter of anticipation.

Slow steps, nonchalance, look content. Then she heard a deep voice that sent tingles down her spine.

"Where did your escort get off to, Ms. Hayden?" Randy stood there in the dim light, smiling. He held out a glass of punch.

Taking it, she moistened her lips then sipped. "Thanks for the drink. I'm not entirely sure. My escort seems to have misplaced me."

"His loss, another man's gain. I would never be so careless." He grinned and his eyes looked mischievous, like a boy with a sparkler.

"Now, Randy, where's your date this evening? You seem quite critical of mine."

"Until tonight I hadn't found a woman who interested me enough to promise an entire evening to."

"Oh, I get it," Hayden teased, taking his arm. "You got turned down."

He laughed a deep husky sound that had Hayden wondering just how old he was. "You got me all figured out, don't you." Together they strolled toward the corrals, neither leading the other.

Hayden nodded. "And the only reason you are out here now, is that you don't have a clue about me."

"That's not fair." Randy chided. "I know more about you than you think."

"Like what?" Hayden slowed, eagerly looking into his eyes for his summation of who she was.

"You occasionally wear glasses, though I doubt you need them." Hayden's mouth dropped open. "You claim to be a hunter, yet your game is a small fox. You detest propriety and I doubt that you have ever held a paintbrush but you claim to study art."

Hayden pulled away. Her chin up, ready to unload an arsenal of newly developed thoughts she had about him.

Randy was quick to take her arm again. His hand gently tucking hers back into the crook of his arm. His voice softened and he leaned in.

The baritone of his voice rumbled in her ear deliciously. "You also are by far the prettiest girl here tonight." The touch of his finger as he traced her jawline had her holding her breath. "You're witty, clever, and I imagine a handful to keep track of. And however innocent your stroll away from the party appeared, I'd bet it was planned as a way to lure me after you."

Hayden, both impressed and intimidated, found herself in a rare place of near silence. He was going to be a challenge. She racked her brain for a witty retort. Finding none, she opted for an honest response.

"Well done. I suppose you do your homework before following women off into the night."

"My homework was half done before I met you. I'm the deputy. You spoke to my brother, the sheriff, a few days ago."

Hayden pursed her lips and smiled. "Ah. I was at a disadvantage from the start, huh?"

"Not at all. I must say though, my brother's description of you did not do you justice."

Hayden released his arm leaning against the fence. Her blonde hair danced in the breeze. She could feel his eyes as they roved over her. "I never would have guessed that you two were brothers. He was very disapproving, but you seem," She narrowed her eyes, "intrigued?"

"I would agree to that. I'm sure that you can imagine how little excitement happens in this place. Then you show up and there are dead bodies..."

He laughed as she hit him companionably in the shoulder. "That's not something to tease about. Have you discovered anything?"

"Only that we suspect the killer to be in town, possibly heading west with the wagon train."

Utter fear spread through Hayden's veins. *No, please no.*

If he was in town, he could be here now. Her eyes darted to every shady patch searching for someone spying.

"Don't worry. You're safe with me. In fact, my brother has been encouraging me to head out with the train to check out the travelers and make sure that our man doesn't slip by or kill again."

"Kayra! I'm sorry I have to find Kayra." Hayden hurried toward the noisy crowd.

"I'm sure she's safe." Randy fell into a fast pace beside her. "Why would you expect her to be in danger?"

"I... It's just..." Hayden fumbled. "The whole murder thing has her terrified and I was stupid to leave her alone."

"We can head back, but you need to tell me everything that really happened. You obviously know more than you told my brother. It'd help us solve this and keep folks safe."

Hayden's mind worked through the dangers and benefits of sharing. The thought of describing the awful thing that the girls had done to Uncle Johnny's body made her cringe. Both girls had heard the town gossip, how one body was more horrifically mutilated than the others because it was burned.

Rumors were circulating about how the killer had probably slept there by the light of the drifter's body, how he'd cooked his dinner in those same flames. Hayden knew that the talk was foolish, they had done the best they could, given the circumstances, but owning up to it was something else altogether.

"I don't know what you're talking about. I gave the sheriff all my information. If you want to scrutinize it, then go read the report."

"I'll let it go but if you remember something, promise that you'll tell me. Don't go to anyone else. Just me."

Softening, she brought her eyes to meet his intense stare. "I promise if I remember anything, you will be who I come to. As if I'd go back to that sheriff again. Brother or not."

A chuckle escaped Randy's chest. "Now there is the girl I met earlier. Come on, let's go check on your cousin, then you owe me a dance."

Hayden's smile was sincere. Grateful, she took his arm. Almost instantly she spotted Kayra right where she'd left her. Oh thank goodness. She was safe, sitting with a redheaded girl. A gathering of men stood to the side.

"It's none of my business, Ms. Hayden, but your cousin might keep a better mind about who she openly visits with in public." Randy pointed.

Immediately defensive, Hayden looked up and noticed that the redhead was the same girl they'd seen outside the saloon when they'd first arrived in Denver. "How could she?" Hayden seethed, marching toward Kayra.

Kayra's eyes brightened at her cousin's approach. "Hayden! You have to meet Fineese. She's going to California too."

Hayden nodded to the girl without looking at her. "Isn't that interesting? Kayra, sorry, but I have a terrible headache and we must go. Now."

Kayra frowned, but came to her feet. "Excuse us. I guess I must be going. Good luck to you, Fineese." She extended her hand.

Fineese looked around but kept her hands in her lap. "You're too kind, Kayra. Go ahead and go. I understand."

Kayra nodded and followed Hayden out of the square like a child headed behind the woodshed with her Father.

"If you two will wait here," Randy motioned to the fence where they had been so carefree just moments ago, "I'll go find Denny and tell him that I'm taking you back to the hotel."

As soon as he was out of hearing, Hayden fumed. "What do you think you are doing? That girl is a whore." Hayden didn't bother speaking politely about what Fineese was. "Didn't you notice that not a single other woman at the party spoke to her?"

"I did notice and it made me sad. I told you that I won't keep treating people selfishly. She was exhausted and wouldn't sit down because no one wanted her at their table. So, I offered her a seat at mine. I didn't do anything improper and I'm sorry if it embarrassed you but I did something good and it felt good. She needs a friend."

"No. You can't become friends with someone like that. End of discussion. I guess with us leaving, it isn't such a big deal, but from now on you'll stay away from ladies like that, you hear?"

"Hayden, she's headed out west too. I told her that we would help. If you don't want to, fine. But I said that I would, and I will. She has nobody and it's the right thing to do. It's what William would do."

Randy cleared his throat as he approached. "It seems that your escort, Miss Hayden, has left to walk the punch girl home. Isn't that strange?"

Randy

He and Hayden shared a smile before the three of them headed down the street. Hayden set an uncomfortable pace, the click of her heels and small strides clicked like a woodpecker against the wooden walkway. Randy was smiling against his will.

When they reached the hotel, Hayden dismissed Kayra. "Cousin, I'll be up momentarily." She would not smile and Kayra seemed to be searching her cousin's face for a hint of understanding. Hayden's expression didn't soften in the least.

What an odd relationship these girls had. Hayden acted as if she were mother to this equally grown woman. He reconsidered, not equally grown. Though they were close in age, Kayra had a naivety that Hayden had long outgrown. Why were these women alone and what had caused Hayden to grow up so much before her time?

Kayra nodded to Randy. Once she had disappeared through the doorway, Hayden returned her attention to him. It was like she was in one of those shows he'd seen with actors.

"So, Randy," her smile was flawless, but the spark was gone from her eyes. He wasn't about to be part of a play.

"It's okay, Hayden." He smiled down at her. "I guess that you do care, maybe just a bit, about propriety and all that."

She snickered. "I guess I do, just a bit." She shook her head again. "Oh, Kayra and her goodness."

"I'm glad." He reached for her hand and brought it to his lips. His warm breath escaped as he kissed it. With wide eyes, he watched Hayden's shoulders ease, the tense lines on her forehead soften. Her tempting face bewitched him. At that moment, she was sweet and innocent, but he knew full well that she was a lot more than that. The inconsistencies in her overwhelmed his senses.

He needed to discover what was behind that carefully guarded persona. It might take a long time to uncover all of her secrets. First he had to gain her trust. Or should he find out what she knows about the murders first? If she were in some way involved, he'd deal with that later, he decided.

"Randy, I doubt that this is entirely appropriate either."

He chuckled, raising his head. "I suppose one scandal for the night is enough. Besides, I need to start getting my things together for our trip west."

"Our trip?" Hayden raised a quizzical eyebrow. "Now *that* would be scandalous." Her lips curved seductively up and her eyes slit with mischief.

"You are a piece of work, Ms. Hayden. I think that I might actually enjoy my assignment. Don't fret, I won't let my brother know that you aren't entirely difficult, or a 'raving coo-coo.' I believe those were his words, if I recall correctly."

She harrumphed. "He paints with an unflattering brush."

Randy smiled wide. "I, on the other hand, found you to be unique and interesting."

Like a snake, she changed course. "What a kind way of calling me peculiar and ugly. I've never before been insulted with such flattery."

Puzzled, he stared at her taught lips and suddenly wide eyes. Where had the teasing angel he'd had seconds ago gone? She was a hen ready to peck. He wondered, not for the first time tonight, at the lightning quick adjustment in her.

No, he wouldn't give her the verbal battle of wits she was asking for. "I ought to kiss that ugly off of your pretty face, but I won't. This time."

He stepped from the walkway onto the dirt road. At least the spark was back in her eyes. "I'll see you on Monday. Stay out of trouble, please. And go easy on Kayra. She didn't mean any harm." Hayden opened her mouth to speak but he cut her off. "Sweet dreams, Hayden. May they be of me." He turned and headed off in the night towards the saloon.

He could hear her angrily hollering after him. He just smiled. At least she'd keep thinking about him, even if her thoughts were less than warm.

Hayden

"You arrogant, miserable, conceited—" Hayden stomped around the walkway yelling. He never looked back, not once. After pulling herself together, she hoped that he hadn't heard her name calling. Why had she felt the need to pick a fight? And why hadn't he engaged her? It was all very strange and frustrating.

Now, alone on the sidewalk, she remembered the possible danger for herself and Kayra. Her eyes scanned the alley across the way. She saw no one who appeared threatening but an eerie cold swept across her despite the heat. It was like being a child alone in a dark room. She saw no danger but felt its presence nonetheless. She entered the hotel and headed for her room.

Kayra was already in bed. Hayden changed and crawled in next to her cousin. Kayra's back was to her. She was unnaturally still.

"Sorry I was so hard on you. I didn't realize that you would take this whole do-good thing so far." Hayden waited for a response. "I was surprised and I was thinking about what people would think. I know that I need to think more about what you would think."

Kayra turned. "You're getting closer."

Hayden smirked. "What would God think?"

Kayra rewarded her with a smile. "Thank you."

Hayden curled into her pillow facing her cousin. "Believe it or not, I did a good deed tonight too."

Hayden watched as amusement danced across Kayra's features. "What noble deed did you do? Remember, it has to be completely unselfish."

Hayden considered how she had manipulated Amy and Denny. "I guess I did benefit from it in a small way but it was mostly unselfish."

Hayden delved into an embellished version of how she brought two desperately in love, yet lonely souls together.

"Tell me about this Randy fellow," Kayra prompted abruptly.

"He's the deputy." Suddenly Hayden was serious. "He thinks the killer is here in Denver and possibly going west with us. Randy is going to head that way as well, to make sure that no suspect gets away. Promise me that you won't leave my side. I don't know what possible danger we're in, if any. I just have a bad feeling, cousin. Promise me."

"I promise. I won't go anywhere alone." There was a pause. "You like Randy don't you? He's good looking?"

"Well, he isn't bad looking, that's for sure. I doubt I'll pursue it, but he certainly is good at the game."

"What game is it that you are always talking about? I don't understand why you can't just have an honest relationship. Men like you. You just run them off."

"How can you say that?" Hayden frowned. "I do have an honest relationship. It's with you. I don't need anyone else. Who else could I trust with all of my secrets?"

"Anyone you wanted to. You know, more than one person can love you."

"What are you talking about? Is this about William?"

Kayra sat up and looked at her cousin. "This is about you. You can't be afraid to get close to people. I got close to William and his family, and it changed me."

Hayden interrupted, "But I don't want you to change. I've always loved you just as you are."

"I know and I will always adore you for the wonderful, beautiful, crazy schemer that you are but you shouldn't keep that person hidden from everyone else."

"Just what are you saying?"

"Look, I saw you two tonight. Only briefly, but you guys had, I don't know, a spark. It wasn't just your usual trifle with a local boy. Heaven knows I've seen that too many times." Hayden affectionately swatted her shoulder. "Something happened when you went off. I know you enough to know, it wasn't bad. I also heard you hollering at him." Kayra's eyebrows arched. "He flustered you. I think that if you back off, it's because you're afraid and for no other reason."

Hayden considered that. She knew in the back of her mind that everything Kayra had said was true. She'd made a fool out of herself on the sidewalk. Why? That wasn't like her. *Control your mind, control the situation.* She'd definitely ignored her own advice there.

Hayden pulled the blanket up to her shoulders. "I'm not saying that you're right, but I will think about it"

Kayra settled onto her pillow. "Hayden, if he's going west with us, how are we going to pull off the teacher thing now that he knows you certainly are not?"

"I don't know. He knows more about us than you realize. We'll need a new approach. If it's a little off, he won't say anything." Hayden's excitement got the best of her as she began to plan. "You can still be married and traveling to your husband, but I will have some sort of illness that can only be treated in San Francisco."

"What kind of illness?"

"Maybe, I could be going blind," Hayden thought, "You know it could go in and out. So part of the time I'd be seeing and then I could suddenly black out."

"That's dumb. I don't think blindness works that way and everyone knows that the best doctors are in the East, not the newly established cities of the West."

"Hmm, you're right. Oh, I got it! I could be on my way to marry someone your husband has selected."

"You're too pretty to need an arranged marriage. And that's only a new tactic to discourage Randy because you're chicken."

"I am not. You take that back."

"You are too and I won't take it back. Besides, if I'm traveling to meet my husband you don't need to be anything other than yourself. Why can't you simply be my cousin accompanying me on my journey?"

Hayden scoffed. "What's the fun in that?"

Chapter Six

Greely

Muted sounds from the celebration in the town square carried to the steamy bathhouse where Greely stood naked. He considered attending the festivities but decided instead to keep a low profile and stay out of sight as much as possible. The bathhouse, which had been bustling with visitors only hours earlier, was now empty. Greely liked the solitude. Denver City was much too crowded.

He pulled a knife from the pocket of his discarded trousers. He adjusted the small mirror on the wall and began stroking the cold silver blade against his cheek. Little by little, a worn face began to appear from beneath his unkempt beard. He rinsed the knife in the tub and started on the other side of his face. He was careful to leave a tidy mustache but completely removed the rest of his facial hair.

It had been a good ten years since he'd seen his face. He traced the scar across his right cheek with the tip of his knife. His face hardened, remembering his father whipping him with a leather strap. He still heard the snap of the leather in the air as it came down. His anger was kindled afresh as if it had just happened. He never felt sadness when he remembered. Only rage.

"You're in hell now, ain't ya, daddy?" He dug the tip of the knife into the scar, opening it just slightly. He breathed a pleased sigh as the blood trickled down his face.

His crooked finger stroked the wound then he brought it to his mouth. The familiar bitterness awoke his taste buds as he licked his fingertip. A shudder jolted through him at the pleasant flavor. The creak of a door brought his attention back to reality.

"Uh, sir? We need to close up."

Greely took his knife and jabbed it into the dressing table. "I'll be out when I'm done." His voice startled the attendant, sending him scurrying from the doorway.

Angry, Greely stalked toward the roll of clothes he'd just purchased. He slipped into the new pants and fastened the belt. After buttoning the crisp white shirt he turned to see his reflection and snorted. "Well now, don't you look respectable?"

He hardly recognized the man looking back at him. Confident, he folded his blade and shoved the knife into his pocket and headed for the door. The bathhouse keeper was nowhere to be found so Greely didn't bother to leave a payment. If the man came to collect, he'd never recognize him now anyhow.

Raucous noise came from both the saloon and the town square. He considered joining in on the action but decided instead that he needed a drink and a woman.

Men, like flies on rotten meat, swarmed in groups around the saloon. He hated crowds. A lively tune was being played on the piano, and that alone was enough to put Greely in a sour mood.

Not an empty seat at the poker tables tonight as cowboys, farmers and fortune seekers intent on winning the next game battled for the right hand. He had no interest in cards tonight. Stepping up to the long bar he tossed a coin at the tender and nodded toward a whiskey bottle.

The man behind the counter slid the bottle toward Greely and set a glass beside it. Greely poured himself a drink, swallowing it down in one swig. The liquor burned his throat then slid into his belly. The sensation made his shoulders relax. He poured another before turning to watch a nearby table.

He drank his second and third glass. Observing was one of the things that he loved to do. You could learn a lot about people by simply keeping quiet and watching how they interact. In a matter of minutes he'd measured up every man at that table. He knew which ones could lie and not get caught, which ones couldn't judge what was a good hand, and the one man that he had best not play against.

Gray hair and shuffling feet blocked Greely's view. The idiot was looking over shoulders at the edge of the game. He'd be lucky if he didn't end up on his backside like he deserved. Greely turned back to the bar. *Great.* The codger was sliding in the seat beside him. Greely made no eye contact. Discouraging the old buzzard wasn't easy. The man, undeterred by his lack of manners, extended his hand, "You aren't from around here."

Greely made no move to shake hands and spit off to the side. "Nope, I guess I ain't."

The man put his hand in his pocket and pulled out two cigars, offering one to Greely. He took it, nodding his thanks and twirled it around in his fingers.

"Name's Tom." He lit a match and held it to his own cigar before handing it over to Greely. Greely accepted the light with silence.

"You play cards?"

Greely shook his head drawing on the cigar. The tobacco was sweet. He hadn't smoked a cigar in a long while and appreciated the gift. "Thanks." Greely ignored Tom's previous attempt to get to know him.

The old man took his thanks as encouragement and kept talking. "I suppose you is one of them folks headed west in search of gold."

Greely nodded.

"Hopes you don't come across no Indians."

"They should hope not to come across me."

The old man laughed. He was missing a tooth in his lower jaw. "What about that murderer on the loose? What do you think about him?"

A curious smile curved across Greely's face. He drew another breath on his cigar before responding. "I suppose most folks who get killed have done something to deserve it."

Tom shook his gray head and raised an arthritic hand in the air. "I don't know. I hear this guy's a real devil."

"You'd have to be, to kill so many times." Greely took no offense. His pulse raced discussing it. Adrenaline pumped through his veins. He was the talk of the town.

"I hear he burned one fella and cooked his supper in the flames."

Greely's eyebrow shot up. "Can't say I heard that." He answered truthfully, wondering about that rumor. Perhaps there was a killing he didn't know about. "How would anyone know if the killer cooked in the flames of a body?"

The old man scratched his wiry head as if wondering about that for the first time. "Can't say I can answer that. I been hearin' the story though. Some poor guy was killed and drug off to a creek bed and lit up just five days ride of here."

Greely wanted to ask more. He might have made a mistake in not checking that wagon before riding off. He was silent, considering what the new information meant. The man, John, who he'd followed and killed after gambling in that horse camp must have had family after all.

He considered the second man who'd been following him, the one that he'd killed a week and a half back. Greely had guessed that he'd been with John and supposed that the poor guy had made an attempt to cremate his friend and then chased his tracks until finding Greely. *Unlucky for him, he found me all right.*

"I'm sure he'll be caught soon and hanged." He pointed a crooked finger towards the back of the saloon. Two men were deep in conversation. "Them's the law. They don't tolerate nothin' neither."

A muscle in Greely's jaw flinched as he perused the pair. They didn't look so tough. He smiled thankfully toward the man who had proven to be quite useful.

"I'll keep the law in mind, then. Much obliged for the cigar and conversation. Now excuse me but I believe I'm about to become otherwise occupied."

The older man nodded. "Good luck to ya." Then he turned to jabber to the man on his left.

Greely's eyes followed a young redhead who entered the bar and headed for the staircase. She held her arms under her belly. A man came quickly to her side taking her elbow. "Let me help you into bed Ms. Fineese."

"Not tonight, Jimmy. I've worn myself out already."

His disappointment was obvious. He released her arm and stepped away from the staircase. He rejoined his friends around a table and ordered whiskey. One of the men at his table laughed. "Well, Jimmy, I guess you'll be giving me your money instead. Deal him in."

Seeds of frustration grew like a vine coursing through Greely until he was wrapped in anger. He came to the saloon intent on having a woman. Tired or not, that devilish little redhead was going to be it. He slunk to the staircase. No one even noticed.

Fineese

Fineese plopped onto her bed. She wanted to rub her feet except it seemed like such an effort. The celebration had been fun, but she was exhausted beyond what was normal. Her fingers worked to unbutton her dress. With some effort she maneuvered out of the gown. Folding it, she walked to the dresser and pulled out a nightgown. She tugged it over her swollen belly.

A pounding on the door made her speed up the task. She shrunk into her wrap. Her stomach was so large that the material gaped wide across her middle. Cracking the door, she addressed her eager visitor. "Sorry, but I'm not taking callers tonight."

Her apology fell as the door was thrown open and a large man thundered into her room, kicking the door shut behind him. Fineese tasted the fear inside her. She knew what this man's intentions were. She wasn't an experienced prostitute but had dealt with difficult customers before. However, those men were usually drunk.

This man was sober and looked like the devil lived in his soul.

He was as alert as anyone she'd ever met. His eyes were alive with excitement and she was suddenly more afraid than she'd ever been before. Protectively, she placed her hand over her stomach and begged, "I'll do whatever you want, just please don't hurt me." "I'm the one paying here. I'll make the demands."

Fineese considered running for the door but the man in front of her looked determined. Likely, she wouldn't make it and only anger him further. "You know, if I scream, someone will hear and come up here." She reasoned.

He snorted. "Shut up. You heard how loud it is downstairs. No one will hear you. Besides, no one cares about what happens to a girl like you. Now, do as I say." He pointed to the bed.

Fineese sat on her bed facing him. She'd go along with him and get this over with as quickly as possible. "What would you like?"

He took his fist and pounded it into her face.

Blackness replaced her dimly lit room. Fineese was only partially alert now. It was as if she were someone else watching the horrible things happening to her. Maybe that was best. Her thoughts were of her child and his safety. She prayed over and over. *Please God, protect my baby.* The plea was chanted until her torture ended.

Fineese tried to move when she heard her attacker preparing to leave. Her body wouldn't cooperate. She realized rope held her in place. The man paused at the door.

"I know you can hear me and you'd better listen real good. If you say anything, I'll cut that babe from your belly and feed it to the wolves."

Fineese understood perfectly. This man was crazy enough to do exactly that.

The door opened and closed. He was gone and she was alive. Adrenaline flowed through her veins making her want to act. She needed to free herself and get away now, but her beaten body refused to cooperate. She couldn't lift her head from the pillow it rested on. Eventually the battle between mind and flesh ended and she escaped into slumber, exhausted from fear.

Light shone from the edge of the window shade in an uncomfortable line straight across Fineese's face. The bright ray was like a knife cutting into her forehead. Trying to work her jaw, she opened her mouth. Her whole body burned, especially along her underarms.

She was still tied and her hands were painfully numb. It took tremendous effort, but she managed to scoot toward the head of the bed, relieving pressure on her wrists. After a few minutes of struggle, she was able to wiggle her fingers. After painful maneuvering, she finally slid her hands from the restraints.

Memories assaulted her. She felt the blows to her body anew. The desire to escape flashbacks of the previous night, along with the tremendous physical effort it had taken to free herself, had her begging for an escape. Sleep would help. Surely, some peace would come with sleep. She gave in to its lure, drifting into the emptiness it offered.

The second time Fineese woke up, she managed to sit. Her head felt like it was being stomped on. Tears clouded her vision. She had survived the night. Had her baby? She ran her hands over her stomach. *Please move,* she begged. A gentle nudge against her side came moments later. As if it were equally happy about the discovery that they both survived, it moved and kicked at her touch. Resting her head against the pillow a smile spread across her face. *Thank you God for saving my child.*

She reached in her nightstand for a bottle of laudanum. Without measuring, she drank it. Soon her eyes were heavy. She sunk into the peaceful oblivion the drug offered.

The next time she woke up, she wasn't alone. A doctor was standing over her, feeling her wrist. She stirred, becoming alert.

"Ma'am, can you hear me?"

Fineese opened her eyes.

"That's a good sign." He bandaged her face and put ointment on her wounds before directing his attention to the deputy. "She'll live and her baby appears fine. She won't be going anywhere though, not for a long while."

The deputy nodded. "Thanks, doc." The two shook hands before he left.

Randy pulled a chair up to the bed and took Fineese's hand in his. "I need you to talk to me."

She closed her eyes and tears began streaming down her face. There was no way that she would say anything.

"I need to know who did this to you. Tell me anything that you can. What the man looked like, smelled like, anything."

She cried silent tears instead.

"Listen, Fineese, Becky's dead. Apparently he was a customer of hers last night too. She died by suffocating in her own vomit because of a gag he put in her mouth."

Fineese nearly choked on her words. "I can't tell you anything."

"Whoever did this to you two has to pay, but we have no leads. Please give me something to go on."

"I can't."

"Did he threaten you?" Randy leaned forward.

"No. He blindfolded me," She lied, "I never saw his face." She refused to meet Randy's eyes.

"Okay, how big was the man? You didn't have to see him to know that."

"Average size." Again, she stared at her lap remembering his bulk.

"You realize that I can help you, if you'll let me?"

Fineese nodded.

Randy took a deep breath. "Listen, this man robbed you of California. He needs to pay for this. Becky's dead. You're the only one who can tell me anything."

Fineese shook her head. Had she heard him right? "No, I'm going. I have to. If I stay here…"

"If you stay here, what? Tell me. Is the man local?"

"I don't know! I have to leave Monday with that wagon train or he might as well have killed me and my baby."

Randy held out a hand to stroke her head but when she winced, he set it back on the bed. "Fineese, I wish you could go. You're too weak. I don't think you'll be able to make it and I doubt anyone will help you. I'm sorry."

"I know someone who will help me. That girl from last night, the one… oh, what was her name?"

"Kayra." Randy shook his head. "Fineese, be realistic. Another wagon train will come through this way next year. Maybe then–"

"I can't ever sell my body again. Please, understand that. This is my only chance. I can't have a child here with everyone knowing what I am."

Randy exhaled like a steam train releasing momentum. "That's a tall order. You tell me something about the man that did this and I'll see what I can do for you."

She squeezed his hand. "I knew you'd help me."

"A deal is a deal. You give something to go on."

Fineese considered what to tell the deputy. "It wasn't a local man. He was a stranger."

Randy ran his thumb over Fineese's knuckle. "Thank you. I'll fetch Kayra, but I can't promise that she will help you."

Fineese struggled to speak. "I've spent my life dealing with all sorts of people. She'll help. She's different. You'll see."

"Well, her cousin is unlike anyone that I've ever known. She's bound to dislike this. So for your sake, I hope you're right." Randy stood and left the room.

Chapter Seven

Hayden

Monday morning had come like an unwelcome visitor. Hayden sat in her wagon outside the saloon. If Kayra was going to assist that woman, she could at least have the courtesy of getting her loaded before the sun was up and folks saw.

Hayden wore a simple beige dress so old that the material across the bodice was threadbare. It was her most unbecoming dress, but she was so angry with Kayra and Randy that she told herself it didn't matter whether she impressed him or not. Her golden hair was pulled in a loose bun at the nape of her neck. Already strands were falling from the knot making her appear, she hoped, like a servant girl.

She still couldn't believe that her cousin had agreed to assist this woman on their trip to California. Kayra had completely disregarded her forbiddance of contact with Fineese. Now, her benevolent cousin was likely to spend the entire journey babysitting the town's mistress while Hayden got stuck doing all the work alone. Not to mention, they would now be pariahs as far as all of the other travelers were concerned. Yet another reason for not dressing to impress, Hayden supposed.

Randy drove Fineese's wagon up alongside Hayden's and pulled the pair of horses to a halt. "Whoa! Ms. Hayden, you are looking extremely well this morning."

Hayden fought the urge to glance in his direction. She was utterly furious with him for having sought out Kayra's help with the pregnant saloon girl. She would not acknowledge him.

"I see." Easily, he hopped from Fineese's wagon to hers. He settled himself gingerly on the front. His leg touched Hayden's. "You're still upset with me?"

Hayden stared at her lap, removing imagined lint from her skirt.

"Well, that's understandable. Besides," Randy tucked a wisp of hair behind Hayden's ear, "I rather like this silent side of you. The only problem is that I was so looking forward to your cutting insults on our long journey west."

She jerked her leg away, securing the hair herself.

Unphased, he continued his easy conversation. "I imagined you riding alongside me, criticizing everything about my driving. It's a pity really that you'll not have the pleasure of teaching me how one ought to handle these mules."

Hayden had never been good at the silent treatment and gave in to Randy's jibe. "You are not riding with me." Her nostrils flared. Her chest puffed out like a peacock. She pushed at him with all her force urging him off her wagon. "Get out!" She ordered.

"There's the woman I've become so fond of these last few days. Now, give me one of those perfectly practiced smiles."

Hayden's head shook in frustration as she climbed from the wagon. He was the worst man alive. She wouldn't spend a single moment at his side.

Randy leaned back in the seat and began stretching. "That's a good idea, Ms. Hayden. We're going to be cooped up together in this here wagon for a good long while today. Stretching those lovely legs of yours is certainly a good idea."

Hayden turned away from him. Agitated, she paced back and forth on the plank walkway. Her heels clicked against the wood with each volatile step.

"I can't stand you." She spat the acidic words at him. "You said yourself that Kayra should mind the company that she keeps, then you come looking for her to help with the very company you warned about. Now I have to do all the work myself because Kayra says Fineese can't drive her own wagon." She halted her pacing and glared at him, hands firmly resting on her hips. "How's that for fair, huh? As far as I can see, this girl should be your responsibility not ours."

Randy

His eyes followed her appreciatively as she berated him. The dress she wore was likely chosen because it was her worst. It complemented her beautiful tawny skin. She could dress in rags but nothing could disguise the air of superiority with which she carried herself. You could paint a peacock gray and it would still look like a peacock. He'd been expecting this moment. In fact, he had been looking forward to the confrontation that he knew would ensue when she discovered what he'd done. Just this morning he'd prepared a speech as he'd driven to meet them. He had a mind to tell her exactly what she needed to hear.

Why was he so attracted to her? She was selfish, fake, and way too independent.

She possessed very few qualities that one looked for in a wife except perhaps the obvious physical ones (and those she had in abundance). She was the most tempting thing he'd ever seen, while standing on the street bawling him out as if she were his superior. She probably thought she was. Maybe that was the pull she had on him.

She was confident, not some love sick puppy that would come when called and wag its tail. He paused in thought, *uh oh*, she was waiting for a response. *How did that speech start?*

Finally, he remembered the words. "If it were up to me, I'd help her myself. But you see, I'm a lawman and I get elected to that position. I'm good at my job and there's a murderer on the loose, as you well know. I believe that the man who killed the body you found and the other one in the creek bed is the same man that murdered Becky from the Lucky Shoe and nearly killed Fineese and her unborn child. If I help her too much, people simply won't reelect me. Besides that, your incredibly sweet cousin volunteered to help Fineese of her own accord. Fineese is terrified of men right now and I thought she might confide in Kayra and then I would have a lead on who this killer is. The killer *you* want caught and hung. *You*, little Miss Hayden."

Randy leapt from the wagon and grabbed Hayden's elbow more firmly than intended, "You are a selfish, uncompassionate and condemning woman. Think about what this girl has been through. Now I don't claim to know your whole story, but I can guess that you and Kayra are the only family each other has. How are you so very different from her? You will do anything to protect your hide and Kayra's, too, won't you?"

Hayden nodded, but her mouth was just as tight as before.

"That's all Fineese is trying to do. She just wants to get somewhere folks don't know her so she can raise that baby of hers without shame. How can you fault her for that?"

Gently, he eased the pressure on her arm. Her eyes glared at him.

"I'm sorry for speaking to you like that. I just want you to think about it. And it just so happens, you won't have to do all the work alone because Kayra and I decided that I will assist you."

Hayden opened her mouth to protest but the saloon doors swung wide. Randy dropped her arm and stepped to help.

The owner looked outside, saw Fineese's wagon was there and disappeared again. Kayra emerged holding the other door open as the man carried Fineese, like a rag doll, to the back of the wagon. Her dress pulled across her middle. Her legs were limp. She made no effort to raise her head acknowledging Hayden nor Randy's presence.

Hayden

Randy jumped into the wagon ahead of them to help get Fineese situated on the bed. Kayra handed up a bag of belongings and a baby quilt Fineese had started. The squares were sewn together with a wide stitch. Like herself and Kayra, she'd likely never had anyone teach her how to sew or knit.

Despite her circumstances, Fineese was trying to do something as basic as prepare for her child. Hayden caught herself feeling sorry for this girl and fought it. She didn't want to see her as a real person. If she did that, she would have to admit that she'd been wrong.

Compelled, Hayden walked to the wagon and stared in horror at the condition this poor woman found herself in. The parts of her face that weren't bandaged were purple and blue. Her red hair lacked the luster it held when the girls first saw her outside the saloon upon arrival in Denver City.

Hayden's condemning words sounded in her ears as she remembered first seeing Finneese. Even then, Kayra had defended her. Fineese's wrists were marked with what Hayden assumed were rope burns. Painful looking welts and bruises ran up and down every inch of visible flesh.

Kayra came up behind Hayden and placed her hand on her cousin's shoulder. "I told you it was bad. It shocked me the first time I saw her too."

Her throat ached. Taking in the sight of this pitiful woman lying in the back of the wagon, gently stroking her unborn baby was much more than Hayden had expected. "How could someone do that to a person?" Her voice sounded like it belonged to someone else.

"I don't know." Kayra squeezed her shoulder then went around and settled herself on the bench seat.

Randy climbed out of the wagon and took Hayden's hand. "Come on, honey." Hayden, so affected by what she'd seen, didn't object and followed him somberly to her own rig.

He helped her up, then seated himself at her side. Quietly, Hayden stared ahead not seeing the street in front of her. She felt a sting behind her eyes. *No*, she shook her head. *Control your mind, control the situation. Control your mind, control the situation.* She swallowed the ache in her throat. Randy took an arm and pulled her to his side. She continued to stare, not ready to try her voice.

"It's okay, go ahead and cry." He moved his hand to stroke her head when she pulled from his warmth.

"No, I was just taken aback. I'm alright now. Promise."

Randy looked at her with confusion. "Well, if you ever do want to cry or talk about it, I'll be here."

Hayden nodded and gave him a half-hearted smile. "Thanks."

It was another half hour before the rest of Denver City started crawling out of bed.

They joined the wagon train as the procession began heading out. The sun danced in the sky. It seemed the entire town had come out to see the travelers off. Ladies stood along the walkway, waving happily. Children scurried about laughing and playing with their newfound friends. Men shook hands wishing each other well.

It was just as Hayden imagined. Their two wagons made up the end of the train.

Kayra

The amount of well-wishers that had come out to say farewell was overwhelming. William would have loved this. If he were here, this would have been a moment for him that would always play in his mind and bring him joy. He was made of the stuff it took to adventure west.

Kayra had played scenarios in her mind, imagining William stopping her wagon at the last second, convincing her that she belonged with him. How ridiculous. It was too late to change the path she'd started down and his path lay elsewhere.

Now, if she were Hayden, maybe a miracle would happen and he would show up to profess his undying love. Things like that happened to Hayden. But she wasn't her cousin.

It had been a full week since they'd driven away from the Mayers's farm. Had she romanticized their relationship? No, it wouldn't hurt so badly if she had. This should have been the beginning of their journey west, together, but it wasn't. And with each building and smiling greeter that she drove past, she concluded that she was putting another step between her and the man that she loved. Kayra felt none of the merriment surrounding her.

William

William was up before dawn. He'd been searching all morning. At his mother's encouragement, he'd traveled to Denver just two days before, intent on convincing Sister Mary-Katherine to stay.

He'd asked at all of the churches then taverns in town as to where the nuns were, that were traveling west with the wagon train. No one had any idea about whom he sought. Even the Catholic Church, Our Lady of Peace, hadn't heard of the sisters. It was as if they'd vanished from the face of the earth.

Frustrated, William wondered if they'd changed their minds or fell into trouble along the way. There had been stories of a murderer on the loose but he wouldn't allow his mind to dwell on those possibilities. He'd searched through the crowd of wagons early this morning as they began assembling. No one could direct him and there were simply too many to keep track of. He lost count of how many wagons he'd already visited and which ones he hadn't.

The wagons began moving. Panic coursed through his veins. Mary-Katherine was in that procession, his gut told him so, but with the crowd so large and the chaos, how would he find her? If only he had the money to buy supplies, he'd join them. It's what his heart wanted. He could head west and find her on the way. He couldn't leave. Too many responsibilities hung around his neck anchoring him to Willow Creek. As much as the idea tempted his soul, he wouldn't do that to his family. Mary-Katherine was falling from his grasp and so was his dream of conquering an untamed land. Life was cruel.

In the middle of the road, he hung his head, a beaten man, a fool for having hoped. He shuffled into the shade as the last few wagons left the main street. Anger, hurt and disappointment tugged at his heart.

The second to last wagon was a nail in the coffin of wishes. A couple sat together, the young, blond woman blowing kisses to the crowd. Her husband sat tall and proud at her side nodding to people as he drove the old rig. A pang of jealousy cinched around his chest. What a life they would get to build together in the new land.

The last wagon eased out bringing up the tail end of the train. A glimpse of dark brown hair blowing in the morning breeze caught his eye. It was only the back of a head but he darted from the shade of the sidewalk, running down the street pushing people out of the way as he went. Hope built inside him like a pot coming to a boil. He smacked into someone dressed in a work apron. The man grabbed his arm angrily.

"What's the rush, son?"

William jerked free. "I have to stop that wagon. I love that girl and she's getting away."

The saloon keeper halted him with a firm grip. "We all loved her. I know business for me will be slower now that she's gone."

Confused, William stopped as the man's words sunk in. If he knew who was in that last wagon, then it couldn't be Mary-Katherine. Likely, he was about to make a fool of himself. He had to make certain.

"The girl in that wagon, what's her name?"

The bartender smiled, his manner one of sympathy. "Fineese and Kayra."

Unsure, William insisted. "What do they look like?"

"Fineese was a beauty when she came to me, with long red hair and the prettiest face you'd ever see, but now I'd guess she's probably more than seven months pregnant. She's a great woman but she's had a rough time of it. She just made friends with the other girl. I don't recall much about her, except that she's going to be reunited with her husband in San Francisco. He done struck gold and sent for her."

William's throat swelled. It wasn't her.

"Come on young man. I'll treat you to a glass of whiskey. The first two are on the house."

Numbly, William followed the man into the saloon and drank his first taste of fire.

Chapter Eight

Hayden

Hayden bounced in her seat. So many well wishers seeing them off, it was a true parade. She spotted Denny in the crowd, his huge impeccably clean hat caught her attention. He didn't look as if he'd ever worked a cow in his life.

He smiled brightly, his arms waving like a windmill. He cupped his hands over his mouth and yelled, "Good luck, Hayden! And thanks for the advice!"

She made a show of blowing a kiss in Denny's direction. "Best wishes to you, Denny. I wish we could have spent more time together."

The fury that had been with her all night somehow wasn't there anymore. Randy and Kayra were doing what they believed was best. After seeing Fineese this morning, could she even disagree? As embarrassing as it would be to be associated with a ladylike Fineese, Hayden felt it was impossible to turn away from someone in so much need. *I'm not entirely selfish*, she thought.

Since the whole silent treatment thing wasn't going to work, she'd need to come up with a new plan for handling Randy. He admired her "sweet" cousin.

Unfortunately, "sweet" was difficult for her to pull off for very long, so she decided not to go that route. He'd already seen her flirtatious and he'd also seen her throw a tantrum.

Randy interrupted her thoughts. "Hayden, I want to know your story. The truth, this time."

That's a laugh, she thought, shaking her head. "You wouldn't believe me if I told you."

"Try me." His easy smile made her relax but he'd asked for a story, and that's exactly what she was going to give him. *A tale to impress.* She gave him an impish smile.

"Where do I start? Let's see, I was born in France to wealthy parents. My Father had a vineyard. Our wines were sought after by royalty. In fact, the Chinese Emperor drank ours exclusively. We lived in an amazing chateau in the countryside. I was an only child."

Randy interrupted her story. "So Hayden is a French name?"

"Don't be rude, I was getting there. Actually, my birth name is Contessa. I was named after my mother's great aunt The Countess of Stolkshire."

He didn't look like he was buying it. *More believable*, she told herself.

"My American Uncle dubbed me Hayden when I came to New England to study music."

Randy nodded, "Because there were no music instructors in Europe that could compare to ours here in America?"

Hayden sighed. "I told you that you wouldn't believe me."

"I'm sorry, Hayden, go on."

She shook her head. "No."

"Please. I believe you. I should have guessed on my own that no one as beautiful as you could be from an ordinary place like Kansas."

His compliment did the trick. "As I was saying, I came to America when I was twelve to study music. You see, my family's private musician had moved here to instruct my cousins and I desperately wanted to learn the violin. I also wanted to meet my cousins since I had no siblings."

"It must have been terribly difficult for your parents to let you travel across the ocean by yourself at such a young age."

"Well, I was very mature."

"Oh, I can only imagine." Randy smirked.

"I wasn't alone either. My preacher accompanied me. He planned to start a church in Boston."

"I had no idea you were religious."

"There is a lot about me that you have no idea. I played piano for our congregation in France."

"At such a young age?"

"As I said, I had a thirst for learning music and am quite gifted."

"Alright. How did you end up in Denver City with Kayra?"

"Well, we became instant best friends when I came to live with her family. We were close in age. She was like a sister." Hayden made her face appear troubled, adding a dramatic pause, "Then, word came that my parents were killed in a fire that destroyed our vineyard and chateau. I was left with nothing, an orphan in a far off land."

"Oh, that's unbelievably sad."

"I know." Hayden continued. "Then my Uncle made me a servant in his home. I was responsible for all the cooking, cleaning and even caring for his herd of racing stallions."

"How old were you again?"

"Aughhh!" Hayden punched him in the arm.

"Ouch that hurt," he laughed. "But I should have known that you would be so strong after solely caring for an entire herd of stallions at the youthful age of thirteen."

Hayden hit him again but there was no malice in her assault. They both laughed.

"You have to admit Hayden, that one was far-fetched."

"Well, maybe just a bit." Hayden straightened her shoulders and wiggled her hips in the seat.

"So what's your real story then?" Randy pressed for more.

"Equally far-fetched," Hayden looked out toward the field, "but I don't want to talk about me. I want to hear about you."

He looked as if he were about to push the subject, then nodded. "My life has been simple thus far. Then again, I've only just made your acquaintance."

The jest pleased her.

"I was born and raised in Colorado. My father was a fur trader. My mother died when I was born and my father remarried her sister to help raise my brother and me. I did a fair job in school. Loved arithmetic, hated reading. I had a dog named Lucy. She was my best friend growing up. My brother got me to join him in becoming a lawman to civilize Denver City. So, I moved here and have been breaking up bar fights ever since."

"That's the end of your story?" Hayden was clearly disappointed.

"Well, I suppose I did leave out the part where I traveled with a circus throughout the east coast and worked in a knife throwing act."

"You did that?"

"That was when I was ten, I believe."

Hayden raised her arm to sock him, but he caught her fist and pulled it against his chest. Halfheartedly, she fought him. His grip was loose and she could have gotten free if she wanted to. Instead, she let him hold her hand until he needed it to steer the mules.

Disappointed at the loss of contact, Hayden sat back against her seat. It was nearly noon and it seemed that the day had just begun. "I can't believe that it's so late in the day. This trip is going to fly by."

"I imagine I'm more interesting company than the preacher that was with you on the ship from France."

Hayden laughed.

Sobering, she cleared her throat. "Thank you for helping me. I could manage on my own, of course, but this is nice."

He smiled in agreement. "I knew you'd warm up to the idea."

"Don't get too secure, Mr. Deputy. I may still boot you out of my wagon."

"I don't doubt that for a moment. I'll take what I can. I want to learn more about you. I make a pretty good friend. You can trust me."

The last thing she needed was a friend, so she turned the tables on him and headed for more familiar conversation.

"A good friend, huh. I was hoping that our relationship might be a little more interesting than that." Teasing, she set her hand boldly on his knee.

He cut his eyes at her. "You sure you want to play that game?"

Hayden gave him her most innocent smile, her eyes betraying her mouth. "I don't understand what you mean?" She returned her hand to her own lap.

Amusement flooded Randy's face. Hayden had achieved her goal in changing the focus of his thoughts.

"You don't play fair, my sweet Contessa. If you do that again I will kiss you and I won't care who sees. This is your warning." His smile never faltered as he made his delicious threat.

Hayden half considered egging him on, but decided instead to build up the moment so that later when it happened, it would be everything that she had been imagining.

The lead wagon stopped in the early afternoon. Hayden and Randy had been wrapped up in a witty battle for the upper hand in their flirtatious game. Hayden loved every second of their competition. It wasn't everyday she had a worthy opponent.

Randy pulled the wagon alongside Fineese's. Hayden had completely forgotten about Kayra and Fineese. Guilt filled her belly. Kayra's trip thus far must have been terribly dull.

"How is it going?" Randy asked.

Kayra smiled. "Fine. She's been sleeping. The doctor gave her laudanum this morning. He left a bottle but said to be stingy because he didn't know how long she'd need it."

Randy nodded. "Get her up and see if she needs to have a moment's privacy."

Kayra blushed.

Randy hopped out and extended a hand to help Hayden down.

Hayden watched her cousin climb into the bed of the wagon with that woman and heard her gentle voice coaxing. "Fineese. Fineese. Wake up. This may be our only stop until we make camp tonight. You need to get up." Hayden walked to the wagon and listened. "I can't. I don't want everyone to see me like this."

"Don't be silly, Fineese. You need to stretch and do whatever else needs doing."

Hayden knew how to fix that. She hurried to her rig and dug through the costume trunk.

Hayden pushed wide the opening to the wagon bed. "Fineese, come on. We are getting out of this wagon for a while. Don't worry about folks seeing you. I have this hideous bonnet that we picked up somewhere along the way. The bill is so large no one will see your face. Kayra and I will walk with you as far as you need to go to be out of sight."

Kayra climbed over Fineese to hug her cousin. "Thank you, Hayden. You're the best ever."

Hayden smiled. Some of the guilt in her belly washed away. "Oh, knock it off. You know as well as I do that I am only doing this to impress Randy," She winked.

Kayra climbed back over and tied the bonnet under Fineese's bruised chin. Together the girl's scooted Fineese out of the wagon. Fineese stood on shaky legs, leaning heavily on the shoulder of each girl. When she began to step forward it was Hayden who took the lead taking the trio away from the wagons and out of sight. As far as she could tell, they had succeeded in not drawing attention.

Randy

Randy sat tall in Hayden's wagon observing the women as they guided Fineese away from prying eyes. Hayden had come around. He'd figured she would, but imagined it taking a lot longer and only happening after folks started saying things about Kayra. There was definitely more to this girl than met the eye. And what did meet the eye wasn't bad.

Physically, Hayden appeared stronger than her cousin. She had been the one to bear Fineese's weight as she steadied herself before they'd started their trek towards privacy. It wasn't pretty but the trio managed and returned before too much time had passed. He forced himself to stay put as they struggled to get Fineese back into the wagon. Maybe she'd taken too much laudanum.

His interaction with Fineese had to be kept to a minimum for numerous reasons. Primarily because if her attacker saw him, a lawman assisting her, he'd assume that she had enlisted his help and that would put all three of these ladies in danger. It wasn't in his nature to watch a lady do all the work, but this was for the best.

When Hayden returned to her wagon she was greeted by his widest smile. She frowned, shading her eyes. "Stop looking at me like that."

"I can't. I'm very proud of you." Randy reached down and helped her onto the bench.

He held a tin cup out for her. She took it, not meeting his eyes. "I found this in the wagon," He tore a hunk of bread from a larger loaf, "When we stop tonight I'll see that we have meat."

"Are we halfway for the day?"

"Depends. If the Wagon Master finds a valley where we can all fit for the night and water nearby. If so, we'll stop early. If not, we push on."

"Are there many lakes in these parts?"

Randy nodded. "I was raised in southern Colorado, but with a fur trader for a father I'm familiar with the streams, and passages throughout the territory. My dad knew every fishing hole, berry bush and tribe from New Mexico to Wyoming. "

"Are we gonna pass through hostile areas?"

"You mean Indians?" He raised an eyebrow.

Hayden nodded. A terrified expression clouding her acorn eyes.

"Yes, we'll pass through Indian territory. But there's little reason to be afraid. Indians might steal a few horses but they wouldn't be foolish enough to attack an entire wagon train unless provoked. It's been my experience that Indians aren't a threat unless they've been wronged. I respect their way of life and it's becoming harder and harder for them to maintain it. Most just want to be left alone. Besides, if you need someone to watch your back, I'd be more than happy to sacrifice myself in that way"

Hayden sat ramrod straight looking at him as if he'd lost his mind. "I can't believe you think that."

Her reaction was another puzzle. "About the Indians? Well, My thoughts are based on experience. I don't think it's fair to judge people because of horror stories told to keep kids from wandering too far from home."

"Horror stories?" Hayden nearly spat the words. "They're a whole lot more than stories."

He needed to keep his cool, but he wasn't budging on this. "You're wrong. In most cases, they are greatly exaggerated tales."

"No." Color drained from her face. She responded in a quiet, loathing voice. "They are not tales, and I..." She moved as far away from him as she could. "Stop the wagon. I want to ride with Kayra."

"No, I won't stop the wagon. This whole argument is ridiculous. You can't run away just because we happen to disagree. Why do you feel so strongly about this?"

"Stop the wagon." Hayden demanded in an increasingly louder voice.

"No," Randy countered, his own voice louder than it needed to be. "We can have a conversation and not see eye to eye."

As soon as the words left his mouth, Hayden hurled herself from the slow moving rig. She landed in a beige huff on the ground.

"What in the world? Are you crazy?" He hollered down to the fuming pile of fabric, hopping to its feet. "Well go on then, ride with Kayra." Randy clicked his cheek and hurried the mules ahead.

Hayden

Thankfully, it was still light when they pulled into the meadow where camps were already being set up. Randy held her rig, waiting for her and Kayra to come up beside him.

He spoke directly to her cousin. "I think we should fall back and camp behind those folks." He pointed where several wagons had distanced themselves. "It will give Fineese enough privacy but be plenty safe."

"I'll follow you over," Kayla agreed.

They parked their buckboard and Hayden stepped out the side. Should she try to talk to Randy? I mean, she'd actually leapt from a moving rig to get away from him. He was wrong, but still...

Randy made quick work of unhitching and securing the mules by the water. Then, he whizzed past Hayden, rifle in hand to wherever he was going. She definitely was not going to be the first to speak now that he was going to find dinner for them. She didn't need to be dealing with him right now anyway.

Hayden helped Kayra unhitch the horses. She led them to the makeshift corral where they could drink and graze. After assisting and resettling Finneese, Hayden started a fire. Kayra was turning corn cakes in the old cast iron. They'd been talking about what Hayden should do since her dramatic flight from the wagon when she was startled into silence as Randy approached the campfire with an infuriatingly smug look on his face. "Am I interrupting?"

Unable to hide her embarrassment over what he might have heard, Hayden hopped to her feet. "It's about time you came back. I could have already eaten if I'd gone hunting."

She reached for the bundle he carried. Two decent size rabbits were already skinned and propped on a stick for roasting.

Kayra scolded her cousin. "Nonsense. Don't be ungrateful. This looks delicious." Kayra smiled an apology toward Randy.

Randy shrugged off Hayden's words with a laugh. "Then you can feed us tomorrow." He gathered the empty water bucket headed for the stream.

Kayra grabbed a pail from Fineese's wagon and some rags. "I'm going to go make up some cool compresses for tonight. Watch the fire." She hollered over her shoulder hurrying to reach Randy.

Randy

He heard her say that he was arrogant. If anyone on this entire trip was arrogant it was Hayden. Where did she get off being so–

"Randy," Kayra called to him as she rushed along carrying a pail, "Mind if I join you?"

Randy halted. "I could have done that for you."

Kayra wiped at the brown hair covering her eyes. "Actually, I need to talk to you."

"Did Fineese say something?" He hoped some new information would lead him closer to the murderer.

Kayra was taken aback. "No, it's not about her." She paused.

"Well come on, we can talk and walk at the same time." Randy was less interested. Hayden had probably sent her.

"I know that you and Hayden had words in the wagon."

Randy shook his head, he was right. "It was a fight. And that cousin of yours was unreasonable and outrageous. You saw."

Kayra bit back a smile. "Yeah, thankfully we were in the back and not many others did. Though they probably heard. You were pretty loud."

Randy hung his head and brought it back up, grinning. "I was, wasn't I? She's got this way of just taking anything I say and twisting it like…"

"A dagger, a knife, a sword." Kayra provided her own words. "She does. You know that about her, but what you don't know is that you aren't the only one who has had experience with Indians."

Randy halted and spun her to look at him. "What do you mean?"

Kayra wouldn't look up. "She said that you went on about how your opinion was based on experience and hers was foolish because she'd never met an indian."

"That's not exactly what I said."

"That's what she got." Kayra raised her face and looked Randy dead in the eyes. Her lip trembled as she spoke. "Hayden will literally kill me if she finds out I told you, but we both have had experience with Indians. It's not my story to tell, but we lost our parents and our home. Hayden is too proud and maybe too scared to open up about a lot of things, especially this. Neither of us talks about it. But she likes you and I don't want her to miss an opportunity because she's proud, stubborn, and foolish. "

"Well those are definitely words I'd use to describe her." Randy held his hand on his hip. He was an idiot. For once, she'd been showing a part of herself that was real. And he'd continued blathering on, teasing and arguing, trying to win the hand. Stupidly, he'd lost the entire round. Hopefully, the game was salvageable. How was he supposed to know when she was genuine and when she wasn't?

By the gleam behind Kayra's lashes, Randy knew how much this admission had cost her. "Both of you are really special, you know? Hayden is lucky to have you."

Kayra shook her head, her thick brown hair swishing along her shoulders. "No, Hayden is the only reason we've made it this far. She's my rock. I'm the lucky one."

Randy took the pail from Kayra. "Go on back. I'll fill this half way and put the bandages in."

Kayra nodded. "Thank you."

Randy shook his head. "No, thank you. I was angry. I didn't know."

Hayden

As darkness enveloped the campers, Kayra suggested that they help Fineese out of the wagon. The ladies propped Fineese on a pallet near the fire. Her bonnet was so large that all they could see were shadows beneath its bill.

Hayden and Kayra were careful to include her in their conversation whenever they could. Folks were settling down and going to sleep for their first night on the trail.

Kayra asked Fineese, "Is there anything you'd like before turning in?"

Fineese smiled through her swollen face. "I usually have my quiet time. Would you mind reading my Bible to me?"

Hayden spit water all over the glowing fire.

Kayra disciplined her with a scowl.

"Of course I can. Just tell me where it is."

As soon as Kayra was gone, Fineese struggled to sit. Hayden came to her side and helped her get into a better position.

"I suppose it does seem out of place for a woman like me to spend time with God each day."

Hayden was well aware of her poor manners. "I'm sorry Fineese, it's just that I..." Hayden sighed, not knowing what to say.

"You don't ever need to apologize to me. I know what I've done, what I've been. That's one of the reasons that I love to read the Bible. The people in there aren't perfect either, but God gives them second chances."

Hayden moved Fineese's hair off of her shoulder. "You will get that chance."

Kayra returned with a well worn Bible and opened to where a golden ribbon marked the page. She started reading in Second Samuel.

Hayden sat back and listened to the story.

She'd heard of King David and knew about him and Goliath, but this side of David was new. Her mouth dropped when Kayra read of his sin with Bathsheba and his hand in the murder of Uriah. Finneese was right. David was little better than Fineese herself.

She frowned. *Why on earth, would God fill up a book with the likes of him?*

The women helped Fineese into bed. She'd been fighting to stay awake for the better part of an hour. Kayra began tidying. Hayden stoked the flames and scanned the field for Randy. Once the camp was in order, Kayra walked into the glow of the fire.

"Want me to wait with you?"

Hayden smiled. "You're the best. It would look less obvious if you were here."

Kayra sat down on a stump. "It amazes me that we are going straight through those mountains. I don't see how our wagons will ever make it."

"Randy says that this stretch will be the slowest part of our journey, that we'll likely be so sick of mountains after it that we'll build homes in the desert."

"I imagine he's right." Kayra giggled. "Build a home. It's a nice thought, isn't it?"

It wasn't long until most campfires had been doused. Darkness filled the valley. Randy emerged from the shadows startling the women. "I figured you two would be asleep by now." He sat right beside Hayden and reached for the bit of rabbit that was kept warm on the rocks by a pile of embers.

Stretching his legs, he reclined on an elbow.

"It's late. I think I'll turn in." Kayra kissed Hayden lightly on the cheek before climbing into Fineese's wagon.

"She's great, isn't she?" He commented.

Hayden beamed. "Kayra is the best person that I know."

Randy took another bite of his dinner. "Well, you haven't known me all that long, I guess."

Hayden cocked her head, her eyes alight with mischief. "Long enough. Did anything appear out of place?"

"No." He chewed with deliberate, slow concentration. "I'd be willing to bet that Fineese could identify our man if she wasn't afraid. Without her description, I have nothing to go on and that makes this a dangerous situation for everyone. Someone has to get her to confide in them." He took another bite and glanced at her. "You could, if you had a mind to. I imagine that you could get just about anyone to do anything you wanted."

Hayden smiled. The request pleased her. "I'll see what I can do."

Taking a deep breath she squared her shoulders and spoke. "I'm sorry for the way I acted earlier." She closed her eyes for a second before continuing. "I don't think that I can talk about what happened with anyone. Kayra and I don't even discuss it, but I shouldn't have behaved like that."

"If you ever do want to talk about it though, we can. You can trust me, Hayden. I won't judge you or feel pity. I want to be your friend."

Hayden was quiet before responding, which was an uncommon experience. "I suppose I could use a friend. Thank you." She dropped her hand to his leg. "I mean that. Thank you."

Randy

He shot to his feet. In a sweeping motion he had the water bucket in his hand and made quick work of dousing the fire. Smoke circled around them like a dust devil. He pulled Hayden to her feet, hauling her into his arms. "I warned you that if you did that again, I'd kiss you. So I guess you asked for this."

He tilted her head to meet his. Hayden instinctively closed her eyes and parted her lips when his mouth came down on hers.

His belly flip flopped and he felt as if his bones had been turned to butter. His hands trembled as if he were a school boy stealing a kiss out behind the church. To his delight, she put her arms around his waist.

Randy leaned his head against hers, his heart beating unsteadily. "I've wanted to do that from the moment I saw you walk into the town square with Dennison Harvey." His lips curled up as he squeezed her waist teasingly, "Dennison? Of all the men in Denver? "

Hayden smiled up at him. "Now what's wrong with Denny?" She came on tip toes and opened her mouth to kiss him again. "Was it at least worth waiting for?"

"I don't know," Randy teased, "I'd better try again, to see."

Hayden laughed and let him kiss her long and deliciously.

He gave a final caress of his lips against her forehead. "I hate to say good night, Hayden, but we really should."

She giggled. "Alright then. I'll go to sleep. Where are you bedding down?"

"It looks like a storm's coming in. I'll sleep underneath the wagon. Now you had better haul yourself up there before I change my mind."

Hayden smiled like an angel and Randy closed his eyes shaking his head. What was he getting himself into?

As Randy situated himself with a thick wool blanket and an extra set of clothes tied into a pillow roll, he started thinking about the stakes they were up against. He was completely at a loss for who the killer might be.

His instinct was rarely wrong, and it was telling him that the killer was someone with the wagon train. He'd visited with a new group of travelers throughout the evening during his rounds. Not any of the men he'd met seemed to pose a threat. Still, he couldn't shake the thought that the man was there right under his nose, waiting for the time to strike again.

Hayden had to get the information out of Fineese. He believed that she could, but there was no telling how long it might take. Fineese was afraid–and rightfully so. Before she would tell anyone what had happened to her, they'd have to become friends. He prayed that friendship came soon.

His mind drifted from his work back to Hayden. A smile curved his lips. He didn't know exactly how their relationship would play out. He still intended on leaving the wagon train once he caught the murderer. The plans he had for himself never included anything close to a partner in life, yet he couldn't help listing off all the ways that Hayden fell short of what a dutiful wife ought to be, almost as if he were talking himself out of falling for her.

And in all honesty, he really didn't know her. He wanted to, but she was unwilling to share her real self with him. All that he really knew about this woman was that she was beautiful, difficult, passionate, had a strange relationship with her cousin, and hated Indians. He had about as much to go on with Hayden as he had about his killer.

The wind blew the scent of wet earth to him as the sprinkling rain turned into a downpour. Randy scooted over until he was directly in the middle of his shelter. He tugged his blanket up around his shoulders and laid his hat across his face. His thick cover could dry tomorrow as they traveled.

The sound that the rain made as it thumped against the wagon above him was a cherished one. It brought back memories of his childhood as the dibble-dibble-dop-dop hit the canvas. There was nothing like a gentle rainstorm. The smell of wet earth being renewed reminded him that the creator always provided for another day.

He started to drift off. In his half alert state he heard a voice above him, then crying. He crawled from beneath the wagon, barely noticing the rain pelting against his now soaked skin.

"Hayden," he called. No answer. He lifted the canvas door and peered inside.

Hayden was drenched. He inspected the tarp in search of a leak but found none. She jerked in her sleep, frantic, thrashing her head back and forth. "No, no... I have to... Kayra.... run, run..."

She was having a nightmare. He grabbed hold and shook her foot in an attempt to wake her. She kicked off his hand and lunged against the side of the wagon. He climbed in. Her struggling form fought against him as he pulled her in his arms.

"Shh. It's all right. Shh you're just having a bad dream."

Hayden called out one terrified scream before waking. As she did, Kayra threw open the flap. Shock shot through her eyes. Hayden was in her nightgown and Randy sat fully clothed holding her across his lap. Kayra stepped back, closing the tarp as quickly as she had opened it.

"Kayra, wait."

There was a pause, then Kayra spoke. "If you're alright, Hayden, then I'll see you in the morning. Sorry. I thought you were having *the* dream."

Randy watched bewilderment fill Hayden's face. "I did have the dream, cousin. What are you talking about?"

In an instant, understanding hit him. Randy laughed aloud at what sweet innocent Kayra thought she was seeing. Hayden scrambled across his lap to open the canvas door.

"I did have the dream and I was screaming. Randy woke me up." She insisted.

Kayra breathed an audible sigh.

"Cousin, you thought that..." She pulled the flap open wide and pointed inside at Randy and then at herself. "He– I...We..."

Kayra nodded, an awkward smile on her face. The rain had already soaked her through. "It did look as if..."

"Nothing happened. You have to believe me. I had the dream and then I woke up and you were staring at us."

"I do believe you. Are you alright? Should I sleep with you? Fineese is snoring. I doubt she'll need anything."

Hayden shook her head. "I'm fine now. Just shook up and terribly embarrassed."

"Well good night then." Kayra called, running back to her shelter.

"Thank you, Cousin."

Randy made himself comfortable laying on his side, resting his head on her pillow. He felt a wide smile spread across his face just as he received a firm punch to the arm.

"Ouch. Are you a cat or something? How'd you see my arm? What was that for anyway?"

"I know that you're smiling like a fat pig who just found an apple bushel. I could die."

"Nah, It was a misunderstanding. Though I can only imagine what Kayra thought." He made no motion to move.

"Thank you," she said, "for waking me. The dream can go on and on like that."

"It truly was my pleasure. You were a vision to behold sleeping that way." It was a lie. She had been a pitiful sight. She looked as if she'd been dunked in a river and was on the verge of drowning, clawing at the air, fighting for life. "Do you have nightmares often?"

"It's only the one. And yes, it is often."

"Do you mind telling your rescuer what it was about?"

Hayden was silent. Randy regretted asking. He'd pushed her again. "If you don't want to, that's alright. I can think of something else to pass the time."

Again, Hayden swung at where his shoulder ought to be. This time, he anticipated it, grabbing hold of her arm. He pulled her down on the pallet beside him.

"Don't worry. I only want to hold you. I promise not to do anything else, at least not now."

She smiled, nestling her body against his. "Though, you may need to worry about me," she teased.

He'd already considered that but decided that he would earn another punch if he said so. She was wet with perspiration, her skin clammy. The long blond hair he loved fell in tangled strands. She fit against his side as if she belonged there. He wondered for the first time how old she was. He was twenty-four. She was probably closer to twenty.

"How old are you, Hayden?"

"Fifteen."

He threw her away from his body as if she were a snake. Her giggling made him feel like a fool. He should have known that she wouldn't give him a straight answer.

"How old are you, Deputy?" She trailed her finger along the buttons of his shirt.

"None of that." He stilled her hand. "I am twenty-four. Now you."

"I'll be twenty-one next month."

Randy whistled out his loud relief.

Hayden snickered at him. "You were scared for a moment weren't you?"

He nodded. "Yes, I was."

The rain had stopped falling. He kissed Hayden's knuckles and sat up.

"You're leaving?" He could hear the pout in her voice.

"I'd love to stay, but how would that look? Besides, if I do stay, your cousin might get herself a real story." Before she could hit him, he climbed out of the wagon and crawled underneath it. His bedroll was damp. It would be filthy tomorrow, but he didn't care. What a terrible, glorious night.

Chapter Nine

Hayden

The wagon train was like slow growing moss traveling up the Rocky Mountains. Were they making any progress at all? The nearly-invisible trail they followed was crude to say the least. The path was so narrow the wagons had to be driven half-on and half-off the trail. They'd known that this was an exploratory train, but it had been done a few times before. You would think that the path would have been smoother by now. And when there *was* a visible path, it zigzagged back and forth.

A few weeks had come and gone. Everyone had fallen into a routine. They rose with the sun, gulped down coffee, repacked and got a move on, eating whatever was left from the night before en route.

The first half of the day was when they made the most progress. If a difficult pass was ahead they'd use the slow break to go to the restroom or switch passengers. A hard turn could take two hours to cross.

Before the sun dipped in the sky the wagon master would select a meadow or valley, even if they had only covered a few miles, reasoning it was more important to stay together than speed along.

Hayden was not good at routine. Boredom was her pastime. Each day she stared at two brown rear ends poking along. As she'd suspected, she was stuck doing all the work by herself because Randy was always busy working with the men.

Apparently, he was familiar with the territory knowing it better than the scout they hired. He'd been asked to ride ahead of the group and designate route and stopping points.

Everything about the situation was frustrating. The few moments each day, when he could drive her wagon, left her confused. Because she was mad that much of the time he was gone, so she acted aloof, letting him know just how disappointed she was.

Except, like an idiot, everytime he was able to show up, she couldn't hide how happy she was to see him. A conundrum, that's what it was. At least she thought that was the word.

Hayden slapped her reins. The mules cautiously veered around a steep, sharp turn. About half the wagons had maneuvered through the abrupt switchback. Amos and Chloe tugged and pulled until Hayden's wheel scurried up a boulder and bounded onto the ground again, righting the rig.

"Good job." She hollered at her team. They had managed very well thus far. She couldn't help but compare. Several other wagons had taken much longer and some needed a push from behind. That was mules for you. Well, that and her own expertise.

She would never let on, but the lectures Randy had made while driving her animals had proven quite helpful. She was now getting more work out of the pair with less effort.

Hayden spied Randy astride his horse further up the mountain. Surely he was watching her. She hoped he was.

When she caught up with the wagon in front of her, she groaned aloud. Like a serpent from Hell, a wide river loomed just ahead, thrashing wildly. Hayden was not at all ready for this challenge. Thankfully, a few men were directing people across.

Her wagon crept to a stop where the river appeared most shallow. One, then another wagon entered the water. To Hayden's delight, their beds were mostly out of the flow. Maybe her's wouldn't get soaked. The horses seemed steady as their drivers coached them along. She could swim, she reasoned, and Chloe and Amos didn't spook easily. Still, she'd never driven across a river.

Randy loped up beside her. "Kayra's through, you can go on in."

Hayden forced a smile. She hadn't even thought of Kayra and whether or not she'd be able to make it across.

"Thanks." And yet, Hayden just sat there.

Randy looked up in the sky. "Wagon master wants everyone across tonight so that anything that gets wet has the chance to dry out."

"Makes sense."

Randy leaned back in his saddle, grinning. "You need me to do it?"

"Of course not." Hayden scoffed.

"So what's the hold up?"

"Well," Hayden began. "I was waiting for the mules to catch their breath." Hayden felt a blush. Both animals contentedly nibbled at the grass by their feet.

Randy surveyed the team. "You're right, they do appear tuckered out."

Hayden cut her eyes, lifting the reins. "Come on guys, let's go."

Reluctant to stop their snack, the animals inched forward toward the water.

Randy

Perhaps he should insist on driving Hayden across. She'd never accept him offering again, he would have to insist. He decided against it.

Why did he always want to bail her out? He couldn't tolerate a needy woman. Hayden certainly wasn't needy, but he needed to help her. Just like now, he knew that the trip across the river was an easy one, but he had to force himself to stay put and let her manage alone.

Truth was, he was having a hard time coming up with a real reason to stay on with the wagon train. Things were more than settled down. Sometimes it was downright boring. If it weren't for the time he got to spend with Hayden arguing or kissing, he'd have left a week ago.

It was time. He needed to head back to Denver City. The killer wasn't with these people, maybe he'd been caught and hung already. A few more days, that's all he'd delay. He wanted to make sure Hayden could manage tasks like this on her own. But boy, he dreaded telling her his plans.

The thought bit at his gut. *What was it about her?* She wasn't the prettiest woman on the trip and she might be the orneriest. If she'd been a good girl and barked on command he wouldn't mind putting a mountain range in between them. But she was certainly no trained dog.

When had the thought of not quarreling with someone become a bad thing? Whether or not he wanted it, soon enough he'd have his peace of mind back.

Hayden glared back at Randy. He motioned her forward.

He adored the way she stiffened her back and cocked her chin in the air before clucking to her mules and rushing headlong into the river.

Too fast! He started after her, but the wagon master had already seen her mistake and ordered her to lessen her pace.

She obeyed and slowly made a straight path across the river. He exhaled the breath he'd been holding.

Hayden

Her feet and skirt were wet but other than that it seemed everything was dry. She steered her wagon behind the one in front of her into a field. Like a caterpillar they moved together, the front end waiting for the back end to move forward and halt.

It was a good place to camp and she was ready. She'd crossed her first river and, proud as she was, she was more than happy to save her next triumph for tomorrow.

A warm breeze blew Hayden's hair across her face. She tucked it behind her ear for the hundredth time. Her rear end hurt, actually her whole body did.

Each day she felt a little more worn out...and her reflection showed that it too. What would she look like when the trip was finally over? She had a sunburn or a wind burn again, whatever it was, it hurt. The wind was terrible, constantly chapping her face. The small amount of cream she'd brought was gone. The palms of her hands were blistered too and raw from managing the reins all day. As if her skin weren't enough to make her feel like an ugly duck, her dresses were not even snug against her anymore.

Kayra, on the other hand, looked like she belonged in the mountains. The fresh air and sunlight tanned her. She had never looked so beautiful. Her hair glistened, long and thick like melted chocolate. Fineese had convinced her to wear it in different styles and it looked wonderful. Kayra had blossomed. It was no surprise. She liked work. She was task oriented and there was no lack of tasks on this trip.

Kayra said that all of the work helped keep her mind occupied so she didn't spend too much time thinking about William and his family. She explained that whenever her mind strayed to him, which it did about ten times an hour, she would quickly redirect her thoughts to some chore that needed doing before they stopped for the night. Who wanted to do that? Hayden was thankful for her own imagination. It was her only source of entertainment these days.

Hayden often imagined the life that her and Kayra would have in California. Recently though, she had to wonder if it would ever be just her and Kayra again. She was a jumble of feelings about the relationship her cousin and Fineese had developed. She'd been glad to see that Fineese had started on her baby quilt again, but when she found Kayra working on that same quilt, she was instantly angry. Because of her recent awareness of right and wrong thanks to her cousin, she knew she shouldn't feel that way and didn't want to, but there it was anyway.

Fineese was recovering. Her face was no longer swollen; only vague yellow blotches marked where she'd been hit. She continued to wear long sleeves no matter how uncomfortable she had to be. Her hair was full of life again and her dark eyes were bright and hopeful for the first time since they'd met. She talked constantly about what she was going to do when she arrived in California.

She planned to open a restaurant. She'd saved a good amount of money and had a mind for business. Genuinely, Hayden hoped that she would do just that. She deserved a fresh start and it was a good way to provide for herself and her baby. And, Hayden realized, if Fineese was on her way to taking care of herself, maybe she would get her cousin back.

The women had become friends in the past weeks, all three of them. Fineese was delightful, much to Hayden's surprise. In the beginning, she hadn't wanted to like her, but now Hayden found that she not only liked her, but admired her. No matter what circumstance they found themselves in, Fineese faced it head on, never complaining. She was funny and had an ability with style and fashion. Hayden told her that what she needed to open was a fancy dress shop. Her trunks were filled with beautiful dresses in expensive fabrics. Neither girl had ever seen so much luxury in one person's wardrobe.

Fineese knew which colors flattered her and had such elegant taste. She encouraged Hayden and Kayra to try on all of her things. It was fun playing dress up, but where would they wear such gowns? Fineese had answered, "Here and today. It's all we have. There is never a promise of tomorrow."

HAyden

Kayra pulled her wagon alongside Hayden's. "That was fun wasn't it?" The sunlight glowed off of her nose.

"Aren't you just content?" Hayden's voice scratched through cracked lips as she wrung out the bottom of her skirt.

Shrugging, Kayra smiled. "I guess I'm doing pretty well, considering that you were the one who wanted to go west and not me."

"Ugh," Hayden frowned, climbing from the wagon. She took her elbow in her hand stretching. "Don't remind me."

Kayra laughed, climbing from her seat. She stopped to take in the mountains surrounding them. "This view is incredible."
"What are you talking about?"

"This," Kayra motioned with her hand to the landscape, "I mean, have you ever seen such beautiful sights in your whole life?"

Mountains loomed all around them. Were they challenging her or simply mocking her? Shadows played along the crevices making them look unreal. The shear height was mind-boggling. Near the mountain tops, the trees thinned before giving way to sparse shrubbery then nothing but rock.

It was incredible, but Hayden noticed none of the beauty. "I don't think I can do this anymore, cousin. I think maybe we should–"

"No way. We're almost to the top. I want to see the other side."

"Why? All we're going to find is another equally impossible hill that we are going to have to inch our way across."

"Probably, and that is exactly what we'll do. It'll get easier. Besides, you would never forgive yourself if you gave up. I have a feeling that something grand is waiting for us just over these mountains."

Kayra took a bucket from Hayden's wagon and headed for the stream. "I'll take care of this for you, since your boyfriend isn't here to anticipate your every need." Kayra, teased.

"Oh Cousin, stop. He just feels sorry for me because I'm such a wreck."

"I never thought I'd see the day that you would play 'the damsel in distress'." Kayra feigned desperation holding a hand to her brow dramatically, then giggled, disappearing.

Is that what people thought? She wasn't a weak woman. She was more than capable of taking care of herself and anyone else for that matter. This "being taken care of" stuff wasn't doing her any good.

Randy may not ride with her each day, but as soon as they made camp he handed over some animal for the women to cook. He unhitched the mules and brought water from the river right to her fire. Speaking of which, he usually had a bundle of branches and kindling for that fire ready to go. She'd let Randy get too close. By becoming comfortable with him, it was easy to rely on his help. She should have never let things get this far.

No longer was she the strong, independent woman that had begun this trip. She noted all the ways that she'd given him control. How she was letting him have the upper hand. A decision was made right then and there that she would stop this ridiculous behavior before he completely ran her life. As if she'd just been given a strong dose of gumption, she grabbed her rifle.

Tonight *she* would provide their food and have it cooked by the time Randy settled into camp. A sniveling little girl she wasn't, and it was high time he recognized that.

Greely

Greely had been keeping his eye on the three women traveling together. They always made up the end of the train. That pesky lawman was sniffing around their campsite too often. Of course, he didn't like the fact that the law was tagging along at all. When he spied the deputy kissing the blonde he let himself relax. Maybe it wasn't business that had him sign on with the train.

The whore he'd nearly beaten to death had more pluck than he thought. He was surprised when he'd seen her and her angels of mercy that first day. The woman could barely stand, but here she was.

He smiled remembering their night together.

There was something about her that had made him leave her alive. Becky might have had a chance if she hadn't had such a big mouth, asking about the scar across his cheek. When he'd warned her to shut up by slapping her across the face, a tooth had fallen out. Then, she'd gone to clawing. He hadn't intended to kill her. Tying her up and gagging her was supposed to make her feel humiliation. He imagined her being found like that the following day. Except morning hadn't come for her.

He wanted a woman now. As that thought crossed his mind he spied the deputy's blonde wandering off and she was alone. The lawman was guiding folks across the river, so that left little miss independent unprotected. Grabbing his knife, he surveyed what was going on around him. Everyone was engrossed in what they were doing. No one would see anything.

She was fast. He caught sight of her nimbly scaling a rock twice her size. If he followed directly she would see him, so he crept around the side of the mountain. The wind was strong, making it difficult to hear. He had a decision to make. Would he kill her when he was done?

She'd put up a fight, he was sure, so he might have to. He could always throw her body off the edge of the cliff. Then again, if he did that, her lawman boyfriend would probably hold up the whole wagon train looking for her. That wouldn't do. He needed to get to a town as soon as possible.

Hayden

There it is.

Hayden dared to breathe. From behind a copse of trees, a white-tailed deer alerted Hayden to the presence of dinner. In a slow, silent movement, she raised the rifle to her shoulder.

Except, something wasn't right.

A premonition forced her to abandon her kill and turn. With lightning reflexes she spun and found her gun pointed directly at a man.

There was nothing remarkable about him. A dirty brown hat and work clothes were the uniform of every man she'd seen in the last few weeks. Relieved that it was just a man from the wagon train, she blew out the breath she was holding. "Are you crazy!" She scolded, "I almost shot you. I thought you were an Indian."

The man ran a hand along his chin. "No ma'am. You are safe with me." Something about the mad look in his eyes made Hayden wonder if she was.

She still held her weapon. "You one of us? Headed to California?"

The man nodded and with barely perceptible steps moved closer to her.

"What are you doing out here?" She demanded.

"Same as you." He answered. His blue eyes narrowed as his lips crooked to the side. He was staring at her with such a strange expression.

Hayden knew that after making camp, any of the men would go into the nearby woods to find game. This man however held no rifle. She looked to his hip to see if a holster was there and saw that he had a knife poised in his grip and his belt was unfastened falling wide open to expose an open trouser front.

If he was one of the people on the wagon train, he was not out hunting like her. Unless she realized, she was the prey.

It was when understanding dawned on her that his grin curved up his face and a purple scar brought the smile clear to his ear. He looked positively wild. She felt completely exposed as his eyes made their way over her body.

Taking a deep breath, Hayden stepped back, dangerously close to the boulder's edge.

"Easy there little miss." The man's hands went in the air, in a position of surrender. Who did he think he was fooling? Nothing about him looked like he would surrender. In his fist he gripped a knife. "I ain't gonna hurt you. I just want to talk to you."

Her aim remained steady. She'd never looked down the muzzle of a gun to a person. *Was killing a man the same as an animal?* Her fingers flirted with the trigger. *Do it,* she told herself.

As if in a slow dance, he shuffled forward, lowering his hands.

"Budge a muscle and I'll shoot." She warned.

The man paused, his eyes calculating. "Now, you don't want to do anything you'll regret. Put down the gun and I won't hurt you."

Hayden's hands trembled as she maintained her aim. "Who are you?"

Lunging, he seized her rifle and tossed it aside. It cracked and fired as it fell off the cliff to the rocks below. His fingers grasped the front of her blouse and ripped the fabric from her neck to her waist. It was such brittle fabric, it did little to put up a fight. Instinctively, her arms went to shield her chest.

He was smiling. Air escaped her lungs as big hands encircled her throat. She kicked at his shin before bringing up her palm to slap him across that moon shaped purple scar on his cheek. He laughed at her attempt to dissuade him.

"I've been watchin' you and waiting. Now I get to taste you." He pushed her to the granite floor thrusting his body against hers. "I like that fire you got. Do it again." He spit the words into her mouth. His face against hers.

She felt the breath hot and wet on her lips as her body was crushed into the solid ground. He was on top of her, his weight pinning her down. Never before had she been more terrified of what was to come and she'd had a lot of terrifying experiences. *No,* she thought to herself. Not this man, not like this. She brought her hands to his, digging her nails into his fingers, prying his vice-like grip from her neck. All her scratching and tugging was getting her nowhere. She had to try something else and she had to do it before her head exploded.

With one hand he held her neck. Easing off her, he reached to his waist. Hayden took the brief moment and moved into action. Her vision fogged at the sight of his empty eyes when she jerked to the side, bringing her knee to his groin.

He gasped and the hold around her neck loosened. She scrambled from under him gasping for air. It took only a mere second for him to right himself and move for her again. She rolled away and leapt from the rock. Her only thought was of getting away from him no matter the cost. His fingers darted for a handhold gripping a chunk of hair. Better to die trying to get away than to meet her fate with him.

Her body smacked against granite. Pain seared her face but that was nothing compared to the feeling of her tresses separating from her scalp. The ground met her, bruising and scraping her body. The sky and earth flipped and flopped in front of her.

Finally, the world righted itself and she realized how close she was to the cliff's edge. Scrambling to her feet she crouched against a conifer tree. Not far above her, brush crackled and heavy breathing snapped her to the present. She had to get away. Ignoring the ache in her shoulder and the blood trickling down her chest. Like a rabbit, she bolted.

That man was behind her, his footsteps heavy and steady. Hayden was fast. How was he still right there?

She refused to be caught, hopping roots and darting bushes desperate to put distance between her and her pursuer. Her chest ached. She'd gone too far from the camp. *I have to get back, just make it to the valley.* She wanted to scream but she could barely breathe. She sprinted through the trees. Her body was giving up and his breathing seemed to be getting closer and closer. From somewhere in her gut, she managed a blood-curdling cry, hoping the breath she used would not be wasted.

Please someone hear me, she prayed.

Six shots sounded.

Never slowing, her arms covered her head. *They heard me,* she assured herself, *surely he's dead.* The pain in her chest slowed her and the trees around her clouded as she collapsed in a heap on dry, yellow grass at the field's edge.

The next thing she knew, Kayra was pouring water on her face and a crowd had encircled them. She curled into a ball still fighting for air. Her lungs ached with each strained breath.

Kayra fell to her side shaking her shoulders. "What happened? Was it Indians?"

Unable to speak, Hayden shook her head and stared from one face to another, hunting for those terrible eyes. "No Cousin, it was him, the man that killed Uncle Johnny." She blurted her thoughts. "But, they got him. I heard the shots. They got him. Cousin, we're safe."

"Quiet." Kayra shushed. "You aren't making any sense. I don't know what you're talking about."

A boy came running into the field and over to the crowd congregated around Hayden.

"He got away. I shot into the air as soon as I heard the screaming. I thought it was an Indian or a bear but then I saw a white man chasing her. I tried to get him, but he got away. I seen him head straight up the mountain like an animal or something." The boy looked at Hayden. "I sure am sorry ma'am, but he got plumb away."

The gravity of what had just happened landed in her lap. She'd almost been killed and who knows what else, then the killer got away and then she'd gone and blurted out her connection to the trail of murders. What a tangled web she found herself in.

An older man with a long, scraggly beard scratched his chin as he ordered. "Grab your guns and spread out. Any man that isn't here with us, you find him and you bring him back. I don't care if he's your pa or your brother. If he isn't here now he's a suspect and I want 'em all rounded up."

Men scurried about grabbing rifles and heading into the mountain she'd just fled. Hayden rested in her cousin's arms regretting her rash words. Now everyone would know what they had done to their uncle's body. The killer must have figured out who they were and that was why he'd come after her.

If that boy hadn't been hunting nearby, what would have happened? She wouldn't cry. Tears were weak. Against Kayra's gentle resistance, she came to her feet.

Blood caked the back of her head where she'd dangled from her attacker's hand before her locks gave way, ripping her scalp. A hot iron couldn't have hurt more. It felt like she was still being branded. In silence, Hayden headed toward the pond and knelt to wash her wound.

The cool water burned. She brought a handful to her mouth, drinking it in gulps. It trickled down her face, cooling parched skin. Uncaring about the spectacle she made, she waded in. Beige fabric pooled around her legs. The billowing flow of water wrapped her hot flesh in its relief. Plopping below the surface, she soaked in its refreshing coolness, vaguely aware that every woman stood nearby watching her float, her dress bobbing up and down.

When Hayden dragged herself from the stream, the weight of her sopping dress was like carrying flour sacks around her legs. It hung in yards of oatmeal-colored fabric, sticking to her legs and tripping her steps. Kayra guided her, calm as ever.

When they reached camp, Kayra climbed into the wagon with Hayden and helped her out of the dripping clothes. She tossed the heavy garment on the ground and pulled a pretty blue dress from the trunk. Without the need for words, Kayra tugged it over Hayden's head and tucked her arms through the sleeves. Hayden sat limply while Kayra buttoned the back. Before, the dress had fit a little too snugly, but not anymore.

"Are you in much pain?" Kayra asked, finger combing her cousin's straggly locks.

"It hurts, but I'll live."

"Can you tell me what happened?"

Hayden nodded. "I was stupid is all. Went off to hunt. That man found me and would have killed me. I think he meant to force me..."

Kayra leaned forward resting her head on Hayden's. "I'm so sorry."

Hayden continued. "I jumped from him. I'd rather be dead than let him touch me. He took a handful of my hair, but I got away. Then I heard shots and I assumed he was dead. I just ran until I saw the wagons."

"What did he look like?"

"I don't know." Hayden stared into the distance. "I only saw his eyes. They were like ice."

"Let's get you a dose of Fineese's laudanum. Then you can rest."

"No," Hayden shook her head firmly, "I want to see all the men they bring in. This guy had a scar." A shudder ran through Hayden. "I need to talk to Randy." She took a breath to steady her nerves. "I'm fine now. Don't worry about me. You stay with Fineese. I may have put you in danger earlier by what I said."

Kayra leaned over and hugged Hayden. "I love you. I don't know what I would do if anything ever happened to you."

"You'd do whatever needs doin', Cousin. But you don't have to worry. I won't pull anything stupid like that again."

Chapter Ten

Randy

The sky was orange by the time Randy charged into the field, his eyes fixed on Hayden's wagon. Ignoring everyone around him, he rode through camp and leapt from his saddle. His horse, lathered in sweat, huffed heavily from its run. Free at last, he loped toward the creek. Randy threw open the canvas and breathed a sigh of relief when Hayden smiled at him. Her cheekbone boasted a painful looking scrape and the purple outline of fingers on her throat made him gasp. Whoever had attacked her had tried to strangle her. How could anyone touch that perfect neck with cruel fingers? He traced a bruise before she took his hand from her throat. She could have been lost to him so easily, but she wasn't. She was here and alive. It took him a moment to notice the bandage at the base of her scalp.

Not caring what folks would say, he climbed into the back of the wagon and pulled her to him, holding her until he realized that she was struggling to breathe. "Are you alright?" He searched for unseen wounds, inspecting both arms and her neck before she brushed his hands aside.

"Randy, I'm fine. I swear it."

A deep breath escaped his chest and he pulled her against him tenderly now. He was careful not to touch the bandage at the base of her skull as his hands directed her head to rest on his shoulder. She held him, clutching his shirt in her hands.

She's alive, he reminded himself. His heart raced as if she were still in danger. He couldn't squelch the panic he felt.

"I'm fine. I promise. Just a few scratches, that's all."

"This is my fault."

"What?" Hayden looked incredulously into Randy's face. Her eyebrows scrunched together.

"You shouldn't have been left alone. Not for a minute. I let my guard down, was doing too much away from you. I'm not letting you out of my sight again."

"Randy, that's ridiculous. You can't be my guard every second of the day. Besides, I can take care of myself." Hayden pulled away from him. She was serious, as always, too confident. *Didn't today teach her anything?*

"You were lucky, Hayden. If that boy hadn't been nearby God only knows what could have happened to you."

"But it didn't. I got away."

Randy held his tongue. The last thing that he wanted right now was an argument. She'd had to be independent in her life. Up until now, that attitude had only been a mild irritation. But it was time for that to end.

"Hayden," he paused. Anything he said would lead to confrontation, so he let the fight leave him with a heavy swallow. "Thank God you're alright."

She smiled and leaned up to kiss him. It felt so good to have the woman that he loved safe in his arms. Suddenly, he stopped as the enormity of what he'd just admitted to himself hit him. A smile spread across his face and he stroked her cheek with his hand.

"What?" Hayden smiled up at him.

"You're so beautiful." He kissed the top of her head not bothering to hide his smile.

"What is with you?"

He shook his head but his grin remained fixed. If he told her how he felt, she would surely run from him, so he'd keep it to himself. For now.

A change of topic was in order.

"Tell me everything that happened."

"Well," Hayden began. "I went into the hills, right after we made camp."

"Okay," Randy interrupted. "Why didn't you take Kayra with you?" No other woman was leaving camp alone.

Hayden frowned. "She was occupied. Anyway, I went into the hill and was sitting on a rock when–"

"What were you doing?" He wanted every detail and she wasn't skirting any of them.

"I went to pray."

"Oh," Randy replied. What could he say about that?

"As I was saying, I sensed someone was behind me so I turned and my gun was pointed directly at him."

She had a gun. *So, not praying.* Thank goodness she'd had that gun with her. He wouldn't point out the flaw in her tale.

"What did he look like?"

"He was big, probably as big as the wagon leader, Foster. He had on work clothes, nothing out of the ordinary, a dirty brown hat, like just every other man here. Otherwise, I can only remember this purple scar across his cheek and empty blue eyes."

Randy knew that he had to keep her talking. "Describe them."

"They were blue. Blue like a frozen pond. And they were evil. The man has no soul, I swear it."

Randy took her hands in his. He hated to make her relive a moment of this. "What happened next?"

"He said something like, 'You don't want to shoot me.' I knew that I should, but I wanted his name. I paused too long and he lunged, knocking the gun from my hand. We fought and finally I jumped from the rock and fell down the mountain. When I stopped, I ran screaming towards camp, hoping that someone would hear. Then I heard shots. I kept running. The boy who'd fired said he got away. That's about it."

"What happened to your head?" He asked as he traced his finger gently along the bandage.

"When I jumped, he reached for me and only could get a handful of hair. It hurt like…well it hurt bad. Tore loose."

He imagined that, shaking his head. It was a horrible image. "By now they will have rounded up the men that weren't in the field when this happened?"

"I heard that was the plan. Are they ready?"

"If you're up to looking them over?"

"Yes," Hayden moved toward the opening in the wagon, "If they're here, let's go."

Randy's chest swelled with pride. She was nearly fearless. Any other woman would be terrified at the prospect of identifying her attacker, but Hayden was anxious and confident that she would find him and he'd pay. "Alright, if you think you're ready, let's go."

The wagon creaked as together they climbed out. Randy held Hayden's hand as she found her footing.

"I'm sorry." He said looking toward the crowd of people waiting for them. "We should have discussed this outside. It doesn't look good that we were alone in the back of the wagon."

"Are you kidding me? I was attacked. You're the sheriff. Of course you would come and talk to me."

"Yes, but I would never have gone into the bed of a wagon with any other woman like that." As they approached the group, an older gentleman who'd been organizing the men met them.

He addressed Randy, "One man's missin'. It's probably our guy. His name's Sam Greely. Don't know much about him, 'cept he joined in Denver and sticks to hisself. She should look over these others, but I imagine that Greely feller is our man."

"Sam Greely you say? The name's familiar. In my line of work, knowing a stranger's name is usually a bad thing. I'm sure I've never spoken to him or I'd have picked up on the name." Hayden touched his arm. "Can we get this over with?"

"Follow me." The older gentleman led them through the crowd to address the men. "All of you who were out hunting when the attack happened, line up. We just want to make sure that this guy isn't among us, so we can make preparations for finding him."

About fifty men waited to be cleared as nothing more than fellow travelers.

It didn't take Hayden any time to decide. "He's not here."

"I figured as much." Turning his attention to the older gentleman, Randy asked, "Where's Greely's wagon?"

The two men walked to a buckboard. They found a bedroll and a few supplies in the back. The old timer pushed a few canned goods against the wooden trunk pointing out the very few belongings. "There's not enough here to get all the way to California. Perhaps he wasn't planning to make the whole trip."

Randy agreed. "Then again, he probably assumed when he needed something he'd just take it."

Hayden

The buzz of conversation filled the camp.

"You alright, Cousin?" Kayra put a hand on Hayden's shoulder.

"I'm fine." She answered, but her interest was elsewhere.

A middle-aged woman with a tight bun and weathered face was talking to her daughters. And it was that conversation that held her attention.

"Now, you see why you don't associate with that type of person. She's been helping that saloon girl and look where it's gotten her."

Hayden felt a jolt shoot through her at the harsh words. Worse than that, she could see Fineese across the way, her red head shrinking to the outskirts of the crowd. Anger simmered inside her making her back stiffen and her hands fold into eager fists.

Before Hayden had fully considered her actions, she was in the woman's smug face. "Who do you think you are?"

The woman stepped back, nervously offering a placating smile that didn't meet her pale eyes. "Excuse me?"

"I heard you. And you know nothing about me or Fineese for that matter, so you have no right to make judgments on either one of us."

Kayra was instantly at Hayden's side, taking her wrist. "Come on. This isn't going to do any good."

Hayden jerked her arm free and looked back at the woman who didn't even have the decency to apologize or be embarrassed by her words. Simmering anger was about to boil over.

"You owe us an apology," Hayden ordered.

The woman balked. "I will not apologize to her," She glared in Fineese's direction. "She shouldn't even be here with respectable folk." The woman paused only for a second before continuing. "You shouldn't either, for that matter."

Hayden closed the distance between herself and the lady.

Through taught lips she asked, "What do you mean by that?"

The woman found a bit more nerve and met Hayden's eyes. "I mean that you and those two whores traveling with you should never have come on this trip."

A hush fell across the onlookers, as raised voices drew their attention. The two women stood face to face. Kayra's mouth fell open and tears escaped down her cheeks. Fineese remained in the background silent, her hands resting protectively across her stomach.

"You will apologize, to all of us, now. As I said, you know nothing about any of us." Hayden barely held her temper in check. Her fingers flinched, anxious to be used.

"I know all about her," The woman spit out. Her worn face scrunched with pain. Instantly, she appeared years older. "I know that she makes good, God fearing men leave their families at night by tempting them with her sinful lust."

A deep, male voice broke in, "That's enough, Beth-Anne."

The woman turned her anger on the man at her side. "You would defend her. I knew all along that it was her you been seein' or is it the dark haired one?"

"I said that's enough." Angrily, he took her arm and tried to lead her away but she jerked free.

"You see," she spoke wildly to her humiliated daughters who stood helplessly watching their parent's spectacle. "This is what comes of good men when women like *them* come to town."

"Beth-Anne, not another word," He warned.

"All three of them are sluts, but you already knew that."

He spoke low and cold to his wife. "I warned you. You owe these folks an apology, especially those girls. You don't know a blasted thing about them. I ain't even met those two before. And her," he said pointing toward Fineese, "she's been more of a wife to me since she came to town than you've been in fourteen years of marriage. You'll apologize to them now."

Collectively, everyone held their breath. Not a person moved, every ear eager to see what was going to happen.

Smoothing out the front of her dress, Beth-Anne spoke, "I'm sorry," before turning to walk away.

Randy

Before she could retreat, Randy was in her path holding up his hand, his jaw set like an ax blade. "Everyone here needs to understand that I will not tolerate any talk against my wife." He was beside Hayden with a few determined strides. "She's done nothing wrong. This Greely fellow is a threat to all of us and it could have easily been you or one of your daughters attacked today." He draped his arm across Hayden's shoulder. "No one will speak a word against my wife for what happened today."

He pointed to Fineese. "As for her, she's helping me with the investigation concerning Sam Greely. I don't care what she was before, she's working with the law now to protect you." Expressions of surprise passed amongst most of the wagon train.

He walked to Kayra and put a hand on her shoulder. "This is Kayra, and she's a nurse from back East. Her husband is in San Francisco waiting for us to get her to him. She's agreed out of the goodness of her heart to assist with Fineese when the time comes for her baby. There is nothing disreputable about her behavior or character. Any one of you who challenges either thing, will answer to me." The crowd accepted every word he said without question.

Finding no resistance, his galloping heart slowed to a trot. "Now as most of you know, I'm a lawman from Denver. I'm on this trip to catch this man. I believe he's killed at least three times and he won't think twice before hurting a woman. I want to talk to every person who has had a conversation of any sort with him. Come to me and tell me about it. I don't care how insignificant it may seem. I want to know. From now until we reach Grand Junction, all of you will do as I say and hopefully nothing bad will happen again. We're gonna camp here for a few days, and then whether or not we catch him, we'll set a rapid pace to make up for lost time.

"That man has neither his gun, nor mount. He'll be wanting those back. Any man willing, get a rifle and meet by the creek. Everyone else, circle up. We're putting Greely's buckboard and crazy horse in the center so he won't be able to steal it during the night. Keep fires blazing, stay alert. If anything seems suspicious, use caution. No one is to go off alone for any reason. Everyone stays at camp until told otherwise. Are there any questions?"

One young man shifted his weight while cocking his head. It was obvious that he wanted to say something.

"If you have something to say, spit it out." Randy urged.

He scratched at the sparse nest of hair on his chin. "I just wanna get to California. No disrespect, but I think that me and Martha here is gonna keep on. I seen a map and the trail is obvious. Besides, a smaller group could make better time. I suppose, I'm askin' if anyone wants to join us." A riot of whispers ensued.

Randy shook his head. "I won't make you stay, but you got a real pretty wife there and I sure would hate to see her stolen from you or killed. This is dangerous territory you are heading into. You don't know where water is and I doubt you know much about the Indians in Utah neither. We got a killer on foot who would probably like a mode of transportation. I hope he doesn't decide he wants yours. Sam Greely is dangerous. He kills and takes his time doin' it. We're going to make up for the lost time, I suggest you stay and help."

The man puffed his chest and crossed his arms. "I can take care of myself and Martha. Remember sheriff, it was your wife who was attacked. Mine was safe with me." He smirked.

Martha closed her eyes and visibly shrunk under her showboating husband's words. She pulled a worn shawl around her shoulders, focused on the ground between her feet.

Randy locked eyes with the young man. They stared at each other a moment before he spoke. "As I said, I don't advise it, but you're welcome to make up your own mind."

The sour feeling in Randy's stomach mimicked the look on the cocky boy's face as he escorted his young wife to their wagon. Her head remained down. She wouldn't look at a soul. They had no business going off alone, but there wasn't anything you could do with a man like that to make him listen to reason.

"We all got work to do, let's get it done." Randy motioned the crowd to disperse. People bustled into action like ants at a picnic.

"Follow me." He grabbed Hayden's hand and a bucket en route. They had to get out of earshot so that he could explain. When he heard that woman's bitter words he just opened his mouth and the story flew out. Luckily, it seemed to fit. The crowd accepted it without question and it gave the women a cover. No doubt he was about to get bawled out, so he decided to put some distance between them and the other travelers.

Randy crouched down at the edge of the lake to fill the bucket. "I'm sorry about what happened over there. I said the first thing that came to mind. I apologize for putting you in this position but the gossip will stop and being my wife will make you safer." There'd be hell to pay and he'd said he was sorry but he wasn't at all sorry for the lies he told.

He looked up so that Hayden could say her peace.

Hayden

She couldn't help but smile. When his eyes met hers, relief flooded his face. In one motion, he stood to take her in his arms, sloshing water all around them.

"You're not mad? I figured I'd be skinned for sure." He nearly laughed. "You just about scratch my eyes out for one thing or another, and then when I flat out lie to the world about something, you look at me like that?"

Hayden nodded. How could she be angry? "This'll be fun. Thank you for what you said. Kayra was devastated by that horrible woman. Then, you were magnificent. You just swooped in and took control. You made everything better. I didn't even know what I should do, then, you just did it. It was fantastic."

She grabbed the collar of his shirt and pulled him closer to her. "I'm proud that you're my husband." She considered that for a second. What would it be like if he actually were her husband? The desire to kiss him right then and there was stronger than any desire she'd had before. There he stood, dirty from his long day riding, shaggy black hair covering his ears and the look in his eyes…had anyone ever looked at her like that? She tilted her head and turned flirtatious eyes his way.

"You are choosing now to give me that look?"

"I just wish you didn't have to leave me tonight. I mean, considering it's our honeymoon and all."

He laughed and engaged her in the game shaking his head. His calloused hands reached out and pulled her into his arms. Boldly, Hayden tilted her head up so that her chin rested in the crook of his neck.

"Hayden, you had better watch that or you will get a honeymoon."

She feigned shock but knew he could see right through it.

"I gotta get going. I imagine Greely's still around. He probably plans on stealing a horse."

"You really think he'll come back?" She'd only ever been afraid of Indians before, until this Greely man. She should tell him. She should tell him what they had done to Uncle Johnny but…not yet.

"Makes sense doesn't it? Where else would he get a horse? Besides, I think that he wants his horse. The wagon leader's sleeping in Greely's buckboard. With all the wagons surrounding him, I doubt that Greely will try for his mount, but he's gutsy. You be careful."

He ran his finger across Hayden's cheek. "I have a spare revolver in my bedroll. Can you use one?" Hayden nodded. "I want you to sleep with it. I won't be back till daylight or after. It might be a good idea for you to stay in the wagon with Kayra and Fineese. It'll be crowded but I'd feel a lot better about leaving you if I knew you weren't alone."

"I'll be fine. You go and get that man. Be careful too. He's not right. If you see him, shoot him, don't take him prisoner."

"Hayden, I'm a law man. I can't just shoot him unprovoked."

"Well…be as safe as you can. I…"

Randy's face shot up. The muscle in his jaw twitched.

"I…I just want you to come back in one piece."

"I will." He promised. "This is what I do and I'm good at it. Don't you worry about me." He kissed the top of her head. "I'll be back. Let's get back to the group."

Hayden watched as he checked his pack. He secured the cinch and went to wrap Hayden in his arms. "Don't go doing anything alone, please. I can't do my part unless I know you are doing yours."

""I'm too tired to cause any trouble tonight. Don't you worry."

Randy nodded, accepting her at her word. "I think Fineese might be more willing to talk now that you were hurt. We know who we are looking for, but not a whole lot about him. She might be able to fill in some blanks."

Hayden ran a hand along his arm, resting it in the crook of his elbow. "I'm on it boss." She smiled up at him.

He leaned down and kissed her lightly on the lips before swinging into the saddle headed to where a posse of men assembled.

It wasn't thirty minutes later when the foolish young man and his bride drove their wagon, along with one other couple, out of the field disappearing behind the mountain.

"God, be with them," she whispered.

Chapter Eleven

Hayden

Wagons belted the travelers. Half the men had headed into the hills in search of Greely. A fire burned in front of each camp site, casting the entire field in an orange glow. Five men stood guard by the horses who were tied to trees behind the wagons. Each volunteer was jumpy, with a trigger finger posed and ready.

Hayden joined Kayra and Fineese in front of their wagon. A fire burned feet from the women. Fineese perched on a log, writing in a journal, while Kayra's fingers pushed a needle through the blanket. It was a joint project that they were making for the baby. Hayden sat beside her cousin.

Kayra smiled. Her eyes were no longer sad as they had been just an hour earlier.

"Are you two okay? I mean about what happened earlier." Hayden asked.

Fineese's soft expression reassured Hayden. "You don't have to worry. It's certainly not the first time I've been called names. It was, however, the first time anyone respectable has ever defended me. You two have no idea what your friendship means."

Kayra was radiant in the fire's glow. The warmth in her expression reached across the campsite reflecting Fineese's. They had become very close in the past weeks. Hayden felt a stir of jealousy and scooted closer to her cousin.

"That was really something." Kayra turned her attention to her cousin laying aside the quilt. Her voice, just above a whisper. "I hoped that you would make your way over here tonight. How did that happen? I mean I've thought from the beginning that the two of you were well suited, but then when Randy started his speech and said that you two were married, I about died. Luckily all eyes were on you or I'd have given away everything. I know to expect the absurd from you, but I never figured him for being a smooth talker."

Hayden beamed. "I know. Wasn't he amazing? I think that my problem with this whole trip has been the redundancy. Now it's interesting again." Hayden's head bobbed in animated delight.

Kayra shook her head. Fineese looked on in silence.

Kayra explained, "I told you that Hayden was a master at playing parts. You see, now she has a role to play, as if being attacked by a lunatic killer wasn't enough drama for the day."

Fineese

Fineese stomach churned as she thought of Hayden finding herself at Greely's mercy. Remembering that night in Denver always brought on panic. Her eyes filled with tears. It seemed that she cried constantly these days. "I'm sorry that he got to you."

Both girls faced her in surprise at the direction the lighthearted conversation had gone.

Fineese's back shook as tears rolled down her face. "This is my fault. I'm so sorry, but I didn't think that he was on the trip with us. I swear, I didn't know or I would have..." Her sentence trailed off as she recalled the stern threat he'd given her. *If you breathe a word about this to anyone, I'll kill that babe in your belly and feed it to the wolves.*

"The truth is," she continued, "I wouldn't have done anything. I was too scared. That man was the craziest man that I've ever met. He said that he would do horrible things to my baby if I told. I couldn't. I didn't realize that he would hurt somebody else. Hayden, I'm so sorry that he found you. You have no idea how lucky you are to have gotten away."

Hayden put her arm around Fineese's shoulders. "This is not your fault. And besides, I'm all right. Now that we know who this man is, do you think that you can help me describe him to Randy?"

Fineese closed her eyes. She was still for a long moment contemplating what might result from her agreement to help. "Yes. It's the least I can do. I'll never be able to feel safe with that man loose. I'll tell Randy everything."

Hayden

Hayden hugged her. Randy was going to be very pleased with her when he got back. She'd accomplished his request and only after a day of being married. Her bubble of enjoyment burst as Kayra interrupted her musings.

"Hayden, we should tell him the truth too–all of it. You already mentioned what happened when we found you. Someone's bound to say something. It's in your best interest to tell him first."

Her logic was sound, but Hayden wanted that secret to always remain between the two of them. If she told, he would have a host of other questions as to who they really were. Hayden's world only consisted of her cousin and herself. She didn't want to let anyone else into her heart even if he was already needling his way through. People came and went too quickly.

"I can't." Hayden stared into the fire.

"Hayden, it has to be done." Kayra added, "If you don't tell him, then I'll have to."

Color ran up Hayden's face at Kayra's challenge. Only in the case of Fineese had Kayra usurped her authority. Questioning, debating, and disagreeing with her ideas were as common as the sunrise, but until recently, Kayra had never threatened to disregard her wishes entirely. It stung as if she'd been slapped in the face.

Kayra wasn't even trying to explain or convince her. She'd stated her piece. As much as she hated to concede, if Hayden were to save her dignity, she would have to be the one to give in. What a strange feeling, to be giving in to Kayra not out of love but out of necessity.

When exactly was it when Kayra had gotten some of the power in their relationship? It didn't sit well, mostly because Hayden felt that she was losing not only her control but her dearest friend.

"I'll tell him." Hayden said, trying to keep the bitterness from her voice. Her eyes focused on the ground between her feet. "But I tell him in my own way."

As if she were trying to lighten the mood, Kayra came to her feet. "You'll have to excuse me. I was asked to stop by Mrs. Turner's wagon tonight. It seems that her small dog, one Mr. Gomez, has not been eating these past couple of days. She imagines it's all the excitement and trail food, but she's just about sick herself with worry. Since I'm now a highly trained nurse, she figured I could examine the little mutt, and assure her that he is healthy."

Hayden tried to remain stoic, but Kayra's predicament was too funny. The whole camp knew Dana. She was a hoot. The middle-aged lady who wore bright colors and gaudy jewelry was always quick to visit and laugh. And laugh she did. Her amusement reverberated through the whole mountain when she got tickled.

Randy had commented that it was a good thing that they weren't making the trip during the winter because her laugh would surely cause an avalanche. Hayden liked her. Most folks on the wagon train were preoccupied with finding food and safely getting their wagons over the next ridge, but Mrs. Turner was always holding up the line so that her small dog could use the bathroom or walk a bit. She was so apologetic and sweet when she held folks up, that no one said anything to her about it. They just sped up the pace and caught the front of the train as quickly as they could.

Her husband was always shaking his head. He'd learned in their many years of marriage that where Gomez was concerned, it was best to just let her have her way. She had after all agreed to move to the other side of the country for him to pursue his dream of opening a mule farm.

He was convinced that mules were more reliable and resilient than horses. He figured that in the west where folks had to work long days that they would be quick to trade in their flashy horses for its dependable counterpart. He had complimented Hayden on Chloe one afternoon. Said how rare it was to find a mule with such height and that if she ever considered selling to let him know.

Hayden thought that the couple went together perfectly, though they could be heard arguing about twice a day.

Hayden stood up and said, "Well no one is allowed to go anywhere alone so we had better go too. Come on, Fineese."

Fineese shook her head. "I don't think so. You go on ahead."

"They aren't going to say anything bad to you." Kayra touched her shoulder. "These are good people. I wouldn't take you unless I knew you'd be welcome."

Fineese frowned but followed along.

"Besides," Hayden said, "If Nurse Kayra has to perform surgery, she'll need assistants." The ladies laughed and headed for the little dog.

The day had felt endless, and by dusk most folks were tucked in for the night when they returned to their own camp. Kayra and Fineese made room in the wagon for Hayden and she obediently placed Randy's gun on the pillow next to her.

In a matter of minutes, Fineese was snoring and Kayra's breathing evened. Hayden lay there unable to sleep. Worry about Randy plagued her mind and the thought of closing her eyes and missing him coming back to the camp kept her wide eyed. Her brain wouldn't quit playing scenarios where he got hurt or killed. Her heart skipped a beat every time she imagined the confrontation the two men were bound to have sooner or later.

She considered all of the possible outcomes. She practiced what she would say and how she would act if Randy were killed, being the grieving widow and all. It wasn't difficult for tears to fill her eyes.

Hayden had never before gotten to play the part of a widow. To lose a loved one and then have to pick up the pieces of a shattered life and carry on, well, that took strength and maturity. Both qualities she admired. The injustice of being left alone, young and eternally in love with a man that was no more, it was such a romantic role that Hayden decided she would use it someday.

She hoped that day wasn't anytime soon.

With a sigh, Hayden forced her eyes shut. In the darkness all she could see was Randy's handsome face with his amused smile and dark eyes staring lovingly down at her. She drifted off as dim firelight filled the wagon with its eerie glow.

Hayden

Hayden awoke to frantic voices. An intense heat radiated through the canvas. Smoke engulfed them. Before she could scream, the flap opened and Randy's face appeared. He scanned the wagon until his eyes met Hayden's. His shoulder's dropped and he exhaled the breath he'd been holding. "Get Fineese up," he ordered. "Get out of the wagon and down to the water."

Kayra came to, and started screaming. Hayden assumed that the memory of the night their family was murdered and their houses burned was what stunned her now. Without time to be understanding nor gentle, Hayden slapped her across the face. It seemed to do the trick. "There's no time. Take my hand." Like a child, Kayra grabbed Hayden's hand and Fineese grabbed hers.

As frightening as it had been to not know what was going on, it may have been better. Hayden's stomach dropped to her toes as she took in the site of her wagon completely swallowed by red flames claiming her sanctuary. It wasn't much, but it was her home and had been for a long time. All she could do was stare, couldn't even muster up the words to comfort her cousin.

The entire camp had come awake. Men formed a line filling buckets that ran from the wagon to the creek. Women tugged at their wraps and held tight to their sleepy eyed children. Hayden jumped into the line alongside the men.

The wagon was swallowed by flame and the heat was like what the preacher hollered about during service on the trail, 'Flee the fires of hell.' Kayra stumbled away.

Hayden took charge, "It's too late to save the wagon. Soak the ground around it. Let's keep the fire from spreading."

She heaved a bucket and dumped its contents onto the ground. The men obeyed, following her example. In a matter of minutes, the fire had consumed the wagon and was burning itself down.

Through the thick smoke Hayden searched for Kayra and Randy. Fineese had rescued her baby blanket and journal. Hayden jogged towards her.

"Where's Kayra?" She called, the crackling still loud in her ears.

Fineese shook her head. "I never saw her."

Fear, like lightning, coursed through Hayden's body. Panic consumed her. She ran from the commotion calling Kayra's name. Hysterically, she darted from wagon to wagon. *I can't lose her. I can't.*

No one had seen Kayra. Hayden, desperate, laid eyes on a horse that looked as terrified as she felt. She hauled herself onto the back of Greely's stallion and raced through the field yelling, "Kayra, Kayra!"

The horse was faster than any she'd ever ridden. Hayden gripped its mane. She was unused to riding bareback and flexed her thighs around the horse's back. Her bare heels dug into its sides making the beast run as frantically as she yelled. The smell of smoke was everywhere. Thankfully, vision improved as she put distance between herself and the camp.

She had no idea where to start looking and even less of a clue what to do if she found her with that man. All she knew was that she had to do something. The revolver that was probably still resting on her pillow would have been a good thing to have grabbed. She cursed her carelessness.

A rider in the distance was heading her way. *Randy*. It was Randy. Her heart filled with hope at the sight. She turned toward him, his face like the first taste of water after an afternoon of work, like the feeling of a full stomach and a cool night with the company of the spring cicadas.

He would know where to find Kayra. His horse was galloping straight for her but Hayden had no idea how to stop the animal beneath her. The rope he'd been tied with drug under him and it was all she could do to not fall off.

As Greely's stallion darted past Randy, there was Kayra, sitting behind him. *Thank God.* She was alive. No doubt she had a story to tell about how she got there. All Hayden wanted to do was turn around and hear every detail. The horse she rode had other ideas. It seemed to gain speed with each lurch forward. The horse showed no sign of slowing and Hayden realized the danger she was in. Applying pressure with her foot, she managed to turn away from the mountain and back toward the field.

She wondered at the wisdom of her actions. The hill would slow the animal down and tire him, but the thought of putting distance between herself and Randy was terrifying. What if Greely were up there?

A plan developed. She would simply allow the animal to run itself out. Then, when it slowed she'd hop off. After several minutes, the horse tripped on its rope, stumbling. Hayden felt herself slipping. The horse righted himself and was off again with the same speed as before.

Hayden's white knuckled fingers gripped the black main. If she fell at this speed, she would be hurt, but her legs trembled and her balance had her dangerously teetering. The gown she wore was slick providing no traction. All control was lost. She braced herself for the fall that was inevitable.

"Hold on." Randy's voice ordered. She wanted to obey but she felt herself sliding. Desperate, she reached for a new handhold of hair and grasped it as the tall grass tickled her leg. *That can't be good.* Barely on the horse's back, she strained with all her might.

Then hoofbeats were racing beside her. She doubted that Randy's horse could reach the stallion she clung to, determined to last another few seconds. She willed her numb fingers to keep a hold of the animal's mane. This horse was as crazy as Greely. Then a strong arm was around her waist, jerking her free. The stallion reared onto his hind legs as she ripped a handful of mane from its neck. She didn't take the time to consider the irony of the situation. Randy slowed his horse and pulled Hayden against him. Her heart beat wildly matching the drumming in his chest. The clump of hair she held fell from her fingers.

The night surrounded the couple as they held to one another. The moon was covered in a haze. Its dim light cascading onto the field. The camp wasn't that far off but it felt like they were the only two people alive.

Haydens arms encircled his chest. She clung to him, unable to believe that he had been able to rescue her. "Kayra...where is she?" Hayden breathed out, "I saw her, you had her. Didn't you?"

Randy calmed her, running his hands up and down her back. "She's fine, she's perfectly safe. I wasn't the only man out looking. I left her with Foster right after we saw you."

Hayden's shoulders heaved her relief. Her throat burned and she felt the familiar ache in her eyes. Randy held her against him. "Go ahead, cry. Let all of that out."

There was no way that she was going to cry, not in front of him. She brought her face to rest in the crook of his neck, still catching her breath. She tasted the salt from his skin on her lips.

The horse carrying the two whinnied. Randy grabbed the reins with one hand, careful not to release Hayden. Slowly, he steered the animal toward camp. After several minutes, Hayden took a deep breath and raised her head.

Her voice whispered. "I'm sorry. It's been a very long day."

Randy chuckled. "I'm just glad you're alright...again," He said pointedly.

Hayden allowed a smile to curve her mouth. "It would take a lot more than that psychotic horse to do me in. Thank you, for saving Kayra though. I couldn't find her."

"Don't I get a thanks for saving you?"

Hayden nibbled her lower lip, biting back a smile. "I would have been just fine."

Randy laughed. "Hayden, you were dangling like a man in a noose."

Hayden's eyes argued the situation that he'd found her in. "I had a plan."

"I bet you did."

Randy and Hayden locked eyes. He sighed, "It looks mighty right for you to be sitting here, on my horse, in my arms. It's not the first time today that I've wished you really were my wife."

Her lips parted in invitation. Randy dipped his mouth to hers and halted the horse while they held each other. There was a lot said in that kiss.

It felt good to be alive. The adrenaline of the frantic ride was simmering down, replaced by a warm peace. That relief flooded into action. The kiss they shared turned to more. That more, continued like an avalanche covering all sense of reason as they reassured each other that they were alive. Finally, Randy held her away. "We can't do this. You want to now, but you'll hate me later."

Color ran up Hayden's face. She distanced herself and straightened her night dress.

"Hayden, don't do that. We're both high on adrenaline and lost our minds."

"We aren't talking about it." Hayden made herself as small and distant as one could riding double. "Let's go."

"Fine." Randy fixed his hat and clicked at his horse. "Hayden, I'm sorry. I didn't…"

"It's done." She changed the topic. "What happened with Kayra?"

Randy sighed. "Best I can figure, the fire on your wagon was set as a distraction. Kayra wandered out of the crowd and he swooped down on her. He took a horse as soon as the men left to get water."

"How did you find her?"

"I heard her scream, jumped on my horse and headed toward the sound. I couldn't shoot because of the smoke, afraid I'd hit her. I chased him into the mountain. When Greely realized he couldn't make a clean break carrying her, he threw her from the horse."

Hayden wiped the hair from her face. "She must be terrified."

"I had to let him go because I needed to make sure she was okay. He must've known I'd choose her over him. She's bruised from the fall, but she's fine. You two seem to have more luck than a herd of cats."

"Hurry, she needs me."

"The camp's just up ahead. Almost there."

Randy announced their presence while they were still a ways off. "Randy here, coming in." He rode past the men guarding the horses. He guided Hayden's foot to the stirrups and eased her down. Then slid beside her. Her legs trembled.

He steadied her. "You got your feet?"

She nodded. "I'm going to Kayra."

"Figures." He winked. "Now a good wife would make her man a cup of coffee first."

Despite all the emotion of the night, it made her smile. She shoved him as she walked past. He laughed out loud and if any of the men saw the exchange they pretended not to notice.

Hayden

Hayden peeked into Fineese's wagon and spied Kayra in the darkness, her eyes red and swollen. Puffy bags outlined them, making her look positively haggard. Kayra practically jumped over Fineese's sleeping form in an effort to get to her cousin.

Hayden held the flap open as Kayra climbed down and hurled herself into outstretched arms, sobbing. Her back heaved as she leaned on Hayden for support. Hayden stroked her head, relishing the simple truth that the sun would rise and they would both live to see another day. Her eyes were heavy, but Kayra needed her so she whispered reassurance. "It's alright cousin. Shh, we're both fine."

Her gentle touch and calming voice brought a tapering to Kayra's tears. Before long, she was quiet.

Slowly she pulled away from Hayden holding tightly to her hands. "You weren't hurt?"

Hayden shook her head. "No. Randy saved me without so much as a scratch."

"It took you so long coming back that I was sure something terrible had happened." Hayden would never admit what had kept them from hurrying. "I'm sorry I scared you, but the horse ran quite a ways off. And there was a lot of smoke in the field."

"I'm just relieved you're alright." Kayra rubbed her arms.

"Me too." Hayden squeezed her hand. "We should go inside and get some sleep."

"Yes." Kayra sighed, leading the way.

Randy

Randy observed the girls. It was strange, the motherly way that Hayden behaved toward Kayra. He watched as she smoothed her cousin's hair and helped her inside. Then he saw Hayden climbing in after and smiled.

One of the men gathered around the coffee urn brought his attention back to the conversation at hand. "Randy, what do you think?"

Randy took a swig of his drink. "The fire was deliberate. I doubt he planned to take Kayra. That was sloppy, but he knew who she was and took advantage of the situation when it presented itself. Thank God we heard her."

His companions listened with avid interest. They each held a cup of thick coffee in their hands. The drink was strong and hot. Randy was grateful to the wagon master for having the pot waiting when he returned. The liquid filled the void in his gut. His stomach growled, reminding him that it had nearly been a full day since his last meal. Until just then, he hadn't thought about anything except Hayden and Greely.

"Randy," One of the farmers laughed, "You should have seen the way that wife of yours charged off after you and that nurse. She looked like a regular Indian brave hopping on that stallion and tearing up the ground as they beat it out of here. We all called to her to stop, but she wouldn't listen. She just took off faster than any of us could, and without a saddle, reins, or nothin'."

The men chuckled as they recalled the scene. Randy enjoyed the image he conjured in his mind.

"You sure got yourself a live one, didn't you? My Beth sure could use some of the spirit in that gal of yours."

Another cut in. "Don't mind us sayin' so but she sure is a sight too. When did you get hitched anyhow?"

Randy's grin widened. "You're right about her. She is going to be a handful. We married the night before we left Denver City."

"Not much of a honeymoon, huh?" The farmer shook his head and gulped down the last of his drink.

Randy had no time to respond when he heard Hayden's squeal from inside the wagon. He dropped his cup, sprinting. By the time he got there all three of the women were climbing from the wagon as if a rattler were coiled inside.

His gun was drawn. "What happened?"

Hayden's eyes were huge but she managed to squelch down her fear. Randy could barely contain his.

"Sorry for frightening everyone." She explained pointing in the wagon. "My gun was tossed off the rock, earlier with Greely. When I laid down just now, it was there by my pillow and yours was gone."

Randy threw open the canvas and saw her rifle propped up against the fabric wall. It could have been slipped in from the side without disturbing anyone, but how had no one seen Greely do it? When would he have had the chance between all the watchful eyes?

A sloppy bow was tied around the bent barrel. It took his eyes a second before he realized that the bow was made from a long blonde lock of Hayden's hair. Slowly, he turned from the wagon. His dark eyes met hers and they stared for a long moment before he pulled her to his side.

"Now he has a gun and a horse, maybe two. This is a warning to all of us, his way of gloating. We had better say our prayers. This man is a lunatic."

The men nodded agreement and went back to their posts. Randy took the gun from the wagon, emptied the bullets and threw it in the fire blazing beside him.

"You two need to sleep." He encouraged Kayra and Finesse. Hayden turned to follow. "Not you," He ordered.

Hayden halted, but when she turned to face him her expression was anything but obedient. "Don't order me."

He took a deep breath, not wanting to fight. "Hayden, honey, please sit down. We have to talk."

"I'm not discussing it. All I want to do is sleep."

He patted the stump beside him. "About Greely." With hunched shoulders she sat down. She did need to sleep. She looked...weary?

He'd just come out with what was on his mind. "Tomorrow we need to leave. We need to get to Grand Junction as quick as we can."

"Of course," She said, "I assumed that was the plan."

His head came up in surprise. *She's not gonna fight me on this?* Her easy consent was not at all what he expected.

"Good. You'll need a dress from Kayra or Fineese, but not much else. We'll need a couple blankets and a canteen. Bare minimum. You'll have to ride one of your mules, whichever one's fastest. Don't worry, we'll get you new clothes when we get to town–"

Hayden held out her hand. "Wait. You think I'm going to hop on a horse and go alone with you to Grand Junction, just because of what happened earlier? We aren't really married."

Of course it wasn't going to be easy. He ran his fingers through his black hair. "Hayden, this has nothing to do with that and we are going to have to talk about it, but you have to listen to me." He sighed, calming his voice. "I won't leave you alone again. Not for a minute. So get used to it. I'm a deputy and it's my job to get the word spread about Greely. Grand Junction is the only place he can go. He's bound to at least stop in for supplies. I reckon he'll beat us, but we have to go."

Hayden stood and put her hands on her hips. The motion caused her chest to jut forward. Randy concentrated on her face.

"I'm going to California." She dared him to disagree with a hard stare.

"I never said you weren't. The wagon train will stop in Grand Junction. We'll just be there before them. When they catch up, hopefully, I'll have caught Greely and you can continue with the group."

"What about you?" The question hung in the air like a warning sign. Her eyes begged for the right answer.

Randy dipped his head choosing his words carefully. "I don't know. It depends on the situation with Greely. I'm a lawman."

Randy took her silence as understanding. Good, the confrontation was over. He stood up and took hold of her arm. She flexed under his fingers. He dipped his face and ran his lips across her burning cheek. Her eyes darted to the sky as if she bore his kiss. He sensed the resistance and assumed that it was due to the openness of their location.

"You're my wife, as far as these folks are concerned this is perfectly acceptable. Why don't you sleep out here with me, by the fire?" He coaxed, scratching her back. He wanted to hold and comfort her, where he knew she was safe.

She jolted away hissing. "Is that all you want me for?" Her hushed condemnation stunned him. "I'm not your wife and you had best remember that." She stepped toward the wagon.

Randy intercepted her. "I just wanted to..."

"Oh, I know exactly what you want. I can't believe that I let you seduce me out there." She practically spit venom at him.

"What?" He demanded, his mouth tight. His whispered voice carried with it all the anger he felt. "You were the one who seduced me. You started all of that, and I even tried to hold you off."

She guffawed. "You're a liar."

"Of course you couldn't have possibly done anything wrong. Well, at least I learned that early on in our marriage." He snorted in frustration, his sarcasm mocking her.

Her smile filled with arrogance and pride. Just the look on her smug face was enough to make him scream. He tried to hold his temper in check.

Hayden replied, "Yes, thank goodness. It will surely save us from years of you trying to figure it out."

Her eyes lit through him. He paused before responding. When he did, his voice was controlled. "Hayden, I need you to stay with me tonight so that you're–"

"Your needs are not my concern," she cut in. "Go find yourself a prostitute for all I care."

"What?" Randy's eyes went wide.

"Oh, never mind." Hayden stomped. "I'm sleeping with the only one here."

Ridiculous. There were no other words. He felt a rolling chuckle in his chest. Her face pinked, and then she was smiling sheepishly.

He took her hand.

"Listen, I will not touch you tonight, not like that. We both need a few hours of sleep and I won't get any unless I can feel that you are beside me, safe. It'll be daylight soon. So, will you please sleep beside me, in your own blanket, outside, next to the fire?" He chose his words so that she would not be able to twist them.

"Of course." She raised her face and kissed him chastely on the cheek before scrambling into Fineese's wagon.

When she climbed out, he had folded his blankets and was tucked inside. He patted the ground next to him so that she lay on the unopened side of his covers. Hayden obeyed his gesture and folded her quilt in the same fashion so that the folded edge lay alongside him. She nestled easily into the crook of his shoulder.

"Yep, I sure got my hands full with this one."
"Did you say something?" Hayden murmured.
He patted her arm and gave into exhaustion.

Chapter Twelve

Hayden

The first rays of sunlight broke through the clouds cascading their glory over the grassy field. The sky was painted with pumpkin and rose colored wisps on a clear blue canvas. The air was crisp, the suffocating smoke became a memory. Hayden sank lower in her quilt. "It's too soon," She whimpered.

Randy knelt beside her, peeling the blanket from her face. "Good morning, beautiful." He tussled her hair.

Hayden's chapped lips cracked into a sleepy smile. She knew that there was no way that he actually found her beautiful right now. She ran a hand through her tangled strands of flaxen hair.

Yawning, she sat up. He handed her a steaming cup of black coffee. She made a face but took the mug letting the steam moisten her parched skin.

Feeling more awake, she looked up to find Randy smiling down at her. He was clean. She could smell his soap. His face was smooth, his raven hair slick against his head. You could practically see the sun rise in his boots. He looked good, which made Hayden very aware of the wretch she was.

"You've been up a long time." She nodded to the tidy bedroll already stowed on his mount.

"Well, with you snoring so loud," He teased.

She shot him an easy smile and cocked her head. The hard lines of his jaw softened as he grinned.

"As soon as you can, we need to get going."

"I know." Hayden gulped down the last of the coffee in her hands. She handed the cup back to him and stood stretching her arms to the side.

"You know I can see through your gown when you do that."

Hayden closed her stance. He strode over to her and pulled her into his arms. She wanted to embrace him but her pride still hurt. He wasn't necessarily planning to stay with her after they reached Grand Junction. She wanted him to. The realization brought her head up. She really wanted him to stay with her.

"Give me thirty minutes and I'm all yours." With that, she kissed his chin and darted away.

Randy

What would today bring? Grand Junction wasn't too far away. With any luck, he'd be able to both catch Greely and turn him over to their sheriff there.

He didn't want to leave Hayden in a couple of weeks, but he'd do what he was sworn to do. He'd been sworn in as Deputy Sheriff, and that meant he had to see this through. Would she go on without him if his work wasn't done? He'd follow if she did but only if she wanted him. He had no idea what she wanted.

He'd have to be respectful and keep their physical contact to a minimum if he was going to win her over. And he needed to do that.

He was determined to make her love him but the harder part would be getting her to trust him. This trip to Grand Junction was a golden opportunity to build these things. Surely, by the time they got there, he'd know where he stood.

No matter how hard she pushed, he would not fight with her and he would not take her to his bed. He would make her his wife first, hopefully when they arrived in Grand Junction. Until then he would be a gentleman and pray that she cooperated.

Hayden

The three women carried fresh clothes and headed toward the creek. They found a brushy area and took turns looking out so that the others could bathe.

Fineese stood guard first. Hayden was grateful that she got the chance to be alone with Kayra. The water was frigid after the cold night. Hayden held her breath before dipping below the surface. Her gown clung to her like a second skin. Kayra laughed and did the same. Hayden began scrubbing awkwardly underneath the nightdress.

"I'm leaving with Randy today."

Kayra smiled. "I wondered if he would take you."

"Is that okay?"

"Of course it is, but I want you to tell him. He should know."

Hayden nodded, "I will."

Kayra dipped her long brown hair in the water, lathered it up, then knelt again to rinse the soap.

Her teeth chattered. "It's too cold. You finish up. I'll trade with Fineese." She held her arms together and ran from the creek, causing silver beads of water to splash Hayden.

A few seconds later Fineese waddled in. Even out here, she was naturally flashy. Some women were just lucky, she guessed. Next to her, Hayden felt like a plain, ordinary no-one. Fineese squealed when her belly touched the water before plunging right in. Hayden felt for the edge of the bandage at the base of her head.

"Let me help you." Fineese took the cloth from Hayden's fingers. She rinsed the linen. "Turn around. Let me wash your hair."

"You don't have to," Hayden began, but Fineese hushed her.

"I can see your wound a lot better than you can." Gently, she lathered the soap.

Fineese's hands paused before she spoke. "I hope that I'm not interfering in your personal business, but I heard you talking last night."

Hayden's heart caught in her chest. "I'm sorry Fineese. I wasn't thinking. I was just so angry and confused."

"Ssh," Fineese interrupted, "No apology is necessary. I thought what you said was rather amusing. And I think Kayra was asleep. I want you to know that Randy never came to see me. His brother did, but not him. Becky neither. She had a terrible crush on him, but he never approached her."

Hayden sighed with relief.

Fineese chuckled. "He's a good man. Better than any I've ever met. And he's crazy about you. I can tell."

Hayden wanted to believe what she was hearing and if she could tell anyone it was Fineese. "No, he only wants me because he thinks I'll..." Her eyes burned and the admission stuck in her throat. At least Fineese wouldn't judge.

Fineese turned Hayden's shoulder so that they faced each other. "You're wrong. I, of all people, know when a man is only interested in sex." Her bluntness made Hayden blush. "He loves you. I would have given my right arm to have the man that I loved look at me the way he looks at you."

"Was it the baby's father?"

Fineese nodded.

Hayden shook her head. "I feel like I've sent mixed signals to him and I want to... Oh, I don't even know what I want."

"You said that there was a lot of smoke last night, but it had blown the opposite direction. You were gone a long time."

Hayden nodded and felt her cheeks burn.

"You did something you regret and wonder if that changes things?" Fineese continued gently massaging Hayden's scalp.

Hayden turned to look into her wise eyes and nodded. "We didn't...you know. I never felt that way or got that lost in someone like I did last night. Now, I feel like I crossed a line that I never even knew I'd drawn. So, I don't know. Does it change everything? I've never thought about marriage before. I want to be courted and pursued with sweet kisses and poetry."

Fineese stifled a giggle. "He loves you. Isn't that enough?"

"Who's to say that he even wants to marry me? I saw him in Denver City. Every girl at that party was after him, and when we get to Grand Junction he said he's leaving."

"That's true enough about the women chasing after him, but he was only interested in you. I won't pretend to know his mind about what happens next, but I know the look on his face means that you're in his heart. He is completely smitten with the challenge you provide. He's not about to give that up."

"But what happens when the challenge is over? When–*if* he wins?"

"You will always keep each other on your toes. Maybe you'll learn to trust, give yourself to another person. Anyhow, I've probably said too much and butted in enough."

Hayden turned and rinsed her hair. "Thank you, Fineese." She took the woman's hand in her own. "I wanted to talk to someone but Kayra wouldn't understand."

Fineese nodded. "Don't worry, your secret is safe with me."

Instinctively, Hayden hugged her. Then she walked from the water and over to Kayra.

While Hayden pulled a clean dress over her sopping body, Kayra made a declaration. "Hayden, I want us to become Christians."

Hayden moved her straggly hair from her eyes so that she could better see her cousin. "We are, aren't we?"

Kayra grinned. "No Hayden, not really."

"Are we Catholic?"

Kayra stood and helped Hayden fasten her dress. "I've been reading the Bible with Fineese and, after talking to a few people, I think we need to be baptized."

Hayden shrugged, adjusting the front of her dress. "Okay. But can we talk about it later? Randy's in a hurry."

Kayra sighed. "Hayden, I'm serious about this. It's too easy to die out here. You understand that."

Hayden frowned. Kayra was as serious as she remembered seeing her. "I'm not at all against it, Cousin. I'll do whatever you want where God is concerned. I told you that when we left the Mayer's."

"It can't be because I want it for you. You need to understand and decide for yourself. At least think about it and when we catch up, will you study the Bible with me?"

Hayden hugged her cousin tight. "Of course I'lll study with you, and I do pray. Sometimes."

Kayra snorted. "That's good. I'll be praying for you."

"I'm sorry, but I really need to get moving." Hayden kissed Kayra on the cheek before leaving.

Fineese had given her more questions than answers but she accepted that Randy was not a crush that was bound to dissipate in a few weeks. He had worked his way into her heart. She calculated that they would have about two weeks alone. That is, if he didn't have to leave town to hunt Greely.

There was a lot of work to be done if she were to sort out her feelings and learn his. She hoped Fineese was right.

Hayden

The pace Randy set had Hayden cursing by noon. They trudged up and down switch backs, and he was all but oblivious to his riding partner.

It irritated Hayden to be ignored. She'd imagined their ride into Grand Junction being as light hearted and comfortable as it had been the first few days with the wagon train but no, he was totally engrossed in the ground of all things. She figured he was looking for tracks, but the least he could do would be to explain why it was more interesting than she was.

"You know," Hayden hollered, "You might want to look back once in a while to see if I'm still here." She waited for a reaction.

Randy called over his shoulder. "I can hear your mule."

Frowning, Hayden kicked Otis, bringing her animal alongside his. Randy slid to the side allowing her space.

Huffing, Hayden slowed her animal and fell back in line behind him. He clicked his horse forward. *So, he thinks he can ignore me? He'll notice me soon enough.*

She turned her mule and started in the opposite direction. That got his attention.

"Hayden, what do you think you're doing?"

"Well, I'll tell you what I'm not doing." She turned her head just enough to be heard. "I'm not swallowing your dust and looking at your horse's butt all the way to Grand Junction."

Head high and shoulders back, she continued her path down the mountain. It was her turn to ignore him.

"Hayden, stop."

His order made her more determined. She kicked Otis to speed up. "What in the world?" Hayden was lassoed. Her arm cinched to her sides, she squeezed her legs together in an effort to stay atop Otis. "This isn't funny." She yelled, throwing her leg over the saddle and sliding from her mule. She fell to the ground landing on her bottom with a string of epithets that she'd never said before. The lovely, mint dress she'd borrowed from Fineese came to her knees as she scrambled to stand. The rope still pinned both arms.

He smiled down at her.

And I was going to be so agreeable, and win him over. I'd rather scratch his eyes out.

He clucked to Otis who followed obediently. Randy turned his animal and the group paraded back in the direction of Grand Junction. Hayden resisted walking until the ropes tightened uncomfortably. She cursed again and trotted along behind.

"I hate you. Do you hear me?"

After a couple minutes, he slowed. When she moved to free her arms he jerked the rope taut again. Then he pulled out his canteen and took a long drink. The water spilled from the lip of the bottle down his chin.

Hayden was silent. Randy held it out to her, but she refused with tight lips.

"If you can behave, I'll let you get back on Otis and we can keep going. If not, I am quite willing to drag you all the way to Grand Junction."

Angry, Hayden jerked the rope from her arms and climbed onto the mule. She settled herself into the saddle, her chin out.

Randy

Guilt strangled him. Why was he acting like this? Nothing had changed. From the beginning, he knew that she was hiding something, some connection to the murders. At the coffee table this morning, while Hayden was finishing getting ready to leave, he'd been told what she'd said after the attack. He wondered why it bothered him now. It did though.

He'd been trying for weeks to get her to trust him and he'd felt like an idiot when asked about her comments and had no good response. He couldn't very well explain what she'd meant because it was the first he'd heard it. He'd looked a fool. Now seeing the expression on her face, he felt like a jerk too.

"I'm sorry, Hayden. I didn't mean to hurt you."

She sniffed and tilted her head regally. "Why did you do that? One minute you're sweet as honey on a biscuit and the next I'm no better to you than a mule."

She was right. He was downright awful. "I'm sorry. Listen, there's a small lake up here. I reckon it's about time to give these animals a rest and have a bite to eat." He led her from the path.

Randy slowed, allowing her to catch up. Still, they didn't speak.

A wagon was up ahead by the lake. He'd found the water source two days earlier when he'd been scouting. As they approached, he saw another one just over the hill.

"Stay back." He warned.

His horse hopped into action, darting for the wagons. In his hand, Randy held a revolver, ready for whatever menace lurked.

Just as he feared, these wagons belonged to the smart mouthed boy and his friend who had gone on ahead. There were no signs of life. A campfire had burned itself out and a charred rabbit lay in the ashes.

With his gun he lifted the tarp and held his breath. The boy's neck had been slit, blood soaked his shirt. His eyes darted from the boy to his bride. She was naked. Her wrists held the same burns that Fineese's had. Randy cringed at the thought of what the poor girl had experienced in the last few moments of her life.

He closed the tarp.

Tugging at the reins, he went to investigate the other wagon. Solemnly, he pulled aside the canvas and took in the two bodies that lay on top of each other. A bullet had gone into the back of the woman's head. Her hair was a sticky mass of matted brown strands. The man had been shot through the chest.

Closing the curtain, he climbed down. Where were their horses? If Greely had taken them, then he and Hayden had little hope of getting to Grand Junction anywhere near the time he would arrive.

He spotted Hayden. She hadn't stayed put, of course. She was staring wide-eyed into the bed of the first wagon. A hand covering her mouth.

He ran to her, scolding. "Why won't you listen to anything I tell you?" He pulled her into his arms. "I didn't want you to see that."

She nodded and brought herself away from him. "What do we do?" It was a question that haunted her, a question that she'd had to answer when Kayra had discovered Uncle Johnny's body.

"We can't just leave. I'll wrap them in a blanket and we'll have to bury the bodies. This is gonna be a big delay. I suspect Greely intended that. You okay?"

Hayden nodded.

Randy found a small shovel along with other tools tied to the side of the second wagon. He held it out to Hayden. "If you think you're up to it, I could use the help. That mound looks like a good spot."

Taking it, Hayden walked from the lake to a hilly area and began shoveling. Her arms quivered from the effort. By the time Randy brought the horse around with the carefully wrapped bodies, she had half dug a shallow grave.

Hayden placed the shovel in Randy's outstretched hand. She shot him a grateful look for the reinforcement. Otis nibbled the grass. She stroked the old mule's neck and took her canteen from the saddlebag. Then she led him to the lake and refilled the bottle. When they returned, she offered Randy a drink.

They worked together taking turns until they had a wide grave dug about six foot deep and six foot long. It was dark when they finished burying the dead. Randy tore a piece of wood from the wagon and scribbled a note. He didn't remember all of the names, but he wanted the wagon train to know who was buried there, when they came through.

"We aren't staying here tonight." Gently, he rubbed Hayden's back. She turned into his arms.

They hopped on their horses and rode wearily through the evening. The moon was full, giving them plenty of light. After at least an hour of traveling, Randy reined in his horse near a clump of trees. He helped Hayden from her saddle and spread his blanket on the ground.

She sat silently and let him take off her shoes. She laid back and he covered her with a quilt. It wasn't long before her breathing changed. He slept on top of the blanket, holding her close, smelling the lavender scent of her hair and feeling each breath that she took against his chest.

"I love you." He whispered the words into her hair as she rested, then closed his eyes.

At the first bit of light Randy awoke to find Hayden sprawled out beside him, her knee on top of his, her head resting across his chest. What a picture she made.

He eased her leg off and gently lifted her head so that he could slip from beneath her. Carefully, he set her head down on the blanket. By the time Hayden awoke, Randy had a small rabbit cooked and was preparing the horses for the long day ahead.

Hayden

Hayden had felt Randy ease out from under her, but couldn't make herself get up. Now something smelled good and her stomach insisted. When she forced her eyes open, Randy was there at her side, reclining by the fire.

"Mornin', sunshine." She crawled to him, snuggling against his strength. It was so easy to wake up like this, almost as natural as mornings with Kayra.

They ate and were headed down the Rockies before the sun was fully in the sky.

The day's ride was longer and more difficult than it had been the day before, but much more pleasant. Randy explained to Hayden what the different tracks meant. By noon, she was able to spot the differences between a hoof print and a deer track, between the markings of a finch and a sparrow.

She knew exactly which tracks belonged to Greely as opposed to the three horses he led. The knowledge that Randy was pleased with her had her beaming as she pointed out different things about this print or that track. Apparently, she had an eye for detail.

When the sun set, they made their camp by the creek that flowed through the mountain range. Hayden was tired but not exhausted. She made the fire while Randy stood nearby hunting small game.

Hayden decided to take advantage of the privacy while he was occupied and walked to the creek. She slipped from her dress and under garments, down to the flesh. The water was deep and slow moving. She sunk into its caressing waves and kicked as she let the flowing ripples cool her muscles. She dipped below the surface, soaking her head. It was wonderful. She floated about the creek, carefree as a fish. The sky was gorgeous and clear. Hayden stared up at the moon. It was so big.

She wondered about Kayra and how she and Fineese were managing. Her mind wandered to the conversation she'd had with Fineese. It was discouraging that she'd made so little headway where Randy was concerned. He was irritable one minute and adoring the next. It was so confusing. She needed a strategy to find out what she meant to him. Once she was sure about his feelings, she would be safe to explore her own. What was it that made him different? She decided that she would somehow get him talking. And it would happen tonight.

Her eyes sprung open at the sound of a rifle. She came to her feet scanning the darkness. There was no one there, but that sound was unmistakable. She was modest beneath the water and dared not step from her safe haven. She hadn't heard so much as a twig snap.

"You're careless." Randy's gruff voice came from the trees behind the creek. She breathed in relief.

"Where are you?"

"You shouldn't be out here like this without a gun."

Hayden frowned as she looked through the trees. "Don't worry, I have a gun. Just there by the rock."

Randy stepped from the shadows. "You need to get out of there."

"What if you came in instead."

Randy jerked his hat off his head and wiped at the brim before shoving it back on his brow. "I'm not playing Hayden. Get out!"

Hayden considered disobeying. There he goes again, all angry and irritated. "Fine. I was about to get out anyway."

"I'll be back at camp. Hurry up!"

What had she done so wrong? She bathed nearly every chance there was water to do so. Often, he kept a look out so the girls had privacy.

Finally, she sauntered into camp as if nothing had happened. Ignoring Randy's sour face, she started preparing for the night. Randy had killed another rabbit.

He handed her the roasting stick and rested back against his saddle.

"Why are you so angry?" Hayden asked.

He frowned. "I'm not angry with you. I'm frustrated with you. I'm more angry with myself."

"It feels the same on my end." She pointed out.

"You regret what happened the other night, when Kayra was taken."

That was days ago. "Do we have to talk about this?" Her face burned at the mere mention of the night.

"We do."

Hayden stiffened. If she was going to have to talk about it, whether she wanted to or not, she decided to be honest and get it over with. "I do regret it. I don't know why, but I wish it hadn't happened." She bowed her head in shame.

"Then why did you ask me to join you in the water tonight?"

Her face burned even more. "I don't know... I guess I just want you to want to be with me."

Randy sighed. "I do, that's the problem. You can't act like you want more than you actually do. It's confusing." He sat forward resting his arms on his knees. "I'm trying here, but I'm not a saint, Hayden. I won't let anything like the other night happen again, at least not until I'm sure it's what you really want and we can have each other the right way."

Even Hayden's toes were blushing. This was quite possibly the most embarrassing talk she'd ever had. She wouldn't consider what he meant by "'at least until." She just wanted the conversation over. Trying to end this torture, she asked, "Are we okay then?"

He ran a hand through his hair, "Yes, we're fine. We can be done with that."

"Good because this fat rabbit's hind end is about to be burnt."

Randy sat up. "He is a fat sucker isn't he? You look like an angel, you know."

"And you look like the kind of man that my uncle always warned me about."

"Then he did his job," Randy laughed.

Randy

After not getting a noonday meal, they ate so much that Randy was uncomfortable at the end of supper. Hayden remained quiet. *What could be going through that mind of hers?* He'd finished eating and was laying out their blankets. She stared at the flames of their campfire.

Suddenly, she blurted out, "There's something I have to tell you."

Her eyes were wide and scared and Randy hoped with everything in him that she was finally going to open up. He finished buckling the satchel he'd been rifling through before coming to join her by the fire. "Shoot."

She took a couple deep breaths. "You need to know the truth about me and Kayra. It's a lot and I've never told anyone before." Her shaking voice matched the tremor in her hands.

Randy took her hand into his. He looked her dead in the eyes, hoping that she could see how much this meant to him. "No matter what you tell me, nothing about us is going to change, at least not for the worse."

"Don't say that until you hear what I have to say."

"I'm listening."

As the story of her life leading up to where she was today unfolded before him, he had to control his emotions in order to let her finish. Her voice wavered, but a tear never fell from her eyes.

He cried.

He couldn't help it.

He knew that she was jaded, and distrustful. Now he knew why. He wondered how she hadn't broken into a thousand pieces.

When she shared about the night when Indians had raped, scalped, and killed her mother while she hid behind a trunk, he also felt hate for the tribe that did that. She had only been brave enough to run from the smoke-filled house when she could no longer see her mom's dead eyes staring at her. No wonder she hated Indians. And he'd been all ego trying to correct her for what she thought.

Randy thought of that night when he had found Hayden drenched in sweat reliving some horrible nightmare. "Is that what your dreams are about when you wake up screaming?"

Hayden nodded. "Kayra has them too."

With everything inside him, he wanted to take those images from her sleep and wrap her in peace.

When she told him about her uncle and how he had used them to run scams pretending to be dozens of different things in order to con people out of their money, his gut caught as he considered some of the ways he may have made money off of the girls. He hated to interrupt when she was really sharing, but he had to know. He had to know everything. "Hayden, sweetheart did he ever...I mean did he let any men..."

Hayden raised a hand to her chest. "No. He never touched Kayra or me and he kept us away from men as best he could. He wasn't a dad, but he did right by us there."

After she'd assured him that he had never laid a hand on either of them or allowed anyone else to, Randy was able to relax a little.

And when she confessed to burning Uncle Johnny's body, so much finally made sense. Although she was ashamed and scared to let the law know what they'd done, he found himself bursting with pride over how she had handled an impossible situation. No other woman he knew would have had the strength of body or mind to do what she had done. She was brave and strong, a survivor.

As she explained how they ended up in Willow creek with a cheeky grin, he had to laugh out loud. He pictured Hayden in a drab black dress, her blonde hair and perfect face peeking from behind a head covering. It was too much, even for her.

"You actually posed as nuns?"

Hayden's voice was strong now. A little light had finally made its way back into her eyes. "Yes, and I was *very* convincing."

"I have no doubt that you were. Wait, there was a man in Denver, just before we left. He was looking for two nuns leaving with the wagon train. He came to the sheriffs station to ask if we had seen them. Said that he had to stop them. I had no idea what he was talking about then, but he was looking for you wasn't he?"

Hayden jolted upright. "He came. He actually came and tried to keep us from going? That's so romantic." Her faraway dreamy expression was like a punch to the gut. "I wish we could tell Kayra."

"Why would she care?" Randy snapped. There was no mistaking how the mere mention of that man had changed everything about Hayden's demeanor. She was suddenly all starry eyed. As she brightened he could feel his own mood change from compassion and admiration to anger. "Is that farmer why you play all these games? Is it because of him?"

Hayden frowned before a slow smile spread teasingly across her face. "Do you believe in star crossed lovers? I do."

Randy's jaw was tight. Jealousy raged in his stomach. He needed to get away from her and clear his head before he said anything he couldn't take back.

When he went to stand up, Hayden grabbed his arm and made him look at her. "Oh sit down and stop being like that. You asked why Kayra would care." Hayden's brows arched as her hand slid to hold his. "She'd care because that farm boy, William, is in love with her. And if he came into Denver to stop her from leaving, it is the most romantic thing that he could have done. She would be over the moon."

Ego and relief plummeted in his heart. For once, it was Randy who felt his face burn.

"You were jealous." Hayden tilted her head like a coquettish vixen. Her eyes danced as if she suddenly recognized the power that she held over him.

Randy smirked. "Well I... I– Of course I was jealous!"

Hayden giggled and rested against him again. "May I continue?"

He scooted closer to her, leaning against his saddle. She easily slid into his arms, settling into the curve of his body. He cleared his throat. "Please continue, Sister Hayden."

He felt her giggle. Thank goodness she was no longer in that dark place she had been mere minutes before. "It's Sister Hannah, actually. Anyway, when we left William's home," she adjusted her hair so it wasn't pinned between them, "we headed for Denver City. I came up with a story that would adequately give reasonable covers for why two respectable ladies might be traveling alone to California. I was going to be a spinster teacher escorting my sister to her beloved spouse who'd struck gold."

Randy chuckled. "That explains the spectacles my brother was talking about."

"Yes it does." Hayden took a deep breath and let it out. "We came across the second body while I was hunting. We were so hungry. I killed a fox, as you know, and when I went to collect his body, I found that poor man. At the time I figured that it had to have been Indians but now I know that Greely must have sold his soul and become one of them."

"Hayden not all...."

She cut him off. "Please. Let's not argue."

"You're right. You have good reason to feel the way you do. I'm sorry."

"After that, we came to Denver as fast as we could and told the sheriff what we found. You know the rest."

Randy hugged her against him. "Hayden."

She turned in his arms. He lifted her chin. Her vulnerable eyes as she looked into his were so enticing. He always wanted her in his arms, but now he needed her. Needed her to know he was safe and would protect her from all of the bad things in the world. There was so much to say, but when she closed her eyes and leaned toward him, he captured her mouth in a kiss.

His heart exploded with a depth of feelings. She had bared her world to him. every traumatic, terrifying and embarrassing thing that she'd been carrying for so long. She had been real and the real Hayden was even better than the mysterious one.

Before things could get out of hand and he completely lost his sense, he broke their kiss. Hayden's lips were full. She seemed as disoriented by their moment as he was. He eased her away from him. "Thank you for trusting me."

They were both exhausted and emotionally spent. "Come on. We need to get some rest. They moved to settle into blankets that he had set up earlier. She faced away from him, resting her head on his arm. Randy stroked her hair and ran his finger along her back. "I love you."

Hayden's back stiffened before her deep breaths evened again. Had she heard him? He almost hoped that she had. She shifted and curled against him. He held her and thanked God for bringing this woman to him.

Life couldn't get better than it was at this moment. The night was cool and the sounds of the breeze in the leaves above them lulled him to sleep.

Randy

As they had the past few mornings, Randy woke to Hayden's body entwined with his. He held still, just wanting to feel her in his arms a bit longer, but the sun was already up.

"Hayden." Gently, he shook her. Her head moved to the side as she snuggled down in the quilt. He brushed the hair out of her face. It was soft and shined like silk. The scrapes on her face were healing but her lips were chapped. When they got to Grand Junction, he would see that she got all the lotions and creams needed to restore her to her previous self. Not that the girl sleeping in his arms wasn't beautiful, but he wanted her to feel beautiful.

She snored indelicately. It was a sound that he had never heard from her. He laughed and tried again to rouse her.

"Hayden, sweetheart, we should already be gone." He rubbed her back with his free hand and she wiggled away in order to give him better access.

"Nope," He stood up, "We're late."

"Well, let's get going then." She stretched languidly before making her groggy way to stand. "I need a moment and I'll be ready."

When she came back, Randy had already folded the blankets. He handed them to her. She tucked them away and hefted her saddle over the animal. After tightening the cinch, she climbed on.

"Let's do it." He mounted up and kicked his horse into action. Hayden rode beside him.

"How long 'til we get to town?"

Randy sighed. "If we push it, we could be there tonight."

Was that a flicker of disappointment in her face?

"I wish we could stay like this." She said softly.

"How badly do you want that?"

"What? For us to stay out here?"

"No, I mean for us to stay together?" He pulled his horse to a stop taking the reins from her.

Hayden

He was serious. For once, she was slow to speak. Her mind spun around all the possibilities. He'd said the words to hera few nights ago as she was falling asleep. The words that she needed to hear. That was important.

Besides Kayra, she doubted that anyone loved her. Fineese's question sounded in her head.

He loves you. Wasn't that enough?

They had a definite attraction to each other. She admired him.

He was unlike any man that she'd ever met. Besides that, the entire wagon train already believed them to be married. Hayden was good at playing parts, but this was real. And what of Kayra? It would never again be just the two of them. Hayden's eyes filled with tears. It would be the end of that part of her life. Yet Kayra had practically thrown Hayden with him and didn't seem jealous at all. That puzzled Hayden because she had been terribly jealous of William when he was stealing Kayra.

Randy reached out, stroking her cheek. "At least you haven't blurted out no. Listen, you don't have to answer me now. I wasn't planning on asking you like this. It's just that until I met you, I never even wanted a dull life with a boring wife and a houseful of kids. But now I realize that making you a part of my life would only make it better and it would certainly never be dull. I can't get you off my mind. I think about you every second of the day and twice a second at night."

Hayden breathed a laugh. She placed her hand over his. He was saying all of the things that she wanted to hear.

"I need you to be a part of me. I need to be with you and know that you're safe. I want to teach you to trust me and be there for you when you wake up from your nightmares. I'm being selfish because I know that you don't need me the way that I need you. I know that you can take care of yourself and anyone else that gets in the way, except Greely, maybe." He smiled at his joke. "I sound like a romantic fool." He shook his head. "I'm asking you. If you want me, I want you to be my wife. Just think on it."

He leaned across his horse and captured her mouth with his. She kissed him soft and slow.

Reluctantly, Randy pulled away. "We need to get going if we're to make it tonight."

Hayden took back the reins of her mule and continued down the trail. She had a lot to think about, after all.

Chapter Thirteen

Hayden

After about an hour, Hayden noticed that the track they'd been following changed. She studied the ground for a long time before mentioning it. She didn't want to be mistaken.

"I don't see all of the horse's prints anymore."

Randy halted his horse and stared at the trail below him. He tipped his tan hat back on his head and looked at the trail behind them. "He's smart. I was busy searching the horizon for signs of him waiting for us and just checking that we were following some tracks. The deepest one isn't his. I guess I was following that one. When did you notice it change?"

"Probably a quarter mile back. I wanted to make sure before I said anything. Two of his horses are still tracking normally, but I think his horse, the crazy one isn't with these others, or he's covering them somehow. The fourth horse's track is gone too."

Randy nodded his head. "You're right. Absolutely right. I should've caught that. I'm usually a good tracker. Thank you for catching it. You are a natural at this. Maybe you should turn the city on its ear and become a law lady." His smile was more rewarding than any praise she'd ever recalled hearing.

Hayden was dead tired when they finally saw the flickering of lights from the town below them. It was beautiful. As far as she could tell, the town wasn't large but it sure was exciting to be near civilization.

The nightlife was in full swing as they rode down the main street. The small bakery and the dry goods store were dark, but across the street a saloon was bright and alive with activity.

There were numerous 'ladies' standing outside. Hayden guessed that Grand Junction must have an actual whorehouse instead of just a few prostitutes. She looked out of the corner of her eye to see if Randy was looking at them.

He was certainly looking at the saloon, but his expression seemed more business than pleasure.

"Is he in there?"

"I don't see him."

They came upon the small sheriff station and Randy paused. "I know that you are as tired as I am, but I have to talk with the sheriff before I can rest. Do you mind? If you'd rather, we can check into a hotel and I can come back."

Hayden shook her head. "You're a lawman first, remember?" She teased him with his own words and smiled playfully in his direction. The one he returned was tired.

He climbed from his horse and helped Hayden from Otis. She limped a bit and rubbed her sore rear end following Randy into the office. The jail was tiny. Only one cell and a desk furnished the room. Randy walked to a door off the back and motioned for Hayden to stay put.

"Excuse me. Anyone in there?"

From a dark corner of the room she heard a startled, "Yes, hold on a moment."

Randy shook his head and walked back to Hayden taking her hand and whispering in her ear. "He has company."

Hayden wasn't exactly sure what he meant by that until a short blonde dressed in bright red silk tight flounced out of the dark room. Hayden felt a flutter of irritation as Randy smiled at her. Her bosoms were as creamy and exposed as a cow's udders during milking. What was going through Randy's head? She'd only seen Kayra and Fineese naked and neither of them had a chest like that, and Fineese was with child, which she was sure meant that her bosom grew alongside her belly. The woman paused in front of him and placed a solicitous hand on his arm.

"I'm Lisa," She breathed the words in an intentionally sultry voice. Then her gaze fell to Hayden and met her glare. The woman was not young, but she had an undeniably pretty face underneath thick makeup. She took in Hayden, dismissing her as a threat with a smug smile. She turned to Randy and ate him alive with her eyes.

"I'm over at Mae Bell's. You look like you could use a shave. And a bath. I give a good one." She promised, sliding her hand down his arm before leaving the room.

Hayden grabbed hold of his arm and stood up straighter, like a lion protecting her lair. He put his arm around Hayden as the sheriff came strutting into the office.

He was tall and thick with an odd mixture of boyish sweetness and manly swagger. His hair looked as if it had been tousled. Except for his cowboy hat that was laying on the floor in the idle of the walkway, he was fully dressed down to his badge and gun.

He extended his hand to Randy. "Timothy Neuhold. Sorry to have kept you. I was...in the back when you arrived." His face was as red as Lisa's dress had been. "What can I do for you?"

Randy shook his hand. "My name's Randy. I'm a deputy in Denver City. I'm looking for a man, Sam Greely. He's killed seven times that I know of in the past two months, raped at least three women and tried to kidnap both my wife here and her cousin on a wagon train that's coming through."

The sheriff's face was ashen.

"I have reason to believe that he is either in town or nearby. He was heading west and now has no supplies. I'm sure that you have a wanted poster for him in that stack over there." Randy pointed to a pile of papers on the sloppy desk. "I need to know if you've seen him."

The sheriff grabbed his discarded hat from the floor beside him and went to the desk. He fumbled nervously through the papers until he pulled one from the pile. In bold black letters was the name they'd been looking for. Samuel Robert Greely. Quick to assist, he handed the wanted poster over to Randy.

It was Greely all right, Greely with a full set of whiskers that is. Randy read the complaints against him. Hayden was right beside him looking at the accusations. It was a long list from robbery to rape and murder. He was wanted in three states besides Colorado, which didn't even appear on the list.

"That's our guy." Randy handed the flier back to the young deputy. "He's clean-shaven now. Seen him?"

The sheriff shook his head. "I ain't even the real sheriff. I'm just filling in for my uncle while he's visiting my Gram in Utah. I don't know what to do with a real criminal. He said all I'd have to do was lock up a drunk or two."

Randy breathed deeply through his nose.

"Well, get a wire to him that he needs to get back here. Is the telegraph office open?"

"I don't think so."

"First thing tomorrow then. I need to send a wire too, where's it located?"

The man gave him directions and asked, "You think he'll cause trouble here?"

"I don't know. He's smart. He might buy supplies and lay low, but he's also bloodthirsty. He has a taste for saloon girls. We might want to warn the ladies."

Hayden butted in. "Randy, you don't need to handle that. He can do it. He already seems friendly with them." Randy huffed a laugh and kept talking.

She wished that she had kept the thought to herself. She was always saying things out loud and regretting it later.

"I'll start hunting for this man tomorrow. Is there a respectable place in town where we can stay?"

"Saw Mill Inn. Just up the road, can't miss it."

"Thanks." Randy again shook the man's hand, then took Hayden's arm and escorted her from the office.

The lobby was small. Dark wood covered every wall. An old man was sleeping in his chair, feet propped up on the desk in front of him. He didn't stir at their approach.

"One room or two?" Randy whispered.

"What?" Hayden whispered back.

"Do we get one room or two?"

"Oh. It doesn't matter. I don't have a cent, so I guess whatever's cheapest." That was an easy way to handle it.

"Don't worry about money. If you want your own room I'll get it for you."

Hayden tried to hide her hurt. Does he want his own room? Perhaps so Lisa can visit him. Her face flushed at the mere thought of his intentions for his own privacy. *Well, she won't be visiting if I'm in his room.*

"One room," she declared,

Clearing his throat, Randy managed to rouse the old man. "I'd like a room for my wife and I for the next week at least."

The old man adjusted his glasses and began writing in a ledger. "A week you say?"

Randy nodded. "Give us the nicest room you have."

Hayden overheard the request and blushed at the way the man looked past Randy's shoulder at her.

"Yes sir." He smiled greedily at Randy and passed him a slip of paper with the amount written on it.

Randy pulled out several bills and handed them over. "I'd like a bath drawn in the morning for my wife and we will take breakfast in our room around eight."

"Sorry sir, we don't serve in our rooms."

Randy pulled out another bill and handed it to the man. "Make an exception."

The man smiled. "Yes sir. Eight o'clock, you say?"

He handed Randy a key and pointed to the door at the top of the staircase. "Do you need help with your bags?"

"No," was Randy's clipped answer. He gave Hayden the key and sent her up the stairs. "I'll tend to the horses. You go ahead."

Hayden paused. The thought of Lisa went through her mind. She didn't want to believe that he would abandon her and go see that woman on their first night in town, but he had wanted his own room and now he was excusing himself.

Randy sensed her reluctance and guessed at her train of thought. "Hayden, sweetie. Go rest. I promise I'll be quick."

"Quick like ten minutes or an hour?" She challenged.

"Quick as in, I can't wait to get upstairs to sleep beside you."

With that, her fears took a back seat.

"Good," was all she said before scurrying up the stairs.

With the lamp from the hallway she found a lamp in her room and lit it. Heavy blue draperies hung from the ceiling clear to the floor. They were sure to shut out every speck of light come morning.

The coverlet on the huge mahogany bed was the color of champagne and so fluffy that Hayden couldn't wait to slip under it. She tugged off her shoes and let her feet sink into the thick rug. The heady scent of flowers wafted through the air from the arrangement on a bureau. She dipped a washcloth in the bowl of water and washed the trail dust from her face.

Seeing her reflection in a mirror she frowned before vigorously finger combing her straggly hair. Spying a robe hanging behind the walnut dressing screen, she slipped from her dress down to her pantalets and wrapped herself in its soft warmth.

She turned down the indulgent coverlet and sank beneath it into the crisp sheets. It felt heavenly to rest. There was a knock at the door. She hauled herself from the bed to open it for Randy.

Randy

He smiled to himself at the sight of Hayden in a thick white robe. It suited her. He pulled his shirt from his jeans and unbuttoned it down the front. Then he sat on the plush chair next to the window and tugged at his boots and socks. He reached to unbutton the fly of his pants then stopped to glance over at Hayden, who sat trustingly on the edge of the bed. He decided they were best kept on. He strode to the basin that Hayden had used and rinsed his face, splashing water all along his neck and chest.

He caught sight of Hayden behind him in the mirror as she climbed up onto the huge mattress and settled down in the covers.

He sniffed at his underarms and decided to put the shirt back on.

He heard Hayden giggle at his predicament. Turning, he shrugged into the shirt and climbed on top of the shiny blankets, grinning.

"This room is wonderful. Thank you."

She leaned over and kissed him softly on the lips. He returned the kiss but was careful not to touch her otherwise. She pulled away and snuggled back down. Randy was glad to have been able to spoil her in this way. He rested, thinking of all the exciting things that were in store for her tomorrow.

⊷← →⊷

Hayden

The room was cast in shadows when Hayden awoke to a staccato rapping at the door. It took her mind a moment to recall where she was. She threw her feet over the bed and found a small pair of slippers, sliding her narrow feet in them. She pulled the robe tight across her belly and walked to the door.

"Who's there?"

"We're here with a bath."

Hayden cracked the door and an old lady and several boys invaded the room each toting a large barrel of warm water to the long porcelain tub. In minutes, the tub was steaming as the young men hurried back out the door.

The lady smiled a plump face up at Hayden. She tested the water, adding a few aromatic sprigs of lavender in the tub followed by eucalyptus leaves, and a powder that Hayden had no idea about.

Smiling like Hayden was her child, she motioned her forward. "Off with that robe now, missy. I'm Lana and you are supposed to be primped and clean for your breakfast appointment at eight o'clock, so come on, dear."

Confused, Hayden obeyed, slipping shyly from the robe. She stepped into the water and sank down in an effort to conceal her nakedness. The warm water was heaven. She wanted to spend the entire day in that tub. Her eyes closed. It had been so long since she felt clean.

Lana wasn't going to allow her to lounge though. She handed her a bar. "You do the scrubbin' and I'll help with your hair."

Even the soap felt luxurious. For a moment, Hayden felt guilty remembering Kayra out in a cold pond, but it passed once her hair had been washed, the woman put an oil in her pudgy hands and worked it into her scalp. She said nothing about the raw portion of Hayden's head.

"Now out with you, missy."

Lana gathered her belongings and her bottles. She picked up Hayden's dirty dress and headed for the door.

"Wait, please. That's all that I have to wear." Hayden explained.

Lana smiled. "Miss Hayden, your husband has other plans for you."

Hayden felt as if her face and neck had been dipped in hot wax.

"I mean, you have another visitor waiting to dress you. I'll send them up."

Less than a minute later, there was another rapping. Hayden opened the door to a serious looking woman with a basket. On her pointy nose rested a pair of square cut spectacles. Behind her, two young women strolled carrying armloads of premade dresses.

An elaborate display of gowns were laid on her unmade bed. The seamstress led Hayden behind a wooden dressing screen.

"Off with the towel. Girls, bring the creams."

Hayden stood there naked, awkwardly wondering what was expected of her.

The girl peeked around the partition and smiled. "I'm Delores. This is for your body." She handed a large jar of cream to Hayden. "Rub it in good, so it doesn't mark your new gowns."

Hayden obeyed. Whatever it was, it smelled like heaven. She thoroughly moistened her dry body. Then Delores peered at her face and selected an amber bottle. "Face oil." She passed it to Hayden.

When she was done, another girl stood next to her holding undergarments. Hayden stepped into them before slipping a fluffy petticoat over her shoulders. Hayden wished that she could wear that all day. That is, until the seamstress handed her a lavender hued gown. "This will flatter you."

She helped Hayden into the dress. It was too long. The woman narrowed her eyes. "Two inches from each gown." She ordered, and the girls scrambled to alter her new dresses. Hayden was dying to see herself in the mirror, but the stern woman stood her on a stool and began hemming the dress she wore whipping a needle in and out with long, competent fingers.

The seamstress led Hayden to a chair. "Have a seat."

Hayden obeyed and when the woman returned she carried three boxes of shoes. She tried on all three pairs. One was a fit.

"I'll see that another pair in your size is delivered this week."

Before she knew it, Hayden had on stockings and shiny brown shoes to compliment her dress. One of the matching seamstress girls approached her with a brush. "You have the perfect hair, you know, for the latest fashions."

Hayden smiled shyly. "I'm afraid I have no idea what the latest fashions are."

The girl laughed, patting her shoulder. "Not to worry, when I am done with you, you will be able to fit in at the finest tea in London."

Hayden could imagine what that would be like. It was a fun prospect. She sat up tall and straight watching the girls in her room alter her dresses and fix her hair under the strict, watchful eye of the dressmaker.

It took some time before the woman arranging her hair stood back to examine her handiwork.

"It's some of my finest work. Take a look." She handed Hayden a mirror and stood back while Hayden stared in awe at her reflection.

Tears filled her eyes. Her blonde hair was arranged partially on top of her head, softened by girlish strands that fell teasingly around her face. The missing clump at the base of her neck and the raw skin were concealed entirely. She had never seen herself look so fashionable. The morning glory color of her dress made her skin brilliant. It brought out the hues of color along her cheekbones.

Her self-inspection was cut short. "I hope those are happy tears."

Looking up, Hayden realized that all of the ladies in her room were watching her hopefully.

"There were no tears." She was quick to assure them.

They shared a warm smile amongst each other. "Of course, no reason to cry when you look as beautiful as you do." The seamstress assured her. "You must be a very special girl. You know, your husband was quite generous to us. Normally we don't make house calls seeing as this is not a large city, but he insisted we make an exception. And I must say, he's going to be pleased with the result."

Again, Hayden looked at herself in the mirror. "Thank you. All of you."

"Well, it's almost time. We'd better scurry." The seamstress motioned to the door and the matching women hopped to their feet.

"We'll return this afternoon to finish the other gowns. Never fear though, the one Mr. Parker selected for this evening is ready."

Hayden swallowed her emotions. Randy had picked out the dresses and made special plans for them. More disturbing than that was the use of Randy's last name. Hayden realized that until that moment, she had no idea what it was. Mrs. Randy Parker. Not half bad.

The women filed out and Lana returned. When she caught sight of Hayden, she looked her up and down. "Well, don't you look fine?"

When she passed Hayden she patted her back. It had her eyes filling again. What was wrong with her? She did not do this.

Lana busied herself hanging the gowns in the armoire and tidying the room.

Hayden, uncomfortable, just standing there while the nice innkeeper went about her work began making the bed.

"No, no Missy. I'll take care of that."

She took the pillow from Hayden's hands and made quick work of the linens. Lana hung the white robe on the hook behind the dressing screen and neatly set her slippers beside it.

"Breakfast is comin'." Lana left and returned with two boys in tow. One carried a small table and the other held two dining chairs. They tried not to make eye contact with Hayden, but the older of the two was blushing. They set the things in front of the window and Lana placed a silver covered tray in the center, plates and silverware.

"Coffee and juice, coming up."

Alone at last, Hayden looked once more at herself in the large mirror, preening. She walked to the tray and lifted its lid. Eggs, sausage and pancakes stacked high on top of each other. Hayden felt her stomach growl at the feast. How would she breathe once she ate? Her corset was as tight as a cinch. But when she put her hands to her waist and felt its smallness because of the constraint, she decided that she would manage somehow.

Footsteps in the hall made Hayden hastily recover the tray. She turned as Randy waltzed in. He was clean-shaven and wore new clothes as well. The white shirt emphasized his broad shoulders. Raven hair lay smooth against his head and a very satisfied smile was fixed on his face as he appreciated Hayden.

"You're so gorgeous." He flattered, taking her hand in his. He held her arm in the air while his eyes roved over her. He whistled his approval.

Confidence beamed from her face...until she remembered Lisa from the previous night, and her salacious offer to give him a bath and shave at Mae Bell's. The smile slid off her face. Had he actually met with her? Noticing the change in her demeanor, he raised an eyebrow and had the gall to look confused.

"You look nice too." Hayden said stiffly. "Where did you go to get cleaned up? You know we have a tub right here. Is there perhaps another place you've spent your time here?"

He simply laughed."Hayden, you don't have to worry about that woman. I only want you." He took her hand pulling her against him. "Besides," he teased, "there are so many ladies at that place, I couldn't even find her this morning."

Hayden swatted him in the arm. He laughed again.

"Now, there is the girl I know and love."

Hayden glanced up at him demurely.

"Shall we?" He motioned to the meal and held her chair out for her. She took her seat spreading the napkin across her lap.

They had just served their plates when Lana knocked. Randy opened the door for her and took the drinks. She looked over his shoulder at Hayden and smiled.

Randy kicked the door closed behind him and set a crystal goblet of orange juice in front of Hayden. He filled his own cup with coffee and sat back.

"Thank you for everything, Randy." She stared into his eyes until it became too tense.

"It is truly my pleasure."

"How on earth did you pay for this?" She had wondered about it all morning.

"Well, even though you think you have me all figured out, there is actually a lot about me that you don't know. You may not like all of it." Randy made slow work of pouring syrup on his pancakes.

Hayden leaned forward, eager to hear. "Everything that I told you is true. My father was a fur trapper, we will talk more about him later, but my mother was the daughter of a very wealthy English Lord who passed away about six years ago and my brother and I inherited his estate."

Now that was ridiculous. If ever a tale was told, that would be it. She remained silent, contemplating the possibility. "You're making fun of me, trying to top my upbringing in France. Now, tell me the truth."

Randy looked into her eyes, his smile filled with warmth. "I will tease you, but I won't ever lie to you. You gotta trust me. The irony that this does sound like one of your stories is not lost on me, but I promise you, it's the God honest truth."

Hayden sat back. "Then why do you work as a deputy?"

"I have to fill my days with something. My brother and I were lawmen before any of this occurred with our Grandfather and we like our jobs. We're good at it. We traveled to England to see our estate and felt entirely out of place." He took a drink of his coffee. "You, however, would love it. Someday I'll take you and you can see our stables and servants. The main house alone is…. I can't even describe it in a way that will do it justice."

"If you hated it so much, why didn't you sell it?"

"I didn't hate it. I just didn't fit in. There are things about me that made me…not easily accepted. However, we own a substantial amount of land. It will be the legacy of my children if we– I have any, and they may want to take their place in court."

He was serious. How did she not pick up on this? What difference did it make? If she married him, it would have to be for bigger reasons than that. She would have never known that he had any more money than she did. That's important because Hayden despised rich, arrogant people who thought that they were better than everyone else.

"You're suddenly very thoughtful." He shoved a bite of pancake in his mouth.

Hayden did likewise. "It's just that… I never would have suspected that you were…"

"Well, I'm not royalty or anything. I do hold a position of status but that is in an entirely other country. I'm just me, Randy. I hope that this doesn't affect your decision as to whether or not you will accept my proposal."

"If I do agree," She looked him square in the eye, "it will be because I care for you and for no other reason. No amount of bribing will win me over, although I do love my new gown."

Randy set his fork down with a clatter.

"I don't want you to marry me because you care for me. I want you to marry me because you love me, because you trust me to always be there, because you see us building a life together."

Hayden took a deep breath. Letting it out was more of a challenge. "I don't know if I can?" She whispered the words across the table. "I want to."

Randy's face softened. "You can, and I'll wait. For the time being, though, we have to pretend. Actually, we have to pretend a lot. I don't want Greely to know that we're here. I signed us in last night as Randal and Rebecca Parker. We, my dear, are traveling to Salt Lake City. I'm a cattleman and we're interested in building a ranch either here or in Salt Lake."

Hayden's eyes gleamed with the thrill of a new assignment. She clapped her hands. "I like that, Rebecca Parker. Is your real name Randal?"

"No and I'm glad you're so amused." Randy didn't give her the opportunity to respond. "Turns out, there's a shindig tonight for a local rancher who died. They're auctioning off his things and a dinner is planned, proceeds go to the widow. I had no idea that my cover would get us invited, but the fellow I spoke with this morning, while creating this story, is responsible for the gathering. So, we'll rub shoulders. We need to leave about five. I believe the dress I picked out is ready for you."

Hayden nodded. The excitement was building and she had an exceptionally good outlook considering the extent of their problems.

Randy took another large bite and wiped his mouth. Hayden noted that the food on his plate was nearly gone and she had barely touched her own. He drank down his coffee and pushed his chair from the table, scraping the floor as he stood. He picked up his hat and held it in his hand.

"I need to follow a lead on a stranger in town who purchased seed. I doubt Greely would buy that, but that's all I got."

He leaned down and kissed Hayden on the cheek. It felt comfortable, natural. She smiled up at him.

"What am I supposed to do all day?"

"I don't care what you do, but don't leave this hotel. If you like, I'll have some books brought up."

Hayden nodded and Randy stood in the doorway looking at her with brows raised. "I want to hear you say that you will not leave the hotel."

"You have my word," She promised.

"I want to hear the actual words."

"I Hayden, no, Rebecca Parker promise my husband, Randal Parker, that I will not step foot out of this hotel until tonight, escorted on the arm of my handsome beloved."

His smile sent shivers up her back. He left the room and Hayden returned to her huge breakfast.

It was delicious.

Chapter Fourteen

Kayra

Kayra was soaking with sweat and exhausted by the time she and Fineese dragged their wagon into the camp where the others were already going to sleep for the night. It was late. They'd barely made their way in before dark.

Ever since Hayden and Randy left, the wagon master, Foster, had been pushing the group doubly hard. The pace he set was difficult for several of the passengers, Fineese among them.

For the past three days, Fineese had been cramping and there was blood in her undergarments. The baby wasn't expected for nearly a month. Fineese laid in the wagon with her feet up. She was taking what remained of her laudanum for the cramps. As an effect of the drug, she slept for days.

Kayra was as gentle driving the wagon as she could be. When she saw a rut that couldn't be avoided, Kayra cringed at the agonized cry that came from Fineese, even in her sleep, which was why they were lagging behind today. An old couple had slowed their pace to stay with the girls and Kayra was thankful for the safety in numbers.

Harce and Annie were a Godsend. Being in their seventies, the journey was hard on them, but they had a passion for this unseen land. Both Harce and Annie were like miniature people, neither one reached Kayra's shoulder. They were the sweetest couple she'd ever seen, not because they were beautiful but because they thought that each other was beautiful. They smiled from their eyes, holding hands as they adventured through the Rockies like teenagers out courting. Their spirits were young.

Instantly, Kayra had taken a liking to them. After Hayden left, there was a void and Annie was quick to jump in helping with Fineese. She'd been the one to suggest that Fineese prop her feet. She said that it would be harder for the baby to come early if gravity worked against it. Kayra wasn't sure if there was any validity to her theory, but just having a plan to stop the child from being born too soon had eased Fineese's mind.

Harce pulled up alongside Kayra and helped Annie from the wagon. Stiffly, the couple walked a while before Harce took the buckets to the stream. Annie came to the back of the wagon and looked in on Fineese feeling her head. She was feverish and her skin was damp.

Kayra set a hand on Annie's arm. "Is she going to be alright? I'm scared out of my mind."

Annie frowned. Her eyes didn't meet Kayra's. "I don't know, honey. I've seen a couple of women in this condition pull out of it and carry their babies long enough, but she seems to have some illness that I can't place." Straightening her back she forced a smile. "You are a God-fearing woman, aren't you Kayra?"

Kayra nodded. Recently, that is. Ever since her time with Will and his family, she had begun to think about God and her need for him. Now, she prayed often, for herself and

Will, for Hayden, Fineese and her unborn child. It had become a peaceful time for her as she drove the wagon alone each day.

Annie smiled solemnly. "It's in His hands. Let's take turns trying to bring her fever down. If it gets any higher, then it could make the child come that much sooner. In the meantime, we need to be preparing for the baby just in case it comes early."

Kayra's eyes filled with tears. Annie squeezed her arm. "Don't worry sweetheart. I've delivered six of my ten grands and you're a nurse for heaven's sake. She's your friend but it will be just like the other babies you have helped into the world."

Kayra fell into Annie's arms crying. "I'm not a nurse, Annie. Randy just said that to end the ugly things folks were saying about us. I'm sorry. It isn't true. It isn't even close to true."

"It's alright now, sweetheart. I wondered about that when she started getting so bad off." Annie pulled her away and made her look into her old eyes. "People are ugly sometimes. It did stop the gossip anyhow. We will get through this just fine. I know what to do if it comes to that. And Harce and I, we won't leave you, no matter what."

Kayra looked into the wrinkled face and gray eyes that were so strong and courageous. Instantly she felt better. She wrapped her arms around Annie's small shoulders.

Annie

Fineese slept through the night, Annie at her side, cooling her ague with wet cloths. Kayra was exhausted and Annie knew that she needed to keep her strength up for the day ahead of them. It was likely to be a difficult one. She ran her fingers across Fineese's emblazoned cheek.

A pained expression crossed Fineese's face and Annie watched as her stomach hardened and lifted.

Annie let tears slide down her cheeks remembering the child she'd lost in birth. She'd been sixteen and he'd come too early. There was nothing they could do. He lived only a few terrible minutes, gasping for air. She bowed her head and prayed that if this child was born early that it would make it.

Kayra

With the morning came the bustle of animals as the other travelers hustled to get on the trail before the sun was full up in the sky. Kayra came to the wagon and pulled open the flap.

"You're an angel, Annie. I meant to trade out with you, but I never woke up. How did she do?"

Annie shook her head. "I think there's nothing we can do to keep this child from coming. We should expect it today. I don't know how Fineese will fare. She's weak. You need to be prepared for whatever happens." She took Kayra's hand in hers. "We can do this, but we won't be following the train today."

Stunned, Kayra nodded. She was petrified but if Annie was willing to stay calm and take care of business, she would too. How would Hayden handle this situation? Hayden knew as much about babies and childbirth as Kayra did. Their experience together added up to a bunch of nothing.

Still, she desperately wished that Hayden were here, for her blind confidence that they'd manage like midwives, no problem. She'd at least have a plan of attack, not to mention her ability to keep Kayra together.

She sighed. *I have to do this without her. I can handle this*, she reassured herself.

"Alright, Annie. Shouldn't we boil water or something?"

"Yes, let's do that and we need to get her gown changed. That one is a mess already. We'll need clean blankets and whatever else you two have made for the child. I'll tell Harce and see if he can hunt us a deer. If we can keep Fineese awake, some broth may help her regain enough strength for the birth."

Kayra swallowed. "Let's get to it, then."

Annie climbed from the wagon. Kayra opened the canvas door, tying it back so that the early morning sunshine flowed in. The other travelers were gone and the small field that they camped in seemed much larger in the daylight. Kayra gently pulled the dirty gown from Fineese's naked body and put a clean one on her.

Fineese became coherent, but her mind was still clouded with the drug she'd been taking. Kayra watched as her stomach tightened, the child kicking against it. *At least it's turned the right way.* She propped Fineese against a pile of things softened by her pillow. She combed out her hair, tying it in a braid that laid like a brick plait down her back.

Fineese shook her head as she struggled. "Water."

Kayra ladled up a spoonful to her cracked lips. "Fineese, Annie says the baby's coming. Today, probably. We need to get you ready."

Fineese shook her head. The effort seemed to take her breath away. "Can't...too soon."

Kayra gathered all of her strength and tried to sound like Hayden. "This is happening Fineese. We can do this."

"Can't." A tear slid from Fineese's hooded eyes.

"We don't have a choice. I don't know what you'll need to do, but as soon as the baby is here, it won't hurt anymore."

Fineese shut her eyes, then opened them again. When she did, they were clear. "Get the ... quilt ... the trunk." Then her eyes closed again.

Kayra climbed over Fineese and opened the old wooden trunk. Inside was the quilt that the two women had made for the baby and a few gowns, one pair of crocheted socks and the journal that Fineese spent her evenings writing.

Kayra lifted the book in her hand and ran her finger along the spine. She looked toward Fineese who was watching her. A weak smile turned up the corners of her mouth.

"I love...love...baby...Tell her...for me." Fineese breathed the words, barely spoken.

Kayra's shoulders shook with the emotion spilling from her eyes. "No Fineese, you will tell her that. You are going to be a terrific mother."

Fineese looked at Kayra. "You love her."

Kayra grabbed Fineese by the shoulders and shook her before she realized what she was doing. "You can't die. I need you. This baby needs you. Stay with us. *Please.*"

Fineese shook her head as tears ran down her face. No sound came from her throat. Kayra grabbed the rag in the water bucket and began to dab it at Fineese's forehead. She talked incessantly about nothing in particular. She just wanted to keep Fineese with her as long as she could. After an hour or so, she realized that Fineese was not going to wake up anytime soon.

She grabbed the journal and opened it to page one.

Hayden

Hayden moved from the chair in her room to watch the street below. She'd been a good girl up till now, following her husband's wishes that she not leave the hotel...but after hours of sitting around, she'd become restless and couldn't focus any longer on the poetry books that he had sent to her room. Poetry was dumb. She always thought she would like poetry, but turns out, it was boring.

The seamstress had come and gone along with her entourage a long time ago. Once alone, Hayden had indulged herself in trying on each dress and prancing about, preening in the mirror at her reflection as she pranced around like royalty. She loved the expensive fabric and cut of the gowns.

She'd thought about what Randy had told her, about the estate and title that he held in England. It boggled her mind. The question of marriage was consuming as well.

He wanted her hand, but only if she truly loved him. Did she? She wondered for the fiftieth time. She had to be sensible. She'd wanted courting and spoiling and poetry, well, until she realized that poetry made no sense. Randy had done all those things since their arrival in Grand Junction. So what was holding her back? Kayra, she needed her sound council now more than ever. Soon, hopefully soon.

Her watchful eye caught sight of that Lisa girl strutting up the street like a pig on parade. Her tight black dress barely held in her thick stomach. Her lips were as red as strawberries and the feathered boa that she held in her hands was ridiculous considering the early September heat.

Then, Hayden spied Randy coming up the walkway opposite Lisa. His even stride covered the plank boards, he was on a mission. Lisa spotted him and made a beeline not allowing him to pass. Hayden huffed. Her fists angrily poised on her hips. Her deep intake of breath made her corset uncomfortable. *I have to stop doing that,* she thought as she eased the air from her chest but kept a cautious eye on the exchange below.

Just then, in the middle of the day, in front of God and anyone else who happened to pass by, Randy took the hussy by the arm and led her into the alley beside the dry goods store. Hayden still had a view but she couldn't read their lips. It definitely was too friendly for her liking.

Randy leaned down and Lisa whispered in his ear. Then she handed him something. He pulled out his billfold and just gave her money, it looked like more than a couple bills. Hayden's stomach churned as the bold little tart stood on tiptoe to kiss Randy's cheek. He smiled and glanced around before emerging back onto the crowded street toward the hotel. Lisa stayed behind a couple of seconds before turning and walking the opposite way.

Hayden fell back into her chair. *How dare he do this to me?* He swore that he'd not been to see her. Maybe he hasn't yet. Maybe he's planning to stay with her tonight and that was what the money was for, some sort of down payment.

The doorknob turned and instantly Hayden reached for her Kipling and pretended to be immersed in its verse.

"What a perfectly domestic image."

Hayden looked up with sharp eyes. At least he'd wiped the lipstick from his cheek.

"You look beautiful. Did they finish the gowns?"

"Yes. Left an hour ago." She bored holes into the page.

He walked to her and knelt beside the chair. Randy touched her hair and turned his face to kiss her. She offered her cheek. He obliged with a chaste kiss then stood lazily and ambled to the window. He was staring in the direction of the dry goods store.

In regal form, she came to her feet. Kipling thudded to the floor. That got his attention. He turned. The carefully put together clothing and hair could not contain the uncivilized woman who was about to tear into him.

"See anything interesting down there?"

Randy shook his head and pursed his lips. "Not really."

"Well, I did." She stomped her foot and threw him a look filled with poison, like a rattler coiled to strike.

Randy sighed. He took off his hat and ran long fingers through his black hair. Setting his hat on the table, he crossed to her.

"Hayden, it's not what you think."

"Oh of course not. It never is, is it?"

"It's truly not."

"How do you think that makes me look, huh?" She used a southern voice to make her point. "Did you see that Randal Parker stepping out on poor Mrs. Becca? She sure must be dumb not to know what that snake is all about."

Randy

Randy kept his voice even, which was quite a task considering that the woman he was about to officially propose to, was more than ruining the moment.

"Hayden, stop hollering at me and listen. Would you please sit down?"

Uncooperative, she paced to the other side of the room. Opening the armoire, she found her new parasol and stomped toward the door. "You'll have to excuse me. I believe that there's a place in town where a lady can find a caring companion for a couple of hours. I believe it's called... Bobby Joe's."

He couldn't help himself. He flat out laughed. "Are you threatening to go visit a male prostitute? Well, that would be a first. Besides, I think that they only have those in France, but you would know that since you were raised there."

Randy blocked her passage from the room. "Now stop this foolishness and listen."

Defiant, Hayden turned her chin to him. It was a common expression. He had come to know it all too well. "I am listening. I simply don't believe you."

Randy dipped his head, defeated already. He pulled a white envelope from his shirt pocket. "I wanted to do this in a special way, but I can see that you won't be satisfied to simply trust me about what you think you saw."

Hayden harrumphed at the mention of that devil wench.

Randy cleared his throat. "I have no interest in that woman or any woman besides you. I went to Mae Bell's because that is where you go when you want something kept private."

Hayden's mouth dropped in astonishment. "You admit it?"

"I told you that I wouldn't lie to you. I promise that I did not go with any of the ladies there. I don't sleep with prostitutes. I went to see about getting a wedding ring and the possibility of hiring a preacher if it comes to that."

The paper envelope crackled as he pulled out a gold band and held it out. "You see, if folks are to believe that we're married, like I want to be, then you should have some symbol of it on your hand. I knew that Mae Bell would be discreet and could help me get what I needed before tonight."

Hayden swallowed down the lump in her throat. Her eyes filled and she threw herself into Randy's arms knocking the piece of gold from his fingers. He held her against him. Thankful that she finally believed what he'd been trying to explain.

She tilted her face to his. She kissed him, she kissed him like she never wanted it to end. Her whole body relaxing into his and this moment.

He pried himself away and looked drunkenly into her eyes. "You really need to put a little more effort into helping me keep my promise of not touching you til we're married," He chided

She giggled, and reached her hands up, pulling his face down to hers.

His fingers ran along her side. "They sure got you cinched in. I don't see why white women wear these things."

Hayden's head shot up.

Great, he'd gone too far again. A sweet kiss had turned into what might happen, and that turned Hayden angry. He pushed her away and turned to gather himself. "I'm sorry. I promised to not do any more than kiss you. But Hayden, I love you and I want you to be my wife. Not just want, I need it. I need you to marry me and I don't even care if you can't admit that you love me. I can't go on like this."

She hugged her arms against herself, visibly withdrawing. Her brow furrowed and she looked plain confused. "I made you angry again? How? I didn't do anything."

"This makes me crazy," He motioned between the two of them. "You can't keep teasing me. If you don't want me, I'll deal with it, but I can't keep holding you in my arms and then pouring water on the candle. I'm not some puppy dog crush you can play around with."

Her eyes blinked several times. "I'm not teasing you. You just said something that caught me off guard."

Randy rubbed his temples. "What? What did I say?"

Hayden shuffled her feet. "It doesn't matter. I'm just sorry that this happened, again."

Randy ran his finger through his hair in an effort to get it out of his eyes. "I'm sorry, too, but what I just said is true. I want you to agree to marry me and I want an answer by the end of the night."

He softened his tone. His eyes implored her to take mercy on him. "I'd decided to wait and let you decide in your own time, but I need to know eventually."

He walked to the gold band lying in the thick rug and slipped it on her trembling finger. "Wear this now." Then he pulled the envelope from his pants pocket and pulled out a small diamond ring. "And if you will be my wife, I want you to have this too. It's not as nice as what I would like to give you. But it's what I could find here."

He smiled at Hayden. Her eyes grew as she jerked the ring from his hand, shoving it onto her small finger. She wiggled her nails for him to see. "It's perfect. I don't need to think about it anymore either. I will marry you," She held out her hand, "but you have to agree to a couple of things."

Randy stood at attention waiting to hear her conditions.

"First, Kayra is a part of me and she goes wherever I go."

He nodded obligingly.

"Second, you will be faithful to me. No other women. Ever."

He smiled and nodded adamantly.

"Third, you don't take over my life and make me into some dream you have of the perfect wife."

Randy sighed. "That's it?"

"Those are my conditions. Should we shake on it? I mean, I don't want to lead you on, or tease you."

He grabbed her and kissed her possessively. She liked the commanding way that he took her in his arms.

He pulled away. "Hayden, there is something else that I need to tell you. You'll need to sit down for this."

He ushered her to the chair by the window, catching sight of the way she smoothed her hair behind him. He paused, pulling out his pocket watch. "Nevermind, there isn't time. We're very late, sweetheart. You have to change now or we won't make it at all." He moved to the armoire and pulled a jade colored gown from the closet. It was a stark contrast to her light skin and hair. She would look stunning in it. "Turn so that I can undo all of these ridiculous buttons."

"If you're sure that it won't tease you too much," She muttered

"I'll manage. I can wait till tomorrow when we get married."

Hayden spun to look at him. "That soon?"

"It's best to do it before the wagon train gets here since they already believe that we are married. Besides, I don't want you to change your mind." He winked at her.

"I wanted Kayra to be here. I couldn't possibly do this without her."

Randy considered the need to hurry up with the ceremony. He certainly wanted her as his wife now but he didn't want to start off married life with her regretting the way it was done. They wouldn't be able to have a large ceremony, so he could at least give her this small request.

"If they're here in the next week, then I agree to wait, but if not, will you go ahead anyway?"

"Yes." Her eyes sparkled.

"And darlin', after this whole mess with Greely is done, I would like to take you to England for a honeymoon."

"What about Kayra?"

"I imagined that she could go on with Fineese and help get her set up in California. We can join them there if you want. I imagine that there are all sorts of unsavory types in San Francisco who need a deputy to teach them manners."

"So, do I have a say in any of this or are you just going to plan everything from here on out?" She bristled.

Randy shook his head. "I'd go and do just about anything you asked. I was only thinking of the things you might want to do, nothing more."

Hayden looked like she was considering whether or not to believe him. "Well. We better get a move on or we will be late."

Chapter Fifteen

Kayra

Kayra read the tragic events leading up to Fineese's life as a mistress. The turn of events that had brought her to Willow Creek. She sat back and smiled in surprise at the coincidence that both her and Fineese had ended up in Willow Creek. Just the mention of the town brought tears to Kayra's eyes.

She missed Will.

Each day she expected the emptiness to diminish, the hope that she might see him again to die down, but so far that hadn't happened. She was plenty busy, so she didn't sit around feeling sorry for herself but she felt as if a part of her was missing.

She spent her nights remembering the quiet conversations that she and Will shared. She thought often of the dreams he'd shared with her and how alike their goals were.

The thought of those last excruciating kisses and the look in his eye, still brought butterflies to her stomach.

Kayra had decided that, with or without Will, she needed to become the person that she wanted to be. So, she'd been doing that.

She was kind and brave, well at least braver than she'd been before. She was searching to fill the spiritual void deep in her soul. She'd been looking for God, and she found him in the towering mountains that they drove through.

He was there with the sunrise while the dew shined like silver on the grassy fields. She found God in her acceptance of the horrible things that had happened in her life.

For the first time, she was able to remember and not feel bitter. She was finally able to let go of the pain that she'd experienced as an orphaned child. It helped her deal with the horrible things that had happened since Greely had come into her life. She saw God in the people that she loved. Harce and Annie were a perfect example of that.

Annie had been staying awake with Kayra till late in the evenings, reading from her little brown Bible and talking about the stories and God's power. Annie was a great help in teaching Kayra that God cared personally for her. That he watched over her and hurt when she hurt. Kayra was overcome with the idea that all along, even when she thought no one but her cousin loved her, that God had been there holding his hand out, waiting for her to reach up and take it. She wanted to share all of this with Fineese. If anyone needed to find the healing and unconditional love that Kayra had found, it was Fineese.

Fineese stirred and Kayra set the journal down, coming to her side. "What do you need?"

"Cold," Fineese's lips trembled.

Kayra felt that her head was hotter than before. She'd already used every blanket they had. She grabbed the small patchwork quilt and laid it over Fineese's shivering body.

Finesse wailed as pain claimed her. Her eyes frantically held Kayra's.

Kayra held her hand. "This must be it Fineese. I think the baby's coming."

Annie appeared and struggled to kneel beside them. She lifted Fineese's gown. Her voice whispered. "I don't see it yet."

Together they waited through two hours of horrible screams before Fineese's body gave way and she passed out. Kayra looked at Annie. "Oh no, what does that mean? What happens now?"

"It might be easier this way. Something's wrong. The baby's head starts to come out then it seems to be pulled back in."

"Will they die? We have to do something! They can't."

"I have seen it before, when the cord that feeds the baby is wrapped around its neck. It can kill the child."

Terrified at the thought of losing both Fineese and the baby, Kayra begged. "You have to do something Annie, you just have to."

"Well," The old woman wiped the blood from her gnarled fingers onto her apron. "I'm not steady enough, but I can guide you."

"Me? No, I...I don't do things like this," Kayra cried, "If there is any other way, please. This is my first time even knowing a pregnant lady. I know nothing."

Annie smiled. Her sweet eyes gleaming with unshed tears. "Kayra, if we don't do this, both of them will die. Fineese can't last much longer. We need to get the child out as quickly as possible."

Kayra breathed deep and nodded. She shook out her hands and took a couple steadying breaths. "Okay. Okay. I'll do it."

"You need to find a sharp knife or scissors, if you have any. Let them boil a moment and wash your hands with lye. I'll prepare here."

Kayra nodded and slipped from the wagon. When she returned, Annie had pulled Fineese's gown up to her stomach and had spread her limp legs. Fineese was asleep. Under her hips was a blanket folded over and over.

"Come here, child." Annie moved to the side so that Kayra was in the center of the wagon. "You see that there?" She instructed, "That's the head. When it pulls back, you have to cut as quickly and as straight as you can along here and here." She showed Kayra exactly what needed to be done.

They waited. Kayra held the scissors in her trembling hand. "There it goes, Kayra. Do it."

As the baby's head disappeared again, Kayra held her breath and cut exactly where Annie had said. Annie held a clean towel to the opening.

With bated breath they waited until Fineese's stomach pulled together in a visible bulge near her belly button.

Annie smiled, "It's here." Kayra had never seen anything like it. Tears of emotion, both joy and fear spilled from her eyes as the child's head pushed through a few times before slipping into Annie's waiting hands. It was covered with gunk and the most precious thing that she had ever witnessed. Annie was fast wrapping the infant in a blanket, and wiping at the tiny face. It was an awful shade of blue.

"Untangle the cord from his neck. Quick." Annie ordered.

Kayra took hold of the thing that both gave life and was taking it now. She dug a finger under it and pulled it over the infant's head. "Now what? Shouldn't it cry?"

"Stick your finger in his mouth and clear any gunk. Then rub his back, hard."

Annie was pressing an already red soaked towel against Fineese. Kayra felt like a giant with huge thick fingers as she swiped into the tiny mouth. Nothing. She flipped the baby into one of her hands and started to rub, frantically. Finally, the baby made a sound, then a small yelp turned into a loud cry, full and strong and wonderful.

Annie's voice crackled with emotion. "Thanks to Jesus." She raised her eyes heavenward. "Now go ahead and clean this little guy up. I'll do what I can for Fineese."

Kayra nodded and climbed from the wagon with the baby. Despite the situation, Kayra couldn't help but stare in awe at the tiny child that fit into her hands.

His eyes were scrunched shut, his little hands clenched in angry fists shaking with each massive shriek from his mouth. The water she had used earlier to clean the scissors and knife was still hot. Kayra mixed some of the steaming water with some cool water until it felt right, then she sponged the baby.

He was so small, hardly bigger than a kitten, and slippery. If she wasn't careful, she'd drop him for sure. She laughed through tears as his temper tantrum grew more persistent. He did not want to be pestered with this bath.

Carrying the naked bundle back to the wagon, she selected one of the gowns that Fineese had made. The outfit that they thought was so tiny and cute swallowed him. Kayra couldn't get over the idea that the baby they had been so anxious to meet was finally here. She wrapped him in a quilt and hugged the bundle to her chest. "Your Mama made this quilt for you. She loves you very much."

Annie called from the wagon. "Kayra, come quick. She's awake."

Kayra jumped and ran to the wagon. Much to her relief, Annie had tidied up magnificently. A thick blanket sat in between Fineese's legs. Kayra didn't want to think about that. She had been educated enough for one day.

Fineese attempted to raise her head as Kayra leaned across her, so that she could see her son. The effort was too much. Kayra propped Fineese up with one arm, cradling the babe in her other one. Fineese's lips parted and the edges of her mouth turned up. Her eyes shone, alive once again and glowing with love.

Oh so carefully, Kayra laid the squalling infant across Fineese's chest. Her arms found their way to wrap around him. Kayra kept a hand on this wriggly back to ensure that he didn't roll. Finesse lifted unsteady fingers and caressed the baby's cheek.

Kayra whispered, not wanting to interrupt their special moment. "It's a boy, Fineese. And he's perfect."

"Actually, he's very small." Annie murmured. "But I think that his size will soon catch up to his holler."

Kayra laughed at the truth of her words, smiling as her dear friend met her son. "What are we gonna call the little guy?"

Fineese had that faraway look in her eye again. Her words were little more than a whisper. "Michael Kayden...for...you...and Hayden."

Overwhelmed with the honor that Fineese was giving her and her cousin, Kayra looked at the woman she had come to love and admire so much. She wrapped her free arm across both Michael and Fineese.

Silent tears spilled from Fineese's face. "Take him." Kayra slid from behind Fineese and held the infant against herself. As soon as the baby was off of Fineese's chest, her arms dropped to her side. Kayra realized what an effort holding Michael had been for her.

When her eyes closed, Kayra stroked Fineese's cheek. "Don't worry, Annie knows what to do. We'll let you rest." She rocked the angry infant, shushing his howls. "Harce is skinning a deer and we'll have some broth for you in a bit. That should help get your strength back, then you can feed your son." Kayra smiled naïvely at her friend.

Fineese shook her head, her eyes remained closed. "You must love him for me."

"I won't hear that." Kayra scolded. "You're going to feel a lot better come morning."

As Kayra stepped from the wagon, she had another question. "Fineese, what is Michael's last name to be?"

Tears spilled from hooded lashes. "Mayer."

Kayra's head shot up. Stunned, she scrambled from the wagon, air was trapped in her chest like a rock in her throat. She leaned against the wagon. Her lungs wouldn't cooperate as her mind told her to breathe.

She recalled the diary entry where Fineese had come to Willow Creek. It just couldn't be. She focused on sucking the air in and blowing it out slowly until she had a hold of herself.

Annie was beside her in an instant, taking the child from her arms. She escorted Kayra to a stump. Kayra sat, grateful that her legs didn't have to support her any more.

"Are you alright? You nearly fainted." Concern showed on the old woman's wrinkled face as she held the squalling infant, who apparently liked her more than Kayra because his cries tapered off. Annie's voice, hard with age, softened and pitched high as she bounced up and down talking to the baby. "There, there you sweet boy. Don't you worry, Annie has an idea and we are gonna feed you. Yes we are."

Thank God Annie was there and at least had an idea of what to do until Fineese could care for the baby on her own. "Sorry, I'm fine now, but I need a minute." Kayra had to find out if the child was Will's. She was terrified at what the journal would tell her.

Mayer was an unusual name here but perhaps Will had more family in the area that she didn't know about. It wasn't crazy to think that maybe an Uncle and cousins lived nearby, was it? The alternative answer to the puzzle was unthinkable. Fineese had said little about the child's father but what she had said was deplorable.

"I need you to tend the baby, just for a bit." She reached out a hand pleading with her old friend.

"Go on. I can manage." Annie asked no questions.

Kayra grabbed the diary and walked slowly toward the mountain behind them. She needed to be alone while she read what she feared would break her heart.

<h1 style="text-align:center">Chapter Sixteen</h1>

Hayden

Hayden dressed in a hurry. Although her hair wasn't as elegant as it had been earlier in the morning, she declared herself exquisite. The selection of the rich fabric against her creamy skin was gorgeous. The gown was cut low, but not inappropriately so; the skirt of the dress, unbelievably full.

Hayden laughed as she walked from her hotel room because she could feel the sides of the fabric and bustle push through the door jam. It was the kind of dress that little girls pretend to wear while playing house.

Randy looked as happy as Hayden felt. He reached for her palm and twisted the rings on her left finger. Then lifted her hand to his lips and kissed them. "You have made me a very happy man tonight, Mrs. Welch."

Hayden's eyebrows came up and she smiled whispering, "Is that your last name? I mean your real last name?"

Randy laughed. "Yes it is. You weren't too used to Parker were you?"

Hayden shook her head.

He tilted his head thoughtfully. "You were going to marry me and you didn't even know my last name?"

"We will have years to learn all that stuff." Hayden waved her recently bejeweled hand dismissively in the air.

Randy

The benefit resembled ones he'd been to before. It was held on an old ranch outside of town. A corral full of beautifully groomed horses pranced while folks set their minds on an offering price.

Randy climbed from the new buckboard he'd purchased earlier in the day. When Hayden asked him why he'd spent money on that, he said that if they wanted to look like normal traveler's then that was the least conspicuous thing to do. He offered his hand and Hayden slipped hers into it. She descended from the buckboard in a fluid motion.

Randy wondered if she had planned her graceful descent. Her behavior recently seemed much less planned and more real.

He smiled at the thought. *Maybe she is finally just being herself.*

She raised her chin and cleared her throat. When she opened her mouth the words that flowed from it were smooth as honey and thick with a slow, southern accent.

"Shall we, Mr. Parker? I am simply dyin' to meet all of these fine people."

Randy barely kept a hold of his desire as he ran his fingers through her neat hair and kiss her. Just when he thought she was ready to be herself.

"What's with the accent, love?"

"Well, as you know, I was born and raised in Georgia on a plantation. I love this part of the country but there are just some things that I have been unable to adapt myself to, like the odd speech that you all use."

Her demure smile made Randy question the wisdom of his agreement to wait a week to marry the creature in front of him. He figured that she was well aware of the delicious image she made. "After you, Rebecca."

The couple caused a lot of heads to turn as they entered the barn. Randy felt out of place, though he tried not to let it show. The rancher who invited him saw them enter and made his way over. He pumped Randy's hand with his beefy palm.

"Randal," he remarked, "You told me you were married, but you failed to mention how lovely your wife was."

Randy draped his arm around Hayden's shoulder. "I find that my words don't do her justice. Pete, meet my wife Rebecca."

"It's a pleasure, ma'am." He shook her hand much more cautiously than he had Randy's. Hayden smiled sweetly.

Exaggerating her accent, she lowered her lashes. "We appreciate the invitation. I have been looking forward to this all day."

Pete couldn't take his eyes off of the woman before him. Randy cleared his throat bringing the heavy man's attention back to him.

"Well, then, enjoy yourselves. I need to get this auction moving." With a tip of his hat, he was burling away.

Randy turned his amusement toward his wife. "And I thought you only worked that hard to flirt with me."

Hayden took his arm as they made their way through the crowd to the stands. Every man was given a number if he cared to bid. Randy accepted number 35 and began explaining how an auction operated.

At first, Hayden seemed giddy with excitement but after an hour of tack and tools going for pennies on the dollar, she looked desperate for a break. Randy took her hand, "Let's get some air."

Hayden followed him from the barn to the corrals. He passed a cursory glance at the horses running inside, his interest was on Hayden. Eager, he put his arms around her until she stepped into an embrace, resting her head on his chest. He kissed the top of her head.

"You know, we aren't the only ones out here."

"I know. And all those men over there by the hay bales, they're pretending not to notice us but inside they're jealous that I'm out here holding you."

Hayden grinned up into his face. "Shall we tease them a little bit, Mr. Parker?"

The innocent gleam in her eye was replaced by the look of a temptress.

He raised an eyebrow. "Not until Kayra get's here."

Hayden giggled. "That's fair."

"Would you like a horse, Mrs. Welch?"

Hayden's eyes lit. She squealed in answer and he turned her attention to the stock. They walked to the fence and Randy leaned against it. Hayden, ever anxious, climbed up and sat on the top post, her dress taking up an entire section of fencing.

Randy laughed out loud at the inappropriateness of what she'd done.

If she had tried to get the attention of the cowboys clustered together, she couldn't have been more successful. He came around behind her and encircled her waist.

"That one's nice. Just there." She pointed to a young appaloosa.

If it was broke at all, it was green. Randy chuckled. "You would pick the least broke one in the bunch." As he said the words, the horse charged forward at full speed to nowhere in particular, proving his point.

Hayden turned to look at him from the corner of her eye and bit her lower lip. "The same could be said of you. I don't guess it's such a bad thing."

Randy considered the woman in front of him. "If that is the one you want, then you shall have it. Are you a good enough rider to manage a creature like that?"

Her smile reeked of confidence. "I can manage anything I put my mind to."

He kissed the top of her head. She turned in his arms sliding indelicately from the fence. He righted her and stepped back, keeping his promise.

He peered past her shoulder and sucked in a sharp breath. "Look, those four." He pointed to a group of horses that without a doubt had belonged to the couples Greely had killed enroute to Grand Junction . "Do you recognize them?"

"Should I?"

"The two white ones belonged to that kid and his wife who left the wagon train and those other two, the black one with white markings on his left leg and the gray, they belonged to the other couple."

Hayden reached for his hand squeezing. "Are you sure?"

"Yes. I made a point of knowing the different men and their horses in case something happened. They're definitely ours. Take my number and bid on that horse of yours. I need to ask some questions and I can't have you distracting them." He smiled at Hayden, hoping that she didn't see how preoccupied he suddenly was.

Hayden took Paddle 35 and headed for the barn. Randy sauntered over toward the men.

"Are you men deciding in which order these animals are to be auctioned off?"

"Yep, we send 'em in, in the order of their worth."

"Well, my wife is eager to bid on that appaloosa." He slid the man who spoke to him a bill. "If you'd send him out first, I'd be much obliged."

"Sure thing, Mister."

The man whistled to a hand who came out and roped Hayden's horse. He led him inside the barn.

"There are four other horses I'm curious about. The two white ones, the black and the gray as well."

"What about 'em?"

"Who owns them?"

"I think Davis brought 'em in."

A lanky cowboy who looked barely old enough to shave piped up. "He brought 'em here. I was kinda wantin' the black one with the markings on his leg."

Randy smiled, "Don't worry son, I wasn't planning on bidding against you. I just recognize them."

A look of relief spread to the boy's eyes as he came forward to shake Randy's hand. "Name's Josiah. I'll take you to meet Davis."

"That'd be great."

He followed Josiah into the barn. Randy saw Hayden waving her number excitedly as the auctioneer pointed out the worthy attributes of the horse. Two people kept upping the bid. Hayden stood and approached one of the men bidding against her. She sat beside him and said something. Her eyes were so beautiful and she tilted her head very effectively. She'll get that horse all right. Randy shook his head.

Josiah interrupted his thoughts, "That's Davis." He pointed to a middle-aged man with long wiry whiskers. The few teeth he had were yellow with tobacco stains. "He's...prickly, let me get his attention."

Randy leaned against a post observing the exchange between the two. With catlike caution, the grizzled man made his way toward where Randy stood. They shook hands as Josiah introduced them, his leery eyes peered into Randy's as if he wasn't sure if he was friend or foe.

"Josiah says you got questions 'bout my mounts. I bought 'em fair and square. They's mine to sell."

"You misunderstand. Can we talk outside?"

The man nodded and led the way from the building.

The men walked from the light toward the shadows of a tree.

Randy heard Hayden's shriek of pleasure and the crowd erupted with laughter. He smiled. She got her horse.

"I'm more interested in the man who sold you the horses than the animals. You can ride 'em, sell 'em, or eat 'em for all I care."

That changed the tone of the meeting entirely.

"Can't tell you much 'bout him. A stranger came to my place and offered to sell me those horses real cheap. I saw the deal and took it."

"When did he come to your place?"

"Yesterday morning."

"Did he say anything about his plans?"

Davis scratched his filthy head trying to remember. "He said something about unfinished business."

"What else?"

"Think that's it."

"He didn't say where he was going?"

The man shook his head. "He headed east though, towards the Rockies."

Randy's stomach turned. He left the men standing in the shadows and sprinted toward the barn.

When he entered the building, Hayden was radiant with the glow of her purchase. "I did it. I got him."

Randy smiled at her but he didn't feel it anymore.

Her face immediately fell. "What happened?"

"Greely. I think he's headed for Kayra and Fineese. We have to leave, now."

Hayden's face flushed as they darted outside. Randy found Josiah, pulling him aside. "I have urgent business that I need to tend to." He pulled out his billfold. "Store my buckboard, the horses too. I'll return as soon as I can. Take care of this, and I will pay you more when I return. I need a fast horse." Josiah led Randy to the corral.

"The one your wife bought is fastest in the bunch, then I'd say that paint or the tall horse by the trough."

"Pick one for me and get it saddled up." He handed the youth more than enough money to accomplish the task.

"Yes sir."

Randy found Hayden by her new horse and he quickly paid the man holding the animal. Hayden had bid more than the animal was worth, but the look on her face as she stroked that horse's neck was priceless.

"We need a saddle."

"Sorry mister, we don't have lady's saddles."

"Any saddle will do."

The man handed one over and Randy shoved money into his hand. He helped Hayden get the horse ready, then she climbed up and he led her to where Josiah stood.

"That's a fine horse, Ma'am."

Hayden smiled at the young man, making him blush. She ran her hand down the animal's neck and patted it gently. "What's your name?"

"Josiah."

"Then that is what I will call him."

Randy cast Hayden an irritated look and climbed in his saddle. Josiah stammered around, smiling like a half grown kid. Randy realized that that is exactly what he was.

Randy called out, "Thanks, Josiah. If I'm not back in a week, go to the Saw Mill Inn and tell them to store our things. We'll collect them later." Then he clicked to his paint and Hayden followed. Her horse was anxious and darted ahead of Randy's mount.

This is going to be a very long night. Randy thought to himself. "You have to rein him in or he'll get the better of you."

She cast him a look of defiance and kicked Josiah's belly, making him leap and snort.

Chapter Seventeen

Kayra

Kayra set the journal aside. It was now too dark to continue, but she had gotten the information she needed. Her red-rimmed eyes blurred again at the thought.

The father of Fineese's baby was not William, but his father. *How? He'd seemed like such a good man. How could he betray Ingrid that way?* She could picture the lovely woman's smile as she went about her chores.

He'd certainly fooled her. Did his family know? What would happen if they ever found out? Fineese had loved him and thought that Gregor had loved her too.

She wrote about the way he surprised her with trinkets. He'd been like a father to Fineese in many ways. Fineese had never really had one. Then, he'd devastated her when he'd found out she was carrying his child.

Her thoughts were interrupted by Annie's call. "Kayra, come quick."

Jumping to her feet, Kayra ran to the wagon. Outside, the baby lay sleeping in a basket near the fire. Harce was nowhere to be found. Annie was inside holding Fineese's limp hand.

Kayra climbed in and took her place at Fineese's side. Her breathing was shallow and nearly rattled. Her dull eyes found Kayra's as she placed a hand on hers. Sobs escaped Kayra's chest.

It was time she accepted that Fineese was dying.

"She asked for you." Annie silently slipped from the wagon.

Kayra laid down beside her friend and cuddled her weak body. She stroked her hair and wept for the girl at her side. She wept for the tortured life that she had lived, that she wouldn't get to see Michael take his first steps or ride a horse, and for the pain and suffering she was fighting now.

After a while, Fineese opened her mouth. No sound came out.

Kayra smoothed her brow and told her what she needed to hear. "It's alright. Michael will know how much you loved him. He will know what a wonderful person you were." She struggled to make her own voice heard and fought the ache building in her throat. "I will love him as if he were my own. I'll protect him and he will be so special to me and Hayden."

Kayra tasted the salty tears that had found their way into her mouth. She sniffed to keep her nose from running. *Stop bawling,* she told herself but she couldn't.

She needed to make this easy for Fineese. It wasn't about her. She pulled the woman into her embrace and whispered in her ear. "We love you Fineese, all of us, me, Michael, Annie, Harce, Hayden, and Randy."

Fineeese's lips turned up in the corners, just slightly. Then she closed her dark eyes and took her last rattling breath. It's a harrowing thing to witness, the moment of death. So Kayra cried, helpless to the grief. She held Fineese in her arms, willing her to wake up. It had all happened so fast. The loss hurt more than she thought that it could.

She climbed from the wagon and looked up at the sky. It felt like night had come suddenly. She walked to the basket where Michael slept. She traced the ridge of his tiny nose. "Your mama was a great woman, Michael. And she loved us very much."

Annie came to her and pulled Kayra into an embrace. "There, there. Harce is digging a grave, over by the oaks. We have to figure out how to feed this little guy."

The thought hadn't even entered Kayra's mind. They had no milk, and no animal to get it from.

"Annie, what do we do?"

"You'll need to take your son and try to spoon feed him the broth we been cooking. If he keeps it down, he'll be alright, if not we'll think of something else. Grand Junction is close now."

Kayra stared at her old friend. *My son*, she thought. *I have a son.* William's brother. Oh the irony. She'd been entrusted to care for someone who was a part of the man that she loved and would never see again. God had brought William into her life after all.

Michael fussed. She lifted him from the basket and kissed the top of his downy head. He was very much like Will. Soft blond tufts of hair stuck up like a baby duck, and his skin was darker than Fineese's.

"Loving you won't be hard at all."

Randy

Randy and Hayden flew through the trees in search of the trail leading back into the Rockies. He knew the direction they were headed, so they'd cut through a forest to save time.

Hayden was quiet and Randy was glad for the silence. Randy was scared. A man who was wanted and hunted, fled. They laid low till things cooled. Even vengeful men were smart enough to wait till the time to strike. Greely was an exception to all the rules. If he were headed back up the mountain, then his need for revenge was more powerful than man's instinctive need for self-preservation. If a man wasn't concerned with saving himself, then what was there to stop him from doing anything he wanted?

The trees opened and the foreboding shadows of the Rockies loomed ahead. The night was so dark that tracking Greely at this point would have been impossible. Randy could barely make out the well worn path. He let his horse find the way and trusted the animal to stay on course.

After hours of steady climbing in the dark, Hayden broke the silence. "Randy I can't see a thing."

"Trust your horse. They see better at night than we can." As the words fell from his lips, his horse stumbled. Hayden screamed. Randy righted himself and patted his horse's neck.

"Well, usually they see better than we do. We're on the trail. I don't want to stop. Greely's been running for hours. He's bound to rest and if we are to catch him before…"

"I know. We can't stop. Let's just get to them." With that, she clicked to her horse and came up beside Randy.

Her beautiful soft voice was barely above a whisper. "What if we're too late?"

The question made Randy's jaw tighten. He would never forgive himself if that were the case. If Greely had outsmarted him and killed Kayra, he'd never be able to look himself in the mirror again. That woman was too pure and good to even think about the possibility of that monster finding her first.

He had to believe that they would get to her first. Not only for her sake, but he had to protect Hayden from losing anyone else.

"We won't be too late." He assured her with confidence he didn't feel.

Just before sunrise, Randy allowed them to break near a stream. Hayden didn't recognize the terrain. She slid from her horse and when her feet touched the ground, her knees buckled. She fell in a pile on the crackling grass. Her horse whinnied and Randy was at her side helping her to her feet. She leaned on his arm until she felt secure again.

"Sorry, that'll happen when you aren't used to riding long stretches."

Hayden turned her face, but not before Randy saw the look in her eye. It was a kick to his gut. He knew he was pushing them but he had to.

"I'll stretch a bit." She walked past him to nowhere.

Randy's shoulders shrunk. Maybe she wanted a break from him. Did he even blame her? Kayra and Fineese were in serious danger, as well as the rest of the wagon train and it was his fault. If only he'd not gone after Greely. If they hadn't followed him uselessly, then he would be there to protect everyone when Greely returned. He had to fix this.

Hayden drank greedy gulps from the stream. Then, she found a private place to go to the bathroom. The task was harder than she imagined in the gigantic gown. When she finished, she walked back to Randy who'd led the horses to drink.

"If the wagon train is coming this way, as quickly as they intended to travel, then we should cross them sometime today."

"Really?" Hayden's eyes beamed with hope. "Then, let's get moving."

He'd never met any woman like her. She was dog tired, but determined, ready as ever to do what needed to be done. That was a quality he respected. Dark circles hugged her eyes. If only he could hold her and let her rest in his arms for a while.

"You know if you took off that corset and petticoat, you'd be much more comfortable."

Hayden stared at him like he'd grown a second head.

He continued, "You've got to be miserable."

She put a hand to her waist, then nodded. "I am. It's awful. I'll need help with the buttons though." With near shyness, she turned her back to him.

He accomplished the task with great speed. She slipped out of the petticoat under her dress and held the bodice of her gown to her chest as he undid the corset. Deep lines etched her skin showing him how truly painful the garment must be. His finger traced the lines on her back.

"That should be better." He turned away, allowing Hayden privacy to slip the corset from around her sides and arrange herself back in the dress.

He buttoned the gown only hesitating briefly at the sight of her bare back. When she was dressed, she turned.

Randy's eyes filled with tears. "I'm so sorry that I let him slip by. I'm gonna stop him before he gets to them. I promise."

She went into his arms, pulling him to her. "You can't promise that. I never should have left her. This is my fault."

Randy raised an eyebrow, disbelieving what he heard. "Hayden, none of this is your fault. I'm the one sworn to protect folks, not you."

"No," She corrected, "I am the one who protects Kayra. She needs me. She can't handle the big stuff by herself."

Randy chose his words carefully. "Kayra isn't as weak as you think. If she has to, she'll take care of things. Look at how she's handled Fineese. Choosing to help a girl in Fineese's situation, that takes a lot of gumption. And look at the way she's handled the trail, driving a wagon alone, keeping up with all the work. I know that you've always been there for her, but she's very capable."

Hayden's expression changed. Randy couldn't take the time to figure out what was going on in her head. Hopefully his comments hadn't upset her. "We have to go."

She nodded and released him. "Let's do it."

Kayra

The sun rose and Kayra breathed a sigh of relief at a new day. They'd fed little Michael from a cloth they'd knotted and dipped in broth giving him something to suck. He awkwardly gnawed at it. Apparently, he'd gotten some of the broth in his belly because he threw it up for hours afterwards.

They thinned it and tried again. He eagerly took hold of the cloth nipple, only to throw that up too. Annie then brought out tea leaves to try. It pacified for a while. Kayra had watched him most of the night, afraid he'd start gagging and she wouldn't wake up.

Finally, he slept. Taking advantage of the solitude the early morning provided, she strolled to her friend's fresh grave. Harce had dug it and he and Annie had buried her during the night. They were exhausted, but she couldn't have gotten through this without them.

Kayra sat by the grave and prayed. "Dear God, be merciful on Fineese's soul. She did the best she knew how. No one taught her and she sought you out. She's led me to you. Lord, be with the Mayer family. There is so much there that they are bound to discover. Guide their paths. Help William to be the rock for those children, for his mother. Thank you Lord for putting people in my life who've shown you to me, for William, Finneese, Harce and Annie. Thank you for Hayden, she's a mess, a beautiful mess. Guide her so that she'll want to know you too. Let her open her heart to more than me. Finally God, show me the way. I'm so afraid. There's so much I need to do. Help me to help Michael. In Jesus' name, amen."

When she opened her eyes, the sky was brilliant, exploding in color over the mountaintops. *God is showing himself now*, she thought.

Harce and Annie climbed from their rig. Still bent from the few blessed hours of sleep they'd gotten, they hobbled around finding their feet.

Kayra came to hers. She'd never been more sure of what she was about to do but she couldn't put it off another moment. In the commotion of Fineese's unplanned delivery and the excitement with Michael, she'd let her spiritual concerns take a back seat. Now, beside Fineese's grave she realized there was no promise of tomorrow.

She plucked a stem of sweet yellow clover from a clump nearby and laid it on her friend's grave. "I wish you'd been given more time." She kissed her fingers and pressed it to the wooden cross that would be Fineese's lasting marker.

She smiled and strode to where Harce was building a fire. "I'm ready, right now. To be baptized like we talked about." Kayra bit her lip waiting for his reaction.

Annie shouted, raising her hands to the heavens. "Praise the Lord, honey. He's been waiting for this."

The three of them walked to the river. Annie set Michael's basket on the bank and sniffled as Kayra and Harce stepped into the chilly water. Kayra's teeth chattered as she followed the small, old man.

When the water danced around her waist she held her hands to her mouth and bounced in place while Harce explained how he would baptize her. She nodded her understanding and covered her mouth, plugging her nose.

"Kayra, because of your belief in Jesus Christ as the son of God and your desire to receive his gift of salvation from sin, I now baptize you in the name of the Father and the son and the Holy Spirit for the forgiveness of your sins."

One of his hands was under her head and his other across her shoulders. She closed her eyes and felt the flowing water run over her whole body. When she came up out of the stream she grinned from ear to ear. She hugged Harce. "Thank you for showing me the way. I knew that I wanted to be right with God, but didn't know how. You and Annie have changed my life for eternity. I can never thank you enough."

He wiggled his nose to keep back the tears that welled in his eyes. "God did all the work, you just had to be willing to receive his blessing."

As she emerged from the water Annie ran forward, wrapping her in a tight embrace. Kayra giggled, squeezing back. "You're a member of the Lord's church now, how does it feel honey?"

Kayra wrung the water out of her long chocolate hair. "It feels almost like coming home. I feel free." She couldn't stop smiling.

Disgruntled, Michael started to fuss. Kayra lifted her skirt and hurried to him. His tiny mouth vibrated as his chest rose and fell with his furious, clenched fists. How demanding he already was.

Despite everything that had happened the last few days, she felt peace, finally. In her wildest dreams she never imagined that she would have to deliver a baby, but she had. She was more confident than ever before and even though she had no idea how she was going to feed the little guy, she trusted that God would show her a way. He was on her side.

Randy

Hayden picked out Greely's tracks as soon as they could see. How was it possible that she'd found them before he had? He was a tracker, a lawman. He had years of practice. The prints led off the main trail and up the mountain along a narrow path. The main trail was the fastest way to meet up with the wagon train. But Greely had taken the mountain path. They headed in the direction the tracks led.

The sun had barely been up when Randy spotted two of Foster's scouts. He couldn't contain his smile as he galloped their direction, Hayden right behind him.

The two men shook his hand, nodding to Hayden. "We thought that you two would be in town by now."

"We were," Randy explained, "but Greely doubled back so we're tracking him again."

The two men exchanged a somber look. The older one folded his hands across the saddle horn. "We found those folks you buried."

Randy nodded. "He hasn't tried anything with the wagon train yet?"

"Not that we seen. We left early to find a camp for tonight."

Randy sighed his relief. A glance at Hayden showed the vast weight that had just been lifted from her. He wanted to hug her. Instead, he held out his hand. Hayden reached for it and squeezed, smiling at their luck at having gotten there ahead of Greely.

"That's wonderful." Hayden piped up. "I can't wait to see Kayra. How far back are they?"

The two men exchanged another look that set very badly with Randy.

"Uh, Mrs. Kayra and her group...they didn't come in last night."

Randy's harsh voice thundered. "What do you mean, 'Kayra and her group'?"

"Well they was comin' in kinda slow like and we was travelin' faster 'en before. That woman with her was feelin' poorly, so they was takin' their time. E'ry night they'd make it into camp with us, but..."

The other man spoke up. "Last night they didn't. I wanted to go back for them or at least wait, but Foster said we couldn't waste anymore time."

Randy and Hayden stared at the men. *How could this happen?* Foster had led several groups west. First rule, stay together. Here they had ridden all this way and found the group before Greely had, just to discover that the train had abandoned their friends to what, make better time?

"You," Randy pointed to the less seasoned fellow, "Head back for the group and tell them that Greely is here. Make sure that Foster knows I'll be dealing with him when I get back." The threat hung between them.

"I'd like to help you, Randy." The other man said.

Randy nodded. "Hayden, you'll go back with the train. I'll get you as soon as I can. You'll be safer there. Greely's gripe isn't with them."

Hayden's regal air of superiority dared anyone challenge her. "I won't do it. I'm going after Kayra."

Randy looked at her. "Can you not fight me on one single thing? Please." His eyes beseeched her to understand.

"Have I slowed you down?" Randy shook his head reluctantly. "And who found Greely's tracks?"

Randy considered her arguments. He saw the deep set of her jaw and the firm hold she had on her horse. If he sent her on, he'd have to restrain her to accomplish the task, and she would undoubtedly sneak off in the night and come after him anyway. If he agreed to bring her, he could at least keep an eye on her.

"Agggh." He growled at her. "You can come. But you do what I say, no matter what." Hayden nodded.

The scout interrupted his thoughts. "We didn't leave the girls alone. Harce and Annie stayed back with them."

Randy's clipped tone left little to be said. "I don't imagine either of them will be much good against Greely, do you?"

The man said nothing.

Randy loaded a gun and handed it to Hayden. "Use this if you need to. But if you shoot, it's to kill, don't hesitate."

Hayden nodded, taking the pistol. The threesome galloped through the mountain-pass headed for Kayra and Fineese.

Chapter Eighteen

Greely

Greely squatted behind an outcropping of rock, watching the two wagons in the valley.

He'd found Kayra alone, or nearly so, and it tickled him to think of what would come next. That old man would be no trouble when the time came. He'd been fumbling the past hour. Only, Greely was worn out. The last few days of running and hunting people had him blinking his eyes just to see straight. He was a jumble now of exhaustion, and excitement.

When he'd ridden up in the night and found that Kayra was alive he was giddy.

He'd taken her on a whim, but once he held her struggling against him, he'd fallen in love. Who knew that love was a real thing? He wanted her more than any woman before.

Now he would finally have her. He'd keep her too, always.

Why had it taken him so long to notice her? He hadn't paid her any mind until she wandered from the fire that night, but seeing her alone, her figure outlined in the orange glow, it was as if she had drawn him to her. She'd screamed for help before he could cover her mouth and that deputy had heard. Some day he'd catch that waste of a man and he'd be sorry he ever heard of Sam Greely.

Ever since that night he'd been obsessed with the image of the girl he had almost taken. He wasn't planning on coming back for Fineese when he headed toward Grand Junction, but his mind just snapped at the memory of Kayra and what he had lost by having to toss her aside in order to get away. He shouldn't have done that. He didn't know if she could forgive him for letting her go. Once he had her again, he'd explain why he'd done it.

He shook his head to stay awake. These two wagons weren't going anywhere and he wanted to be able to clearly see the look on Kayra's face when she realized he'd come for her. She should be as happy as he was, and if she wasn't, time would teach her.

Kayra

Kayra had fed Michael the tea and was tearing strips of cloth to make diapers. She was surprisingly happy as she worked. She let Harce and Annie rest, taking over the chores of making a fire and making their breakfast. They deserved the break. Harce had changed and laid his wet clothes out to dry alongside Kayra's skirt and blouse.

She had so much to tell Hayden and after all the awful things that had gone on, two beautiful things had happened that meant new life. God sure must be smiling down on her.

Tushon

Tushon, Powai and Emat crept along the ridgeway of rocks leading to their prey. They were silent as they approached. After tracking the white man who had disgraced and killed Tushon's wife, they had finally caught up. And there he was. That disgusting muskrat of a man with his putrid odor was asleep on the cleft of a rock. That hidden overlook gave him a perfect view of the valley a hundred feet below where a couple of wagons camped.

Powai motioned toward the meadow. He held up three fingers, made the symbol for a man and held up one. Tushon watched as the women entered and exited one of the wagons.

The sun was setting. Why was this white man, whom they called 'Wicked One,' asleep? Why was he there at all? Tushon assumed that his intention was for the dark-haired woman. The other was old, but if that were his plan, why had he waited and not killed them already and taken his prize?

The three braves stepped away to talk, and it was Emat who pointed out how tired 'wicked one' had to be. Although he was hidden from the valley and the mountain above, it was foolish to sleep during the day. Perhaps he was drunk. A man only slept that hard if he was at peace, drunk, or crazy.

Powai told Tushon, "Kill him before he wakes up and hurts those people. They are harmless. It would be a good thing to do."

Emat disagreed. "There is no honor in killing a sleeping man."

Powai raised his eyebrows, shrugging his shoulders. "Then wake him."

Tushon made the final decision. "I will wait. I want him to be able to look into my eyes and see who is spilling his blood. I will go and cleanse myself. You two, keep watch. If he wakes up and I must return, signal me."

The two braves nodded. Tushon padded silently away. He would spend time with the Creator, cleansing himself in the traditional way. If the Great Spirit were to bless his retribution, he'd need to perform the rituals that would bring along that blessing.

It was nearing dawn when Tushon re-emerged. The faint hint of day was beginning to show across the horizon. He jaggedly cut his long hair. It was greased, slick against his head. He'd painted his face and felt strong. The Great Spirit would bless him now. He had been right to cleanse his soul first.

"The wicked one slept through the night." Powai said. "We found the black horse. It's just there, by the quaking aspens. It walks in circles without stopping."

Tushon nodded, determined to complete his task. Gazing into the valley he watched the woman near to his Kachine's age trying to feed a baby.

Emat spoke up. "A child was born. That is a good omen, when new life comes as one leaves."

"The baby is not hers." Powai told him. "They buried the mother."

Tushon was thoughtful, "It's time."

The two braves came to their feet. Tushon held his hand out, halting them from coming along. "I will do this alone and I will avenge Kachine, or I will die, but this is my task."

Tushon crept across the mountain. His feet made no sound as they padded over the dry hillside.

The foul odor of the white man met Tushon's nostrils before his eyes found him. The wicked one was waking up.

Tushon watched as he peed near where he'd slept. Even animals found a different spot to relieve themselves. This man was worse than an animal. He killed without reason. Tushon felt the pang of anger rise in his chest like the sun was doing now.

The wicked one still had no idea he was being watched. He laid on his belly like a snake watching the valley. With a slow motion, he grabbed the rifle that had been resting beside him and aimed.

Tushon was not about to let this wicked man take another life. In one motion Tushon leapt, landing on Greely's back. The gun fired twice. They could not see the valley below as the two men rolled on the outcropping of rock. Tushon smacked the weapon out of the wicked one's hands. It scudded across the ledge landing by a pine tree.

The wicked one flailed back and forth trying to free himself. Tushon held on, refusing to let go. His dark hands felt the soft supple neck of the man that had taken his wife. He encircled that throat, squeezing, choking.

But the wicked one was strong. Stronger than Tushon had expected. With Tushon clinging to his body, the white man stood up like a bear. As one, they staggered away from the ledge, toward an enormous boulder. Tushon felt waves of crushing pain as the wicked one slammed his body against the granite. Again and again, Tushon was crushed between the stone and the weight of the man he hated, but he held fast to the wicked one's thick neck, hoping the Creator would hear his thoughts and give him strength.

When Tushon could no longer feel breath coming from the wicked one's body, he let go, falling to the ground. The big man collapsed as well, both men gasped for air.

Tushon was first to hop to his feet. He roared and ran toward the wicked one who leapt up with the agility of a much younger man. He raised a beefy hand, pounding Tushon in the chest. It knocked the wind out of him. He was momentarily frozen from the staggering impact and the wicked one swept his leg out from under him, sending Tushon to land with a thud on his back.

He still could not breathe. With one hand, the big man held Tushon's wrist, the other hand twisted his leg in a direction contrary to human anatomy. Tushon felt his knee give as it smacked against the ground. Blinding pain surged through his body. When his vision cleared, Tushon saw the silvery glint of a blade flash in front of him.

Was it finished? There was nowhere to go. He could not retreat. His body ignored all commands to move quickly. All he could do was brace himself as cold sharp steel pressed against his neck.

No! No. He would not die like this. He was a mighty warrior. Kachine's murderer would not take his life too. Adrenaline spiked and gave him breath. He threw his head back. His skull smacked against the wicked one's face. The force gave him a dizzying throb and he shut his eyes tightly at the crunch of cartilage. The knife clanked to the ground.

Tushon broke from the wicked one's grip and clutched at the tomahawk hanging from his pants, raising it in his right hand. It was time.

The wicked one was stronger and crazier than Tushon had given him credit. When he first arrived, he had planned to kill him with his hands, but now he realized he needed to be content with killing him quickly.

Tushon struggled to stand. His leg screamed against him as he raised himself to his full height. He strode forward dragging the leg behind him. The white man scurried like a mouse toward the rifle that had earlier been tossed aside. Tushon threw his tomahawk. It sailed head over end, landing mid back in the wicked one. He gasped and grunted at the shock. The handle was all you could see as the man's back colored with bright red blood. Tushon exhaled his breath. Surely, it was now over.

The wicked one stumbled forward. Blood spilled from his mouth. Still he whistled, a shrill eerie sound. With heavy, staggering steps, he made his way to a steep trail leading to the valley below. Tushon watched with a mixture of awe and horror as the wicked one refused to die. Instead, he stumbled away.

Tushon's leg drug behind him as he followed. The putrid man persevered down the switchback like a wounded grizzly intent on getting to his den. They had named him well. The wicked one. Was he an evil spirit?

From out of nowhere, a big black horse galloped to the white man. It was the crazy animal that had fled up the side of a mountain carrying the wicked one and Kachine from the Indian camp the day before. Tushon felt fury rise in his chest. If this evil man got away again, it would dishonor the death of his wife.

If only he could run, and lunge at this wicked one, but his head pounded and his leg wouldn't cooperate. He could barely think. The wicked one was escaping. The Great Spirit had not blessed him today. Tushon could not stop this beast heading for the valley. The wicked one was atop his horse disappearing from his sight before Tushon could shout.

A woman's shrill scream sounded. Had Kachine sounded like that? Tushon grabbed his leg, forcing it into place. He yelled out in agony, but managed to limp ahead.

When he entered the field. The wicked one was off his horse, staggering forward, his arms extended in front of him. He plodded toward the dark-haired woman, choking on the words he called out, "I came for you."

An infant wailed in the distance. That woman, with blood covering her, shoulder to belly, raised a rifle to her shoulder. She cried out in pain as she did it.

The wicked one gagged on the blood that ran down his chin spewing like a fountain from his mouth. The dark-haired woman screamed again. A shot echoed off of the rocks behind him. Finally, the wicked one collapsed with a thud at her feet.

She had completed his task. He was at peace with her victory.

Chapter Nineteen

Kayra

Greely thundered to the ground. His remains lay in the golden meadow, blood drenching the earth below him.

Kayra dropped the rifle and collapsed. She had nothing left. At least now they would die by someone other than Greely. The world was slipping away. Michael cried and Annie wailed somewhere behind the fog in her mind.

Someone lifted Kayra into their tanned arms and carried her to where Greely lay. It was the Indian that had come out of nowhere. He tore a strip from the bottom of her dress and wound it around her shoulder. It ached, as if there was a blade in her arm. He was pressing the wound sending shocks through her that wracked her whole body. Why was he bothering with her shoulder? He was just going to kill her. She teetered in and out of consciousness. *I have to stay awake. Please.*

Two other Indians appeared. They ransacked the wagons. Kayra heard Annie. Was she crying? No, she was humming. Kayra fought against herself to see the older woman. Annie rocked back and forth, Harce's silver head in her lap. Would they kill her too?

One of the Indians was holding Michael. His staccato cries reverberated through the valley. If they were going to die, she wanted to be the last face Michael saw, but she couldn't move. When she opened her eyes, a horrible red striped face stared back at her. She could feel the hot breath escaping from his brown lips. His hands held her shoulders to the ground. He was saying something soft, repeating it over and over. What were those words? He raised her to a sitting position and forced her hand around a blade. Was he going to make her kill herself?

She hadn't the strength to fight it. He guided her hand to Greely's head. She tried to pull away but the man's calm words, purred in her ear. She would be doing whatever he wanted. He held her fingers over the knife and pressed the blade. He sliced Greely's head then shook the knife from her grip. He took her fingers and forced them to grip Greely's hair. Greasy, warm, wet blood bathed his locks. Understanding what the Indian wanted her to do, she seized his hair and ripped the scalp from Greely's skull. Tushon threw his head back and let out a warrior whoop. Kayra closed her eyes, tears spilling down her face.

Tushon raised her hand in the air holding the scalp. His friends cheered like wild animals. Then, he carried Kayra to his horse and hefted her up in front of him. They were taking her. No!

"Michael," She cried. "Michael!"

Tushon motioned to his companion who had crudely tied the infant to his chest. Kayra didn't like the way he was being carried, but he was being taken along. She closed her eyes and fell into the oblivion of sleep.

◆← →◆

Randy

Hayden, Randy, and the scout were making steady progress when they heard the distant sound of a rifle. Twice it went off. Randy and Hayden exchanged a terrified look before Hayden hollered and kicked her horse into a jolting speed.

Randy was close behind her, gun drawn. The horses charged wildly through the trees jumping rocks and dodging limbs.

They rode for what seemed like an eternity until they came to the valley where Annie sat. A large figure lay on the ground. He recognized the hefty form as Greely's. Randy slid from his horse to the man's lifeless body. He'd been shot in the face. He'd also been scalped. It had to be Indians, but the tribes in these parts didn't allow their braves to use firearms. Randy recognized the familiar way that the Cetewas scalped.

There were three basic shapes that this band used for marking the conquered. Each method was directly related to the worth of the person being scalped. If one was found to be a worthy opponent, then their scalps were taken in a triangle. If they were weak, the scalp was taken in a large circle. The last method was reserved for only the most despicable. A man was scalped from crown to neck, as Greely was now, only when they were betrayers or criminals. How had the warrior known Greely's transgressions?

"It's him isn't it?" Hayden slid from Josiah's back and started forward. Randy came to block her view of Greely's mangled head.

"It's him alright, but you don't need to see it." He tried taking her in his arms but she shoved him away. "Hayden, don't," He warned.

Ignoring his plea, Hayden darted past him and stopped short. The blood drained from her face. She staggered away.

"Kayra, where is she?"

Hayden's wild eyes darted in unsteady circles, scanning for danger. Her hand still held the pistol that Randy had given her earlier in the day. She stepped away from Greely's body, pointing her gun in front of her. He knew better than to touch her.

"Hayden, look at me." Randy spoke with a quiet, slow voice. She stared but he didn't think she heard his words.

"Hayden. Put down your gun, sweetheart."

With terrible timing, the scout rode in, shattering the calm that Randy was trying to create. Hayden spun at the sound of the approaching rider and aimed.

"Hayden, no." Randy dove, knocking the gun from her hand before she fired.

Stunned, Hayden stared at the man on top of her. Randy saw recognition enter her eyes. Relief washed over him. She was back, but the reality of the situation wasn't good. It was her worst fear, after all.

He helped her to her feet. And yelled to the scout to check on Annie.

Randy was quick to retrieve Hayden's gun. "I don't have answers right now, but I will. Are you with me now?"

Hayden nodded.

Annie's feeble figure sat in the grass. She rocked back and forth holding Harce's upper body in her lap. There was no sign of Kayra or Fineese.

If only Hayden had stayed with the wagon train. How was he going to tell her what he feared? He knew a bit about the tribe he suspected. They weren't known to hurt people without reason. Hopefully he was right. If Kayra and Fineese had been taken, it was likely that little harm would come to them by the hand of their captors.

Randy approached the old woman cautiously before crouching beside her. Annie shook her head and held out a hand to stop Randy from coming closer. She managed a cracked whisper in his direction, "Kayra's hurt. Shot in the back. They took them. Her and the baby."

"Who? Who took Kayra?" Randy urged.

Annie shook her head, gasping for breath, before falling into her husband's neck in sobs.

The scout went to one of the wagons and grabbed a shovel. He walked to where a fresh mound lay and began digging beside it. *Fineese must be in that grave.*

After convincing Annie to let him take Harce's body over to where the grave was being dug, Randy came back to face Hayden. He sat beside her on the ground. Her shoulders slumped. Dark circles ringed her eyes like a raccoon. Her dress was streaked with dirt and sweat. Her fancy hair fell from its pins in wispy tangles. The light in her eyes was dim and Randy feared it would go out altogether when she heard what he was about to say.

He knelt in front of her. "Hayden, you know I love you." She tried to smile but the sides of her lips wouldn't cooperate. "There are still some things about each other that we don't know." She looked at him, suspicious. "I was trying to tell you before the auction but time was short. I have to tell you now. And this isn't how I wanted to."

He sat Indian style. This was as hard as he figured it would be. She stared, silent, waiting. Reaching over she took his hand in hers. The tender gesture made it difficult for Randy to find his voice. When he did, it croaked and scratched.

"Hayden, I... My dad..."

Interrupting, Hayden came to her knees resting on her haunches, her face level with his. She took his other hand in hers. "I've been sitting here, thinking. We don't even know if Kayra is alive. And you can't promise me that you will save her."

Randy shook his head. "I'm pretty certain she's alive."

"But we don't know for sure. The point is, I'm afraid. I'm afraid that Kayra is lost. I'm afraid that Fineese is hurt, but I'm not afraid of you. You are the one thing that has been solid, protecting me through this. I have to say it and you have to believe me. I love you."

Randy shook his head. "I have to tell you..."

"It doesn't matter. Whatever you have to say won't make me love you any less."

His eyes locked with hers. The drum that beat in his chest made him painfully aware of his heritage. She said it wouldn't matter but he knew it would. His voice was lost. He tilted his face and Hayden leaned in. This time was different from all their previous kisses. The usual stirring of raw attraction was there, but beside it simmered a deep, ingrained devotion born of love. For a few brief moments the world only consisted of two lovers clinging to each other in the breath of morning.

How could he tell her now? He lowered his face. "I'm going after Kayra. Fineese died last night after having a son. Some Indians took Kayra and the baby with them."

A flicker of hate sprung into her eyes. He knew its source.

His pulse surged. "You will return to the wagon train with Annie and the scout. I won't hear an argument." Her brows scrunched together but she didn't fight it. "I think that I can...buy Kayra back. I'll need to take your horse and mine as well. They're fine animals and the Cetewas respect a man's mount almost as much as a bride. I will talk to whoever took her and when she's well enough, we will meet you in Grand Junction."

"What do you mean, when she's well enough?" Hayden held her breath.

Randy ran a hand through his black hair. She was not going to take this well either. "Annie said that she was shot in the back before she was taken."

"That murdering savage. I ..."

"Hayden, Greely had to have been the one to shoot her. This Indian wouldn't have done it. Cetewa seek justice over wrongs done to them, but they don't hurt people unprovoked. I'm not sure why they took her, but they took the time to wrap her shoulder before they did, so they don't mean to harm her. Cetewas are a good tribe. She will be healed before anything else happens, and if he has plans to marry her, then they will treat her as well as they would any other family member. Since she's been shot there really is no better place for her than with them. They're known for their healers."

"How will you talk to them? They'll kill you before you get a chance to explain." She spoke the fears of her heart. "What if I lose both of you?"

Randy took a deep breath. "No, they won't."

"How can you know that?"

He dipped his head. "I speak a similar dialect to theirs. Someone in their tribe will be able to communicate with me." He sighed. "Everything that I have told you has been true. My mother is from England, but my father is...my father was half-white and half-Cheyenne. I favor my mother's fair skin but I'm Indian too."

Hayden

Hayden blinked in rapid succession. She fought to keep her face from spilling out all the emotions coursing through her brain. For the first time, she noticed how black Randy's hair was and how wide his cheekbones set. She saw the ebony eyes, like coal and wondered how she could not have guessed it before. That explained a lot. That must have been why he was so quick to defend the evil ways of the Indians, of his people. She was stunned. She'd said that whatever he told her wouldn't make a difference, so why did she feel betrayed?

She released his hands and came to her feet. "If you can get my cousin back, do whatever needs to be done. I imagine that the sooner you head out the better."

Randy remained seated in the grass, looking up at Hayden. She avoided his eyes. It would take time for her to adjust to this new information, but time was a novelty they had little of.

Hastily, he came to his feet and walked past her to her horse. He grabbed the reins and yanked the animal to follow. He went to his own horse and lithely lifted himself into the saddle.

He was a powerful sight. His dark eyes guarded, lips trembling, the only sign of his emotional state. Hayden wanted to run to him, assure him that they would be fine but she didn't. He rode to her and paused. She averted her eyes, hiding.

"I love you, Hayden. I'll do my best to bring Kayra and the baby back to you."

Biting her lip, she nodded.

"Hayden, I'm still the same man I was yesterday and I will be the same man tomorrow."

Hayden forced a smile. "I know. Be safe...and come back to me. I'll be waiting." She forced her eyes to his. Relief rushed through his gaze.

"I will." He clicked to the horses and raced into the mountains. Hayden stared long after he'd disappeared over the ridge.

"Please God, bring them back."

Chapter Twenty

Kayra

The aroma of boiled venison tickled Kayra's nose. Somewhere close by, children laughed. What wonderful sensations. An animal was keeping her warm. Fur tickled her neck. A cool breeze blew on her shoulder. She moved her arm, pulling the skin further across her chest. When she did, horrific pain shot through her upper body. An agonized cry escaped her lips. Opening her eyes, she realized that she was not in the wagon with Fineese.

Oh no. Fineese. Michael! The memory ascended upon her like a bird of prey. Panic encouraged her to sit, though when she tried, the sharp pain that ran down her back and arm sent her back against a fur mat.

A young girl with soft eyes and flowing black hair was at her side. She called out something that Kayra didn't understand and smiled. She spoke abrupt, guttural words.

A heavy-set woman with skin the color of creamed coffee cheered, holding her hands in the air as she walked into the tent. It was then that Kayra realized where she was. She was in a teepee, but why she was here and why everyone seemed so happy to see her awake was unclear.

The woman knelt beside her, stroking her hair. She wasn't an old woman but Kayra doubted she had a child as young as the girl who'd been there when she awoke. Perhaps she was the child's grandmother.The girl asked something and the woman nodded enthusiastically. The child raced away hollering. Before Kayra knew it, the small space was full of women and children.

It was very confusing, but not scary. The people obviously meant her no harm. Still, she could only think of her son.

"Michael?" She implored, searching the older woman's kind eyes.

The woman spoke "Haika Tanpa, Haika Tanpa."

A girl younger than Kayra stepped out in front of the crowd. Baby Michael's white face sucked greedily from beneath the woman's leather shirt.

Tears filled Kayra's eyes. He was eating and so much bigger. How long had she been asleep, and why was she here?

A gruff voice sounded outside the teepee and the crowd of women and children made a hasty exit. Only the older lady and Kayra remained in the shadowy space. The woman chattered as she pulled the skin covering down to Kayra's waist. Gently, she rolled Kayra onto her side and peeled back a bandage. The woman went through a bag and removed a hunk of some thin sticky web like threads. Then she took a small bowl and dumped sumac in it. She mixed the two things together and called, "Tushon!"

A man entered the teepee. He observed Kayra with penetrating eyes that made her want to hide. The cadence of his speech made Kayra's head bob up and down.

The man and woman laughed when they noticed what she was doing. Kayra felt her face burn as they carried on their conversation. The woman spread a hot mixture on

Kayra's back. Kayra darted her eyes at her nurse. The woman clucked her disapproval and held Kayra in place until it cooled. Then she stood and walked from the tent.

Alone in the darkness with the intimidating man before her, Kayra was fearful for the first time and incredibly aware that she was naked under the animal skin.

The solid man patted his chest. "Tushon."

Kayra understood and said, "Kayra."

He shook his head. Pointing at her. "Kachine."

Kayra shook her head. "No, Kayra." She insisted.

He strode towards her. Emphatically, he patted his chest. "Tushon." Then pointed at her again. "Kachine."

Kayra understood that he intended to call her what he wished and decided not to push the issue.

"Kachine." She conceded.

A wide grin spread across his face to reveal straight white teeth. He went behind her, inspecting her back. When he removed the fur, he inspected her naked body as well. She felt her skin flush. Seeing the redness in her cheeks, Tushon laughed. He mocked her? She closed her eyes, humiliated. He returned the fur to her body and left.

Randy

It had taken Randy nearly three weeks to locate the Cetewas that had taken Kayra. They had released two horses in a direction opposite their path and he had stupidly followed the wrong animals. It galled him to have made such a foolish error and that had cost him valuable time. With each sunset he feared that he would be too late. His chances of getting her back without violence diminished with each sunrise. Finally he crested a hill overlooking the Montrose valley and spied the group he'd been seeking.

Cold wind whipped against his face. He sniffed, watching the women scurry about the camp preparing skins and storing fat for the winter ahead. This band of Cetewas was small in number. Only ten teepees were erected in the field. A few old men sat in a circle around a large fire. The young men must be out hunting. It was the time of year to hunt before snow set in. The familiar sight stirred him.

He was no stranger to a camp like this. His father had taken him along to trade furs and to visit his family many times. As a boy, he'd loved the trips and played happily with his cousins, but as he got older it became harder and harder to feel at home among his people.

He felt more white than he felt Cetewa. It wasn't his light complexion that set him apart, but annual visits weren't enough to make him feel a part of the tribe. He knew the customs, the dialect.

He respected their ways, but he didn't truly fit in. He'd not been back to visit in three years. Seeing the activity below him, feelings of a home he loved but never fully fit into stirred in his gut.

Kayra

Kayra sat on her knees curing Tushon's hides as best she could. The woman she had come to call Grandmother was patient as she showed her how to do the simple work. Kayra tried to follow her example but somehow Kayra's hides were stiff and rough, where Grandmother's were soft and flowing.

Tushon was cross when he inspected her work. He chastised her with words she didn't understand. Each time she was reprimanded she tried to keep from crying. That seemed to please him and for whatever reason. Kayra found herself wanting to please him. He either scowled at her or delighted in her achievements. His satisfied nod of pleasure at a task well done made Kayra proud. Praise wasn't given out frivolously here.

Her arm still ached. The strange mixture of the first day was packed onto the bullet wound nightly. Kayra had figured out that Greely had been the one to shoot her. Yet she remained in the dark as to why the Indians were there at all when it happened. She was glad they were or she might be dead. They were treating her as one of their own. The whole situation was a puzzle. The work she was given was hard but she was expected to do no more than any of the other women. Her portions were equal to theirs and, except for feeding him, she was the one who cared for Michael, who was adored by all.

His cheeks were now round and full. He hardly resembled the tiny baby she had helped into the world. Kayra was proud that he was hers. Tushon, for all of his grunting and gruff speech, spent a lot of time holding the baby. From what she could guess, she was in his custody. He gave the orders where she was concerned and she slept in his teepee. He asked her a question every night and laughed at her confusion. His wives lay quiet, giggling at the exchange.

As the days passed, it became more obvious to Kayra what he was likely asking her. She continued playing dumb and he left her alone.

She finished a hide and shook it. It billowed. *Finally.* It was good, as smooth and soft as any. She was really getting the hang of this. She anticipated Tushon's return from the hunt.

He would be pleased. Kayra smiled, then frowned. How could she be so content when she knew that Hayden was likely sick with worry over her disappearance? Harce and Annie, too.

It was only when she thought of Hayden that she felt the draw to go back. She had no idea if she would even be allowed to leave this tribal sanctuary that she'd found. Did she want to? Yes, she wanted to assure Hayden that she was fine and show her Michael. How much of each other's lives they had missed these past weeks. *Had Hayden given her heart to Randy? Had they really married?* She hoped so. Kayra prayed each day that Hayden was being taken care of the way she was.

Here, Michael was growing strong and healthy and the tribe accepted her like William's family had. It was as if she belonged right here in this wild territory with these people that she had once considered her enemies.

Thoughts of Will bombarded her less often these days. She had to move on. Hope of ever seeing him again was gone but he would always be in her heart. Her future wasn't hers alone anymore. Michael was her priority now.

No matter how confusing her feelings were, this was where Michael needed to be. So, she worked alongside her new friends and put her energy into Michael and learning the language. So far she knew several words and each day her vocabulary grew. She would surprise Tushon with a word or phrase now and then and he would give her a proud smile. Those looks were something Kayra coveted.

Tushon was a good man. The other men came to him for counsel and although he was young, he sat with the elders in their circle. The only thing that really bothered Kayra about Tushon, was that he had multiple wives. Two other women slept in their teepee. Kayra imagined that she was expected to become a third. If she were the only one, she might consider it, but sharing a man with other women was not something she thought she could do.

Kayra was preparing a meal of roots when excited cries brought her out of the teepee. As she exited the dark tent, her eyes fell on a stranger that was tall and lean with short black hair and olive skin. His dress, entirely native, right down to the ornamented moccasins on his feet and his leather breeches. He sat cross legged in the elder's circle. They shared their pipe. It took Kayra a moment before recognition set in. That Indian was Randy.

Her belly flopped in her stomach. She had to go to him. He looked positively native. She tugged on one of her own dark braids and realized that she must too. He made brief eye contact. Something in his stare halted her steps. She hadn't seen any woman disturb the men in their circle. She stared from a distance. He talked easily with the men but his attention kept drifting to her. One of the elders noticed that he was distracted and turned to see the cause of his straying eyes.

Kayra ducked her head and pretended to be walking somewhere, only to discover that there was nowhere to go. Her face burned, she turned directions and headed back for her teepee. Once alone in the room, she fell to her knees and thanked God that someone had come. At least Hayden would know that she was alright.

Nervous, she stirred the stew that bubbled in the center of the room. After about an hour the young woman who nursed Michael brought the infant to her. Kayra was glad for the distraction. She was going crazy. The stew could only be stirred so much. The beadwork that she had been practicing was a mess now from her shaky stitches.

She held Michael to her and softly sang a German song that Ingrid Mayer had taught her. Shaking her head, she laughed to herself. *Here I am, a white girl, dressed as an Indian, in a teepee holding my orphaned child and singing in German. I bet in Hayden's wildest dreams that she never would have imagined playing this role.* In fact, she considered for the first time, since awakening in the teepee weeks ago, her greatest fear had been Indians but the entire time she lived among them she had yet to witness a single thing that would invoke such fear. She knew that all tribes were different, and the horrible things that she had seen as a child were in no way a diluted memory, but in this tribe she was safe.

Tushon entered the teepee and let his eyes adjust to the dim light blinking several times. "Haawka." Kayra greeted him.

The sound of her voice brought his eyes to her. "Haawka uma-ah, Kachine."

He took Michael from her arms. Holding the boy away from him, he spoke tender words to the child. Kayra found herself joyful at the attentive way he addressed her son. He was as adoring as a real father could be. She noticed his strong arms glistening in the firelight and the dip of his tight stomach. He was nothing but sinewy strength with blunt features, harsh like the words he spoke.Something in the combination of power he exuded and the gentleness he showed with Michael made him strangely appealing.

Kayra looked up and found that she had been caught admiring him. He smiled and something in his eyes made heat radiate from her neck. She came to her feet and began scooping stew into a bowl.

"Atewa utum." Tushon pointed to another dish that sat by the fire. Kayra was puzzled. He had never before asked any of his wives to eat with him, but he acted as if he wanted her to fill a second bowl. Hearing the pad of feet outside her teepee, she looked up.

"Haawka, Tushon." The voice saying hello belonged to Randy. Kayra spilled some of the stew on the ground, receiving a hard look from Tushon.

"Haawka." He greeted in return. Randy entered the teepee and touched his wrist to Tushon's. His eyes fell on Michael. He smiled at the infant in Tushon's arm, never once acknowledging Kayra.

The two men sat together while Kayra served the meal. Once the bowls had been placed, she took the baby from Tushon. She went to her mat in silence, trying to understand the words being exchanged. It was familiar, but Kayra knew enough now to decide that they were speaking something she wasn't used to hearing.

After the meal, Tushon lit a pipe and he and Randy took turns smoking it. One of the elders came to the teepee and called Tushon. He said something to Randy before leaving him alone with Kayra.

As soon as he was gone Randy came to his feet and hugged Kayra. "Are you alright? Have they hurt you?"

"No, I mean they haven't hurt me. How did you find me? How is Hayden?"

Randy's smile was like a hawk gliding towards the sky. "Fine I think. It wasn't easy to find you. Annie said you were shot."

"They took care of me. I woke up here and they were doctoring me and tending to Michael."

Randy ran his hand along the baby's cheek. "He's so small."

"He's big now. You should have seen him before. Etanya nursed him."

"I'm going to try to get you back, but Tushon has lost a wife. Greely killed her. She was young and pregnant. He sees you as a replacement. I'll offer to buy you. I have two high quality horses. I hope it's enough. If that doesn't work I don't know what we will do. He hasn't... I mean, you aren't his wife yet, are you?"

"I wondered. I didn't know about his wife or child, but he insists on calling me Kachine and he adores Michael. I haven't been forced to do anything, if that is what you mean, but I sleep in here with him and do the same work as his wives."

Randy frowned. "He probably is still mourning. Kachine was his squaw's name. Greely killed her on his way to you and Fineese. Greely's the one who shot you... and he killed Harce." Randy's forehead wrinkled and his jaw flinched.

Kayra's eyes closed. Her heart ached.

"I'm sorry Kayra, I shouldn't have told you like that. It's just that we don't have much time."

Kayra shook her head and wiped her face. "What should I do? Tell me and I'll do it."

"It's best if you don't let on that you know me. I will try to buy you and gamble for the baby."

"He's already lost one mother, Randy. I won't leave him."

Randy nodded. "Then I had better get Tushon drunk, because it has been a long time since I have gambled Indian style. He won't let the child go easily. He has talked proudly about his son."

"His son?" Kayra was caught off guard by hearing Michael referred to as Tushon's son. The thought had entered her mind, but she hadn't realized that although he hadn't made her his wife, the child had already been made his son.

At the sound of shuffling near the door, Randy hurried back to his position by the fire and was sucking on the pipe when Tushon entered.

Tushon glanced around the room and smiled toward Kayra before seating himself. Randy spoke and Tushon considered something before motioning towards the door. Randy led him from the teepee.

Neither came back until Kayra was asleep.

She awoke sometime in the night and felt a warm body sleeping beside her. Instinctively, she knew who it was. She dared not move. The man in her bed turned over and pulled her against him. Kayra swallowed, frozen with panic. Her hand flinched and brushed against bare flesh. As if she had been scorched, she jerked it away. Tushon stirred. He slid his arm across Kayra's belly and resumed snoring.

Kayra relaxed her body. Her unsteady breath was like thunder in the quiet night. Only one other time had a man held her while she slept: Her sweet William. She pushed his face from her mind. He was gone and she would never feel his arms around her again. She couldn't live in a memory.

Tushon was sound asleep. The rhythmic snoring was something she'd become accustomed to. Laying beside him in the cold night was oddly comforting, but when sleep carried her away, it wasn't Tushon that held her.

Chapter Twenty-One

Hayden

A crackling fire eased the chill in the air. Hayden wrapped Annie's blanket around her shoulders, barely more than skin and bones. The woman hadn't spoken. She seemed locked in her own world. She muttered, but the words were no more than a jumble of sounds.

Dana strolled past the fire with her dog. Hayden gave a small smile and waved at the woman. Dana ambled over and held her free hand to the warmth.

"Hello, Hayden, Annie." Her sad gaze took in Annie rocking back and forth, oblivious to the world around her.

"She hasn't eaten today. I tried to feed her some broth but she won't take it."

"That will pass. Soon enough she will find someone who needs her and it will pull her out of this trance." Compassion spread over Dana's Face. "Harce was her world. They had what I see in you and Randy. Love changes with time. You won't always be stealing kisses by the creek." She winked. "It gets bigger somehow. You'll see."

Hayden couldn't imagine what she was talking about but it sounded good. "I hope you're right. I just don't know if..."

"Oh, he'll make it back. That boy is too in love with you to let those red savages get the best of him."

Hayden frowned. Why had she allowed herself to fall in love? If she were truthful, he frightened her now. When she pictured his face, it changed from her perfect Randy to an awful image of him striped with war paint. She was sick over how easily emotions were betrayed. She was sure that nothing could have altered how she felt about him, but this was unlike anything she'd imagined.

She stared into the dirt beyond Annie not wanting Dana to see the truths in her eyes. There were strange markings right there in open sight. Her heart skipped in her chest, then began beating like a hummingbird's wing. Recognition slapped her in the face. It was Greely's horse's print. She was sure of it. She had tracked it for days on the way to Grand Junction, but this was much more recent. The print was etched deep in the wet.

Hayden crawled closer and knelt, running a shaky finger over the crooked markings that made it so very distinguishable. Randy had gone in the wrong direction. This was without a doubt, Greely's print; and the Indian that had stolen Kayra had taken his horse. They'd been here. Kayra had been here!

Dana came up beside her and stared at the ground. "Did you find something honey? They say that in this part of Colorado you can come across gold just like that. What is it dear?"

Hayden brought herself up and used cautious steps to move from the depression in the dirt. "Dana, you have to help me. I have to get away from here tonight. Randy went the wrong way. The Indian that took Kayra is headed straight up that cliff." She pointed toward the steep mountain looming ahead of them. "I have to go."

"That's craziness. You aren't a tracker, and even if you could find them, how would you get her back? You'd be kidnapped too."

"I know," Hayden paused, "but at least we'd be together. She needs me. I'm all she has. If I don't go, it will kill me as surely as Harce's death is killing Annie."

"Randy'll skin you, when he finds out." She paused, "Then he'll skin me."

Hayden nodded. "Yes, he probably will."

Dana stared into the eyes of her young friend. She frowned. "What you are considering is–''

Gomez, Dana's small dog, sniffed at the markings in the dirt and yelped, "Well, he thinks it's a good idea. Kayra's lucky to have you. I don't have any idea how I can help though, and I doubt any of the men will go along. They're anxious to get into Utah before the first snow."

"I can do this myself." Hayden assured her. "Just watch over Annie. Get her to Grand Junction if you can. There's a woman there who runs Saw Mill inn. Her name is Lana. She'll remember me, well she'll remember Mr. and Mrs. Parker, it's a long story. Leave Annie in her care, tell her that she will be doubly compensated when I get back. Annie won't make it to California." Hayden put a loving arm on the woman's spindly back.

Dana nodded. "I can do that for you. What else?"

"I need your fastest mule. The best one you have. And you can't tell your husband what it's for."

"He'll not let one out of his sight. He sleeps with 'em."

Hayden implored her. "I have to have a mule. I'll never get up this cliff in the dark on a horse. Find a way, please."

"I'll try." Dana picked up her dog to leave.

Hayden began gathering a blanket and canteen for her trip. She wouldn't weigh herself down with anything except a gun, water and one blanket.

Her items lay in a pile by the fire as she made a torch. She investigated the tracks. They led right up to the base of the steep mountain. From where she'd been sitting earlier, she'd seen the mountain as a cliff, but as she studied it now, she realized there was a crude trail zig-zagging up its face.

Dana led Lacey, her husband's pride and joy, saddled and ready.

"You're a lifesaver." Hayden took the mule and added her things to its back before swinging onto its saddle.

"You sure you know what you're doing?"

Hayden had a moment's panic. Did she? It was ludicrous. Then an image of Kayra gagged and tied popped into her mind. "I've no choice. He went the wrong way." Her voice trailed to a whisper.

Dana reached up and clasped hands with Hayden. "You be safe, honey."

"I will." She hoped. "How did you get the mule so quickly?"

Dana smiled, rolling her eyes. "Oh, I just picked a fight and Pat wandered off grumbling with his whittling block. I'll make it better later. You go on."

Hayden smiled her thanks and shoved her few supplies in a saddle bag before heading into the darkness.

Hayden

The steep trail narrowed as she traipsed the mountainside. She doused her torch so that the men in the camp wouldn't see her leaving and force her return. Hayden squinted to see, but it was no use.

She might as well have been blindfolded. Thank goodness Lacey seemed to be able to. Just as the thanks crossed her mind, the mule lurched awkwardly making a sharp turn. The trail must have narrowed even more because Lacey slammed Hayden's leg against jagged rock. Pain shot from her knee to her ankle and warmth ran down her calf. "Whoa!" She called. Hayden's leg was pinned between the granite and her mount. As the mule swayed back and forth, Hayden's leg scraped against the rock tearing her skin.

Hayden cried out again. Lacey lunged forward, nearly throwing her from the saddle to topple down the face of the mountain. Hayden scrambled to stay aboard, despite what the ride was doing to her. They must have come to a slightly wider area because Lacey came to an abrupt halt. Hayden righted herself.

"Good Girl." She tried to reassure the animal, patting her neck. "Just don't move."

Lacey pawed the ground and Hayden heard debris fall from the trail down the hill side.

She tore at the sleeve of her blouse. Luckily the clothes she'd borrowed from another traveler were well-worn. The sleeve ripped from its seam. She pulled it apart lengthwise and lifted her skirt. The mule, either unaware or unconcerned of her dilemma, began walking.

"No, no girl, wait."

Lacey didn't listen. She'd have to manage tying the fabric around her knee en route. She breathed out, steadying her nerves. Her mantra repeated in her head. *Control your mind, control the situation.* As they rounded a bend and her throbbing leg was once more on her free side, Hayden leaned out lifting her damp skirt. *It stings like the dickens.* Hayden wrapped the strip around the kneecap securing it with a knot. There wasn't anything else to do but hold on and hope they made it to the top. She sat up straight and gripped the saddlehorn.

Five minutes hadn't passed when her leg began to tingle. It prickled like tiny sparks were landing on her skin. Groaning, she reached down to loosen the tie. It was considerably more difficult to undo the knot than it had been to fasten it. She loosened the first section, her fingers fumbling with the second when the mule rounded another corner. She jerked her hand free not wanting to crush it. Her head smacked against the mountain wall. She cried out again. "Woah, Lacey. Woah!" Lacey jumped at the shrill sound, darting forward all too quickly.

Hayden closed her left eye to keep the blood from running in it and desperately clung to her animal. *So much for mules being unflinching.* Her fingers ached with the hold she had on the saddle horn. It wasn't long before the mule calmed, but by that time Hayden was too shaken to release her grip on the saddle horn.

Blood trickled into her mouth. She spit it out, wiping her lips against her shoulder. The wind began to pick up and although she was already cold, she welcomed the breeze because it dried the blood before it oozed into her eye. If it was flowing slowly enough to dry like that, then she was probably fine despite the ache.

She tried once more after Lacey rounded a corner to undo the tie strangling her knee. This time she was successful. Blood circulated once more through her leg. She wiggled her foot to help rid her-self of the awful tingling sensation.

Looking up, she didn't see the usual expanse of stars. Her mind wandered to her cousin. Kayra had become pretty religious since they'd left Willow Creek telling her to put it in God's hands. Did God even have hands? Hayden had made it a practice to depend on herself, but she was alone now and wasn't sure she would even survive this climb. Her heart pounded through her chest, fear freezing her movements.

This was out of her hands. If she lived or died was either up to this fool mule or Him. She needed help. What she needed was a miracle. *What if I can't get there in time? What if they rape her? What if I fall off this mule and we both die?* Questions of terror flooded her aching head. She closed her eyes and talked to God with her whole heart, for the first time in many, many years.

"God, I don't know what to say to you. I've done things that are wrong, or at least Kayra tells me they are. I haven't been in a church house or looked in a Bible for years, but I really need your help now. Help me. Help Kayra. She does read your word and lives right. Please protect her. Let me get there in time. Please, God. I've hurt Kayra. Because of me, she lost William.

"Forgive me for the lies I've told and the money I've taken. I'll do anything now to save her. I'd give up my life to make her alright, but I don't want to fall off this cliff. Please, God, don't let me die like this. Help me survive this night. I think Jesus said, 'not my will but thine be done', and, well, I'm askin' for our wills to lie together and that you answer this prayer, if you are there, and you're listening. Be with Randy too, Lord. Keep him safe and let him find us. I love him, God. Amen."

Hayden opened her eyes and tears were rolling down her face. She did nothing to stop them, as if she could. It felt good to let all of the emotion and fear and hope pour from her soul, to ask for help, to dare hope that it would come. Her voice sounded in the darkness like a wild animal as it escaped her chest. She couldn't hold back the tears or the noise she made. Had God heard her? Why was she so relieved?

After her well had run dry, her eyes grew heavy. She cracked her neck and shook her head to ward off the sleepiness that seemed determined to overtake her. She rubbed her ears to keep from dozing. When she nodded off again, she began singing to stay awake. There was a song she remembered from church as a child. She couldn't remember all of the words, so she hummed the tune, Amazing Grace. After several minutes of that she gave in and let her eyes fall shut.

William

William Mayer looked out over the cliff watching the campfires burning below. They were little more than tiny match tops scattered across the valley. He scratched his head and wondered how on earth he could have gotten so far off the trail. It was so obvious to him where it was leading and then he decided to push his small group ahead in hopes of covering more miles. Now those he hoped to catch up to were in the valley hundreds of feet below them and he had no way of getting down there. He just stared, hands solidly on his hips, pursing his lips at why this happened and how was he going to fix it.

Thomas, his twelve-year-old brother approached him. "Will, Becca's got to go again. Can we get out of the wagon?"

Will slapped his hat back on his head. "Yes, I got us lost anyway. I won't be able to see how to find the trail 'til morning. We'll camp here. But we're leaving at first light, so no goofing off."

Thomas ran to tell the others. William's family, all of his brothers and sisters piled out of the wagons and began making camp. William strode back to the wagon barking orders about bedrolls too close to where they made a fire. He unpacked some of the dried meat they'd brought. The kids were too glad to be out of the wagon to eat. They darted past him, tagging one another as the older boys tried to light a fire.

"I'm serious about leaving at first light," William warned.

Calla, his younger sister, sat down beside him. "Oh let them have their fun. They can sleep tomorrow."

She was an almost identical image of their mother with deep set eyes and a mouth that always carried half a smile. Her golden hair lay in a sloppy braid across her shoulder. William looked away. Sometimes he almost mistook her for his mother. He could tell that she wanted to talk. How much longer could he put it off? Hopefully another night, so he decided to put a stop to a conversation that he didn't want to have before it could start. "You're right, but *I* can't sleep tomorrow so if you don't mind…"

"Will, are you sure we can catch the wagon train and that sisters Mary-Katherine and Hannah are even with them? You said yourself that you tried to find them before they left Denver City and no one had heard of them. They're kind of hard not to notice, you know."

"I know." William laid down and blew out a deep breath. "We're lost Calla. The wagon train is right beside us but at the bottom of this mountain. I don't know how I managed to get us so far off the trail, but I saw their fires. I can't explain how or why, I just know that Sister Mary-Katherine left with the train from Denver. Tomorrow we'll have to backtrack, but we will catch them, hopefully by the time they reach Grand Junction. Then I will hunt every wagon bed and trunk till I find her. I won't lose her Calla, God knows that I need her, that we all need her."

"I can raise these kids. I'll help you do this."

"And give up your life? No Calla, I won't let you do that."

"What's the difference? Either I give up mine or you give up yours."

"Calla, I won't discuss this anymore. You're gonna be a nurse. I know what it's like to want something and to be powerless to achieve it. You'll have your dream and I won't listen to any more."

Calla sighed. "It is useless to reason with you. You're stubborn. I won't speak of it again tonight, but you are not the only one who is dealing with our new life, and I won't let you have me be a burden. We will find the wagon train and Sister Mary-Katherine."

Calla came to her feet, "You can see them down in the valley?"

"Yep, they are right there, mocking me."

She stood brushing the leaves from her skirt. "We'll reach them. I can't wait to be with people again. Your company is getting old."

William snickered, "Yours too."

She turned to leave and stopped mid step. "Do you hear that?"

"What, the children playing, when they should be resting?"

Calla peered over the cliff and startled backward. "Will, get your gun. Someone's coming."

In less than a heartbeat, he was on his feet ordering the children to pile into the wagon. Dutifully, they obeyed. He came running, his rifle in tow to where Calla stood.

She pointed down and sure enough, there was a narrow path along the mountains side. "How on earth..."

The huffing and clomping were unmistakable. No matter how insane anyone would have to be to scale the cliff, someone was coming up it.

"Calla, get behind me." He ordered. "Who's there?"

No answer. He cocked his rifle and aimed. After a minute or two he made out the dark figure of a horse steadily climbing until it crested the top. When it did, William realized it was not a horse. It was a mule and there was a lady rider on top. She looked to be in trouble. Her arms draped on either side of the animal's sweat lathered neck. Was she alive?

He set his gun down. They were not the ones in danger.

He and Calla ran to the animal. He eased the woman from her saddle and carried her to the firelight. Once laid across a bedroll, Calla took over, feeling for a pulse.

The children peeked from their hiding spot. Calla ran to the wagon and brought back a pail of water and a few of her doctoring supplies.

Calla washed the blood from the woman's face, careful not to reopen the gash that had scabbed over. Her hand stopped mid cheek.

"Will, come here." He came quickly.

"What is it?"

Calla bit her lip and pointed to the woman who had yet to regain consciousness. "Don't you recognize her?"

"Should I?"

"It's Sister Hannah."

William fell to his knees, studying her face. The woman did resemble Hannah, but this woman was no nun.

"It could be her." He conceded.

"It is her, Will." Calla locked eyes with her brother.

"If it's her, then Mary-Katherine is in trouble too." He leapt to his feet and ran to the cliff, starting down the narrow trail. It was like a ridge cut out of the rock that Sister Hannah had rode up. He stumbled, losing his balance and steadied himself against the mountainside. Slowly, he climbed back to the safety of level ground. His mind raced at the possibilities.

He ran to Calla, who was closing a gash across the woman's forehead with her needle.

"Is she awake?" He wanted to shake her into consciousness.

"No, and I hope she stays that way until I'm done. Her leg is bad. Take a look. If you'll start cleaning it, this will go a lot faster."

Impatient, William stared back at the cliff's trail. He wanted to go find Mary-Katherine but Calla was right. They needed to tend to Hannah, first. Then, maybe she'd provide answers. His gut tightened. Something was very wrong. Why else would she be covered in blood, riding alone, so late in the evening, up a cliff that no man or beast should dare climb in the daylight.

He lifted her mangled skirt to just above the knee and poured what was left of his canteen over her leg.

"I've never seen anything like this." How would he touch the raw wound without doing more damage? He needed something strong to rinse it, but he'd refused to let his sister bring along any alcohol. She'd kept insisting that if there was an emergency, it would be needed, but he'd dug in his heels.

"I can't clean this. It's too bad."

"You mean, it would be nice to have the alcohol bottle you insisted I leave behind?" She raised a brow, challenging him.

"Yes, I do. I was wrong." He sat back on his haunches.

"And lucky for Sister Hannah, I ignored you. It's here in my bag." She motioned with her head to where her bag sat.

He grinned, pulling the amber bottle from her pouch. "For once. Thank you Calla for being headstrong and disobedient." Stingily he poured it over her leg. When they found Mary-Katherine, she might need it too.

Calla chuckled. "Well, when someone is being stupid, you do what is best sometimes, not what you are told." She shooed him aside and began examining her knee.

William was happy to stand back. He was inadequate when it came to this. Too many times recently he'd felt this way.

Thomas led the children from the wagon. They came to stand beside him like a funeral parade.

"Is Sister Hannah going to be alright?" Becca asked, sadness filling her small voice.

William lifted the child into his arms, leaning his blond head against hers, he did his best to reassure. "I hope so, my *kleine schwester*." He kissed her cheek. Thanks be to God that Calla was here. He wouldn't have been calm enough to do what she was doing, and he didn't doubt that her stitching was a sight neater than his would've been.

Calla finished her work and rinsed her needle and scissors, then poured a small amount of the whisky over her tools. "I'm going to change." Her dress was smeared with Hannah's blood.

The kids gathered around Sister Hannah, watching her sleep.

"I knew Calla could make a good dress, but I never knew she could sew a face up so good." Thomas pointed with pride at his sister's handiwork.

Becca looked over to Will. "We should say a prayer for her."

They all looked at him. He nodded. They knew to turn to God. That should have been his first thought. He came and sat in the circle around the Sister. "I'll do it."

The children bowed their heads and William prayed. "God, heal Sister Hannah and lead us to Sister Mary-Katherine. Too much has happened to people we love. Please don't take two more from us." His voice cracked. He could say no more.

Thomas jumped in. "And thank you, Father, for William and Calla and what they do to keep us safe. Amen."

When he finished praying, the kids looked to William for direction. He wanted to be alone, to figure out their next step. "You go on to bed now. Sister Hannah won't go anywhere while you're asleep." Before long, the antsy children were settled and only William lay awake.

Hayden

Hayden felt the warmth of a fire before she came to. Her whole leg felt like it was being seared with a branding iron and her head ached as if held in a vice crushing her skull. Raising her trembling fingers to her eye was an all-encompassing task. She moaned and a strong pair of calloused hands stopped her.

"Don't touch it or you'll split the wound again." He had an odd accent. She opened her eyes and blinked. Was she back with the wagon train? Who was this man? "Sister, it's William. William Mayer. Talk to me. Where is Mary-Katherine?"

Hayden fought the impulse to fall back into sleep, but his question was the same one she needed answered. She managed to speak. "She needs us."

William fell to his knees beside her, shaking her shoulders.

Hayden's voice whispered. "They have her. I have to get to her."

William was insistent. "Hannah, who has Mary-Katherine?"

"Greely took Kayra and Indians. I have to get to her." Hayden tried to sit up and managed with some effort. The fog was lifting. "We have to go after them."

Hayden looked at the big man lumbering in front of her. "William?" It looked like him, but he hadn't shaved in a long time and a short beard covered his face making him appear older than she remembered.

William grabbed her shoulder. "Yes it's me, William Mayer."

Hayden began shaking her head, but the pain stopped her. "How did you get here?'

"It doesn't matter. Where is Mary-Katherine?"

It was the miracle she'd prayed for. He was real and he had heard her. She stared with shock into William's frantic eyes. "God is real. He brought you to me, for Kayra."

"You aren't making any sense, Hannah. What are you saying? Who is Kayra?"

"I am making sense, William." Hayden sat up straighter. "Kayra is Mary-Katherine." She didn't have the strength to hide anything or ease what they had done. "I am not a nun. We are not nuns. We aren't even Catholic. I thought that we were going to die, but God brought you here. It's going to be alright. He answered my prayer."

"What are you talking about? You know who I'm talking about don't you?" William asked.

Hayden nodded. It hurt to bob her head. She focused on the man in front of her. His eyes bore a pained expression of confusion. She put her palms to her eye sockets and rubbed. Then she blinked several times clearing her sight.

"I'll try to explain." She took a deep breath and started with the death of her uncle. She told all about their con and plans to go to California. She told about Fineese and Randy. She spilled out all of her concerns and feelings, the things she held so close to her chest. Then she told about Greely, Annie and Harce and how Indians had taken Kayra. She told him about finding the tracks and how she thought she would die until she woke up and he was there. How God had led her to him when she desperately needed someone who would help. He was quiet. It was a lot to process, Hayden knew. She took the moment to sip from the canteen laying at her side.

"How on earth did this happen? Poor Mary-Katherine– no, Kayra." he corrected himself. Do I even know her? I am," He amended his words, "We were crossing the Rocky Mountains to find her. I brought all of my brothers and sisters and it was a lie." Tears filled his eyes. "I don't even know her?"

"Yes William, you do. The girl that you fell in love with was Kayra. She has a different name but it's her. You have to believe me. She never would have lied to you. That was my fault." The guilt she had been waiting to feel landed squarely in her lap. "I wouldn't let her tell you, and then it was too late." Hayden reached a hand to him.

"But ..." He shook his head.

"She loves you William. And she needs us. Please, you don't have to forgive me but forgive her. She needs you, now more than ever."

Pensively, he sat back. "What about you? You said that this 'Randy' deceived you. That he lied to you about what he was. You said that you didn't know where that left you, the fact that he was an Indian. Can you forgive him?" William challenged her.

Hayden was shocked into silence. She had not considered that her own deception was as similar as Randy's had been. He was the same person now as the one she had fallen in love with.

"Hayden," William searched her face, "Are you alright? Should I get Calla?"

She forced her eyes to meet his. She stared, unblinking. "You're right. Yes, I can forgive him. I do love him still and nothing is going to take that away from us."

William was silent, his gaze spoke of his internal struggle. "Then I can too. Truth is I need your cousin now more than ever before. My Mother, she died. The man I called father, he will never see us again. I'm responsible now, for all of us. I was chasing after the wagon train, praying that we would meet up with you and that Mar– Kayra would help me raise these younger ones up and be my wife."

Hayden smiled in spite of the pain she was feeling. "She will. She hasn't been the same since we left you. She does what needs doing, but she says that there is just a part of her that she lost in Willow Creek."

William smiled shyly. "She said that?"

"Yes, more than once." Hayden grabbed William's strong hand. "At first light, we have to go and rescue her. Will you do this with me?"

"You're not in any shape to go off looking for Kayra."

"You don't get to make that decision. I'll be ready by morning. And I won't slow us down. I'm going with or without you."

He nodded. "Very well, but I'm not much at tracking. I couldn't even track the wagon train."

"Don't worry about that. I am. And it wasn't your lack of ability that brought you up here instead of down there. It was God, William. He knew that we needed you."

William opened his mouth and laughed at what Hayden said. "That certainly is better on my ego."

Hayden liked William. He was easy to talk to and as warm-hearted as Kayra had said. He was very handsome too. No wonder Kayra had fallen in love with him so quickly. It was obvious he felt the same.

"We can't take all of these children with us and they are my responsibility."

"I promise you that they can catch the train by early evening. I know the route. I've been across it three times now."

"I don't know about leaving them alone." William shook his head.

Calla sat up in her bedroll and dared him to disagree. "I'm taking these kids tomorrow, William. I won't let you give this up. I'm sorry for interrupting but I can't just lay here pretending to sleep while your stupid sense of feeling overly and solely obligated for us wrecks your chance to get Mary-Katherine back, or Kayra, or whoever she is. You do what you need to and I will too."

She stared at him, challenging. Hayden could see his back stiffen and fought the impulse to chime in alongside his sister. She didn't even remember this proud and stubborn girl, but she liked her. The siblings stared each other down.

"Fine." William finally spoke. "I'll let you do it."

"Great, then we will all meet in Grand Junction." Hayden was thrilled with how things were turning out. If only she knew where Randy and Kayra actually were.

Chapter Twenty-Two

Hayden

The treck that William and Hayden made the first day was exhausting. Hayden was weak and still in tremendous pain. She realized in the morning that Calla had stitched her face and leg. Her fingers kept running across the puckered skin on her forehead. How bad would the scar be? She knew that she should be simply thankful for being alive and she was, but she hoped that the permanent reminder of last night would be small.

The tracks had been easy enough for her to find. Just as Randy had taught her, looking in the mud and finding one solid track would lead you confidently to the harder to see ones.

William ran a hand along his short beard. "I never would have made those out." He turned in his saddle which cracked below him. "Kayra spoke very well of you, Hayden. She said you were brilliant. I guess she was right."

They spent the day getting to know who they really were. Hayden couldn't believe how open she was being with this man who was practically a stranger. She shared her feelings and thoughts about Randy. She told him about how exciting it was to be at the auction and bid on a horse. She confessed her previous lack of trust in anyone or anything other than herself and confided that she was considering trying the whole God thing after what had happened in the night.

William shared his own struggle with God after learning about his Father's betrayal and how finally he felt he was on the right path searching for true answers.

For Hayden, it was like an awakening, to have this spiritual side to think about. She wanted to know more and William seemed to have a lot of answers. He was wise beyond his twenty years.

They stopped, only when darkness made it impossible to track even with the lantern. Then, they slept for several hours until the first hints of sun shone on the peaks of the mountains. It was cold now. Colder than Hayden had realized it would be. Her blanket that she draped around her shoulders was little help against the wind. She longed for the warmth of the bed she'd slept in, in Grand Junction. She frowned at her selfish thoughts when Kayra was likely being tortured right now. Nevertheless, the chill was getting to her. She cupped her hands to her mouth blowing her hot breath against them.

When morning came, her feet ached with cold and her cheeks burned with fever. Ignoring her discomfort, she mounted Lacey and found the tracks once more, leading William into the strong wind. She scrunched her nose and squinted as the frozen air chilled her body.

He looked at Hayden and shook his head. "We have to stop and get better prepared."

"No." was Hayden's quick objection. "We can't."

"If we don't, you're liable to freeze to death. We don't know how much further we'll need to travel." He got off his horse and helped Hayden from hers.

Hayden decided not to tell him that she feared she had a fever. "Where do you suppose we are?" Hayden looked around at the changing landscape. They had left the Rockies the day before.

"I imagine Utah territory by now."

They made a fire. Hayden greedily sat beside it, rubbing her arms and hands. William took his rifle and gathered some wood. Hayden was asleep before the fire blazed.

He woke her. "I'll be back and with any luck we'll have a few skins. We can raw cure 'em and that ought to help with the cold."

Hayden nodded. "Hurry." She muttered.

Her mind was powerless against the nightmare that she hadn't dreamt in weeks. She saw her childhood home, her mother. She heard the screams and saw the face of her mother's tormentor. She thrashed back and forth locked in the horror of that night. Then she was running and almost to the safety of the rock where she always hid when someone jerked her up onto a horse and called out in a strange tongue.

All at once Hayden was awake and found herself in the tight arms of a very intimidating copper skinned man. He smiled wide, as he stroked her blond hair and hurried off heading north. Hayden screamed as loud as she could. The Indian grabbed her neck, wrapping his hands tightly around it, choking her. She couldn't breathe. So this was it, this was how she would die. She kicked and struggled against him until she was gone.

When she awoke it was dark and he was tying her to the leg of a horse. There was a fire and the scent of game roasting. He tugged at the cords holding her hands. Her tongue fought with the rope forcing her mouth open. He ignored her, strutting instead to four Indians sitting by the fire. This was her worst fear. *Control your mind, control the situation,* she chanted in her head, but control was nowhere to be found. As if someone were holding a knife to her throat she felt the uncanny security that death was imminent.

The native men it appeared were gambling. They had six pack horses, loaded down with dead animals, she imagined they were taking the game back to their families. Were these the same people that had taken Kayra? Had God led her here so that she could be with her? If so, no matter the situation she was in, at least she'd found them, or more specifically they found her. Her head pounded and she still shook, freezing down to her numb toes. She stretched her leg and wiggled, trying to warm her feet.

One of them noticed, jumping to his feet he yelled out strange words pointing in her direction. "Etsay amaiahan."

The man who had brought her in stared. He came to his feet and brought with him a cup of water. He undid her gag, slowly speaking to her, as one would a child. "Tonse etahono."

Once her gag was free she screamed with all of the voice she could muster. The men who watched from the fire burst out in unanimous laughter. Her captor frowned, slapping her face. Instantly Hayden stopped. He crouched down to her level and held out the cup. "Tonse etahono." He repeated, coaxing her to accept.

Hayden spit at him, which was followed by another roar of laughs. He smiled at her and returned the gag to her mouth. He covered her with a thick woven blanket before walking toward the fire where he was received with obvious teasing. He accepted the jesting with good nature and settled back on his rug picking up dice and shaking them in his hand. The men sobered, getting back to the business of gambling.

Hayden sat there for more than two hours without so much as a glance passed her direction. She fully expected to have been raped and tormented long ago. Now, she was thinking of a way to escape. Things certainly weren't supposed to happen this way. She hadn't worked out the details of rescuing Kayra, but she imagined that the job would be easier if she weren't a captive as well. She was becoming uncomfortable with her need to pee and she wished that she had accepted the drink she'd been offered earlier. All the liquid in her mouth spilled out around the rope gagging her.

She waited as long as she could. When she knew she would wet herself without relief, she began calling out as best she could with the gag in her mouth. The men turned her direction. Ignoring her, they continued playing. Finally, after one of the men gathered the rocks that were used as some sort of winning, Hayden's captor took the cup he'd offered her earlier and walked to her again.

His eyes were full of amusement as she straightened her back proudly against the horse's leg where she was tied. Her eyes were as blue as his were black. Once again, he repeated the strange words to her. "Tonse etahono."

One of the men who stood by the fire watching the exchange said something and the brave beside Hayden chuckled at his comment. "Tonse etahono—Ahh, ahhh." He imitated Hayden screaming in a high-pitched voice, his hand waving in the air dramatically. All the men at the fire stumbled around laughing at his imitation. Even Hayden thought he looked pretty ridiculous. But she didn't smile.

Cautiously, he undid her gag. Hayden opened and closed her mouth working her sore jaw. He held out a cup of water to her. She stared defiantly in his face.

"I have to go to the bathroom." She told him.

He held the water to her mouth. "Osona metewasin."

"I have to go to the bathroom, you stupid idiot." Hayden closed her mouth firmly. She salivated at the thought of a sip but she refused to do what he asked.

He raised an eyebrow.

She had to get the message across so she motioned with her eyes downward. And made a sound. *Pssssssss*, she stared at him meaningfully.

He nodded and held the water to her pursed lips. She sighed in frustration and took a sip. It wasn't water she tasted. She spit out the fiery liquid that burnt her tongue.

Apparently she couldn't have been funnier if she were trying.The men roared. Her captor undid the ties that bound her to the horse. She was grateful to rub her wrists. She'd decided that when he turned his back to let her pee, she would make a break for the trees ahead. He offered her his hand. She pushed it away. He allowed her to get up unassisted. Then he pointed towards a bushy area not more than twenty feet from the fire where all of the men sat staring.

"No. There is no way that I am going over there in front of everyone." Hayden glared at the brave. She thrust her jaw in the air and shook her head.

He motioned toward the bush and pushed Hayden in that direction. She shrugged him off and walked defiantly to a more distant place. He grabbed her arm and painfully squeezed her wrist. Hayden hollered out in pain. He pointed to the bush again.

Hayden knew that she would be unable to get away, being so close to everyone else. She also realized that her modesty was about to humiliate her if she argued about where she relieved herself any longer.

She jerked free and stomped behind a bush near the one that he'd indicated. She waited for him to turn, but he obviously had no plans of doing so.

She turned from him, and difficult as it was she refused to lift her skirt. She fumbled with her underpants and finally got them far enough down her legs that she was able to slide one foot out. Then she squatted and spread her feet as widely as she could. She felt her stomach's instant relief and then was faced with the dilemma of redressing.

She scooped her skirt in her arms and sort of hopped forward to get out of the path and stuck her foot back in her underwear. She shimmied them up past her knees then struggled to pull them up from the outside of her dress.

The trees were just up ahead. Should she run? Could she beat them? The brave grabbed her arm bringing her to the fire before she could make a decision. She shook her head and pointed to the horse where she'd been tied. He placed one of his hands on her forehead, feeling her fever. He increased his grip on her arm and pushed her down on the rug that he had been sitting on all night. Hesitantly, she sat down and stared into the terrible eyes of each man there. She refused to let their horrible faces intimidate her, though her heart raced and panic was rising in her throat. She repeated her mantra in her head.

They said nothing, neither to her or each other. Her captor tied her hands again behind her back and sat in front of her with a plate of meat. It looked close to raw and Hayden shook her head refusing the sustenance that her body craved.

He opened his mouth and pursed his lips at her.

She bit her lips closed, raising her eyebrows for effect.

The men smiled, talking among themselves. Her captor sat the plate down and pointed to his chest, "Kiltosuna."

Hayden understood what he was trying to do but she refused to cooperate. She shrugged her shoulders.

Kiltosuna sat back and crossed his arms over his chest. He frowned at Hayden and announced to his friends, "Abooksigun." He pointed to Hayden.

The group again fell into hilarious laughter and Hayden figured that it was at her expense. She glared at Kiltosuna.

He smiled and nodded pointing to her again while repeating the name. He retrieved the plate of meat and tore off a bite. He held it out to her. She opened her mouth to receive it. This pleased him. Carefully, he brought his hand up to feed her. Hayden took her opportunity and bit hard on his meaty finger until she tasted blood. He slapped her face hard with his free hand and made quick work of reattaching her gag. His friends all shook their heads and repeated the name that he had selected for her. "Abooksigun."

He roughly forced her to her feet and dragged her back to the horse. He shoved her down and retied her. She immediately regretted her behavior. The wind was cold and now she couldn't feel the fire's heat. He stomped back and wrapped his finger. That was the last Hayden heard from any of the men that night, but when she awoke there was a warm hide across her body. Why had he given it to her?

In the night another man had joined them. He was small in stature. He sat in the firelight of the early morning with Kiltosuna playing the dice game that they all seemed so fond of. The scary looking stranger stared boldly at Hayden. She felt her wind-chapped face flush at his gaze.

It appeared that Kiltosuna had lost by the irritated way he handed over a leather pouch to the man. Then the man pointed at Hayden. It was obvious that he was expressing an interest in her. Kiltosuna looked back at her, then down at his finger. The two men talked and Kiltosuna came towards Hayden.

From the first time since laying eyes on her captor, she had wanted to be free from him, but now, she found herself terrified that he was about to gamble her away to the stranger with cold eyes. Kiltosuna had, for the most part, treated her decently and maybe would have treated her better if she had been more cooperative. Now, it appeared that he was fed up and willing to gamble with her as currency.

She was angry with herself. She knew men. She knew exactly how to work them, how to worm her way into their good graces. She should have taken a different approach from the start. It might be too late now, but she had to try or else she might find herself at the mercy of the newcomer who looked about as merciful as a rattler.

Kiltosuna untied her without a word and paused before undoing her gag. Hayden moved her lower jaw back and forth. Once her mouth felt like it belonged to her again, she smiled the most engaging smile she could muster. He smiled back, his dark skin in sharp contrast to his white teeth. Hayden raised her hand up, asking him for his help in rising. He stared back at her before taking her hand in his and helping her to her feet. Then, he led her to the fire where he sat her on his rug, trying again to give her water and food. His companion shook his dice eagerly. Kiltosuna opened his bag and pulled out a silver brush and some hair combs, placing them on the center rug.

The stranger shook his head and pointed at Hayden. Hayden gulped down the bite of hard meat that she'd been chewing, scooting closer to Kiltosuna. She looked pleadingly into his dark eyes and managed a frightened smile.

He shook his head at the man and brought out another treasure from his bag. He laid a gold pocket watch on the mat. The stranger frowned, but threw his dice.

Hayden was instantly relieved. At least for now she was not the ante. Kiltosuna won the game and returned his things to his bag along with some bright beads and a bottle of whiskey.

He tied Hayden's hands behind her back and laid down beside her. The stranger looked anything but sleepy and the prospect of sitting up with him was far worse than faking sleep next to Kiltosuna. Immediately, she laid down and scooted as close to her captor as she could without actually touching him. The stranger muttered something that even Hayden recognized as a complaint and a challenge.

Kiltosuna sat up. Angrily he stared at the man. Hayden sat up too, afraid that the two were going to fight. Their voices raised in confrontation and Kiltosuna hopped to his feet. The other men woke up, but none of them moved to intervene on their friend's behalf. Hayden was scared for him, her current safety–no matter how shallow that safety was. He was lean and muscular, sure, but the other man was fearsome. Big.

The stranger made his move first, swinging at Kiltosuna and hitting him hard in the face. Kiltosuna's head reared back at the impact, but he ran forward and leapt on top of the stranger screaming out in his strange tongue. The men cheered as the pair rolled on the ground punching and grunting at each other.

The stranger lunged forward with a knife and slashed a long trail across Kiltosuna's thigh. The man did not even flinch as the blade dug into his brown leggings. Blood spread from the cut to his whole thigh. Hayden closed her eyes at the sight.

Like Hayden, Kiltosuna's opponent was surprised at his lack of response. He scrambled to get away. Kiltosuna grabbed the stranger's arm and managed to get the blade from his hand. Then he managed to flip the man over landing with his knees pressed firmly against the guy's shoulders. The stranger kicked and cried out.

The men sitting at the fire laughed as Kiltosuna quickly drew a shape on the man's head. Then he yelled out and tore the scalp from the man who had challenged him.

Hayden found herself mesmerized by the activities she witnessed. All thought of escape was gone. She knew that what was happening was barbaric but she couldn't close her eyes to the scene.

Kiltosuna slit the man's throat. The Indian wiped off his blade on the stranger's pants then came back to the fire carrying the scalp. He dropped it beside Hayden who squealed and scrambled away from the bloody mass of black fur. The men chuckled at her before returning to their sleeping positions.

Kiltosuna plopped onto his mat, moving the scalp nearer to the fire so that the flames dried it. He stared at Hayden and sighed. "Do you sew?" He asked, motioning to his bag.

Hayden's mouth dropped open. "You can talk?"

He snickered at her comment. "Yes, in four languages. Can you sew?"

Hayden nodded.

"Then do it." He pointed to his leg.

"You mean, stitch you up? No, I can't do that." The idea terrified her. She could barely sew a straight line with embroidery.

"You cost me this leg."

The fight had been over her. Hayden didn't know what to think about that. "I'm sorry, but I'm no doctor."

Kiltosuna grabbed the bag and threaded a needle. He handed it to her and poured some of the drink he'd won over his leg, sucking back a gasp as he did it. Then he took a long drink and laid back.

Hayden sat there, staring at her captor, holding the needle with her thumb and index fingers. She made no move to work on his leg.

"You're looking for someone, aren't you?"

Hayden came to her knees, crawling toward the man who had fought to keep her.

"Kayra? Tell me, please, where is she?" Her heart leapt.

"Fix my leg."

Hayden nodded and her nervous fingers went about stitching. It felt very different putting a needle through thick flesh than it did through fabric. She cautiously pushed the needle in and blood covered her view. She dabbed at it with the edge of her skirt. She did her best to sew evenly, but when she finished she realized what a sloppy job she'd done.

Kiltosuna laughed when he saw her work. "Lih, looks like lightning."

"Do you know where Kayra is?"

He nodded and laid down.

"Is she alright? She was shot. Is she okay?"

He nodded again. "Today she was married."

"No!" Hayden cried out.

Hayden

The following day, the men that had camped together left as a group. She was pleased to discover that she was feeling better. She was still freezing, but figured it was because of the weather, not fever.

Kiltosuna had refused to speak in English to her again. She had cried and begged, which only seemed to annoy him, so she'd given that up and gone back to her plan of manipulating information out of him. All morning she'd been compliant, almost agreeable.

They crested a ridge and she saw in the valley a small Indian village with about a dozen teepees. She scanned the women looking for her cousin, but she couldn't make her out from that distance. "Please, Kiltosuna. Where is my cousin?"

He sighed and pointed to the teepee in the center of the valley. "That's where she will be for one week. You cannot see her until after the marriage rituals are done."

"No. I have to see her now."

He frowned at Hayden and spoke to her in his Indian tongue. Hayden refrained from arguing further.

The group was spotted on the ridge and several from the valley cheered, running toward them. The men sat tall on their horses. Kiltosuna led the way holding the fresh scalp in one hand and Hayden, his captive, in the other. She didn't fight him. In fact, she clung to him, afraid of the unknown people rushing her.

Once they were in the valley, he helped her from the horse. Her eyes darted in hopeful search, but no one emerged from the wedding tent. He handed Hayden over to a group of squaws who led her to the creek. She stared back in confusion as Kiltosuna raised his chin to direct her to follow them. The woman tried to undress Hayden at the side of the creek. She fought them off, swinging and thrashing as they ganged up on her. The whole tribe watched the scene with much amusement.

The squaws looked toward Kiltosuna in frustration. He walked down to the creek. Hayden was sure that he was going to slap her again. She placed her hands defiantly on her hips, challenging him to interfere.

"Abooksigun," He said. The women giggled, stepping aside so that he could talk to Hayden.

"What is that, Abooksigun? What is it that you say about me?"

"It is your name. It means wildcat." He smiled at her. His black eyes were full of warmth as he spoke. She bit back her own smile. She deserved the name and she knew it.

"They are not going to hurt you. I promise. Do as they say or you will disrespect me and I will have to punish you. I don't want to do that."

Hayden shook her head. "If I do this, can I see Kayra?'

"No." He continued speaking quietly. "She cannot see anyone but her husband until the rituals are complete. Do this and I will not have to beat you with a strap."

Hayden frowned at her options, but held her hands out to her sides in surrender. The women flocked to her and removed her outer garments. Then they tore off her undergarments as well. Hayden objected and modestly tried in vain to cover herself. The men howled with pleasure as the women tried to push her to the water. She fought them off for a while but realized that it wasn't much use and only made her reveal more of her naked body to the observers.

She jerked free of the women and strode proudly into the frigid creek. Her eyes locked with Kiltosuna's. She saw the admiration in his eyes and, although the water numbed her body, her cheeks ignited. The women waded in after her, chanting something while they raised handful after handful of water up cascading down every part of her naked body. Then they dunked her under. The dips were swift and after being submerged three times, they pushed her out of the water. Kiltosuna wrapped her in animal skin and led her to his teepee.

There was a fire burning in the center. She scrambled to get as close to it as she could. Her teeth chattered and water ran from her stringy blonde hair down her neck and down her chest. Kiltosuna brought some cloth and approached her to pat her dry.

"No." She objected. "I'll do it." She took the clothes, then turned from him and dried herself before wrapping herself back in the skin.

"What was that all about?" She motioned toward the creek.

"It was a cleansing. They washed away all of the white from you. You are a Cetewa now."

"What?" She pulled the skin closer around her shoulders. "I am no Indian and I'm not staying here. I have come to get my cousin and take her home. You can't stop us."

He laughed. "I suspected that was your intention, but it is too late. Your cousin is married to a man who will take her to his tribe in a week's time. You will stay here and you will be my wife."

Rage coursed through Hayden. "I will not." She stomped toward him and looked him dead in the eye. "I'll never be your wife. We're leaving the first chance we get."

"You will learn to like it here. We all have in the end." He reached out to touch her. She jerked away from his hand. "Until then, you don't need to fear. We are better than your people. We don't force our women to sleep with us. You'll do all of the things that a wife is expected to do and when you choose, and you will, you will come to my mat and be my wife."

"You will die first. I may come to your mat, but it will only be to kill you while you sleep."

Kiltosuna laughed at the threat. "Get warm by the fire. I will bring meat. Tomorrow you will serve me."

"Where are my clothes?"

"You will get clothes when I am sure you will not run away. A naked wife is less likely to try to escape."

Hayden felt panic rise in her chest. There was no way that she could remain naked in his presence. "You are a filthy pig. You say that you don't force women but you steal us and what about my cousin locked up in a teepee with some man for a week? What is that?"

"Kachine agreed to the marriage, and you will too, in time." He ducked his head and crept from the teepee. Hayden fell to the mat by the fire.

Chapter Twenty-Three

Kayra

Randy entered the teepee where his 'wife' anxiously sat by the fire sewing the beadwork that had come naturally to her. Kayra had heard all of the excitement and figured that the men had come back from hunting. Her stomach growled. She was as eager as the rest of the tribe to taste meat again. Randy said that he would go investigate and bring back their portion. She desperately wanted to leave the tent, but it was forbidden for a bride to see anyone but her husband for a week.

Randy frowned and handed her a pile of raw meat hanging from a rope. Kayra grabbed at the bundle and took several strips of venison, stabbing them through with a metal stick.

"This looks fantastic." She deeply breathed in the aroma as she laid the stick across the fire just out of the dancing flames. Then she caught Randy's eyes and realized that something was very wrong. "What's the matter?"

"Hayden is here." He said flatly.

"What?" In astonishment, Kayra came to her knees. "How on earth did she get here? Is she alright?"

Randy kicked the water bucket, spilling what was left of its contents and paced the small tent. "As far as I could tell, she's fine. Her leg had been sewn up but she looked for the most part unharmed."

"What is she doing here?"

"Kiltosuna brought her in. He intends to marry her. To make it worse, she's already been made Cetewa. By the time I got out there, she was being cleansed."

"What do we do?"

"I don't have any idea. Why that girl can't listen to one single thing that I tell her is beyond me. I actually thought that after this week we would be able to leave here with little Michael to find her in Grand Junction and everything would finally work out. Now, once again, things are complicated and I betcha it's because she did something foolish."

"Oh, Randy. You can't really be mad at her. She does what she feels she has to. It's part of loving Hayden, to accept that about her."

"I know," Randy shook his head for what seemed like the tenth time, "but she just complicated everything and I'm afraid. I don't know if we can undo this one. I pulled out all of my tricks getting you. How am I supposed to get her too?" He ran his hands through his black hair.

"Kiltosuna's a good man. He won't harm her unnecessarily." Kayra reassured him.

"Yes, but with Hayden, it will become necessary soon enough. He has no other wives does he?"

Kayra shook her head. "He wanted to marry the child Ayiana, but her Father said that he had to wait until she reached sixteen winters."

"When was this?"

"I don't know. It was before I came here. He loves her though. All of his animal kills are given to her family."

"I don't know what we are going to do." Randy sat on the rug beside Kayra.

She got on her knees and checked the meat, turning the stick. Her and Randy stared in surprise at each other when they heard the angry voice of the girl they loved yelling at her husband to be. Kayra couldn't make out the words, but Randy grinned.

Kayra was so concerned, yet Randy was amused at her tantrum nearby. "What is funny about that?" She motioned to the direction of the sounds.

"You know what he named her? He named her Abooksigun."

Kayra understood and bit her lip suppressing her own grin. She could only imagine how her cousin had earned that name so quickly. "She hasn't seen you, has she?"

Randy shook his head.

"She probably doesn't know that I'm here either." Kayra's eyes pleaded with him to figure something out. "We have to get word to her. Somehow, you have to see her."

Randy scoffed at the idea. "She's probably going to be confined to the teepee for a while. Kiltosuna is not a stupid man. He has to know that she will run. The only way would be to receive an invitation to his teepee and I barely know him."

"He gambles." Kayra told him. "I've seen him gamble many nights with Tushon in my teepee."

"Does he win?"

Kayra nodded.

William

Will returned a couple of hours after leaving Hayden by the fire. He had killed a rabbit and thanks be to God, a buck. He went ahead and skinned the deer where it had dropped. He brought with him the best cuts of meat and the hide. It seemed wasteful to leave the rest of the carcass, but there was no logical way for he and Hayden to eat it or carry it. He skinned the rabbits as well and figured that they would warm Hayden's hands. He had a sturdy pair of gloves for himself.

As soon as he entered the field and found the wisps of smoke rising from the nearly burnt out fire, he cursed himself for leaving her. He stalked in closer, with his rifle poised and cocked. Hayden was gone.

He found a few prints and was angry with himself that he didn't have more skill in tracking. He couldn't rightly say how many tracks there were, or if the horses were shod or not. He was at a loss for what to do.

He knew that he had to follow the tracks as best he could, but he wasn't at all confident in his abilities. Now he was on a wild goose chase and had no idea of where Kayra or Hayden were. He wanted to scream out in frustration over the whole situation. He couldn't waste any of the precious light, so he stuffed the skins in his pack and galloped off in the direction that he thought the tracks led.

Hayden had tracked in the dark several nights, but he knew better than to try. He stopped when the sun dipped behind the hills. Whoever took Hayden couldn't be too far off but he had learned his lesson with the wagon train. Pushing for mileage at night could make you find yourself a day and a half behind.

He lit a small fire, careful not to make too much light or smoke and cooked his supper. If God had led Hayden to him, why had he allowed her to disappear? He ate, then doused the flames. The last thing he wanted was someone to come across him because he was overzealous with his fire. He covered himself with a wool blanket and tried to sleep. It was a long time coming.

In the morning he got back on the hunt, but the grassy field became thicker and the tracks harder to see until he lost them all together.

Not knowing what else to do, he decided to ride in the same direction until he came across more tracks or at least signs of human life. He was beginning to be more and more lonely without his chatty riding companion and the Utah landscape was an intimidating place to be alone. It was known for its Indians, although he had yet to see one.

He blamed himself for whatever situation Hayden was in. His worry over Kayra had his gut tied in knots as he continued across the open fields of Utah. His thoughts danced between all of the people that he felt responsible for. By now, his brothers and sisters were in Grand Junction. He'd given Calla almost all of the money that Victoria had given him to start a new life. He prayed that she hadn't spent it on anything foolish. How was he going to be able to rescue everyone and meet his family back in Colorado? At this point, he questioned whether or not he could even find them.

It seemed that summer had skipped over fall and given winter full reins. He used the skins that he had taken for Hayden to pad his clothes. Hopefully, wherever the girls were, they were warm.

Randy

It was three days before Randy could weasel an invitation from Kiltosuna to come to his teepee. He'd been trying to make friends with the brave that had captured Hayden, but the man was so preoccupied with her that Randy got only moments in passing to peak his interest in a game. Kiltosuna spent the majority of his days in his teepee, which rankled Randy to no end. He knew just how captivating Hayden could be.

Kayra was driving him crazy too. She was going insane locked up in their teepee and she still had three days of solitude until she could come out without causing a ruckus. He was her only outlet. He tried to be patient but between the two women he was being pushed to the limit.

He found himself falling easily into the lifestyle of the Cetewas. Kayra seemed pretty content here too. She made, he noted, as fine a squaw as any he had ever known. She served him in silence and returned to her own mat to eat her meal.

"Kayra," he said smiling at her, "you know that you can join me at the fire."

She smiled shyly. "I know. I've just gotten used to the customs. It seems right for me to sit here." She grabbed her bowl and walked to him, sitting at his side.

"This is a good people. If you want to stay here, you know you can." He watched her consider that. She already looked the part. Her greased hair hung long and dark down her back. Maybe she was part Indian and just didn't know it.

Kayra shook her head, "After all that you've been through to allow me to leave?" She spooned some of the mush to her lips. "If you need to, you can trade me for Hayden. Michael goes wherever I go, though. Hayden has to get out of here, and soon. I could stay here if I needed to. I would miss you all, but Tushon loves Michael. He would make a fine father."

"What about husband? He would want that back too, you know."

Kayra didn't rush to answer. "I could be a wife to him, if I had too. He treats me well."

"Could you love him?"

Kayra was thoughtful for a long while. Tears filled her eyes. "In time I would grow to have feelings for him, but I'm afraid that I won't ever be able to love anyone again."

Randy nodded in understanding. "When someone gets under your skin that way, it seems impossible doesn't it?"

He fingered the last bit of his acorn mush and licked his fingers. Then he stood and left the teepee without telling Kayra where he was headed. He didn't want to get her hopes up.

His hands trembled as he realized he was about to see Hayden. He'd thought of nothing but her for weeks and now that she was here, the plague was even worse. He needed strength to get through the night. He had a plan and if he stuck to the plan (and Hayden didn't screw things up) he figured that he had a good chance of getting her back. He hoped to do this civilized but if need be he was more than prepared to take her his own way. Kiltosuna would be a formidable opponent. He had forty-three scalps. Many of them were Indian.

Randy found himself at the door of the teepee. He took a long breath and blew it out. Here goes. "Haawka." He called out.

Kiltosuna returned the greeting. "Haawka."

Randy entered the teepee. Kiltosuna sat contentedly beside the fire. In his fingers he held a sloppily rolled cigar made with a white man's tobacco. How had he gotten that?

As soon as Randy was inside the tent, Hayden jumped to her feet and ran toward him begging. "Help me please. I have to get away. Please!"

She clutched the bearskin that covered her still naked body. Randy turned to see the woman whose voice shook with emotion and he swallowed hard at the sight of her. Her hair was a tangled mass of knots. Her skin was pale from her confinement inside. She seemed so thin that he assumed she was starving herself in protest. She looked so vulnerable and terrified. He fought with every ounce of control he had not to pull her into his arms and reassure her that she was going to be okay.

Recognition came into Hayden's light eyes a split second before Kiltosuna slapped her cheek, forcing her back to her mat. Randy felt himself step forward, fingers clenched into a fist. He checked his action, staring at the ground. There was nothing more offensive to an Indian than for another to interfere in his interaction with his family. Randy reminded himself that if he wanted to get Hayden back, then he had to stick to his plan.

Hayden screamed out in anger more than pain. Her eyes focused on Randy's and he shook his head at her hoping that she would not give him away. He saw the confusion, then hope fill her eyes. Tears lingered on the rim not spilling over but glossing her pupils. She was actually on the verge of crying. After everything he had seen her go through, she hadn't shed a tear. His arms ached to comfort her

Kiltosuna shook his head and apologized to Randy for Hayden's behavior. "Umpesono Abooksigun." He explained, chuckling.

Randy forced a smile and nodded. "She is beautiful though." Randy said in Kiltosuna's tongue. Kiltosuna shrugged and stared back at her. She cast him a disgusted look and he returned to her, jerking the robe from her body as a sort of punishment for her lack of respect.

Randy's eyes caught the neatly stitched gash on her leg and audibly gasped at the wound as well as Kiltosuna's action. The proud brave took his noise as pleasure for her form and not as outrage for his action. That was probably a good thing. Hayden held her tongue and said nothing to further upset her captor.

Kiltosuna again apologized for Hayden's behavior. Randy waved it off, forcing a smile. It was not her behavior he was worried about. If the man did another thing against Hayden he was sure he would strangle him with his bare hands. He offered a quick prayer to the Creator.

Kiltosuna sat by the fire and offered Randy tobacco and paper. He rolled a cigar with clumsy fingers, forcing himself not to glance at Hayden. They smoked in silence until the cigars were gone. Finally, Kiltosuna pulled out dice, rolling them on the blanket.

"What shall we gamble for?" He asked Randy.

Randy smiled. If Kayra's words were true and he did in fact love the girl Ayiana, then he had a strategy for Hayden's release. He was about to find out.

"I need horses." He stated matter of factly. "I have found someone else that would please me."

Kiltosuna grinned at the newcomer. "You just took a wife and you want another, so soon. Either married life is very good or very bad, huh?"

Randy laughed. "My wife needs another squaw to better teach her our ways. Ayiana is young but I think that she would make a good wife."

Kiltosuna's smile vanished at the mention of the girl. "You may not take her. She is spoken for."

"By who?" Randy asked. "Her father said nothing of her betrothal."

Kiltosuna grew furious. "I have spoken for her." He threatened Randy with his words.

"I have heard nothing of this. Have you given horses for her?"

"No. She is too young."

"Psh. She is ready to marry. If she waits much longer she will become hard to live with." He motioned to Hayden. "She has waited too long. See how disagreeable she is?"

"I will not gamble for horses. If you have no horses, then you will not be able to take Ayiana as a wife."

Randy laughed. "I have other ways of getting horses. I can buy them. Can you?" His words hung in the air.

Kiltosuna's eyes darkened and his hands shook. "I want Ayiana. She has been in my heart for many years. I will give you my best horse, if you agree not to ask for her."

Randy acted like he was considering the man's offer. His gaze fell to Hayden whose eyes begged him for a sign of comfort. He offered it with a slow smile that Hayden mirrored.

Kiltosuna noticed the exchange. He hurried to his feet and went to Hayden. He pulled her to stand, holding her hands behind her back, he forced her to twirl around for inspection.

Randy reddened at the way Kiltosuna advertised her. Hayden hated being controlled and here she was being paraded around as one would a horse.

"You can have my best horse and her too. She can be taught to be a good wife. She just needs to be broken."

Randy scoffed at the idea of Hayden's strong and powerful spirit being broken. So much of what he loved and admired about the woman was directly related to that spirit that Kiltosuna spoke of breaking.

Randy knew better than to appear eager to accept. "You said that she was a difficult woman. How will she teach my wife to respect a husband?"

Kiltosuna scratched his head. "She's beautiful. I will give you her and my horse and..." he glanced around the room for something of worth to bargain with. He saw his collection of scalps and pointed in their direction, "You can have your choice of my scalps. Take any five you would like."

Randy was shocked by that offer. An Indian's scalps were held in high regard. To not accept an offer of this magnitude would be a huge insult. Randy had no use for the scalps and didn't value them in the same way the Cetewas did, but he was pleased that his plan had worked so well. Maybe, just maybe, he would manage to leave the tribal camp with both girls and the baby without resorting to confrontation.

He walked to the corner where the scalps were displayed and fingered several. He chose five, leaving one red scalp that he knew Kiltosuna would be especially proud of, for him to keep.

"I accept your offer. You have many fine scalps. Shall we still gamble? Perhaps for–"

Kiltosuna cut him off. "No, I don't want to play anymore. We have an agreement, yes?"

Randy nodded. "Agreed."

He gathered the hairpieces and the bearskin and strode to where Hayden crouched. He knelt down and ran his fingers across her cheek. Tears spilled from her eyes. Randy found his own emotions getting the better of him.

Understanding that the woman was no longer his, Kiltosuna spoke brusquely to Randy before leaving them in the privacy of his teepee.

As soon as he was gone Randy wrapped Hayden in the bearskin that Kiltosuna had taken from her and pulled her into his arms. Her cry soon became a sob of relief. She clung to him with what was left of her strength. He gently whispered to her, smoothing her tangled hair.

"It's alright, sweetheart. It's alright now. I have you. You're safe."

Hayden looked into his face and shook her head. "I thought that I would die here and that I'd never see your face again. He said that I could never leave and although I came here to save Kayra, all I've been thinking about is you. I love you."

She caressed his grease-slicked hair and then wiped the slime from her hand on the bearskin making a disgusted face. The two laughed and Randy wiped at his own eyes.

"You have no idea how badly I've wanted to hear those words. What are you doing here anyway? You can't obey a single thing I say and it is down-right aggravating."

Hayden giggled. "I thought that you had gone the wrong way. I found some tracks that belonged to Greely's horse and I knew that you had ridden in the other direction. I just couldn't go on to Grand Junction after that. I had to go after her."

"What was your plan for rescuing Kayra once you found her, honey?" His question pointed out how ridiculous her attempt to rescue Kayra was.

"At least she wouldn't be alone anymore. I can't imagine her here in this place with these people." Hayden shuddered at the idea.

Randy shook his head. "Kiltosuna didn't take advantage of you."

Hayden shook her head and remembered the stranger at the campsite before they came into the valley of his tribe. "Another Indian wanted to."

"What happened?"

"Well, Kiltosuna..." she began. "He fought the man and killed him."

Randy nodded. "You look thinner, so I guess he starved you."

Hayden shook her head sheepishly. "No. I refused to eat the food he offered me. I thought that he would realize how serious I was if I didn't eat."

"That wasn't smart Hayden. You need your strength."

"He did take my clothes."

"Yes, so that you wouldn't run away. If you did manage to run away, where would you have gone? The Kimsenio tribe lives near here and they are not so kind to their captives. It's likely that he saved your life by keeping you here in his tent with him."

Hayden considered what he said. Maybe he hadn't been as awful as she'd thought. But when she considered Kayra, she had to wonder about how he had treated her. "Okay, so let's say, for discussion's sake, that he didn't harm me too much, but what about Kayra? She's been forced to marry a man from a neighboring tribe. Is it that bad one? Where were her choices?"

"Hayden, listen to me. Kayra was not forced. I gambled and bartered with Tushon who was her captor. He was agreeable to my offer for her because he admired the horse you bought at the auction. It was that horse of yours that made him consider giving Kayra to me. He asked her after we talked and she agreed to marry me. I'm the man from a neighboring tribe. I married her."

"You what?" She jerked free of his hold.

"Hayden, it's not like that." He came to his feet, taking hold of her arm again. "We married here, so that we could leave in peace. It was in fact one of Tushon's agreements for letting me take the infant Michael with us when we left. He had already adopted the child as his own son. He believes me to be a good man and he wanted to ensure that Kayra, her name here is Kachine, was not separated from the child. He is a very respected and admired man."

"So you and Kayra never... that is you haven't..."

Randy shook his head. "You are the only one that I want Hayden. When will you believe me?"

Hayden smiled. "So Kayra is still here and you're here too. She's alright, then?"

"She's great. She's done well here. All of the people love her and she has been a fast learner. I don't think that she's even sure that she wants to leave. These people have been a family to her."

Hayden's brow furrowed. "I'm her family."

"And she loves you for everything that you are. Haven't you learned yet that a person can love more than one other person?"

"I have to see her. Let's go." Hayden wrapped the skin tightly around her body.

Randy frowned bracing himself for her disappointment. "You can't, Hayden. I'm sorry. If I brought you over to our teepee it would outrage the elders. Kayra is to be in her matrimonial solitude. It is only a couple more days, then we can all leave here together."

Hayden's eyes slit to angry pebbles. "You are not suggesting that I actually stay here with Kiltosuna, are you?"

Randy nodded. "There is no other way. I'll see that he gives you clothes, and you will not be confined to the teepee during the day, but he will probably restrain you. Remember, Abooksigun, you cannot suddenly be too agreeable or he'll become suspicious. Your role is still as a terrified captive. Can you do this for me?"

Hayden breathed out slowly. "I will do whatever you say. Tell Kayra that I love her and that I am glad she is alright."

Randy smiled. He was surprised at how easily she had agreed. He looked into her eyes and saw no scheming, so he accepted her word for what it was and pulled her into an embrace. That embrace turned into a kiss.

Randy was overcome with the realization that she could have so easily been taken from him. It was a dangerous trip to the valley they found themselves in and thank God the Cetewas had been the ones to come across her. He pulled his lips from hers and ran a finger across her head where she had been stitched up.

"How did this happen?"

Hayden did not have the opportunity to respond because Kiltosuna cleared his throat before walking into the teepee.

His eyes angrily took in Randy. "She is not yet your wife," He chastised.

Randy responded with an equally harsh tone. Words that Hayden didn't understand. Remembering her role to play, she squirmed away from Randy.

He dipped his head to keep from smiling at her show. "Get away from me, you miserable pig." She spit in his direction.

Hayden crawled to her mat and covered herself appropriately. "Get out of here."She yelled. Hayden stared at him with such a convincing look of hate that Randy found himself wanting to apologize to her for his behavior.

"Umpe sestena monga." Randy said to Kiltosuna who was still frowning. "Pecha mose tun."

Kiltosuna nodded and Randy looked one more time to Hayden before retrieving his scalps and taking his leave.

As soon as he was gone, Kiltosuna came to Hayden and knelt beside her. "I'm sorry for what he did to you. That is not our way. He is not from this tribe. You will be happy that he has agreed to take you with him. Your friend whom you seek, is his wife. At least now you will be together again. She cares for him much. So he must be a good man. I don't understand his bad actions just now. He will bring clothes tomorrow and you will be in his care during the day. Until then, you will stay with me."

Hayden was shocked that this brave was actually apologizing to her for Randy's kisses. She fought the urge of defending him to Kiltosuna. It struck her how truly honorable the brave was.

She nodded. "Thank you for what you have done."

He smiled softly. "I do not want to give you to him, Abooksigun." He ran a dark finger along her pale cheek.

"I want to be with Kayra."

Kiltosuna nodded. "Then you will be happy." He stood and went to the fire lying down to sleep.

Hayden covered her head with the skin and smiled, then she remembered William. She never had the chance to speak of him to Randy. Was he still alive? If he were, she hoped that he was heading back to Colorado.

Chapter Twenty-Four

William

Not a single glorious star shone through the heavens. The extra dark nights were somehow longer. As much as William hated to, he doused the fire. What had he done? His hope of finding either Hayden or Kayra was as bleak as the weather. On top of that, he had little idea of where he was. He was no good alone out here. He feared that he would not even be able to find his way back to Colorado. He hadn't recognized a track in three days. He hadn't come across a human or large animal in a week either. His wandering seemed futile, the world empty.

His horse whinnied. William continued his musings, engrossed in his hopeless situation. The horse paced back and forth in front of the tree where he was tied. William paid no mind and tuned out the restlessness of his mount.

William's eyes shot open and he found himself nose to nose with a fierce looking brave who held a gleaming knife to William's throat. He dared not move. He was unarmed and in his present position the brave would likely slit his throat at the merest sight of challenge.

The Indian took William's arms and tied his hands together. Then he gathered some things from the camp and threw them on a horse. He put a rope around William's neck that was tight enough to make swallowing difficult and hopped on his horse. William was silent, breathing fast, shallow breaths.

William had never seen a real Indian before, and this man was exactly like what he'd imagined. The man was powerful and that made him terrifying. His black eyes were cold and hollow. William expected to be scalped and killed. He couldn't figure out why the man was bothering to take him. William silently obeyed the man who held his future in his dark, calloused hands.

The Indian led him to a fire not even a mile away from where William had been camped. Three others watched them approach from around the fire. William took in the strangers and determined that they were all capable fighters. They were smaller than he was but every piece of their body looked like rock.

He hated fighting but had had to do his share defending himself and his siblings when they arrived in this new country. It was against his nature, but he was a big man and could handle himself when he had to. Untied, and in a fair fight, he could beat out no more than two of these dark men glaring at him.

He took in the rest of his surroundings. Another man was tied to a tree nearby. He was Indian, either dead or unconscious. His arms were spread, tied tautly to two different branches. His limp head hung and blood dripped from it to the dirt below. Terror ran through William's heart when he noticed that the man's back had been skinned in long frightening strips. The skin hung like tails across his pants. William's stomach lurched and he closed his eyes.

So that was to be his fate. William turned his eyes to the men sitting at the fire watching as his captor removed the rope from around his neck and cut his hands loose.

The men surrounded him. He walked backwards a few steps and stumbled over a figure that he hadn't yet seen. It was the body of an Indian woman. Her face was black and swollen from an obvious assault. Her naked body held the marks of a horrendous attack. Teeth imprints marred her arm. *Who were these devils?*

The men smirked at his clumsiness. He heard a raspy breath come from the woman and he realized that she was still alive. His eyes searched her face. Her eyelids fluttered open. He saw defeat in her eyes, glassy as they were. He put all his hope in God that Hayden and Kayra weren't laying somewhere out there with the same look. Adrenaline shot through his veins.

The men were closing in on him, their intentions obvious. He might die here tonight, but he would not be taken easily. He would punish these men for what they had done to the woman beside him. He screamed with abandon, fearing that he had nothing left to lose if he was to die anyway, and sailed through the air, landing on his captor.

Taken by surprise, the Indian fell to the ground with William's weight on top of him. His knife sliced into William's back. He bucked in pain and the knife left the brave's grip. William stumbled off of the man, yanking it free. *That was an unfortunate way to get a weapon.*

His hands shook as he put his head down and slammed into the Indian a second time. The two fell to the ground and fought in a dark cloud of feet and dirt. William had the knife in his hand, still wet with his own blood. A moment's hesitation rippled through his body as he stabbed the blade into the man's throat. The Indian began sputtering and coughing as blood gagged him when he stumbled away.

The other men looked at one another. As a unified front, the three warriors ran to William. He intercepted the first with a heavy, leather boot to the face. The Indian fell to the ground holding his busted jaw. The other two grabbed hold of William when he lost his balance. Although he struggled powerfully against their grip, they held his wrists and shook the knife firmly from his grip and led him towards the tree.

One look at the pitiful work they had made of the other man, still dangling from his ties to the branches, made William frantic. He wriggled his strong body, freeing himself from their hold. The two men looked at each other and went after him again, tomahawks drawn. The man that William had kicked was on his feet now. He caught William from behind. William got a handful of dirt in the eyes. For a few seconds he was opening and closing his stinging eyes to the world around him. He shook his head and blinked rapidly.

He heard a frightening war call and, from somewhere behind him, a young brave leapt onto the scene, whacking the man holding William in the back of the head with a weapon.

William fell forward onto the ground, the weight of the dead man on his back. The new fighter seemed to have the same enemy as William, so William gathered his strength and climbed from beneath the lithe, dense body. He wiped his eyes and saw one of the two other men barreling toward him, his knife shining in the firelight. The other one was kept occupied by the unknown warrior.

William grabbed hold of the Indian running toward him and managed to roll with him on the ground using his momentum. William held the Indian's knife hand by the wrist and butted his head into his attacker's. In the stunned second when their heads met, William jerked the knife loose. Then he rolled the Indian away from his weapon and punched the man in the face again and again before William saw the blood and halted his fist. He wanted to punish the man, but feared he might kill him in the process.

To William's surprise, the Indian jerked forward, managing to throw William off of him. He came to his feet as William grabbed hold of the weapon. The Indian was already leaping on William when he saw the silver glint of the knife in Will's hand. It was too late. The knife landed squarely in the left side of his chest, piercing the skin and burying itself in thick muscles. William braced himself for the impact of the man's body. William yanked the knife back and swiveled to find the last Indian to assist the mystery warrior with his opponent.

The new man was outweighed by his rival. His skill level was vastly below that of his adversary, which was obvious by the way that the older Indian held the newcomer on the ground preparing to cut into his raven scalp.

William threw the knife and by some act of God, it landed blade first with the handle sticking out of the older Indian's ear. The man fell to the side, and the warrior stared at him in disbelief. A moment of silence filled only by their heavy breaths fell over the clearing as they wondered at the blessing it was that such a whim would have worked.

William was stunned himself that he had hit his target. *This mystery Indian is anything but a warrior*, William thought. He was little more than a boy.

They knelt there together catching their breath, looking from one body to the next. William's eyes fell to the girl who lay limply by the brush. He crawled to her and looked down into her broken features. It was impossible to tell her age.

The boy who had come to his assistance appeared at his side, carrying water.

William raised the protesting girl to an incline and the boy poured the water over her mouth. Then gently he cleaned her face. The girl made pathetic whimpering sounds. William's eyes filled with tears.

His new friend held back his emotions and continued steadily cleaning the woman's ravaged body.

William didn't have any idea of what he could do to help. He held gently to the woman's small hand. He couldn't bring himself to watch what the other man was doing to patch her up. What was the relationship between this fortuitous stranger and the girl? Was he a husband? A brother? He had no clue, but he obviously cared for her very much and was determined to make her live.

William doubted that it was possible for her to recover physically, and after something like that, you are never the same even if you live. She made no effort to work with her saviors.

Finally, after a long while and much conscientious repair, the Indian motioned to William to lay her flat.

He obeyed, and the young brave stood motioning his head for William to follow him. They went to the Indian tied to the tree. William's arm's went under the dead man's armpits as the brave cut the ropes that held his friend in place.

Carefully they wrapped the body in a blanket and tied him to a horse, who no longer had a master. William tied all of the animals together and came to assist his companion in carrying the woman to a horse.

The Indian climbed on a small, underfed animal and held his hands out to take the woman in his arms. William hefted her fragile form up to him and helped him adjust her so that she sat sideways in front. His arms encircled her and her head fell to his chest.

William looked around. Was he free to go? The Indian spoke to him in words that made no sense motioning for William to follow along. For lack of anything better to do, William nodded. He felt safe with the young man and knew that at least with him, he would stand a chance of not getting attacked again and of finding his way to some form of civilization. If he was lucky, the man might be able to lead him to Hayden and they could get back to the business of tracking Kayra. He prayed that the same tribe that he had just fought with hadn't been the band who had taken her.

He closed his eyes to cover the image of the nearly dead girl they had just cared for, but the darkness only replaced Kayra's face where hers had been. He shook his head to clear the thought.

Kayra

Kayra busily sewed on the final beads to a perfectly cured deerskin dress that she had been working on for Hayden. Actually, she had started the project for herself, but after Randy told her about how their plan had worked and how Hayden was naked in Kiltosuna's tent, Kayra decided that her cousin needed the dress far more than she did.

Randy entered the teepee and took in the sight of Kayra admiring her work. Her eyes sparkled with satisfied accomplishment over her well-completed task.

"That's beautiful. I honestly have never seen better work."

Kayra bit back her smile, not wanting to show how proud she was and flattered at the compliment. "Can you take it to her now, Randy?"

"In a minute I will. She'll love it."

"I hope so. It is an Indian dress. I hope she doesn't mind."

Randy sat down beside her and ran his fingers through his hair.

Kayra sensed his discomfort. "Just tell me. I've been through a lot. I can handle it, whatever it is."

"I know you can. Hayden still doesn't believe that, but I know it's true. Okay, here goes. William, your friend from Willow Creek was coming to find you with Hayden, when she was taken."

Kayra tried to remain calm and let him finish speaking.

"Hayden has no idea what happened to him. He left her to hunt and while he was gone, Kiltosuna rode in and took her. Hayden said that she thinks God led her to him in the night. Her story is amazing–and this one, I actually believe."

Kayra said nothing. Her mind swam with scenarios in which William was hurt or killed. None of them were favorable so she tried to concentrate on Randy's carefully chosen words.

"Hayden said to tell you that he loves you and was coming after you."

Kayra let a few tears slide from her eyes. *Did she tell him that I was lying to him all that time?* Her face flushed with shame over William finding out the truth. *If he knew and he came after me anyway, then he must really love me.* She both doubted and hoped it was possible.

"He's a strong man. He's gotta be back in Grand Junction by now, waiting for us with his family."

"His family?" Kayra was confused by Randy's words.

"I didn't understand it all, but I guess somehow, his Father is gone and his mother is dead..."

Kayra sucked in a sob that refused to stay inside. It came out in an agonized cry of shock and pain for Ingrid and all of her children. In their eyes she was a saint, in Kayra's eyes as well. The woman was the epitome of grace and generosity.

"I'm sorry, Kayra. You needed to know."

"It's fine." She wiped at her face. "What did she say about William? Is he alright? Where are the rest of the children?"

"I guess they are all in Grand Junction waiting for us."

Kayra was quiet as her thoughts turned to Michael. She would never abandon him. He was her son.

Oh, what a tangled mess. William must be hurting so badly right now. She wanted to wrap him in her arms and comfort his grief but she couldn't. If he ever knew that Michael was his father's child could he accept him? Would Kayra even be able to tell him the truth?

Kayra closed her eyes and let her head fall. "Things were almost simpler before you found me."

Randy frowned. "I've told you before that if you want to stay here, you can. Hayden thought that this news would make you happy."

Kayra squeezed her eyes together. "You're leaving tomorrow, after the final feast of the marriage rituals?"

Randy nodded. "You can stay if you want, but it will be mighty hard to explain now that we've been married. Tushon will be suspicious."

"I know. I have to think about what's best for Michael. It's so complicated, Randy. I don't know what to do."

"It seems pretty simple to me. You love this William and he loves you. So what if you've taken in a baby? From what Hayden said, he's taken in a whole slew of kids. It won't be your typical family, but it'll be a family."

A family, my own real family.

"You make it sound so easy."

"It is. Look, I'd go anywhere and do anything to be with Hayden, anything at all. Whatever it took, because I love her. If you feel that way about William, then what's holding you back?"

"I love Michael, too." Kayra said softly, handing him the dress she had finished, "I'll let you know my decision tomorrow. Please, give these to Hayden and don't tell her what I said about staying here."

Randy

Evening was setting in the tribal camp. Kayra was in her tent. Randy sat beside Hayden, who was wearing her new dress, where a communal meal was being prepared. She tried to act disagreeable, but he could tell that she was once again enjoying her role and the sparkle in her eye spoke of the mischief in her mind. She seemed not only unafraid now but intrigued by the customs and practices of the Cetewa. He was glad that her hatred of all Indians had dissipated.

Kiltosuna was always nearby, not completely trusting Randy after that first night when he found them in the teepee. The brave was a man of his word. He kept his distance. Randy knew it was because of his love for Ayiana and that alone.

Tushon was first to see the figures approaching camp. He came to his feet in a flash running to his brother. The tribe as a whole hurried to the group.

Hayden followed Randy's lead. They chased after the Cetewas who were suddenly howling. "What is it?" She whispered.

"Nayati is dead. He's the chief's son, and there is a girl who has been hurt badly. It seems that the tribe nearby who is enemy to the Cetewas killed him and defiled her as well."

They saw the girl resting limply in the arms of a man on horseback. That first time she'd seen Finesse after her attack was an image that rivaled this one.

"Kiltosuna may have saved me from that, huh?" She tentatively touched Randy's arm.

"You have no idea how bad I want to hold you right now." He said.

Hayden gave a sad smile in his direction. They looked at the two men that had brought her in. One brave and a very tall, solid looking white man.

"Will!" Hayden called out his name.

William jerked his face up. His eyes fell to her and then to the Indian man at her side. He searched her face and a wide toothy grin spread across his features.

He jumped from his horse and the two ran to each other hugging. Kiltosuna looked toward Randy. The jealousy over such a display of familiarity between her and the newcomer rankled him. He figured it was William, but she just seemed a little too happy to see him. He did nothing to stop the pair and was well aware of Kiltosuna's gaze on him.

Randy followed as Kiltosuna walked toward Hayden. "Who is this man?"

"My...brother. Actually we're twins. We were born in Canada and came here when we were six."

Randy covered his mouth with his hands to keep from laughing out loud at her flowing lies.

William's companion began talking and everyone gathered around the two of them. Hayden was afraid at first, not understanding their intention. She looked at Randy for assurance and he shook his head at her, smiling. He motioned with his hand for her to come to him. She squeezed William's hand before leaving.

The Cetewa men, each one by one, grabbed his forearm in their respectful way of thanking him for saving the chief's daughter.

Randy whispered in Hayden's ear what was going on and that William was a hero in their eyes. The women helped take the girl down from the horse and carried her away. William's new friend led him to the fire where supper was being cooked. The tribe offered him food first, then his companion.

He took the bowl of meat and made his way to where Hayden and Randy stood. William took in Randy as he stood possessively near Hayden. He held out his hand. Randy shook it. "You made it." His smile grew as William realized that he not only spoke English but wasn't fully Indian either.

Hayden giggled. "Don't give him away, brother," She whispered, "He has rescued us both. Me and Kayra."

William's eyes closed in relief at her words. His smile was so brilliant and white and contagious that Randy had a hard time keeping himself from laughing, right out loud.

"She's here? Where? I have to see her!"

"This is the first time I have seen you look like you weren't carrying the weight of the world on your shoulders." Hayden ran a hand across his arm.

He shook his head. "It feels like it, too. I'd about given up hope. I have to see her."

"You can't," Hayden explained, "I haven't even been able to see her yet. She's been in a ritualistic solitude that ends tomorrow. Randy married her."

William's smile fell and his brows furrowed together. "What?"

"Shh. It's not what you think. She was already spoken for, so he gambled and managed to win her from Tushon. Tushon insisted that they get married so that the baby would stay with Kayra. They only married in name, Will." She assured him.

"Thank God for that." He looked at Randy, unsure of how he was supposed to react to the new information. Randy had forgotten briefly about Kayra. He wasn't sure how she was going to react. Her behavior earlier had been odd to say the least. There had to be something that she wasn't telling him. Whatever it was, it was building a huge barrier between her and this man. He hoped that he could help her work through that wall, and tonight.

"I'll go tell Kayra you're here. I know she'll be relieved that you're okay. Hayden can fill you in on the rest of what has happened."

William nodded. "Tell her..." his voice caught on his emotions, "that I love her." He smiled. "I want her to know that."

Kayra

Kayra was peeking out the flap of the teepee when Randy approached. "What are you doing?" He scolded.

"I heard the commotion."

He entered the room. "He's here. William's here. He wants to see you, of course. We told him not until tomorrow. From what I understood, he was captured by the Kimsenio."

Fear filled Kayra's heart. They were Cetewa's enemies. She had heard horrible things about their cruelty.

"He was lucky to get away from them, in one piece. He's tough. He and a boy beat out four of their warriors, as the story goes. The Kimsenios killed the chief's son and nearly killed his daughter too. William seems fine, but this will probably mean war with Kimsenios."

"He's here, in our camp?"

Randy nodded. "He wanted me to tell you that he loves you."

Kayra turned from Randy and wrapped her arms around herself. She closed her eyes and tried to figure out the mess that she found herself in. Now she was going to have to face him. The reality was scary, but after everything that she had been through, surely she would be able to make it through this too.

"Kayra, what is it that you aren't telling me?" Randy didn't approach her.

She took a deep, cleansing breath. "Michael is Will's brother."

Skeptically, Randy raised his brow. "Are you sure?"

"Yes. Before Fineese died, she said that the baby was to be named Michael Kayden Mayer. That is Will's last name." She paced the small space that seemed to be closing in on them. "I read her journal and she was Will's father's mistress for a couple of years. She loved him, but when she became pregnant, he abandoned her."

"This does complicate things, doesn't it. Why didn't you tell me any of this before?"

Kayra shook her head. "I never thought that I'd see him again. It never occurred to me that I would have to tell any of this, or that little Michael would have to deal with the rejection of his family. Don't you see? If I tell William the truth about Michael, it would devastate the whole family, and there's no way that I can be with him and lie ever again."

"You haven't spent enough time with Hayden then." His sarcastic comment cut the tension making both of them smile.

"I don't know what to do. I won't let Michael get hurt."

"But you'll let yourself? That man out there has come all this way. He's even fought off Kimsenio warriors, all in his attempt to save you, to spend the rest of your lives together. Kayra," He grabbed her shoulders and jolted her, "you owe yourself, him, and even Michael the chance of being a real family. Besides that, he needs you. Hayden said that he's carrying the weight of the world on his shoulders."

Kayra wouldn't look Randy in the eye. "I can't even imagine what he's going through. Of course Will would have taken responsibility for all of his brothers and sisters."

Randy ran a comforting hand along Kayra's arm.

"I have to see him." Kayra was suddenly determined.

Randy nodded. "You will."

"No, I mean this can't wait. I need to talk to him tonight."

"Kayra, what difference will a few hours make?"

"Please, I need to do this." She clutched the leather of Randy's shirtfront in desperation.

"This is a bad idea. Tomorrow, first thing, you can talk to him." Randy shook his head and pulled her hands from his shirt, placing them at her side. "We are so close to getting away from here. I won't jeopardize that."

Kayra nodded. "You're right."

She offered a weak smile and went back to stir the pot atop the fire in the center of the teepee. Randy smoothed out his slick hair. "I'll get back to Hayden and William then."

Kayra nodded.

Randy

Randy sat beside Hayden during the common meal that night. Her dress was the one that Kayra had made. It was a bit longer than it should have been, but the beadwork around the collar and up the side was exquisite. The tawny color of the thinly cured hide made Hayden's light skin glow. She looked as radiant and as confident as the first night that he had met her in the town square.

He was all too aware of the attention the other braves had begun to give her. She acted aloof and difficult, but now it was enticingly girlish and not belligerently offensive. He decided that he would tell her to ease up before Kiltosuna changed his mind about their agreement altogether.

Hayden tasted the strange acorn mixture that was a staple of the Cetewas. She dipped her meat in the mush and Randy laughed when he noticed that she was finished before he was. She smiled and slid slightly closer to him. His arms ached to pull her to him. He winked at her and she motioned her eyes toward the river where she had been washed just a couple of days before.

Randy glanced in that direction. It was dark. Everyone was well occupied by the tales the young men were telling of their heroism in battle. William sat beside Kiltosuna, who for the first time in two days wasn't staring watchfully over Hayden. Randy was surprised to hear him translating the language for William. William was smiling as a story was being told of his prowess.

Randy was dying to have her in his arms again, to feel her arm around his neck. The memory of her moist mouth on his skin was driving him mad. He was consumed with his desire to steal just a moment of truth with her where he could talk to her and kiss her the way he ached to. She was back to her old self again and he was glad for that.

"It's too risky," He whispered without looking at her.

She dipped her elegant, moccasined foot to the ground and let her toe touch his. She smiled as she did it. Randy jerked his foot away and stood to avoid blowing his cover. "You are Satan," he hissed quietly.

She giggled. Randy walked to the outskirts of the fire and motioned with his head for her to follow. She slowly stood up and went around the group on the opposite side.

He came up behind her in the dark, encircling her waist, kissing the crook of her neck. Hayden's head fell back against him before she turned, snaking her arms around his back. It was wonderful to be alive and with the woman he loved.

Randy stopped abruptly at the screech of an owl in the distance. He stilled Hayden with his hands. She froze.

They heard the shrill "LlaaYaaYaaYaa" war call of the Kimsenio warriors and saw the frantic scramble of the Cetewa's in the firelight as they darted about grabbing weapons to defend their small band.

Randy threw Hayden from him and ordered. "Stay here behind the rock. Swear it to me, Hayden."

"Get Kayra!"

"Swear." He pinned her with a hard look.

"I'll stay." Her terrified eyes assured him that she intended to do just that.

◆← →◆

Hayden

Randy darted over the rock and Hayden ducked down, only her eyes and forehead peeked out. She couldn't believe the savage way the Kimsenios were falling on these gentle people that she realized she viewed as friends.

Hayden was awestruck by the fierce way that Randy dove into the action fighting off as many of the enemy that he could. He was terrifying in his assault. As terrifying as his copper-skinned brothers. She found herself proud of this uncivilized side of him.

William was in the midst of it too. She was pleased to see that the stories being told of him were true. His size alone helped to make him a deadly opponent.

She heard the cry. Hayden saw a figure run through the field, holding tightly to a bundle. Her mind lapsed to that awful day from her childhood. She somehow knew that the frantic woman was Kayra.

A dark man on horseback charged the woman, scooping her onto his horse. Kayra screamed, and Hayden realized that the rider was barreling toward her sanctuary. She felt around for anything to save her cousin's life.

Finding nothing, she crouched low in her hiding space and listened until the drumming of hooves was almost upon her, then she sprung with all the force and agility of a wild-cat. Her fingers dug into the sinewy flesh of a Kinsenio.

He cried out trying to shake her loose, but she fought him with every ounce of her strength until as a pair, they fell from his horse. Kayra and the baby were thrown too. Kayra rolled the infant out of danger as her body dragged brutally along the dirt and brush.

The warrior punched Hayden in the face. She fell to the ground, her cheek and eye hot with white-hot pain. The warrior glanced at Kayra who scrambled to her feet running away with the screaming infant.

Kayra

Hastily, the warrior lunged for Kayra and missed, falling to the ground. Then he was running after her. Kayra continued running.

"Kayra!" Came the deep, strong voice of a man in the darkness.

"Help!" She cried.

William appeared in front of her. His tall, powerful figure illuminated by the fire behind him. He ran down the hill to the valley where Kayra fled.

Kayra stumbled. The warrior ascended upon her his arms around her body. He held a knife to her throat. "Icksay tuno." He ordered.

Kayra understood. *Tuno.* Quiet.

Michael let out a blood-freezing cry.

The brave took the blade that he held to Kayra's throat and moved to stab the infant.

Understanding his intent, she screamed out the sheerest, most fearsome war call that she could and stomped down on his foot, unsettling his hold. She wriggled and turned out of his arms. She kicked with all of her strength, her foot landing solidly in his groin. He collapsed, breathless for a moment. Suddenly, William was beside her.

He fell to his knees punching the Kinsenio in the face until his hand bloodied Hayden got there as William stood. "You got her?"

"Yes," he called out.

"I'm going to find Randy." Hayden yelled as she dashed through.

Kayra brought her attention to the man in front of her. She held Michael to her chest and tears fell from her eyes as William, bloody from his participation in the war, collapsed beside his victim.

Kayra crawled to him and knelt, feeling his face and chest for wounds.

"I'm fine." He managed while catching his breath.

Kayra kissed his hand as he recovered. "You came for me, Will. You really came for me."

"Of course I did. I would die for you, Kayra." He held his hand out to her.

She brought her mouth down on his, kissing him over and over.

Michael, still wrapped in Kayra's arms, let out his disgruntled resistance, bringing Kayra back to reality. "We're squashing him."

William laughed sitting up. He took the baby in his arms. Kayra bit her lip, almost not wanting to let him hold the child. "Hey, little guy. We got us a strong woman here, don't we?"

Kayra sat beside William. The fight back at camp had dissipated and most of the Kimsenio warriors were making their escape. She placed her hand on William's strong leg. "There is so much that I need to tell you."·

"Me too." He smiled at her in her Indian dress. "You really look the part, you know."

"What?" Kayra asked.

"When I first met you, I never doubted that you were a nun and now look at you, as authentic an Indian as I ever met."

Kayra laughed at his comment and tugged on her long braid. "I'm sorry that I didn't tell you then, the truth about what I was. I'll tell you everything now."

William sat silent, waiting for her confession.

She ran a loving hand along Michael's head. "This is my son now. I won't ever leave him, Will." She stared into William's eyes.

"I would never ask you to."

"If only it were that simple." Kayra fought back tears that threatened to tumble. She had to say it, but how does one destroy all of the security and love that a person has for the man who raised him?

"I have a lot to tell you too, Kayra. It's bad, worse than you can imagine. My Mother died about a month and a half ago. She got a disease that the doctor said he has treated in saloon girls, only Mutter's was too far gone. I don't want you thinking that she was unfaithful to Father. She was a saint as sure as any ever christened. Father, well, he gave the disease to her. I forbid him to ever climb our doorstep again. He never even tried to, not even when she died."

William's back heaved. Kayra caressed his head, understanding the horror he was feeling.

"Will," she began, "It's okay, take your time."

"Victoria, she came up to me at the funeral. I buried Mother in the clearing where we spent that last night together."

Kayra's face lit with tender emotion over his thoughtfulness.

"She would have liked that."

"I found myself responsible for all of these kids that were hurting and confused about Father, like I was. Victoria gave me a generous gift and told me to go after you."

Kayra smiled fondly remembering her friend. "You know, I liked that woman from the start."

He grinned, "So, I listened. I could only think of catching up to you and making you my wife."

Did he really just say that? She couldn't contain the smile on her face. It had been what she dreamt of hearing ever since leaving Willow Creek, months ago.

"Kayra, didn't you hear what I've been saying about my folks? Are you not shocked?"

"I'm not," Kayra sighed.

Rage flew across William's face. "My father didn't... he wouldn't–"

Kayra was quick to reassure him. "No, no, no Will. He never did anything inappropriate toward us."

William's shoulders sagged in relief.

"I love you so much that it hurts, but I have something that you need to know. I want to tell you about Michael's mom."

"I know. It's alright. Hayden told me what she was."

"If only it were that simple. Her name was Fineese. What she was, was one of the most devoted and strong women that I've ever known. She loved this precious boy before he was even born, with as much love as any person could ever give. She wanted to make things better for him, to give him a good life. I promised her when she was dying that I would do that."

William tried to interrupt. Kayra cut him off. "Let me get this out. You see, Michael is your father's son."

William sat, frozen. No expression whatsoever. He just sat there with Michael in his arms, staring into the baby's cherub face.

"He's your brother, Will."

William came to his feet and carried the baby off a few steps, holding him silently against his chest.

Kayra fought the impulse of going after them. This was something that he had to work out for himself. If he couldn't, then there was no place for William in her future. Her chest felt heavy with her final decision.

As he ambled back to her, he asked, "Kayra, how old are you?"

Kayra was puzzled by his seemingly out of place question. "Nineteen."

"I'm barely an adult myself, and here we are in an Indian camp in the middle of nowhere. I'm covered in other men's blood. I *feel* old." He sighed and looked into Kayra's eyes. "I have found myself playing father to six of my father's kids, one of which I don't even know. You've been raising a baby all this time."

Kayra wrapped her arms around his waist. "If you still want me, William, I will do this with you. You don't have to face this alone."

"If I still want you? I'd die without you. I want you in my life so badly it tore me to pieces when you left my farm. I have wanted you from the first day that you and your cousin rode into our place."

She smiled up at him. "Then it's settled. We have a family. It's not what folks would call ordinary, but it's ours and it will be perfect."

William leaned his face to hers and kissed her with a tenderness that spoke volumes of their love. Their passion simmered below the caress of lips. This was a kiss of promise and devotion, the kiss that Kayra had dreamt of her whole life.

William broke the contact. "So, what does this little guy call me? Uncle Will?" The frown on his face made Kayra smile.

"I think dad will do just fine." She stroked the baby's head, caressing his soft hair.

"We'd better get back to Hayden and Randy. Likely, there are many hurt."

Kayra paused. "Can you please go on ahead? There's something I need to do first."

William frowned.

"Please." Kayra reiterated.

He nodded and carried Michael back toward the camp.

Randy

Hayden ran from Randy toward William as he entered the ravaged common ground. Her left eye was dark and swollen, almost shut. Her stare was wild as she took him in, alone with the baby.

"Kayra, where is Kayra?" She sprinted in panic toward the towering white man.

"She's fine. Perfectly fine." He assured her. "She wanted some time to herself."

A loud, shrill voice rang out in the night and Randy lowered his head understanding what Kayra had stayed behind to do. It was a courageous and powerful thing. Tushon stood erect in his place and answered her cry. His voice rang out and was swallowed by the voices of his people echoing Kayra in the still night.

When Kayra came back to the camp, her hands were clean yet trembled. Gripping fingers held the neatly cut scalp of the Kimsenio warrior that had tried to take her life. Randy stood proud as she marched into the tribal grounds handing the scalp to him. The men nodded, admiring her.

Hayden ran to her in a flurry of unrestrained emotion. Kayra held Hayden's small figure to her chest. "It's okay Hayden. We're safe now."

Hayden sobbed in her cousin's soothing arms. "Are you sure you're alright, cousin?"

Kayra smiled. "I'm just fine, but you're a sight." She fingered Hayden's bruised eye and neatly stitched forehead. "I have an ointment for that."

Hayden smiled. "I just can't believe that it's you. You look fantastic, Cousin."

The two women embraced again, each privately thanking God for their safety. Around them, the low mourning chants began to be sung. Kayra released Hayden and walked to Tushon holding the body of one of his wives.

Kayra had always liked the woman. She had been one of the first to offer help with her chores. She knelt beside the grieving husband and joined his wives in their song of anguish. Hayden buried her face in Randy's chest. William held Michael in his arms. Together he and Randy stood, watching the scene of devastation unfold around them.

Chapter Twenty-Five

Randy

Snow blew circles around the weary travelers as Randy led the entourage through the streets of Grand Junction. It was mid day, but with the storm, it felt like night was setting. Both Hayden and Kayra were dressed in their Indian clothes and wrapped in thick skins atop horses.

Randy's mount whinnied, his breath rising in smoke. They would soon be out of this ice land. He smiled as he looked back at Hayden who was almost completely buried under her fur. What a sight. How he had fought to keep that sight alive.

Kayra

Kayra kicked her horse and caught up to William, who held Michael inside his jacket with his left arm. With his right hand he maneuvered his horse through the blanketed street. "It's beautiful," She sighed.

His smile was brilliant as he nodded. "I can't wait for the kids to meet this little guy."

Kayra stared into his eyes. She hadn't given him the credit he deserved. He wasn't at all distant from her son. In fact, he was as loving and attentive towards the child as she herself was. Already she felt they were a family. After all these years, she was at peace.

Hayden

Hayden was shaking from the cold, desperate to get indoors. She hated snow. The sight of the hotel where she and Randy had stayed came into view. She nudged her horse to hurry. She passed her companions and slid from the animal to the covered porch of the hotel handing the reins to Randy.

He laughed, as did William and Kayra. William took Kayra's reins and handed the baby down to her, careful not to wake him.

"Go on in you two. We will see to the horses." Randy assured them. "Hayden, I need to send a telegram to Denver City and tell them I'm still alive. I don't know if I have a job anymore, but my brother needs to know. It could take a bit to get the horses settled and the message sent."

Hayden waved a hand over her shoulder acknowledging him. "As long as I'm allowed to thaw, you can run all over this town." She paused with her hand on the brass knob thinking of Mae Belle's. "Well not all over and you better remember that," She said pointedly.

The tinkle of bells on the door joined Randy's laughter as she turned the brass knob. The door creaked open. She and Kayra hurried inside the small lobby. Lana bustled out of the kitchen untying the apron about her thick waist.

Her eyes took in the ragged girls with surprise, then recognition spread across her face. She ran to Hayden, forcing her head to her ample bosom.

"We'd almost given up hope. I'm so glad we were wrong." She hugged Kayra as well.

"Oh Lana, you just wouldn't believe what we've been through." Her voice was as dramatic as ever.

"You look it. Half-starved to death aren't you? Now hand me that baby and let's fix him some warm milk. You two come on into the kitchen and I'll fix you a plate of dinner. I was just finishing up the biscuits when I heard the bells."

Hayden smiled at her cousin. "Lana is the best."

"Have you any word of the children? They did find you didn't they?" Hayden asked.

"Oh heavens, yes," Lana bustled around, "Wonderful bunch. I hired Thomas to look after the stable and the young lady Calla, well she went and married that Josiah boy, you know, the one you left your horses to when you ran back into the mountains. They've been married a couple weeks. She helps out Doctor Morgan. She's real handy with a needle."

Hayden knew very well how handy with a needle she was, and instinctively felt the scar that ran down her forehead.

Kayra's mouth dropped in shock. She whispered to Hayden, "Will is not going to like Calla marrying like that."

Oblivious, Lana chattered on, motioning for the girls to take their seats at the table. She ladled and sat two plates of mashed potatoes, chicken and gravy in front of them. Then began a pot of water to boil for the baby's bottle. "Those kids brought with them an old woman. A speck of a thing that Annie is, she has been fantastic with the youngsters."

Hayden stood gaily. "Annie made it? She's alright?" She prayed nightly that Annie would recover from that fateful day.

"Why, yes. She's wonderful and back at the house with them now."

Kayra smiled as she asked the question. "Whose house?"

"Well, it'll be yours I reckon. That Calla made some right smart decisions. When the wagon train continued on and you all were nowhere to be found, she figured that you would be spending at least the winter here and she didn't want to waste any of the money she'd been given on rent and such. See, that young man Josiah, he took a liking to her and helped her buy an abandoned place just outside of town. He got a good deal on it and traded work for a couple animals. The house is small, only two rooms to the whole place but the two of them are fixin' it up. It's cozy-like. Annie has been working her skinny fingers to the bone helping out on the place. She never once doubted that you'd make it back."

Hayden's mind swirled to take in all of the information. There was so much, so fast. Obviously, Kayra would stay with William and his family. They needed her and Hayden, remarkably, was happily moving on to a life she'd never even considered for herself. Whether that ended up here, back in Denver if Randy still had a job, or anywhere else that sparked their fancy. She knew she'd go. No matter what happened, she was never leaving Randy's side.

Kayra was going to be just fine and so was she. How quickly life could flip you upside down. It was all changing at a dizzying speed but it was good.

For the first time in their lives, Kayra and Hayden's lives looked like they may fork away from each other. She'd never imagined a life without her cousin. For the past many years, Kayra was her life and her purpose. She didn't want to leave her, but she realized that she could.

Kayra had proven herself more than capable in one hundred crazy and difficult situations. And no matter what life threw at her she would never again be alone to face them, not with William and his brood wrapped around her. Perhaps they could stay together until the winter passed?

Lana frowned at the two women staring back at her. "Well, eat you two. I can see you haven't had a decent meal in months."

Hayden laughed and dipped her fork into the mashed potatoes. The first scent of it made her stomach growl and before she knew it, the whole plate was empty and she smelled the biscuits baking in the oven. Those would be next.

Michael was halfway done with his bottle when the bells jangled from the front door. Hayden's chair scraped the floor as she hurried into the lobby.

William and Thomas were there, beaming at her. "I don't know what it is but something smells heavenly in here."

"Come on back, Will. Lana is a first rate cook for sure." Thomas led his brother into the kitchen where Lana had already set two more plates out.

Hayden followed them. "Where's Randy?"

William shook his head. "He'll be along. Said he had something needed doin'." He bent down and kissed Kayra's forehead before introducing himself to Lana.

Hayden frowned, returning to her seat. Lana handed the infant to Thomas who was only a little flustered by the baby in his arms. "Give him every ounce of this bottle you hear me?"

Thomas nodded, smiling. "Sure thing, Aunt Lana."

"Now the two of you girls need a warm bath. Come on."

Hayden laughed, taking Kayra's hand and pulling her away from William. She could tell that Kayra wanted to stay, but once she felt the warm water on her parched skin, she'd change her mind. Besides, Thomas was there to fill William in on all of the happenings.

When Hayden reached the staircase, Lana was already at the top ordering her few maids to get the water up here in a hurry. She opened the door to the suite that had been Hayden's before. Hayden was delighted to find it just as she'd left it. "Lana, you didn't have to keep this for us."

"That's what Josiah said, that I could store your things, but turns out, not many visitors have dropped in since you left. I thought that I might as well leave it be, in case you came back."

Hayden and Kayra walked inside. Hayden threw the armoire door wide for Kayra to see all her gowns. She fumbled through them, selecting a lovely yellow one with yards upon yards of fabric. "You can change into this after your bath, cousin. It will look brilliant with your hair."

Kayra laughed at her cousin's enthusiasm. "Am I going to a ball or something? I just want to go to bed."

Hayden giggled in delight as a few of the maids carried in enormous pails to fill the tub.

"Where on earth did you get all of these?"

Lana interrupted the conversation by taking Kayra's arm and escorting her out of the room. "I set you up in a room of your own. The bath is getting cool, so along with you missy."

Kayra looked back anxiously to her cousin who giggled like a child.

Hayden

Hayden undressed and combed through her tangled blond hair before sliding her legs into the silken water. She brought the cake of soap up to her nose, breathing it in. She scrubbed with relish until her skin was pruney from her time in the tub.

She imagined the splendid treatment Kayra was experiencing at the hands of Lana and her pampering bath. After all that her cousin had been through, she deserved this.

Hayden toweled herself off and shrugged into her thick white robe. She was suddenly too tired to fix her hair or put on a fancy dress. She plopped down on the feather bed. Having forgotten how temptingly sweet the bed felt, she snuggled down and was asleep before she could remember to stay awake for Randy.

When Hayden cracked her eyes open to the sound of a door latching, she realized that Lana must have come in and covered her up.

Hayden awoke to the sound of her door unlocking. Randy strode in, wearing a suit. Her first thought was disappointment at the change in his attire. She'd decided she liked the rugged way that his native side looked on him. Then she realized where he'd been. He'd actually had the nerve to go to that bath-house of Mae Bells.

Hayden hated that place and he knew it. "I cannot believe that you went there. Again?"

Randy had a smirk on his face. "I like when your cheeks get pink like that. And yes, I did go to the bath house. I went with William to get cleaned up. We were letting you ladies do that here. Mae Bells is where men go to bathe and I was in a hurry to do that. And do you want to know why I was in such a hurry?"

She looked down her nose at him.

Hayden's straight back and defiant chin made him smile. "I was in a hurry so that I could get back here to you. Because I don't want you out of my sight again." He sat on the edge of the bed. She didn't object. His long fingers reached to stroke her still damp hair. "This whole room smells good. Like you." He dipped his head and kissed her cheek.

She moved so that he could kiss her more fully. "Later," He promised

"I picked something up for you at the seamstresses." Hayden sat up in excitement. "She said it would fit."

"Where is it?" Her eyes glowed.

"It's coming. Lana's pressing it first. I figured you'd be dressed, with your hair all done up fancy."

"What on earth for?" Hayden groaned at the thought, curling down into the bed.

"For your wedding." He was grinning ear to ear.

Hayden froze at his words. "Are you serious?"

"If you are still willing, then I'm serious."

Hayden squealed in delight and hopped from the bed all but running to the dressing table. "Oh, my hair is still wet." She frowned.

"You look beautiful just like that. In fact I think I'll tell Lana never mind about the dress."

"You'd better not." Hayden turned back to the mirror and ran a comb up the side of her hair, pursing her lips to see the effect it made.

"I'll leave you to that. I still have some arrangements to make. Don't tell Kayra. William wants this to be a surprise."

"A surprise that I'm getting married?"

"No, a surprise that she is."

Hayden turned to see his face. "Are you for real?"

Randy laughed, running his fingers through his dark hair. "We both have waited long enough. I'll see you in an hour."

"An hour? I only have an hour?"

Randy made his way to the door. "One hour, not a second longer. Oh, and Hayden, everyone else here in town believes that we are renewing our vows. I told them this was our anniversary."

They shared a secret smile that made Hayden's heart beat quicker before Randy shut the door behind him.

William

William stood outside Kayra's door. Hair still wet from his bath, face shaved smooth. He wore simple trousers and a white shirt. He'd gone to Calla's house to see his family, letting Kayra freshen up and rest. Lana was like a bulldog anyway, not letting him near the staircase. "She's not decent." She kept hollering at him.

He knocked. When the door opened he had to take a step back. She was stunning. She had always been beautiful, but seeing her tonight, took his breath away.

Kayra tugged at the bodice of her gown. Her hair hung long and straight in a thick cascade of Chesnutt silk. Her face was shining from her bath. The scent of rose water met his nostrils. He stared at her in silence, simply taking in the view.

"I was nervous you'd forgotten me. Lana said that you left. I want to see the children too."

"I did leave. Wow, you look..."

Kayra smoothed her hair.

"You're so lovely." Coming to his senses he continued, "But we'd better get going."

Kayra grabbed a wrap that Lana had loaned her and followed William out into the hall. She threw it around her shoulders. "I'll kill Hayden for picking this. She knows that I'd never wear something with a neckline this low."

"I like it." William teased.

"Where's Michael?"

"I took him to Calla," he paused, "And her husband." His frown told Kayra that he didn't approve.

"I wanted to tell you, but there wasn't an opportunity."

"Thomas told me, first thing. Josiah's a good guy I suppose. He's been getting the old house ready for us. He said he'd like to stay there and work alongside me."

"That's wonderful. What did you say?"

"I told him he had as much if not more invested in the place than I do. He knows about horses. I sure don't. I told him the place was his and we would be full partners in anything that is done. He also said there was space to raise sheep."

Kayra smiled at William. "That's why I love you."

"Because I don't know a thing about horses? We'd better hurry or you'll make us late."

"Where are we going? To the farm?" Kayra asked.

William's smile teased his lips. "You'll see."

They stepped out to the porch where an enclosed buggy was hitched and waiting. The snow fell like feathers, light and steady blanketing the road.

"Whose is that?"

"It's your ride."

Kayra looked from him to the buggy and back. "Are you serious?"

"Step in. We have somewhere to be."

She cast him an intrigued look to which he raised his brow and helped her up.

Chapter Twenty-Six

William

The small church on the edge of town was lit up as if it were Sunday. Kayra stepped from the carriage.

"You said that you would be willing to be my wife."

Kayra gulped.

"I don't want to spend another hour without you by my side," He smoothed a snowflake that landed on her cheek, "Will you marry me tonight?"

She wrapped her arms around him pulling his body to her. She cried softly, holding him on the church steps as the snow daintily danced around them.

"Is that a yes?"

"You know it is."

He reached into his pocket and pulled out a simple silver band. "I had this to give you, that last night, when you snuck away. I've kept it with me ever since, waiting for you to wear it."

Kayra's eyes glossed. There were no words to express herself.

William stuck the ring back in his pocket and kissed her cheek before opening the church doors.

Everyone cheered. Lana anxiously ushered Kayra to a small room where Hayden waited.

William hugged the children and joined Randy at the front of the small church.

Randy held out his hand and William shook it firmly and thankfully.

"So, did she say yes?"

William grinned, nodding to his friend.

Annie hushed the kids as the preacher took his place beside the grooms. Becca carried her small basket of dried berries to the back of the church. William saw Calla link her fingers with Josiah.

His sisters were happy. Both of them beamed.

He smiled like a fool at his new brother-in-law who had fixed his gaze on the door at the end of the aisle.

Randy straightened his collar and cleared his throat. Lana motioned for Becca to start down the aisle. The little girl eased her way past the small crowd of people in the church as she clung to the small basket of flowers in her hand. Annie raised her small fists in the air cheering on the little girl.

Thomas awkwardly rocked his fussy brother in his arms.

The doors opened and Hayden and Kayra entered the sanctuary.

Two women couldn't look more different.

Kayra was as fresh as a daffodil as she started down the aisle. She was a vision of sweetness. Her eyes beamed with joy and the soft candlelight lit her angelic face. William had dared to dream of a moment like this and it had actually materialized. What other dreams lay in store for him and this beautiful woman in her silken, buttery gown gliding toward him?

She was everything soft, kind, giving and strong. Her lips trembled as she stepped forward, toward the man who couldn't take his eyes from her face.

Kayra

Her heart was filled with joy over the night that she had dreamt of and imagined since girlhood. For too long her world had been about making it day to day. Six months ago she couldn't have imagined how her life would turn out, but here she was, looking into the eyes of the most amazing man, who loved and cherished her. She was walking into this mariage knowing that she was different than she had been. When she fell in love with William, she was pretending to be something she wasn't. Now, she'd become a lot of what she had been faking all along. Who could have guessed that putting on the act of a deep relationship with God could pave the way toward actually having one?

Now, she had William and soon a whole big family, but first, she'd found God and that made everything about this night so much more beautiful. They were starting their lives together with God guiding the way. He had led William to her and against all odds, he had brought them to this point, to this night. She was blessed and she would never take that for granted again.

Randy

Hayden strode down the aisle with her chin up and wintery eyes locked determinedly on Randy. Her snowy dress showed off her slim figure as it cascaded at the hips into a ridiculously full skirt that pressed up against the pews as she passed. Her skin glistened in the candle light. Long, honeyed curls kissed her shoulders and tumbled down her back. She was beautiful, and she knew it.

Randy grinned, admiring his bride. She was going to be a handful alright. The look in her eye spoke of mischief. She was the most precious thing in the world to him. He couldn't believe his luck in having come across her. She was exciting and breathtaking and he couldn't wait to see how she settled into married life. He could have picked someone who would have been better suited to be his wife on paper, a woman who would be polite and restrained, but in this wild, impish girl he had found himself.

Hayden

Hayden was completely unprepared for this next adventure and therein lay some of the thrill. She had never thought she would find a man who was worth the idea of forever, but she had. Randy was everything. He made her pulse race and her stomach leap. He was full of surprises and liked that she was too. She smiled wider at all the tricks he had up his sleeve to keep her on her toes. He was someone that she never knew she was even searching for.

Had God put him into her life, the way William had appeared at the top of the cliff the night she'd gone off in search of Kayra? She suspected that he had. Whatever tomorrow held for them, she was confident that together, she and Randy would make their way, laughing and fighting and kissing as they went. She looked forward to that.

Annie stood, wiping her eyes, followed by the harsh looking seamstress then a whole slew of others until the women made their way to the altar.

The preacher nodded at the two couples before him. He spoke of love as a decision and a promise. He quoted scriptures about marriage and how God designed it. He explained how men and women compliment each other. Hayden vaguely heard it as she held Randy's solid hand in hers.

The preacher said the vows. Kayra's voice fluidly repeated the promise to love, honor and obey till death do them part. Then William's shaking voice made the same pact to her.

His eyes filled with tears and she smiled at his display of emotion. It was the look in his eye, the adoration in his words and the worshipful touch of his hand that brought awes from the audience. Kayra took a deep breath and squeezed his fingers as he slid the simple band on her finger.

Hayden wasn't jealous. Just watching the two of them together assured her heart that this was right. They were right. In a strange way, she felt a little like a proud parent handing their child over to be loved and cared for by someone else. And she knew William would care for her.

The preacher interrupted Hayden's musing by directing his attention to them.

The preacher had called them Randal and Rebecca Parker as they repeated their vows. Hayden was too wrapped up in the moment to notice the startled look on her cousin's face. From behind her, Hayden heard the preacher. "You may kiss the brides."

Randy smiled and turned to Kayra.

"Hey," Hayden scolded, punching her husband solidly in the arm.

He shrugged. "He said brides, didn't he?"

The church erupted in laughter, then cheers as the grooms eagerly kissed their brides before dancing down the aisle and out of the chapel.

Hayden

Lana hosted a small gathering at the hotel in honor of the nuptials. She served a simple vanilla cake with white frosting. William's brothers and sisters ate several pieces before Annie noticed.

"Oh let them eat as much as they want." Lana countered mussing up Becca's neatly combed hair. "You want some more don't you, missy moo?" The little girl shoved another bite into her mouth.

It was perfect. In her wildest dreams, and they could be really wild, she'd never imagined that their lives would be turning out this way. Kayra had found everything she ever wanted and Hayden had found something that she never knew she wanted. God was smiling down on them tonight. That thought and her belief in a heavenly father filled her with warmth.

Kayra came to stand beside Hayden near the fire-place. Together they watched their new families celebrate. William hummed a familiar tune and Randy spun Addie, Will's eight-year old sister in circles.

Kayra put her arm around her cousin's shoulders. "I guess you don't have to pretend anymore, do you?"

Hayden's heart warmed at her cousin's insightful comment, but she never got the opportunity to respond.

Randy whisked his dance partner toward the two ladies and bowed to his partner. "Thank you for the dance, my dear."

Hayden handed him a cup of Lana's wedding punch. He drank it down in one drink and smiled at his bride. "I've been thinking, Mrs. Rebecca Parker." He set the glass aside and linked arms with his new wife. "What do you say to a honeymoon in London, at my estate?"

"For real?" Hayden squealed, throwing her arms around his neck.

"England?" Kayra asked, amused.

"Oh yes, my goodness. In all the chaos of this past week, I forgot to tell you." Hayden gushed. "So, turns out, Randy is an English Lord. Can you even believe it?"

Kayra shook her head, "No. I thought he was an Indian."

William interrupted. "Well, he could be a priest, or a nun."

"Not tonight." Randy shook his head emphatically and winked at the other couple. Playfully, he lifted his wife into his arms. Her arms encircled his neck as her dress fell in piles, draping down his body. He made his way toward the staircase that led to their room.

"Randy!" Hayden feigned shock as they disappeared.

He laughed and called out behind him. "Good night everyone."

Kayra

William took Kayra's hand. They smiled at each other, a knowing look in their eyes.

"We should get going too." William suggested. "They aren't going anywhere for a while." He reassured her.

Kayra dipped her head shyly and lifted Michael from the makeshift cradle he was sleeping in. William hefted Becca into his arms and ignoring the children's disappointed protests, led them out to the wagon.

On the bumpy ride home, Kayra snuggled herself close to her husband under a thick wool blanket resting her head on his shoulder.

"Will," Kayra whispered, "You said that Hayden and Randy weren't going anywhere anytime soon."

He nodded. "I know it must be scary for you to be apart from her after all you have been through."

"I appreciate you trying to reassure me, but I need to reassure you. It's not scary. No matter what she and Randy end up doing with their lives, you and these children are mine now. It's you I can't be without."

They exchanged a smile that was filled with promise and trust.

The joyful sounds of songs in German cut through the soft cadence of horse hooves padding across frozen ground. She closed her eyes and thanked God for making her dreams come true. She was finally headed home, home with her family.

Made in United States
Cleveland, OH
03 December 2024

11255209R00135